DATASHARK

RYAN JONES

neshui
publishing

DATASHARK

Neshui Publishing
2838 Cherokee
St. Louis, MO 63118

ISBN 1-931190-52-6

ACKNOWLEDGMENTS

The book you hold in your hands is the first fruits of a ten-year odyssey. And the first person I must thank is my lovely wife Carol for being such a brave, patient, and loving companion on my chosen rocky path. You are truly God's gift to me.

.Barbara Sachs-Sloan, the writing teacher who saw a spark of talent and refused to stop fanning the flame until this book was forged. You were my coach, editor and mentor throughout this process. Just as important as your knowledge of the English language and plot mechanics was your intuition on when I needed a pat on the back, and when I needed a hearty shove. Thanks, and keep that red pen handy.

My parents, Russell and Jerry Jones, who had the kindness to warn me of the difficulty of the road I was about to start down, and the wisdom to not let me quit once I had begun. I hope I've made you proud. Thanks for being such faithful lovers for over fifty years. You two are a marvelous example to follow.

Helen and Denny Carter, you two are amazing friends. I couldn't have pulled this off without your help. The Wryter's Inside group for ten years of advice, feedback, and cheerleading. Merri, Emery, Larry, and Norma, this book is a team victory. The best days of our group are just ahead of us!

Special thanks to my good friend and "agent" Ted Povinelli. I owe you a tremendous debt, but consider this book a downpayment.

Michael Kahn for the encouragement and legal advice. Stan Townsend, thanks for the technical test read--I'll try to give your character a bigger role in the next book! Chief Ron Battelle, Officers Steve Deen and Jim Been, Detective Kevin Lawson, and the St. Louis County SWAT team, thanks for letting me walk a mile in your extremely large shoes. To Phil Stern, for his encouraging words in due season. And to Mike Renieri and

Ed Gerding, my past and present bosses who have shown incredible support in all of my endeavors, whether it's creating books or airplanes.

This book is dedicated to all of you.

Quotes in Chapters 9, 10, and the Epilogue are taken from James Bamford's excellent nonfiction book on the NSA, *Body of Secrets*, by Doubleday.

CHAPTER 1

"Democracy becomes a government of bullies, tempered by editors." - Ralph Waldo Emerson

BROADMAN

The late afternoon heat rose in waves off the Hackensack parking lot, baking Tony Broadman's dress shirt to his chest despite the best efforts of his seven-year-old Jeep's air conditioner. Broadman loosened his tie further. He had already sat for an hour in his Cherokee waiting for his overdue contact. Only the occasional shriek of a jet on short final to Teeterboro broke the monotony.

Tony Broadman wasn't an idealist. He wasn't on a quest to change the world. He just wanted to make an honest buck. But some days making that buck was harder than others.

Previous experience had taught Broadman to bring along an assortment of "toys" to help pass the time. The first was a laptop with a prototype wireless modem that promised to "usher in a new era of mobile Internet connectivity." He'd see about that. The claims hardware and software companies made for their wares kept Broadman expecting a computer guaranteed to cure herpes, along with an optional upgrade that fixed speeding tickets.

Broadman loved gadgets. Like a little boy at a toy store, he was always pulled into shops with the latest computer, cell phone, or digital organizer. If it wasn't for the technology "fixes" he received on the job, he might have racked up a serious personal debt.

His technology column for the New York *Times* gave him the perfect excuse for gadget collecting. Whether it was the virtues of the latest pocket PC or the Windows bug fix of the week, Broadman was paid to make sure "The User's Edge" talked about it first. He hoped the upcoming interview could be turned into a week-long feature, if this guy Yoshida showed up at all.

The new laptop's wireless modem *was* fairly speedy. It also threw corrupted data onto the page whenever a jet flew over.

That one would go back to the manufacturer, along with a polite note suggesting more field testing.

Broadman was an electrical engineer, but technical details weren't his true strength. His real skill was making friends quickly. He earned his pay by finding the people who *were* technically adept and talking them into spilling their secrets. Yoshida had promised secrets worth spilling. Broadman's job would be to work those secrets loose.

Broadman was street-smart, but his easy charm put even jaded New Yorkers at ease. He had a smile that lifted one corner of his mouth, then widened until the twinkle in his eyes pulled people in. Strangers often confided in him without even knowing why they had done so.

Too bad his charm hadn't worked on the balky laptop. The next toy was a combination wireless handheld computer and GPS locator. One of the uses the brochure touted was surfing into a nationwide database of public restrooms--he wondered who got stuck with drawing up *that* list--then using the GPS to navigate to the closest one. If his wife got her wish, she might find this extremely handy. A bathroom was something an expectant woman never wanted too far away.

Broadman smiled. Parenthood was a big step, but he was looking forward to it, especially since he knew how much Christina wanted children. She wasn't pregnant yet, but she had openly expressed her hope for a boy, one who would have "the same wavy black hair and luscious brown eyes that make my Tony so handsome." It made him blush, especially when she said it around her girlfriends. But after years of being self-conscious about his average height and slender build, it was a pleasant kind of embarrassment.

Traffic on nearby I-80 was thickening. It would take him forever to get home from here in Jersey if he waited much longer. He reached to put the Cherokee in gear. An hour was the limit of his patience, no matter how important the interview. His cell phone chirped. This guy had better be calling from the hospital.

"Broadman!"

"Oh, I'm sorry," a familiar voice purred. "I was trying to reach the man I make love to."

An electric tingle made him squirm. "Is it time?"

His wife Christina was testing another gadget for him, an electronic fertility monitor called OvaCue. By placing a sensor on her tongue, the OvaCue measured her electrolytes, calculating the optimum time for conception. She had practically ripped the package from his hands when it had arrived from the manufacturer.

Broadman could hear road noise past the breathy voice on the other end. "That's what the little box you gave me says. What's the matter, don't you trust your technology?"

"Oh, *absolutely!*" Broadman had suspected something was up from the very unlibrarian-like black miniskirt his wife had worn to work that morning. In his mind's eye he pictured it riding up as she drove the winding road to their house.

"Then *hurry*, lover man, or I'll start without you!"

That nailed it. Fertility provoked a distinct earthiness in Christina, which he was always willing to indulge. "Hang on, honey! I'm on my way!"

Broadman almost ripped the gear shift from the console. The underpowered V6 seemed to roar with more gusto than usual. He was just yards from the parking lot's exit when a black Honda Civic cut him off. Broadman stood on the brakes, barely stopping in time. The Civic's driver rolled down his window.

Broadman did the same. He was about to vent his anger and sexual frustration, but the other driver spoke first. He was holding a device that looked like an improvised version of the cellular phone scanner an FBI agent had once demonstrated for Broadman.

"Family hour can wait, Mr. Broadman," the young oriental man prodded. "Or should I call you 'lover man?'"

Broadman was fuming. That this punk had kept him waiting and *then* listened in on his phone calls wasn't the only reason. He knew by the time he finished this interview the traffic going north would be thoroughly screwed. He'd be lucky to get home by eight. He swallowed his irritation and followed Ken Yoshida from the lot.

Until today, Broadman had never met a hacker face to face. Hackers were always a faceless, disembodied enemy in his electronic world. They were a danger he warned his readers about frequently. Pointing out such hazards was part of Tony Broadman's job. Professional revulsion had prevented him from interviewing one.

But there was also a personal edge to his dislike of hackers. He had recently spent the better part of a week recovering from a virus hidden inside a software upgrade. He had downloaded it from the MegaComp corporation's supposedly "secure" business software site. MegaComp of course denied any responsibility for the virus, which then infected every computer on Broadman's floor and made him a techno-leper with the *Times'* staff. His stinging editorial against MegaComp never made it into print.

But Kentaro Yoshida was supposedly a "reformed" hacker. He had served federal prison time a few years ago for hacking corporate computers and stealing everything from credit card numbers to proprietary research data. Now he worked as a computer security specialist, charging the same corporations he had hacked large fees to plug holes in their networks' security.

Broadman's Cherokee was hard-pressed to keep up with the Civic. It sped to a run-down apartment complex, the kind with two letters missing from the curbfront sign. Broadman left an apologetic message on his home machine for Christina, then set his car alarm and double-checked it.

He wondered what had drawn the hacker out of the woodwork for this interview. The government had done its best to paint Yoshida as a Public Enemy during his incarceration. They also made sure cameras from every network were at the prison gates to stigmatize his re-entry into society. He had since stayed out of the spotlight, refusing interviews and even a book deal.

Until last week. Yoshida had called *him*, offering to share the latest hacker tricks with Broadman's readers. He refused to give a contact number, insisting their communication be one way only. The cellular number that flashed on Broadman's display was different on each call. It was only after several last-minute cancellations that this tardy appointment was arranged.

Yoshida didn't stop to make introductions, bounding up the uneven stairs to the second floor.

"From your reputation," Broadman called to Yoshida's back, "I pictured you driving a fancier car." Not to mention living in a better neighborhood.

"Even Batman has a second car."

At least Yoshida had a sense of humor. He stopped Broadman at the door. "Did you remember what I said about electronics?"

Broadman showed his empty hands. Yoshida had been adamant. No electronic devices of any kind were allowed. "I even left my cell phone and pager in the car," Broadman assured him. "Is that why you tapped my cell, to make sure I followed the rules?" If he hadn't needed this interview, Broadman would have been tempted to pop Yoshida for that little trick. They *were* in Jersey, after all, where the left jab was a time-honored form of communication.

A knowing grin. "I've found it helpful to know who my clients are talking to right before they talk to me. It's helped me avoid customers who, shall we say, didn't have my best interests at heart. It also lets you know that Big Brother could always be listening. I'm taking a big enough risk using *my* gear. I don't want you throwing any more variables into the mix."

It also shows off the power you have over other people, doesn't it? "Whatever you say." Broadman always agreed to any ground rules the subjects of his interviews requested. It was part of making them feel comfortable. And if they weren't comfortable, they might not talk.

Yoshida motioned Broadman inside and scanned the breezeway for several seconds. He locked the door behind them.

"Expecting visitors?"

"In my line of work, paranoia is a virtue."

It fit, Broadman reasoned. Look over enough people's shoulders and eventually you'll believe someone *has* to be looking over yours too.

* * *

The stretched Econoline bore the markings of the local cable company. The two workers in the van's front seats had corporate IDs and even golf shirts with the appropriate matching logos, but they belonged to a different "company" altogether. Hard hats covered their military haircuts.

Senior Airman Dave Jackson went in and out of a vacant apartment, keeping up the show of an extended but routine service call. Master Sergeant Tom Kramp, the driver, appeared to be on lunch break, but a trained observer would have noted that his steely blue eyes never stopped moving.

In the back of the van, Colonel Carl Richter waited. Two men were with him, one facing a tinted window, the other working at a computer terminal. The window was a design they had "borrowed" from the FBI. A silk-screened cover stretched over the opening. Painted the same color as the van, the cover made the window invisible from more than ten feet away.

Seated at the window, Staff Sergeant Bill Womack motioned to Richter. "Target in sight. He's got somebody with him, too."

Richter squeezed in next to Womack. "How often does he receive visitors here?"

Womack lowered his binoculars. "At *this* place? Never, that I know of. He's always gone to a neutral site for his meets before."

Richter didn't normally allow Kramp to park this close, but it was a good thing he did this time. Through the window they watched a man in a shirt and tie walk away from a Jeep Cherokee. "So who's *this* guy?" Richter asked.

"Never seen him before," Womack said. "I'll run his tags."

Richter keyed his radio. "Let's reposition. Don't want to make him nervous."

* * *

Broadman was even less impressed by Yoshida's quarters. Spartan was the first word that sprang to mind. Monastic was the second. There was no furniture in the living room, not even a couch or a TV. He followed Yoshida back to the single bedroom.

"Be sure and thank your wife for that call," Yoshida goaded. "I thought I was going to *die* of boredom while you were surfing that database of public restrooms. Did you need to use the john?"

Broadman held back a retort. "No, I was just trying out a new piece of hardware."

"Good, 'cause I'm short on toilet paper. By the way, that GPS thing you were using was still uploading your position onto the Internet until you stuck it under the seat."

"But I put it in sleep mode."

"Then it sleeps with one eye open. That's why I was trying to lose you coming over here. Just to show how I could track you down again from that leaking GPS signal."

"Okay. Nice to know." Broadman hoped his shock wasn't too obvious. *That* would certainly make an interesting footnote for his product review.

There was no bed in the bedroom, just a long folding table covered with wires and computer hardware. Two metal shelves packed with computer manuals and books in Japanese were within easy reach. A pile of copy-paper boxes filled the opposite corner, like he had just finished unpacking.

Yoshida made a crash-landing into his chair, his momentum rolling him to the table. He moved in fast forward, powering up three laptop computers and checking the spaghetti-web connections between them with quick, bird-like motions. He hummed *Ride of the Valkyries* fervently, as if preparing to charge into battle.

It took a few minutes for Yoshida to realize there was no place for his guest to sit. He waved a hand at Broadman. "Grab a chair from the kitchen."

The dust on the counters and the smell of three-day-old takeout pizza made Broadman's nose wrinkle. The folding table was obviously used more often as an overflow desk than for eating.

He unfolded a chair at Yoshida's side and pulled out his notebook. Broadman was so used to taking notes with his laptop that paper and pen felt stone-age to him. And he had *never* conducted an interview without a tape recorder.

A physical description came first. Yoshida was in his late twenties or maybe early thirties. He was slightly shorter than Broadman, his build more athletic. Straight black hair fell almost to his shoulders. A prominent brow cast shadows over deep-set, brooding eyes, and his lips were perpetually pursed, as if he was contemplating a puzzle.

Broadman attempted a handshake. "I guess an introduction would be a waste of time, right?"

"Correct." Yoshida shoved a fat folder into the offered hand.

Broadman hefted the file. "What's this?"

"It's you."

On top was Broadman's short bio from the *Times* website. Printouts of several recent columns followed, along with web search pages showing articles by other writers who had quoted Broadman in their stories. Nothing a computer-savvy grade school student couldn't duplicate. "Okay, so hackers can use search engines too?"

"Keep reading." Yoshida was fixated on his task. He stabbed at the laptop's controls with frenetic motions, pushing

ahead to the next web page before the last one had finished
loading.

Broadman continued digging through the folder. He realized he was reading printouts of his own e-mail. And files from
his boss's computer. One of them was his performance ap-
praisal.

"Broadman communicates technical information effectively," the document read, "but his articles frequently lack the
depth and originality readers of the *Times* have come to expect.
He is temperamental when challenged on this and other matters.
He also missed a deadline recently which resulted in a substantial layout change shortly before press time. Because of these
facts, I recommend an average raise of three percent."

"Why, that two-faced little..." She was the *reason* he had
missed that deadline! All because she was afraid his column
critical of the MegaComp corporation might stir up trouble for
the *Times*. Had she ever heard of the truth being its own defense? Or of the *Times'* staff of lawyers?

The slightest of smiles curved Yoshida's lips. "I see you've
found the good stuff. Keep going."

Broadman thumbed through the stack, finding more half-
truths and outright lies his boss had used to minimize his share
of the raise pool. His anger mounted. How would *she* know that
his articles lacked depth? She couldn't troubleshoot a computer
glitch if someone held a gun to her head. "I didn't think they *put*
this kind of information on the computer."

Yoshida snorted. "They make sure the really sensitive stuff
is *only* on the computer. That way if they want to fire you, any
records useful to your lawyer would be--zip--deleted."

"Temperamental when challenged..." Broadman mumbled.
Well, she *did* nail him on that one. The User's Edge was his
baby. Nobody liked changing something they thought was correct as it stood. She just wanted to put her mark on his column
because it *was* popular. But it was the "lacking depth" comment
that really burned him. She couldn't even schedule her computer for an automatic backup without his help.

"Hey, if it really bothers you that much, we can change it,"
Yoshida offered. "I have root access to most of the computers at
the *Times*, just like I was the head sysop. I can't raise your sal-
ary yet, but I could change your personnel records to a more
glowing review. If I time it right, I might even be able to change
the headline for tomorrow's paper. How about, 'Tony Broad-

man is a computer god?' Would that make up for what your boss said?"

A few choice comments about his boss would make an even better headline. "Could you really do that?"

"With root access, I *own* the *Times*. The computer thinks I'm the systems administrator for the whole damned network. I could even program every computer on the network to reject certain words or phrases. So if somebody wrote a story critical of hackers, the system would refuse to print it."

He knew hackers had a long reach, but this was a whole new level. "I'll try to keep my words soft and sweet."

"Never a good idea to piss off a hacker," Yoshida agreed.

* * *

The van had moved to the far side of the complex. Kramp noticed the bearded man in a tie-dyed shirt stalking toward him. He keyed the radio in his lap. "Trouble, partner," he whispered.

"On my way."

The man approached the Kramp's window, his face livid. "Hey man! Your service *sucks!* I called you people a week ago, but now you're here working on somebody else! How long have *they* been waiting for you to show up?"

Jackson returned to the van. The wiry young Airman moved with a quick, confident gait. "What kind of trouble are you having, sir?"

The man waved his hands. "Look, man, like I told you on the phone! Everything was fine one minute, then *bam*, it just turned to snow! Every channel! I've had to go back to the damned rabbit ears, for Christ's sake!"

Jackson kept his smile relaxed and friendly. "Sounds like a bad converter box. We get a lot of those." He reached into the van's front seat and pulled out a spare. "I bet this'll fix you up. Let's go take a look."

That took the edge off their "customer's" anger. He led Jackson to his apartment. The radio in Kramp's lap crackled.

"Everything okay up there?" Richter asked.

Kramp grinned. "Have no fear, cable guy is here."

"Excellent."

"This position is getting a little exposed," Richter told the man at the computer. "How's it coming?"

Senior Airman Tim Feldman reviewed the data they were capturing. The van had TEMPEST gear, able to suck in the faint radio signals from PC and laptop monitors and read their displays. But he had to get close for that, less than a hundred yards for the laptop their target was using. Add to that the interference from scores of PCs and TV sets in the complex and Feldman would have a real headache skimming the target signal from the electronic sewer around them.

Luckily their target had taken advantage of the cable company's broadband Internet service. Using their cover, they had hooked a repeater to their target's computer line in the main cable box. Now Feldman could pick up their repeater's clear, clean signal from anywhere in the complex. The only hard part had been tracking this hacker down. Earlier efforts had succeeded only in locating the empty apartments where their target *used* to be. But even the smartest hacker couldn't hope to outwit the entire NSA indefinitely. It was just a matter of time.

"He's close enough to smell the cheese," Feldman said. "Give him a few more minutes."

* * *

Broadman was sufficiently rattled that he flipped through several pages before realizing the files were from his *home* computer. "Hey! How did you get this? My firewall program is the top of the line!"

Yoshida teased him with an arched eyebrow. "It wasn't your firewall program's fault. Your wife was kind enough to be logged on when I hacked your Internet service provider's server. Then I just slipped down your phone line as another packet of information. *Voilà!* Instant access!"

Broadman drew in a quick breath at the next page. A voluptuous brunette reclined nude on a couch, licking her upper lip seductively. Several painfully familiar pictures like it followed.

Yoshida gave Broadman a smirk. "And *look* what I found under 'Miscellaneous Tax Info!' Does your wife know about those gals?"

Broadman closed the folder, his face burning. "Thanks. I think I've seen enough."

Yoshida feigned astonishment. "You haven't even *looked* at your credit reports yet! I hacked into three different databases so you could compare the numbers! I can even change them if you want."

"Gee thanks, that's nice of you to offer."

Yoshida's smile broadened. "Feeling a little naked, Tony? Take off your clothes and get comfortable. Actually, *everybody's* this vulnerable, it's just that now you *know* it." He resumed typing.

Broadman unconsciously held the file closed, as if the contents might make a break for freedom. He needed to regain control of the interview. "Uh, where exactly are you going?"

Yoshida continued his manic tempo, occasionally sliding sideways to switch laptops. "Ever heard of MINTNET?"

"Some kind of government database, isn't it?"

Yoshida's grin melted away. "Monetary Intelligence Tracking Network. It's the *mother* of all government databases."

Broadman scribbled the acronym on his notepad. "Is that why it takes three laptops to break into their system?"

"Just one to break in. The other two are to make sure I don't get caught. That's where most newbie hackers screw up. Breaking into a computer network is the easy part. You only get to be a grizzled old graybeard like me by covering your tracks."

"Mind showing me how you do that?" He had always wondered how hackers could wander like ghosts over the Internet, undetected until the damage was done. He was sure his readers did too.

Yoshida turned one of the laptops. "The trick is root access and multiple jumps. I'm leapfrogging across four Internet service providers, ISPs, to get to my current target, and I have root access to all of them. I can do everything the ISP's system administrator does, and I can watch every command entered at root level."

The SONY laptop's screen was split into four Unix windows, all idle at the moment. "I planted a Trojan horse program called a root kit at all four ISPs. It deletes my keystrokes from any system logs and defeats any program looking for those kind of system alterations. That's my first line of defense."

It sounded more like the software equivalent of a nuclear weapon to Broadman. "Where would you *get* a program like that?"

"You can download one from any hacker website, but I wrote my own just to make it harder to spot. If the root kit is defeated or if the system administrator at any of the ISPs starts launching defensive programs, it'll show up on one of these screens. But I picked these four ISPs because none of their administrators appeared to be the sharpest knives in the drawer."

"But what if the watchdogs at MINTNET detect you and start running a trace *through* these ISPs? That wouldn't show up, would it?"

Yoshida placed his hands together in a mock oriental bow. "Ah, grasshopper! Truly you begin to think like wise serpent!" He pivoted a Hewlett-Packard laptop to face Broadman. "That's where screen number three earns its paycheck. This monitors traffic through each of my hacked ports. If one of these shows a spike in activity, either someone's running a trace, or more likely an automated security program like EtherPeek was tripped at one of the ISPs. Either way, we sack the hack and disappear."

The way Yoshida used "we" made Broadman feel like an active participant in this criminal enterprise. It was an uncomfortable but strangely exhilarating sensation. "So what makes MINTNET worth all this trouble?"

Yoshida was busy with the Compaq laptop in the center. An MIT web page popped onto the screen. "Years ago, the courts decided a citizen's financial information was one of the last pieces of information the government couldn't traffic in for fun and profit. If the IRS had built a case against Joe Blow for tax evasion, they couldn't just throw the data over the fence to aid the FBI's investigation of Mr. Blow for money laundering. The FBI had to come to court with their own evidence and convince a judge why they needed the IRS's data."

Yoshida clicked on the button for the MIT Supercomputer Center. "Well, you can imagine how that sat with the Feds. Privacy is a four-letter word for them. That's when they created MINTNET. They use the National Security Agency to suck in data on virtually every financial transaction conducted in the US, then they classify it as 'intelligence.'

"They have two hundred people from every alphabet soup agency we've got working at the NSA facility to swap that 'intelligence' around. But share financial data? Hell no! And since everything the NSA does is classified out the wazoo, no judge is going to get close enough to shut them down."

A window opened on the screen. "PLEASE ENTER YOUR ACCOUNT NUMBER." Yoshida filled in the blank.

"WELCOME PROFESSOR ERSTWINE. YOUR BATCH JOB IS COMPLETED."

"What does Professor Erstwine have to do with MINTNET?" Broadman was struggling to get all this on paper.

Yoshida downloaded the file. "Other than his idle account on MIT's supercomputer, nothing. Even though MINTNET is located at NSA headquarters, the agencies who want to access their data still need a pipeline to MINTNET's database. That's what I think I've found."

"MINTNET's back door?"

Yoshida shook his head. "Front door. Actually more like an entry hall. Every agency that wants in has its own door in the hallway and its own password to get through that door. After I picked the lock for the hallway, I dug out an encrypted password file. I was just using MIT's supercomputer to crack the encryption."

Yoshida opened the batch file. A sequence of alphanumeric strings filled the screen. He leaned back in his chair and sighed.

"What's wrong?"

"Nothing, nothing. That's the password file all right, one for each portal into the system. It was almost too easy."

"So what's next?"

For the first time, Yoshida turned from his computers. "Next, Tony, I need you to make a decision. If I'm going to risk my butt hacking into MINTNET again, I need to know whether you'll publish what I find there."

Broadman pushed away, rocking the folding chair back on two legs. "Whoa, wait a minute! A hacking *demonstration* is one thing. Stealing government secrets is way beyond that!"

"C'mon, I've read your material. Isn't electronic loss of privacy one of your favorite rants? I figured you'd *jump* at the chance to expose something like this."

"Well yeah, but only if I can come by the information *legally*. You're talking about hacking into a *classified* government computer. That's one of those things that gets you a ten-year vacation at a federal resort."

Yoshida laughed. "If the NSA knew we were hacking into MINTNET, they would probably kill us on the spot, take my computers, and leave our bodies for my landlady to find."

Broadman's stomach clenched. "Oh good, I thought we were talking about jail time." If he had left that parking lot just five minutes earlier, he might be home making love to his wife by now.

"I'm serious. These guys are using the Constitution for toilet paper. Somebody's got to stand up and say 'Enough!' I'll get the goods on them. That's my part of the bargain, but I need to know that you and your management won't choke on me when I deliver."

"And here I thought you hackers were all anarchists. I hardly expected a civics lesson." A voice in Broadman's head told him his life was about to be permanently changed, regardless of which choice he made.

Yoshida encrypted the password list and filed it away. "Even hackers grow up eventually. And I learned my civics lessons the hard way."

Broadman massaged a growing tightness in his neck. "If they're so intent on keeping MINTNET a secret, wouldn't they come after me if I tried to go to press?" Part of him was intrigued by the information Yoshida was offering, but another part reminded Broadman of how hard he had worked to get his life into its current ordered state.

Yoshida powered down his laptop trio. "They'll give you a hard time, all right. But once you go public, they can't physically harm you. It would just confirm your story."

"That's comforting." As a reporter, Broadman had seen how the government could turn someone's life upside down without laying a finger on them. Yoshida's assurances were really no comfort at all. "And what would they do to you?"

"We would have no further contact. I make the delivery and disappear. Even if they check phone records, I've made sure they can't tie the two of us together."

"I'll have to talk it over with my boss. The one who said my stories lack depth." This was going to be a tough sell. A well-done product review was a lot more popular with his management than testing the boundaries of the First Amendment.

Yoshida pushed back from the table. "I hope I've given you enough material to justify the trip."

Broadman flipped his notebook closed. "More than enough. I'll call you in a couple of days." It was probably a moot point. He could count on the editors quashing any idea that fell outside the narrow scope of his column.

"No, I'll call *you*. Thanks for stopping by."

Broadman hardly noticed the traffic on the way home. He had other things to think about.

* * *

Yoshida was annoyed by Broadman's attitude. Despite what Broadman's boss thought of him, Yoshida had been led to believe that he was a solid guy, if a little immature. His source had said nothing about an underlying streak of cowardice. So much for the *Times* being on the cutting edge of journalism. He hooked his cloned cell phone to a scrambler and punched in the destination number. It was answered on the first ring.

"So are the Rangers taking the Cup this year?" a gravelly voice asked.

"You know damned well I'm a Devils fan," Yoshida replied. "The proposal has been delivered."

The scrambler lent a metallic tone to the voice. "Do we have a sale?"

"Unknown. He'll consider it and get back to us. Maybe we should start looking for another customer."

"Understood. Keep me posted."

"Always." Yoshida ended the call and slid out the phone's battery. Later he would pull the phone's chip and reprogram it with a new electronic personality, but that could wait.

* * *

"He's definitely off-line now," Feldman reported. "If we need to reposition, this would be a good time. He's a methodical guy. He usually takes a couple of hours between hacks to plan his next move."

"Where's he been?" Richter asked Feldman.

"The Supercomputer Center at MIT. Looks like he cracked the password file. Record time, too."

Through the window he watched the Jeep Cherokee leave the complex. "Do we have an ID on this guy yet?" Richter asked.

Feldman retrieved a sheet from the printer. "His tag came up as Anthony Broadman of Mountainville, New York. Yoshida hacked into several accounts of the same name last week. Probably part of his legitimate security business."

"If Broadman's legit, then he's not a factor. You think Yo-shida will hit MINTNET again tonight?"

Feldman snickered. "He's got the decrypted password file right there in his hot little hands. Would *you* be able to resist?"

Richter nodded decisively. "Okay, it's taken long enough, but I think we finally got this bastard. I'll call the Snake Pit. As soon as he gets his pants down around his ankles, he's ours."

THE HUNDRED HACKER RAID

"Every general is on stage" - Frederick the Great

Lieutenant General Jonathan Stoyer's phone rang. He looked up at his reflection in the tinted windows of the Direc-tor's office. The darkness outside National Security Agency headquarters turned the shielded glass into mirrors, allowing Stoyer capture to the moment. The late hour assured him this would be no ordinary call. He allowed the phone to ring twice.

"Stoyer."

"General! We have a massive cyberattack in progress." It was Jeff Archer, the NSA's Deputy Director.

"How bad?"

"Sir, the entire state of Nebraska just dropped off the map. You'd better come check it out." Dread radiated from the other end.

"On my way."

Stoyer went through the ritual of leaving his office at NSA headquarters. He secured his classified material in the Mosler safe concealed inside a cherrywood credenza. He placed his granite paperweight on one of the unclassified documents neatly arrayed on his desk, reminding himself where to resume work when he returned. He gave the granite cube a final pat for good luck. Its inscription said it all:

POWER. FOCUS. CONTROL.

The ride down to the command center gave him a chance to adjust the lines of his Air Force uniform on his thin, wiry frame. The air in the elevator felt electric to him, as crisp and sharp as his graying crew cut.

The elevator halted. With his general's face firmly in place, Stoyer marched into the National Information Command Cen-ter. His office upstairs might be the outward symbol of his authority, but the NICC was the seat of his true power. In this chamber, he was the best-informed military commander on the planet. The communications and intelligence equipment surrounding him here connected him instantly to the NSA's own Army, Air Force, and Navy elements, which included dozens of aircraft, fleets of ships and satellites, even a nuclear submarine.

Just as important as the technology in the NICC were the two dozen people staffing it, the NSA's top-drawer analysts. Most of them monitored data from specific sources: satellites, listening posts, surveillance ships and aircraft. Others searched the full spectrum of the NSA's data stream for specific threats, such as terrorist activity or hacker intrusions. Some of the NICC staff were in uniform, but most wore business suits.

The NSA's first string was having trouble coping with tonight's crisis. Information was their lifeblood, and precious little was flowing. Even with the recent emphasis on homeland defense, the NSA was having more difficulty gathering intelligence on American soil than they would have in some hot spot half a world away. Consternation was mounting as the employees of the world's largest intelligence agency were reduced to flipping through cable news channels or attempting telephone calls into the affected areas, without success.

In the center of the chaos the NICC's watch officer spoke into his headset and the handset of another phone while nodding or shaking his head at notes his subordinates placed on his desk. One of his two pagers went off while Stoyer passed. The watch officer dropped his phone trying to silence the pager and salute at the same time. Stoyer returned the salute stoically, enjoying his superiority over the Army colonel.

The NICC was shaped like a fat pie wedge. Stoyer had entered on the narrow end and mounted the stairs to a glass-enclosed balcony. From there he overlooked the huge central screen and four smaller screens on each side that took up the wide end of the room. A custom-made leather captain's chair placed the controls for the screens at his fingertips. Sitting in the elevated seat, Stoyer exuded the calm and confidence a good officer should exhibit in a crisis.

"Report!" he barked.

Jeff Archer was anything but calm. He had jumped to his feet when Stoyer entered. Now he nervously retook his seat at one of the three stations along the front edge of the balcony. This vantage point let him see not only the screens but the workers on the floor below. Archer would monitor the execution of the General's orders, while Stoyer need only concern himself with the data on the displays.

Archer's fingers danced on a keyboard. "This is the latest spy satellite feed. The view is centered over Omaha."

The central screen went dark, then showed a networked constellation of lights. A gaping void consumed the center of the image, pitch black.

Stoyer leaned forward, not fully able to believe the picture. The blacked-out area closely followed the state boundaries, although it was harder to see in the sparsely-populated panhandle.

"Am I seeing what I *think* I'm seeing?"

Archer nodded, his expression grim. "They cut everything. Electricity, telephone, fiber optic lines, even microwave links. It's like somebody dropped a Nebraska-shaped cookie cutter from orbit."

The sight sent a shiver down Stoyer's spine. "I think someone is sending us a message."

"Anywhere, anytime," Archer agreed.

The blackout area was not entirely unlit. Small orange glows flickered in the darkness.

"Are those *fires* burning down there?"

"My people are trying to find out right now. The watch officer should be reporting back momentarily."

Stoyer studied his second-in-command. A clean-cut man in his early forties, Archer had a doctorate in mathematics from CalPoly and was a detailed but efficient manager. He watched over day-to-day problems, allowing Stoyer to focus on the NSA's future. Stoyer could tell that beneath Archer's professional veneer, *fear* was gnawing on the man's insides.

The phone next to Archer rang. He snatched up the receiver on the first ring.

"Sir," Archer reported, "we're picking up police radio intercepts from all over the state reporting natural gas explosions. One incident in Omaha and one in Lincoln sound pretty bad. They're screaming for ambulances and mobile triage units."

"Great Plains Natural Gas still has their switching network on the Internet, don't they?"

"Yes, sir. We warned them all about that. Great Plains apparently didn't listen."

Stoyer allowed his shoulders to drop. "I assume all the appropriate agencies have been informed?"

"We're ringing the fire bells right now."

"My god, my god. Then it's finally happened." And in the President's home state, Stoyer mused.

There was horror in Archer's voice. "The Hundred Hacker Raid. We warned them it was coming, didn't we, sir?"

Stoyer made sure he matched Archer's tone. "Yeah, Jeff, we certainly tried."

His work here was complete. Damage control was not his concern. "Jeff, it's going to take a lot of detective work to find out who caught us napping. In the meantime, the politicians are going to want me to hold their hands, and I'd prefer to do that with a good night's sleep. Besides, I'd just be in your way if I stayed here."

Archer blinked. "Uh, yes sir. I'll call a driver."

"No, I knew I'd be working late, so I drove myself. Listen, why don't you route my home phone here tonight? I don't want some junior White House staffer waking me up. Tell them I'll brief the President myself at oh-eight-hundred tomorrow morning. Have a car at my house at oh-seven and make sure you fax me the brief before then. If I have any questions, I'll call you on the way."

"Consider it done." While Stoyer was getting a good night's sleep, Archer would get none at all, but that was assumed.

"Thanks, Jeff. You're a good man to have at the wheel."

Archer worked up a half-hearted smile. "You're welcome, sir. Glad to be of service."

Stoyer took one more look at the black hole punched into the very heartland of America, then stepped briskly to the stairs. He needed to visit the Snake Pit right away.

CHAPTER 2

"The natural progress of things is for Liberty to yield and government to gain ground." - Thomas Jefferson

PEARL HARBOR

Stoyer's visits to the White House had taken on a predictable routine. Like a fireman, he was summoned only when there was trouble. He was a bit player in a predictable Kabuki theater, the outcome decided before the performers even took the stage. But today would be different. Without the knowledge of the other actors, Stoyer had changed the script.

He smelled the fear when his car pulled through the White House's Southwest Appointment Gate. It was evident from the increased numbers of Secret Service agents brandishing their Heckler & Koch submachine guns openly, instead of concealed inside the fast-action bags they used around the tourists. As if guns could protect the White House from the type of attack Nebraska had suffered last night.

Several official cars already occupied the VIP spaces along West Executive Drive, the parking lot between the West Wing and the Old Executive Office Building next door. The Director of Central Intelligence's limousine arrived just before Stoyer's Grand Marquis. The DCI bailed from his limo immediately, jogging for the West Wing entrance. Stoyer took a deep breath and waited for the plainclothes NSA bodyguard to open his door. There was no need to hurry. He was in charge today.

The White House staffers inside carried out the expected crisis drill, rushing with stern faces from office to office in the appearance of taking action. It was laughable, but required. The overhanging gloom thickened with every step Stoyer took toward the Oval Office.

President Marshall Adams paced like a caged tiger in front of his desk. His eyes carried a mixture of shock and barely contained anger. By God, he was going to do something, he just didn't know what yet. Stoyer would provide the President with that answer, but only in due time.

Adams was short for a politician. His figure had once been as compact as a right tackle but now required ingenious tailoring of his suits to keep him from being called pudgy. In his late fifties, with thinning hair and a prominent nose, he was more often described as distinguished than handsome.

Stoyer respected the abilities of the former governor and two-term senator from Nebraska. He wasn't just a politician, he was a *leader*. He had even been decorated in battle, for taking command of an artillery battery in Da Nang following a devastating enemy mortar attack. So Adams had been a warrior at one time, Stoyer reasoned, but he had left the true faith for a lesser profession.

The core members of the President's National Security Council sat on the couches, their eyes glued to the screen at the opposite end of the room. It was still dark in Nebraska, as it had been when Stoyer had received the President's summons to the White House. *Come sit with us as I watch television and do nothing*, the message might as well have read. The TV cameras in Nebraska followed a group of firefighters carrying body bags to a waiting Army truck.

The President stopped pacing. "Dear God, is that a replay, or are there more?"

"Two of the worst gas explosions occurred at a nursing home and a homeless shelter, Mr. President," the Secretary of Defense offered. "We were warned the casualty count from these accidents could be catastrophic."

Stoyer had stood quietly in the doorway of the Oval Office. It was time to make his entrance.

"Those were *not* accidents, Mr. President," Stoyer declared.

Every head in the room swiveled toward him.

Stoyer's confidence irritated his Commander-in-Chief. Adams probably wanted Stoyer to feel the same confused agony he was enduring. "I understand you have some theories, General?"

"Not theories, Mr. President, facts." Stoyer took his place at the President's side, opening a folder to read from the brief Jeff Archer had provided.

"Last night at ten o'clock Washington time, the United States suffered its first electronic Pearl Harbor. As with the first Pearl Harbor, we were caught sleeping and totally unprepared for the attack." He read down the list of facilities his hackers had targeted.

"Whose fault is this, General?" The CIA Director sniped. The bald little man was still breathless from his dash inside, but his shifting eyes were already looking for a scapegoat. "I thought the NSA was responsible for our electronic security."

Barton Walsh III was the bureaucrat in charge of the nation's intelligence machine. Officially he was Stoyer's boss, but Stoyer had effectively frozen the CIA out of the NSA's inner workings.

"Enough, Bart!" Adams snapped. "General, continue."

"Right now my staff is examining electronic evidence from the attack. We now know what was hit, and since we can monitor traffic on the global networks closely, we should be able to backtrack the sabotage to its source."

Cynthia Hale, the President's National Security Adviser, crossed her arms. "General, do you really think you can locate the people who did this?"

Stoyer considered his response carefully. Hale was the former chair of the International Relations Department at Stanford, a position she left to become then-Senator Adams's foreign policy advisor throughout his presidential campaign. Stylishly dressed even for this early morning meeting, Hale was neither a socialite nor an ivory tower academic. Past the pearls, designer suits and degrees, she was a tough political fighter who had the President's ear on a daily basis. She also had served at the CIA, although Stoyer didn't know in what capacity. He resolved to fill that gap in his knowledge.

"Ms. Hale, the perfect crime hasn't been committed yet, and I have some of the best electronic detectives on the planet." Stoyer held his fingers a fraction of an inch apart. "If the terrorists who did this screwed up even *this much*, we'll nail them."

"And then what?" Adams asked, posing his question to the group.

Stoyer did not give the others a chance to respond. This was his moment. "Once the origin of the attack has been located, the NSA will present a range of viable responses to deal with the threat."

"The NSA?" Walsh protested. "What business does an intelligence-gathering agency..."

Stoyer cut off his nominal superior. "An electronic attack, an electronic response. I can *promise* you our methods *will* be effective."

The President's eyebrows rose. It was very seldom he heard such certainty from a government official. Most were more concerned with covering their backsides than providing the right answer. The element of surprise was again working in Stoyer's favor.

The TV showed a school which was now a makeshift hospital. The corridor was lined with victims whose injuries were merely painful or disfiguring, not life-threatening. Their cries and moans were like listening to a live feed from hell.

"Damn!" Adams stabbed at the remote to mute the sound. "Very well, General. Since you seem to be the only one here with a plan, I'll excuse you from this wake. Go catch these bastards."

"Consider it done, Mr. President." Without a glance at the other advisors, Stoyer turned on his heel and marched purposefully from the room.

Frederick the Great would have been proud.

TAKE DOWN

Ken Yoshida considered his options. Making a re-entry into MINTNET would be dangerous, but what more precautions could he take? He wasn't using the same intrusion scheme as when he scooped the password file. He was hacking from a different apartment complex, using a different ISP, and a different set of bounce-points to frustrate tracing his signal. He couldn't get any more invisible.

But still. His hacker's intuition made the skin on the back of his neck tingle. Someone was watching.

Hell, someone was always watching. Part of the reason the government set up the Internet was to monitor its traffic. The news media made a big deal when terrorists and militia groups used the Internet, but the government couldn't be happier. It was like setting up a free phone on a high-crime corner, just hoping the criminals would use it. Since law enforcement paid for the phone, they could legally listen in on every word. Just like they did on the Internet.

But his mind was wandering. The fastest way to find out would be to take a stroll through MINTNET. He would take a quick peek, then scoot and see what rolled back down the line. He had an apartment across the complex and another beater car just for that purpose. His books were already packed and his bookcase broken down, ready to move.

If he saw an increase in the number of unmarked vans prowling around afterwards, then he would have his answer. But his superiors in the Resistance wanted the MINTNET data. This intrusion was going forward whether Broadman published the information or not. Broadman was just the mouthpiece for this operation, and mouths were never in short supply in New York City.

Yoshida made his decision. His first step was to access an obscure server in New York City. He found the portal by doing a random address attack around the publicly listed Justice Department domain. Some quiet snooping had identified this as a site where local FBI agents logged in from the field to search criminal databases or send secure e-mail.

Although the server's transmissions were encrypted, he had captured a short message and routed it to another idle account at MIT's Supercomputer Center. That had yielded an agent's ID, his password, and the exact encryption program the agent had used for authentication. Yoshida now used this stolen identity to make his entry.

Once inside the NYC Justice node he went to the databases. Buried beneath the NCIC, ATF, DEA, Customs, and state law enforcement links, there was another category labeled "Special." He clicked it, and a password was demanded again. Apparently not even FBI agents were all privy to MINTNET. He hoped the agent whose security codes he had skimmed was one of them. Shortly another menu popped up, offering choices of CIA, NSA, DIA, NRO, and MINTNET. Bingo.

Yoshida took a deep breath and clicked MINTNET. It seemed to take a very long time, but finally a password window popped up. When the proper information was entered, he was confronted with another challenge.

ENTER PORTAL NUMBER AND PASSWORD.

He pulled up the password file and gasped. He realized he had no idea which portal belonged to the FBI and which belonged to the DEA, IRS, and the others. It was a stupid mistake. He started his watch on a five-minute countdown. When it sounded he was disconnecting, no matter what. Assuming the FBI would be near the top of the access list, he entered the first portal ID and password.

INVALID ENTRY!

He tried the second.

WARNING! INVALID ENTRY!

Yoshida assumed this was a "three strike" system. The third screw-up would kick him out and set off alarms in the Security office. He entered the third code on the list.

WELCOME SPECIAL AGENT JOHNSON. THE FILES YOU REQUESTED ARE READY FOR REVIEW.

He restrained himself from hooting with glee. Not only was he in, but he wouldn't need to dig around inside a hostile system looking for incriminating data. MINTNET was about to hand it to him.

The lights in his apartment went out.

His battery-powered laptops cast an eerie glow in the darkened room. He checked his watch. Three minutes. He clicked on the first file, which began to download. He jumped up and cracked the curtains. The whole complex was blacked out, although he could see the lights of nearby businesses still burning. He clicked on the second file. Less than two minutes left.

Outside, a van pulled up under his window, its headlights out. It gunned its engine and kept it roaring.

With the distraction of the van's engine, Yoshida almost didn't hear the click of the front door deadbolt. Almost. He whirled about in his chair. The lights in the breezeway were out, so all he saw was the shape of a man in the doorway, darker than the night outside. The shape charged toward him.

Yoshida reached under the computer table, his hand seeming to move in slow motion. He found the holster taped there and yanked the nine-millimeter Beretta free. Before he could bring the pistol up, the intruder was on top of him. Yoshida saw a nightstick swinging down toward his head. He raised an arm to deflect the blow and brought the pistol to bear on the man's gut.

Blue sparks flew when the club contacted Yoshida's forearm. An electric charge blasted through his body, arching his back and knocking the pistol from his hand. When he sucked in a stunned breath, the dark figure drove the tip of the club hard against his chest. Yoshida let out a long scream, tumbled sideways and blacked out.

* * *

The team charged the apartment building when the lights went out. Womack was the point man for the take down. After Jackson defeated the front deadbolt with a lock picking gun,

Womack rushed inside, his stun rod at the ready. Richter followed him, ready to use more lethal force if necessary.

Their target didn't even have time to get out of his chair before Womack reached him. The hacker tried to block the stun rod, but there were electrical contacts along the side of the rod as well. That knocked Yoshida's arm down, allowing Womack to stick him in the torso, where the stun rod was most effective. Womack held the rod in place until Yoshida fell out of his chair, striking the edge of the table on the way down. The hacker lay sprawled on the floor, twitching with residual spasms. Only then did Womack notice the pistol beside Yoshida's body.

"Damn!" Womack whispered. "The bastard tried to shoot me!"

"That's why you wear a chest plate," Richter said, lowering his silenced pistol. He surveyed Yoshida's setup, the laptops blazing in his night vision goggles like triple suns. He waved Jackson and Feldman into the room. "Get him off-line and start collecting his gear."

Jackson pulled an air hypo from his assault vest and shot it into Yoshida's neck. That would keep him unconscious for the several hours it would take to reach their destination. He rolled the hacker over. Yoshida was bleeding freely from a gash on his forehead. Jackson reached for a field dressing from another pocket on his vest.

Their radios crackled. "Heads up, guys," Kramp said. "The lady downstairs just called 911 reporting a scuffle and someone screaming. The cops are sending a patrol car."

Night vision goggles swung toward Richter.

From monitoring the scanner, Richter knew the police in this area had a response time of around six minutes. He wanted to be long gone by then. "Okay, we'll get this stuff later. Bag him and drag him."

"He's bleeding pretty bad," Jackson warned. "Gonna need stitches for sure."

"He'll live," Richter countered. "Patch him up in the van. And find his keys! Let's move!"

Womack rolled out a body bag. They stuffed Yoshida inside. Each man grabbed a strap and they carried him outside. Their goggles enabled them to move quickly in the darkness. Jackson secured the apartment. The police would find all quiet and the door locked. They tossed their package roughly into the van and clambered in behind it. A siren wailed in the distance.

Richter slammed the back doors shut. "We're tight! Go, go, go!" The van pulled out of its spot and roared away.

When they were clear, Richter reported in. "Snake Pit, this is Animal Control," he said over the secure phone. "We're inbound with cargo."

GADGET GUY

The User's Edge wasn't the dream job Broadman had envisioned when he sold the idea to *Times* management, but it paid the bills. He was becoming a respected voice in the press, even appearing occasionally as a "talking head" technical expert on CNN. But here at the *Times*, he was just another cubicle dweller with a word processor and a daily deadline. Sitting in his boss's office, Broadman theorized that every job eventually degenerated to this.

"I'm sorry, Tony, the answer is no. Absolutely not."

"But the story is *right there*," Broadman pleaded. "He practically *handed* it to me."

Janet Randall straightened and squared her shoulders, a signal she was about to deliver a lecture. "If this was some software company stealing its customers' financial data, we'd go to press with it. But this is federal misconduct." She interrupted herself. "*Possible* federal misconduct. I don't need the hassle of butting heads with the Feds over the word of one has-been hacker."

Broadman knew Randall was out of her depth as head of the *Times* Technology section. She knew it too. Almost everyone under her had earned a technical degree, and many had written a book in their field. Janet Randall had done neither, but she was a Journalist, which carried more weight with *Times* management. It also made Randall an insecure supervisor who blew up at the slightest questioning of her decisions. And since Broadman already knew he was "temperamental when challenged" in Randall's eyes, he saw little use in reinforcing that opinion.

"So did Yoshida give you enough background to write a general column about hackers?" she asked.

"Well sure, but..."

Randall flashed a fake smile. "Good! Then we're in agreement." She pushed away from her desk.

Broadman stayed put. "Can I at least *see* what kind of information Yoshida digs up before..."

Randall held up her hand. "Stop! Don't give me your 'nose for a story' speech. You are *not* a hard news reporter. You're the gadget guy. Leave the snooping around to the folks upstairs. Hacker column on my desk by press time tonight, and not a word about MINTNET. Thank you."

SPECIAL DELIVERY

Yoshida woke to a pounding headache and a searing pain at his temple. He tried to raise his hands to his head but could not. He blinked against the light. He was in a jail cell.

A guard scowled at him through the bars. "Okay, he's awake!"

Yoshida's hands and feet were manacled, and a thick leather belt constricted his waist. The throbbing in his head made it difficult to focus.

A second guard appeared. "Rise and shine, scumbag!"

Yoshida tried to sit up, but the pain doubled him over. He groaned.

The cell door creaked open. "Awww, is hacker boy not a morning person?"

"Where am I?"

"Hell!" the first declared. Both guards shared a laugh.

They hauled him to his feet. He groaned again. His muscles ached. "Where are you taking me?"

One of the guards jabbed him in the kidney. "We ask the questions here!"

Yoshida kept quiet. He was still wearing his street clothes, but they had taken his shoes. The concrete floor was cold against his feet. The pain in his head was making him nauseous. The belt around his waist felt like it had diving weights attached to it. He would have fallen if the guards were not dragging him forward.

Outside the cellblock, the hallway led a short distance to an interview room with a table and a single chair. A gaunt, suited man with piercing eyes sat waiting, regarding Yoshida with a predatory stare. The guards shoved Yoshida to the center of the room.

"My name is Julius Lockhart," the man announced. "I'm a lawyer for the Justice Department." He leafed through a folder. "Mister...Yoshida. Is that the correct pronunciation?"

Yoshida blinked at the unreality of it all. "Yes, it is." Part of his brain was warning him of imminent danger, but his mind was too clouded to think clearly.

"Mr. Yoshida, you have placed yourself in one *hell* of a lot of trouble. Let's see here. Electronic trespass on federal property, theft of federal access codes, electronically impersonating a federal officer, theft of evidence in a federal criminal proceeding--the list goes on. Not to mention illegal entry into MIT's computers and theft of several thousand dollars worth of supercomputer time. Yep, we're looking at some serious felonies, Mr. Yoshida."

"In that case, I would like to consult with my attorney immediately."

Lockhart shook his head. "No, Mr. Yoshida, that's the *last* thing you want to do. Now, overlooking the charges which would have to be pursued in Massachusetts, the federal charges alone would yield a minimum sentence of ten years, should you be convicted." He turned several pages, then whistled. "And *that* would appear to be a likely outcome, judging from the evidence collected against you."

Yoshida knew something was wrong. The request to see his lawyer should have stopped this interview cold, unless the government had something very special in mind for him, like a trip to Guantanamo Bay.

"However, I am prepared to offer you an alternative to rotting in prison for a very long time." Lockhart paused for dramatic effect. "Would you be interested, Mr. Yoshida?"

He sensed the trap, but his options were limited. "I'm listening."

"You'd better be. Mr. Yoshida, you are clearly a threat to society, to a public that is still learning how to defend themselves electronically. But the government is running an experimental program, where hackers like yourself are given a chance to use their skills for the public good, to shore up the defenses of the United States against computer attack.

"You would enroll in this program under strict supervision for three years. If you serve with good behavior during that period, the charges against you will be dropped. If at any time during those three years you are judged to be extending any-

thing less than your best efforts, you will be returned for trial in
a federal court on the charges previously outlined. Do you understand, Mr. Yoshida?"

The chain between the leather belt and his handcuffs prevented him from rubbing his throbbing skull. Metal tabs on the
belt were jabbing him in several places. He grimaced. "Yeah, I
think so."

"Then what is your decision?"

He sensed the oncoming train rushing toward him. "Say
what?"

"Your decision, Mr. Yoshida. Prison or the offered alternative?"

"I'll need to consult with my attorney before accepting any
plea agreement."

Veins bulged from Lockhart's neck. "You little parasite! I
offer you an alternative to hard time in a federal penitentiary
and you want to dick around with your *lawyer?* Given your
prior convictions, you're lucky we're even *having* this conversation!"

The mention of his criminal record pinched a nerve. "I have
a *right* to consult with my attorney!" Yoshida challenged.
"Speaking of which, I don't recall being read my Miranda rights
before being dragged in here!"

Lockhart almost came across the table at him. "Why, you
ungrateful little piece of shit!"

Lockhart's anger only emboldened Yoshida. "Come on,
I've never *once* met a government lawyer who could pass up
playing head games with a defendant's counsel. You guys *live*
for that crap. What kind of *sham* is this?"

Lockhart flicked a finger toward one of the guards. The
guard pulled out a remote control and mashed the button.

A fiery impact struck Yoshida's back. The battery packs on
the belt passed 20,000 volt charges through his body. He fell
hard on his face, writhing. It was like burning to death in an
invisible flame. When it finally stopped, he gasped for breath.

"Pick him up!" Lockhart spat.

The two guards lifted Yoshida, but his legs were rubbery.
Their hands held him like iron clamps. Yoshida had bloodied
his nose, the fluid running in warm streams down his face. He
could hear the lawyer speaking, but his vision was a blur.

Lockhart spoke in a harsh whisper. "Now that you know
the rules, Mr. Yoshida, I'll level with you. You're right, this *is* a

departure from due process. But a judge wouldn't give you the second chance I'm offering you now. *Don't* blow it. Because if you turn this down, there's a plane waiting to haul your sorry ass to the federal maximum security prison at Marion, Illinois, to be held until trial."

Lockhart pointed a skeletal finger. "And I promise you, if you make me do that, your cellmate *will be* an HIV-positive rapist who outweighs you by seventy-five pounds and hasn't gotten any for five years. You'll *never* see the outside of a prison wall again. You have my word on it!"

Yoshida shook silently.

"Your answer?"

It took an act of his will to even open his mouth. "W-w-what?"

"Do you accept the alternative I have offered you?"

His mind screamed. It was plainly a trap. An illegal trap. But those voices called from far, far away. The electric shocks had jangled his brain. The room whirled around him. It was like asking a man falling down a well if he chooses to fall the rest of the way to the bottom.

"Yes," Yoshida heard himself croak.

* * *

After Yoshida was led away, retired NSA counsel Myron Shapiro, alias Julius Lockhart, opened the door to the surveillance booth next to the interview room. "Now *that* little bastard really made me work!" he laughed. "Normally I just rattle off the charges, they pee in their pants, I dangle the carrot, and we're done. That Yoshida's got some brass! You sure you can keep a leash on him?"

Colonel Carl Richter didn't share Shapiro's good humor. Richter wore a black jumpsuit over his husky frame, devoid of any name tags or rank insignia. His eyes were black marbles under his thick brow. "I'll manage," he rasped in a voice that hinted of a harsh life and too many cigarettes. "You drive a pretty hard bargain. You almost had *me* convinced!"

Shapiro laughed again. "Hell, I spent my entire NSA career telling judges what they could do with their Freedom of Information Act requests. I've faced off with the best of them. Just out of curiosity, what would you have done if he had told me to take a hike?"

One look into Richter's lifeless black eyes gave Shapiro his answer. "So what happens to him now?" he added quickly, changing the subject.

"They'll drive him around for a couple of hours, then bring him back here for incarceration. Thanks again for coming in on short notice, Myron."

Shapiro made a hasty exit. "Glad to be of service. I hope that kid won't turn out to be a problem for you!"

Richter stubbed out his cigarette. "He won't be."

POWER. FOCUS. CONTROL.

General Stoyer didn't fully relax until his limousine turned off the Washington-Baltimore Parkway into the NSA's Ft. Meade complex. He enjoyed Ft. Meade because it was his dominion. Within the dual rings of ten-foot cyclone fence marking his territory, he was god. The barbed wire, the guard dog patrols, and the WARNING: HIGH VOLTAGE signs served only to emphasize that fact to outsiders.

Not that the security was excessive. The National Security Agency guarded America's most vital secrets. Since 1952, the NSA had the daunting task of guarding all US military and government communications against intercept. They also eavesdropped on the communications of every military or government organization on the planet, both friendly and hostile.

The United States had learned its lesson in World War II. Both the disaster at Pearl Harbor and the victory at battles like Midway could be traced directly to the quality of communications intercepts. General George Marshall had solid information that the Japanese were about to attack on December 7, 1941, but he didn't know where.

Later, when the Japanese naval codes were cracked, Admiral Chester Nimitz knew not only *where* he was about to be attacked, but when, by what ships, and from which direction. The lesson was clear: Victory followed successful codebreaking. America resolved to never be caught on the short end of the eavesdropping stick again.

The sprawling complex at Ft. Meade was the result. More than 32,000 employees worked here, in a multi-towered edifice larger than the Capitol building and CIA headquarters put together. Much of that space was occupied by computers. The

NSA usually measured their computer rooms by acreage rather than by square feet. They also employed more mathematicians and scientists than any other government agency, including NASA.

But none of these facts were revealed to the American public. The same top-secret presidential memo that had created the NSA also provided for its near-total anonymity. It stated that Congress shall pass no law "to require the disclosure of the organization or any function of the National Security Agency, or any information with respect to the activities thereof."

Neither had Congress passed restrictions on the actions of the NSA, either at home or abroad. The NSA exercised such a free hand in its operations that the running joke in the intelligence community was that NSA stood for "No Such Agency."

Stoyer's stretched Marquis passed the headquarters complex. Like any large town, "Crypto City" had its good parts and its not-so-good parts. The OPS 2A and OPS 2B towers, where Stoyer's office was located, were modern designs with mirrored black glass windows. These partially hid the squat OPS 1A and OPS 1B buildings, charmless and dilapidated monoliths dating back to the 1950s. The older structures resembled mental institutions, their horizontal slit windows wide enough to admit sunlight but not so large as to allow the occupants a chance at escape. Even with the NSA's security, there were parts of the older buildings female employees refused to walk through alone.

The limo turned onto Ream Road, named after the NSA's fourth Deputy Director. Stoyer rode past the NSA's fire department, beyond numerous supply and maintenance buildings, then onto a gravel road that led deep into a wooded area.

The woods opened to a clearing where a large bunker sat, surrounded by another dual ring of barbed-wire fencing. A concrete guard tower covered each corner of the enclosure. The outer gate opened and permitted the limousine to enter. The driver swiped a pass card through the reader and the inner gate rolled aside.

The big Mercury circled the bunker and slipped into an underground garage. A heavy metal door clanked down behind it. Guards toting M-16s flanked the limo and snapped to smart attention when General Stoyer emerged.

The bunker had originally been built as a back-up to the headquarters facility, to allow codebreaking activities to continue even in the event of a nuclear war. Now it served a completely different but no less important purpose.

Colonel Carl Richter saluted. "Good morning, General! Good to see you again!"

Stoyer saluted mechanically, already heading for the stairs to the bunker's upper level. "Did you find our mystery genius?"

Richter jogged up the metal steps behind Stoyer. "Yes sir, I did. He's looking forward to meeting you."

Stoyer's nose twitched. No matter how expensive or well-maintained, a bunker always smelled like a bunker--that malodor of dank concrete and compacted humanity no ventilator fan could ever drive out. Passing through an airlock, he made an immediate left into a conference room. The guards inside came to attention and prodded the man in an orange jumpsuit to his feet.

Stoyer stood facing the prisoner. He was in his late forties, with thinning hair and a fleshy, pockmarked face. Pudgy hands were clasped underneath his bulging stomach. Stoyer engaged in a short staring contest with the man, who looked away immediately. Good. There was no doubt who was in charge here. That was important.

Richter did the introductions. "General, this is Robert Pittman. He's been with the program for over two years."

Pittman extended a hesitant hand.

Stoyer ignored it. "I understand you deserve the credit for some of the more innovative facets of the attack last night."

Pittman bobbed his head. "If you're referring to cutting the utilities at the state boundaries, yes sir, that was my idea."

"How did you do that? Surely the electrical and phone grids aren't that clearly marked. Some had to cross state borders, but the black-out zones were straight as a knife."

Pittman's face brightened. "Taxes, sir."

"Taxes?"

"Yes, sir. Even if a substation serves a city straddling the border, the utility taxes in the two states will be different. I had the computer search by utility rates, then cut all the nodes with a Nebraska tax scale. It worked for electricity, phone service, even cable TV."

Not bad for a caged monkey. Now to give the monkey his banana. "Damned clever. I assure you it had a very gut-level effect on the receiving end. Colonel, how are we rewarding Mr. Pittman for his ingenuity?"

"We're giving him a leadership role on his next assignment, and he'll be receiving larger accommodations here on the program."

"Very well. Thank you, Mr. Pittman. Good work."

Pittman averted his eyes deferentially. "Thank you, General!"

"You're making excellent progress, Pittman," Richter pronounced. "Dismissed!"

Pittman shuffled from the room, guards in tow. Neither officer spoke until the door was firmly closed.

Richter fidgeted. "Sir, I take full responsibility for the natural gas explosions. When we locked down their pipelines, we didn't anticipate the pressure spike. The gas meters in some of the older buildings couldn't take the load. Then the whole network drained out through the broken valves." His head dropped. "The loss of life..."

Stoyer waved off the apology. "Collateral damage, Colonel. If there's one town that operates on a tombstone mentality, it's Washington. Unless somebody dies, nobody gives a damn. This may be a good thing. The bureaucrats are crapping in their collective drawers, and the President is mad enough to bite a brick. They finally got the message."

Few people would recognize the wall-sized world map at the head of the conference table. It was a world *information* map. The size of the countries on the chart were based not on geography but on computer networks. The United States and Europe took up a great deal of "land area," while countries like Japan and Israel occupied space far in excess of their actual territory. Sprawling expanses like Russia and Africa were reduced to small "islands" at the map's margins. Microwave and satellite links replaced the highways and air routes between countries. Insiders called the whole electronic realm "Cyberia."

Colors on the map were based on threat assessment. Greens were allies, reds were known hostiles, whites were neutral, yellows were developing threats. Many of these threats weren't even countries, but extranational groups like Hezbollah and the Cali cartel. Some yellow nations were theoretically "friends" with the US, others were sworn enemies, but most were developing or declining nations that had a continuing desire to see the US humiliated.

There were twenty-six red and yellow threats on the map at Stoyer's last count. Each of these nations and groups were actively reconnoitering US and European networks, probing for weaknesses. Power grids, telephone systems, and financial networks were all being scanned in preparation for a surprise attack.

But what were the US and NATO doing about it? Appointing a few working groups, conducting a few studies, then complacently concluding the problem had been solved. After the World Trade Center attack, information warfare seemed to be the least of the worries the United States faced. But Stoyer knew that once the US beat back these overt attacks, terrorists and hostile states would be looking for more covert methods of waging war against the Great Satan.

The potential for disaster was enormous. Like a family picnicking on the train tracks, the defense establishment acknowledged the danger, but had done nothing about it.

Until now. By attacking the heartland of the US himself, Stoyer had firmly dashed America's misguided sense of information invincibility. He was forcing both government and industry to address their vulnerabilities *now*, not after the North Koreans or the Iranians had melted down Wall Street or the Pentagon. The casualties in Nebraska were unfortunate but strategically inconsequential.

"Do they have *any* clue where the attack really came from?" Richter worried aloud.

"They only know what I tell them. What steps did you take to cover your tracks?"

Richter traced a red line on the world map. "Each prong of the attack used multiple bounce points, including commercial satellites." He jabbed a meaty finger at central Japan. "But everything converged *here*, at a server in the Mitsusui headquarters in Nagoya. The attack programs then spread out again, using multiple paths before they converged on Nebraska. Even if the CIA does their own independent analysis, they'll stop dead when they hit the server at Mitsusui. It's a smoking gun."

Stoyer noted that Japan was a "yellow" nation. China next door was a "red," but the damage from a DATASHARK attack there would be more difficult to verify. "Very good. Mitsusui has been a real thorn in the latest trade negotiations. They'll *want* to believe Mitsusui did it. And the next phase?"

"It's ready to go. Just say the word."

"No, I'll let the President do that." Stoyer placed a hand on Richter's shoulder. "This has succeeded beyond my wildest dreams. You'll get a general's star for this, Carl, I promise."

"Thank you, sir."

The two officers walked to the balcony overlooking the lower level. Two dozen computer terminals filled the room beneath them, a convict in an orange jumpsuit sitting at each station. FEDERAL PRISONER was emblazoned on each of their coveralls. Guards in black jumpsuits and caps roved the balcony, their shotguns at the ready.

The sight of the captives below caused Stoyer a brief but uncomfortable flashback to his own time as a POW. Perhaps that's why he visited the Snake Pit infrequently, gladly leaving the day-to-day operations to Richter. Richter had never gone through that experience, although he faithfully applied the lessons Stoyer had learned about breaking a prisoner's will.

DATASHARK had originally been staffed by Air Force computer experts, but there was a flaw in that approach. They were government employees--they didn't think like criminals. They had selected military service because they liked to play by the rules, and that mindset was hard to break. Because lying, cheating, and stealing did not come naturally to them, they were at a constant disadvantage.

But these computer hackers had no such misgivings. They lied, cheated, and stole habitually. It was their chosen lifestyle, and they were good at it. Now they used their illicit instincts against targets of Stoyer's choosing, with the original DATASHARK team looking over their shoulders.

He shook his head at the brilliance of it. These criminals had once been a constant irritant to the NSA. They hacked into networks, compromised security, and wasted lots of money getting chased down, only to be released to do it again after some liberal judge slapped them on the wrist. No more. Now these men were working toward a unified purpose, the greater national security of the United States.

Power. Focus. Control.

These qualities set General Jonathan Stoyer apart from other men and made DATASHARK possible. A lesser man would never have exercised such audacity to achieve his goals. Stoyer grasped the iron railing tightly, feeling the cold firmness under his fingers. He drew a deep breath of satisfaction.

"God, this was a great idea!" he whispered.

FANTASIES

Tony Broadman squirmed restlessly. Even his new double recliner couldn't make him comfortable. He flipped absently through the hundreds of channels on his new satellite TV system, trying to avoid the continuous news coverage of the Nebraska attack aftermath. It just reminded him of work.

He slid his seat all the way back. Above him the pine beams glistened, showing off their newness. He should be basking in the fact that he and Christina had finally reached a level of financial security where they could buy their version of a dream home, a spacious cabin in the woods. It would mean both of them going without a new car for a while, but it was worth it. Their nearest neighbor was only visible during the winter when the leaves were down. *Hope you like this place*, a voice told him. *You're going to be making payments on it for the next thirty years.*

Christina emerged from the bathroom, throwing him a smile as she toweled her hair. His sisters had always been jealous of Christina's natural curls. Her spirited raven tresses looked better in five minutes than theirs could with an hour and a pit crew. She spotted his downcast mood from the kitchen.

"What's the matter, gloomy Gus? Fifty sports channels not enough for you?" Christina knew when she married Tony she was also accepting the Yankees and the Rangers as members of her extended family.

Broadman sighed. "Nah, it's work. Iron Jan nixed my Yoshida story. She called me the Gadget Guy. Told me to leave the investigative reporting to the professionals."

She reached into the fridge for one of her noxious health-food drinks. "I thought you *liked* being the Gadget Guy," her voice echoed from inside the appliance. "Defeater of flashing twelves and all that?"

He didn't care how many vitamins and minerals a soon-to-be-expectant mother needed, he'd rather get a rabies shot than drink that sludge. His secret fear was that someday she would bring home a similar slurry for male virility. Wouldn't his family have a great time making him live *that* down?

"Oh, I like being the Gadget Guy, but this MINTNET story was the real deal. I ended up having to file a column admitting the hackers were in control. The best I could come up with was to never be the first guy to load a software update. Like everybody doesn't know that."

She padded barefoot to the double-wide lounger, sitting cross-legged next to his reclined form. She toweled her hair with one hand and shook the algae-colored concoction with the other. "The real deal? Are you having visions of Woodward and Bernstein again? You *hate* those snobby investigative reporters at the *Times*."

Sometimes it was embarrassing how easily she read him. He still had to *ask* her what *she* was thinking. "Well, I hate their *attitude*. And sometimes their technical ignorance makes me want to scream."

Her finger burrowed at a tender spot under his ribs. "And they could have avoided all those stupid mistakes *if only* they had asked the Gadget Guy first, right?"

If he had known he was going to marry a telepath he would have tried to develop a more complex personality. "I'm not asking for a byline."

"But you wouldn't mind it if they gave you one, right? Especially if it was a really juicy story that landed somebody powerful in jail?"

Being an investigative reporter wasn't Broadman's true fantasy. It was just the fantasy he thought was within reach. He had interviewed with representatives of both the CIA and the FBI back in college, but both agencies were looking for "installers," not agents.

The CIA recruiter had eyed Broadman's slender frame and technical degree with particular interest. But crawling up a ventilation shaft to plant bugs in the Chinese embassy wasn't the glamorous image of cloak and dagger he had in mind. Broadman chose private industry after graduation. Journalism had followed several years later.

"No, I'm past fantasies. But some stories really do need to be written. I have a feeling this MINTNET thing is one of them."

Christina swung her legs over his, her toes massaging his thighs just below his gym shorts. "You know, I think Iron Jan just did you a favor!"

"How's that?" Broadman wondered if she knew how hard it was to concentrate when she did that.

"You've always been threatening to write a book. Well, here's your chance! Only this one won't be about computers, it'll be *Gadget Guy* exposing the evil government privacy thieves! Scoop the newsies upstairs and I'll bet they'll treat you differently at work."

He tried to focus on what she was saying and not on the growing fullness near where her soft bare feet were kneading. "The *Times* has a strict conflict-of-interest policy. No book deals without prior review. Fat chance of that getting traction."

A skillful twitch of her little toe made him jump. "Excuse me? They already turned this story down! And if you pursue it on your own time, *you* own it, not them! I say go for it!"

Broadman stared into his wife's deceptively innocent blue eyes. "I think I owe you a retainer, counselor."

Christina nestled her petite form against his, her bathrobe falling open in a way that ensured his thoughts of the day's business would be quickly forgotten. Her lilac-scented hair tickled his nose. "I'm just a humble librarian. I'll settle for a cut of the royalties."

THE SNAKE PIT

The van drove for hours. It took roads ranging from highway to gravel. Ken Yoshida rode face down, spread-eagled with a guard's foot on his back. When they finally stopped, he had no idea how far or in which direction they had traveled.

The rear doors flew open. Blinding lights stabbed into the van. Yoshida was grabbed by his ankles and hauled out to fall face down on the concrete. Men behind the lights screamed at him to stand and jabbed him with cattle prods. His legs had gone to sleep and he was only able to crawl. Shouted orders and stings from the cattle prods drove him on all fours through a doorway.

Finally the barrage of shocks stopped. Yoshida remained on his knees, his arms protecting his head from further assault. His eyes slowly adjusted to the light. He was in a concrete hallway, with steel doors on one side. Guards in boots and black jumpsuits surrounded him.

"Stand *up!*" the closest one to him bellowed.

Yoshida struggled to his feet.

"Strip him!"

Two guards held Yoshida immobile while another cut off his clothes with a razor knife. He stayed very still. Then he was subjected to a rough body cavity search, for humiliation as much as inspection, he was sure.

The lead guard sneered at Yoshida's naked body. "My name is Colonel Richter. If, and only if, I ask you a question, you will address me as 'Colonel Richter, sir!' Is that clear?"

"Yes, Colonel Richter," Yoshida replied.

A cattle prod jab in his back drove Yoshida to his knees again, screaming.

Richter seized Yoshida's ear and yanked his head up. "Did you forget something, *prisoner?*"

The maniac was about to tear his ear off. "Yes, *sir!* Colonel Richter, *sir!*" Yoshida shrieked. The iron grip released.

"Stand *up!*" Richter shouted.

Yoshida complied.

Richter shouted down at him. "You are now under my control! I control every second of your life! Everything you *do*, everything you *say*, everything you *think* is because I say so! Is that clear, prisoner?"

Brainwashing. "Yes, Colonel Richter, sir!"

"Obey me without hesitation for the next three years, and you *may* get your life back. But right now, your life hangs by a thread. If that thread snaps, it will be because you did not obey me instantly and completely! Is that clear, prisoner?"

"Yes, Colonel Richter, sir!"

Yoshida heard a heavy door swing open behind him. Richter stared into his eyes, measuring his resolve. "Does the prisoner have any questions?" he finally asked.

Yoshida was surprised the electric jolts hadn't made him wet himself already. "Yes, Colonel Richter, sir! May the prisoner use the restroom, sir?"

Richter signaled the guards. But instead of leading Yoshida to a bathroom, the guards assaulted him again with the cattle prods. They drove him backward into a tiny space like a broom closet. He barely fit inside. The shocks forced him to the wall. He raised his hands in a vain attempt to fend off the onslaught.

Suddenly it stopped. Yoshida cowered against the cold concrete.

Richter leaned into the doorway. "No, the prisoner may not," he said quietly. "Welcome to the Snake Pit!"

He slammed the heavy door shut, leaving Yoshida in darkness.

CHAPTER 3

"No government power can be abused long. Mankind will not bear it." -Samuel Johnson

DETERRENCE

The last time Stoyer addressed a meeting of the National Security Council, half the members elected not to attend, the President among them. There wasn't a single no-show today, Stoyer noted with satisfaction. There wasn't the normal gaggle of hangers-on either. Usually every glory-seeking lackey who could get past the Secret Service agents lined the dark paneled walls of the White House Situation Room, a cramped space under any circumstances.

But not today. Stoyer had caught a few minutes of CNN while waiting for his car. It reminded him of the initial coverage of the World Trade Center attacks--a great deal of anger and fear, with no one to direct it at. This was not a career-enhancing administrative problem, it was a crime begging for a fall guy. Even Jeff Archer was standing in a dark corner, hoping not to be noticed.

Stoyer had watched the council file in. There were no greetings and little eye contact. In many ways the NSC was just as cowed as the prisoners in the Snake Pit. Stoyer knew that when he offered them a way out, it would be seized upon. Indeed, anyone trying to block his proposed exit would be trampled by the others. In their haste to offer the impatient American public a "drive-through" solution, they wouldn't examine his plan too closely, if at all.

Stoyer had also learned that the best way to herd civilians was to only give them one option. They needed an enemy, and they needed a means to strike back. He would provide them with both.

The President was the last to enter. It was obvious from his dull eyes the Chief Executive had slept little, if at all. Neither had Stoyer, but his insomnia had been from exhilaration, not anxiety. Stoyer had never surfed, but he imagined it must feel something like this, riding the cusp of the wave, flirting with disaster while sharing the power of the wave's crushing inevitability.

"All right, let's get this started," Adams growled.

Stoyer keyed his remote, admiring how the room lights smoothly transitioned from the bright overhead fluorescent lighting to the tightly-focused reading lights over each seat. A map of Nebraska appeared on the screen. "Now that forty-eight hours have elapsed since the attack," Stoyer said, "we have a much better picture of how deeply we were penetrated."

Red dots covered the map. "In addition to the almost-universal interruption of electricity and phone service across the state, there were local attacks on gas and water systems, emergency services, and air traffic control centers. Almost all these attacks were successful in temporarily knocking out the software but left the hardware intact."

"Is that significant?" Adams asked.

"Yes, sir. With the ease that the saboteurs took out their software targets, they probably could have caused permanent hardware damage. But the equipment was left alone, making recovery after the attack fairly simple. I believe the attackers were more intent on delivering a message than creating casualties."

A much smaller number of black dots spotted the map. "These are the fatalities statewide, excluding deaths due to the natural gas explosions. Most were elderly people under home health care or in small-town nursing homes without backup generators. Three were traffic fatalities. A total of fifteen statewide, in addition to the forty-six killed in the explosions."

Adams shifted uncomfortably, the stress of the crisis settling in his lower back. "Your point, General?"

"Upon further analysis, I believe the natural gas explosions really *were* accidents. If truly bent on destruction, the hacker team could have caused hundreds of deaths, not just the sixty-one we experienced."

Adam was wide awake now. "Are you saying they went *easy* on us?"

"Compared to the full potential of an information warfare attack, yes sir, that's exactly what I'm saying."

There was a collective push away from the conference table, the council members struggling to grasp the magnitude of this new threat.

Admiral Chet Holland, the Chairman of the Joint Chiefs and a forty-year Navy veteran, spoke haltingly. "So you're saying...they killed sixty-one people...using nothing but computers...and this was just a shot across the bow?"

Welcome to the twenty-first century, Admiral. "That's correct, sir. Not a single power plant was bombed, not a single utility cable severed. It was all done with a keyboard, from thousands of miles away. And it could have been much worse."

"Hold on," Barton Walsh interrupted. "How do you *know* this came from thousands of miles away? Maybe some militia group has switched from fertilizer bombs to computers."

Stoyer tried to imagine the electronic goose chase the experts at the CIA had been led on, the traces from his attack bouncing from server to satellite and back again before disappearing entirely. *If Stoyer is going to boast about how good his people are in front of the President, let's see him deliver,* Walsh was probably thinking.

Stoyer keyed a number into his remote and the red dots covering Nebraska reappeared, spreading out into a spidery web. "The attackers' initial entry points were at satellite downlinks in the largest cities," he said. "From there, the attack routines spread outward using the victim computers' own communication links." The map zoomed out to show the United States. "Backtracking these signals led through a maze of deceptive paths all over the world." The map continued to zoom out, the tangle of transmission paths resembling a cracked windshield wrapped around a globe.

"That's exactly what my people found," Walsh said smugly.

Stoyer did not reply. Like a draining network of pipes, the tangle of red lines became shorter and less numerous. The lines converged in the Far East, where the map zoomed in. Finally, the paths intersected in one spot.

Adams squinted. "Nagoya, Japan?"

"Specifically, the signals were traced to a computer research facility for the Mitsusui Corporation on the outskirts of Nagoya."

Secretary of State Harold Abramson had just returned from a trade meeting with the Japanese. "Those *bastards*," he whispered.

The President's eyes narrowed. He readied a legal pad. "Tell me what you know, Harry."

"Prime Minister Noguri is a former member of Mitsusui's board," Abramson said. "He's been demanding preferential treatment for Mitsusui in exchange for further access to Japanese markets."

"No conflict of interest there, huh?"

Abramson made a dismissive gesture. "What we call corruption is accepted business practice in Japan. The concessions they wanted would have cost WestStar Corporation alone about three billion in sales next year. When we told them no deal, they walked. I guess this is their next bid in the negotiations."

A cold silence settled over the room.

Adams locked eyes with Stoyer. "General, you said the NSA could provide an appropriate response to an electronic attack. Was that just idle talk, or can you really deliver?"

Backs straightened around the table. Stoyer allowed the tension to build for several seconds before responding. When he finally spoke, his voice filled the room.

"Operation DATASHARK. An offensive information warfare project that will provide an effective deterrent against future computer attacks." A video panned across the high-tech vista of the National Information Command Center at NSA headquarters.

"Using high-speed computers and automated attack programs, DATASHARK can launch a devastating assault against any nation or organization on the planet. The target can be governmental, military, industrial, civilian, or any combination thereof. If they use computers, they are vulnerable to attack by DATASHARK. These attacks are highly scaleable, from shutting down a single computer for a few minutes, to causing permanent infrastructure damage over a vast area. A response to the Nebraska attack is being drafted right now. It will be ready to execute in approximately twenty-four hours."

Startled glances were shared around the table. Jeff Archer looked just as surprised as the NSC members.

"What did you have in mind, General?" Adams asked.

The map zoomed in, Nagoya filling the screen. Yellow circles dotted the city. "The proposed attack would completely shut down the city of Nagoya. Power, water, transportation, communications, and emergency services. However, instead of targeting just their software, we would take their systems down hard. Many of their computers will have to be ripped out and replaced. When the dust settles, the hardest hit will be the

Mitsusui Corporation. I suspect their research and development efforts will be set back several months, at least."

The NSC raised their eyebrows in unison.

The Secretary of State was the first to break the silence. "Mitsusui is killing us in integrated home entertainment systems. Even a few months to catch up would be invaluable to American companies, especially WestStar."

The council mumbled approvingly. WestStar had been very generous to the President's campaign last year. And corporations were even more generous if favors were performed on their behalf.

Seated at the President's left hand, the National Security Advisor spoke quietly. "Mr. President, this *is* an act of war we're discussing."

Admiral Holland was in no mood for doves. "No disrespect, Ms. Hale, but what the hell do you think just happened in Nebraska? We're *already* at war. It's time we started acting like it."

Hale directed her next question to Stoyer. "General, do your computers also predict what kind of casualties will be inflicted?"

Stoyer had anticipated this resistance. "Any casualties would likely be from the interruption of electrical power. The city of Nagoya and its outskirts are almost twice the population of the entire state of Nebraska, so I would estimate twenty to thirty fatalities maximum. If we leave their emergency services alone, less. In fact, phone company computers could be sabotaged so their version of 911 would be the *only* call that could be completed."

Stoyer had great confidence in his numbers. The casualty model had been developed for the Nebraska attack and was refined afterwards to reflect the lessons his team had learned. Fortunately the Japanese weren't big on natural gas.

Hale was not impressed. "Why not attack only the Mitsusui corporation itself? Why drag innocent civilians into this?"

"No Japanese corporation would attempt something like this without government complicity," Secretary Abramson countered. "And since Afghanistan and Iraq, no country or group would dare admit being party to an attack. I'm surprised we have even this much evidence to work with."

Holland joined in. "And if we let even one country get away with this, it'll be happening every other week. We need to make an example of them."

Hale glared at the Chairman of the Joint Chiefs. "Like we did in Hiroshima and Nagasaki, Admiral?"

Holland leaned into the table. "You'll notice we never had to drop an atom bomb on anybody else, did we, Ms. Hale?"

Stoyer tried to reassert control over the meeting. "Mr. President, the nuclear weapons analogy is very apt. There is no real defense against an information warfare attack. Key systems can be protected, of course, but civilians and businesses will always be vulnerable. As with nuclear weapons, deterrence is the only real protection."

"But for deterrence to be effective, you have to demonstrate that you're willing to knock heads in a big way," Holland said.

Adams cut off the debate. "General, the Japanese went to substantial lengths to disguise their attack. Would you be using a similar approach?"

"Their mistake was to leave behind evidence on the computers they attacked," Stoyer said. "Any computers we attack will be destroyed in the process. The only thing DATASHARK will leave behind is smoke and darkness."

Adams looked to his Secretary of State and the JCS Chairman, the two offices historically in conflict over most use-of-force questions. Both men signaled their approval with a nod. The days of waiting for a formal declaration of war from a hostile power were long since gone. "Very well, General, continue your preparations for operation DATASHARK as outlined. Let's take a break. General, Admiral, may I see you for a moment?"

* * *

After ushering Stoyer and Holland into the Oval Office, Adams immediately began typing at a laptop computer. The officers stood silently until he finished. Stoyer had a flash of uncertainty.

Adams pressed his index finger against the dime-sized fingerprint imager, then turned the laptop to face the Admiral. "Witness this for me, Chet."

Holland's eyes widened. "Are you *sure* about this, Mr. President?"

Stoyer's mind raced. What was Adams doing?

Adams's face darkened. "They attacked Nebraska *because* it's my home state. That's personal. A member of my *family* could have been killed when those gas mains started popping."

Holland added his fingerprint beside the President's. The laptop beeped its authentication.

Adams popped out a three-inch CD and handed it to Stoyer. "General, this is a classified Executive Order. I'm amending your operational plans for DATASHARK to inflict a proportional number of civilian casualties when Nagoya is attacked. The primary focus is to remain economic, but I want it to hurt them, and hurt them badly. I take full responsibility for this decision and my authorization protects you against legal sanction. Do you understand, General?"

Stoyer accepted the disk. "Yes, sir!"

Adams's jaw clenched. "I'm not in the business of murder, but I'm leaving this afternoon to attend a memorial service for sixty-one people. I thought the world had learned that killing Americans wasn't going to be tolerated any more, but apparently Prime Minister Noguri didn't get the message. Make *damn* sure he gets it this time, General."

Stoyer was reminded of a news story he had seen recently. A tourist in Florida had been marlin fishing when the shark he had accidentally caught jumped into the boat and bit a large chunk out of his leg. Stoyer suddenly sympathized with the unlucky fisherman. The politician *he* had hooked was a good deal more vicious than he anticipated.

Stoyer stood to attention. "That won't be a problem, Mr. President."

* * *

Director Walsh's first stop back at Langley was the CIA's Information Security Center.

Dr. Ravi Prakash, the head of the ISC, shook his head. "How the hell did they track this down? We were only able to trace *one* of the attack programs to Japan, then it dropped off the map. They tracked this to an individual server *and* confirmed it by multiple paths! How did they do it?"

Walsh shrugged. "If I gave you the NSA's budget and manpower, you might be able to work wonders, too."

"So what do you want me to do?"

"Just verify his answer."

"You think he's *lying?*"

"Now, don't get ahead of me, Ravi! I'm just saying now that you know the answer, work the equation backward and see if you come up with the same result."

"You don't trust him, do you, sir?"

Walsh placed a firm hand on Prakash's shoulder, a warning that his familiarity with the Director had reached its limits. "Always remember the first rule of intelligence, Dr. Prakash," he said with a cold smile. "Trust, but verify."

LOOSE ENDS

Tony Broadman was charged with purpose. His decision to continue with the MINTNET story on his own time had given his morale just the boost it needed.

The hacker attack on Nebraska had also provided ample material for his column. As usual, Americans were overreacting as only Americans could, buying up every portable generator that wasn't nailed down and stealing a few that were. Fights broke out in some stores over canned goods and bottled water. It resembled a repeat of Y2K, with a harder edge of impending panic. An Internet rumor that the Nebraska hackers had cleaned out senior citizen's retirement accounts had even triggered a few bank runs.

His interview with Yoshida helped Broadman better explain the Nebraska attack. Not that Broadman was surprised. He had been warning his readers that this day was coming. The hardest part of the column had been keeping an "I told you so" attitude out of the piece.

Americans were diggers, he wrote. Either we're digging holes to bury our heads in, or we're digging bomb shelters and filling them with guns. It was the same mindset that led to stockpiling antibiotics and gas masks after the anthrax attacks. He understood that panic better than most, since anthrax had been loose in the building where he was sitting.

Instead, Americans should pull together and dig a trench. The bad guys are out there and they want what we've got. Instead of meeting the new threat with individual panic, we need to meet it with collective defensive action. In that respect, the hackers may have done America a long-term favor. Now we know what we're up against.

The piece failed to dazzle his boss. Janet Randall cared only that the text contained words related to the title and it was delivered before deadline.

Broadman wasn't too concerned when Yoshida didn't call him back. Still, he needed to find out if Yoshida was willing to deliver the MINTNET information under the new ground rules. He might have been interested in Broadman only because of his status as a *Times* staff member.

As Broadman inched out of the city toward home, he saw the exit he had taken to his last meeting with Yoshida. What the hell. He might get lucky. And it beat staring at taillights. He dropped out of the gridlock and headed for Yoshida's apartment.

Yoshida's Civic wasn't on the lot. Broadman wasn't surprised. Dropping in unannounced had been a long shot anyway. He circled back toward the street.

Broadman jabbed his brakes. Yoshida's apartment door was open. Broadman parked his Cherokee next to a white van full of cleaning supplies and paint buckets. He climbed the stairs and peeked through the doorway. Two men in T-shirts and painter's pants were spreading a tarp on the living room floor.

Broadman knocked on the door jamb. "Hey, guys, do you know what happened to the man who lived here?"

A worker with stringy blond hair and tattooed arms shrugged. "Hey, man, he bugged out. We just clean up and paint for the next guy."

An aging ponytailed hippie whose Grateful Dead T-shirt didn't cover his ample belly laughed. "Yeah, man, if he owes you money, you're screwed, dude!"

Broadman stepped inside. "Mind if I take a look around?"

"No skin off my hide," Stringy Hair said. "But he didn't leave nothin' behind. Not even loose change!"

"Yeah, and you bet he looked, too!" Ponytail added.

Stringy Hair pried open a can of paint. "Hey man, did I tell you about the time I found a bag of weed some chick left behind?"

"No way! You sure didn't share any of it with me..."

Broadman slipped into the bedroom. The thick curtains were pulled back, the late afternoon sun pouring in. There were depressions in the carpet where Yoshida's computer table and bookshelves had sat, but nothing else. A faint stain on the carpet caught his eye. It was hard to see in the brown fabric, but a large spot was noticeably darker than the surrounding shag. He touched it. Wet.

Broadman knelt and brushed the strands to one side with his hand. There was a rust-colored stain in the carpet mat and at the base of the fibers, fading out toward the tips. It looked like a bloodstain. A bloodstain someone had tried to wash out.

Maybe Yoshida was right about what the government would do if they caught him digging around in MINTNET. If that was the case, then this was a crime scene. But if the government took Yoshida, it would be suicide to call the police. He had an old college friend in the FBI, but to call him would place him in danger too. If anyone was going to collect the evidence, Broadman would have to do it himself. He'd figure out what to do with it later.

He looked over his shoulder to make sure Stringy Hair and Ponytail were occupied. He took out his pocket knife and carefully snipped several strands of the carpet, folding them into a clean handkerchief.

* * *

Wanda the apartment manager gestured frequently. Broadman guessed it was to draw attention to the cheap jewelry that bedecked every pudgy finger. Her thick New Jersey accent was directed mostly through her nose, allowing her high-pitched voice to approximate fingernails on a chalkboard.

"Oh yeeaah, Yosheeda!" she squeaked. "That was the day after the blackout!"

Broadman's eyebrows rose. "Blackout?"

"Yeeaah, that was *so* strange! The lights were on everywhere but here!"

"And Ken Yoshida..."

"Oh!" Wanda said, tugging on her flowery muumuu to show slightly more wrinkled cleavage. "Well, the next day there was this *moving truck* parked out in front! And these men were taking out Mr. Yoshida's things! Not that he had that much. You know, he's supposed to give me thirty days' notice..."

"Was Yoshida with them?"

"No! And the movers just acted dumb. All they said was he took a job in another city and had to leave immediately. And they looked like Marines." Wanda squared her shoulders and pantomimed a flat-top haircut with her hand. "Kinda handsome, though. But after they left, Mrs. Eckhardt, the lady who lived below him, told me she had called the police about a fight in his apartment. She said when the police showed up, everything was quiet and his door was locked, so they left."

Yoshida's offhanded comment about MINTNET was looking more plausible all the time. Broadman made a note to run Yoshida's name against state and federal arrest records in the area. But if it had been a simple arrest, the police would have told his landlady. Maybe Yoshida was just performing another disappearing act and had spilled something on the carpet while packing. No need to get paranoid, yet. "Any forwarding address?"

Bejeweled hands flashed. "That's what I wanted to know! But the movers acted dumb again, said they were just delivering the furniture to a storage locker and he would call me with his new address. You know, if he doesn't call in two weeks he's going to forfeit his deposit."

Broadman sensed the hole Yoshida had disappeared into closing up after him. "You don't have *any* idea where they were taking his things?"

"No! But the truck had Maryland tags, I remember that much."

Broadman tried to remember--was the NSA in Maryland? Or was it in Virginia? Not that the feds couldn't fake tags from any state they wanted. "Any name on the truck?"

"Not that I remember. You know, it's almost like we have a mystery on our hands, Mister...what'd ya say your name was?"

PRISONER 36

The thick walls and door shut out all light and sound. The cell wasn't large enough for Yoshida to lie down. He was forced to sleep sitting up. Sleep was difficult, though. The chamber was cold enough to make him shiver until his muscles ached. The rough concrete was like needles against his naked skin, no matter what position he assumed.

His head still hurt like hell and it itched, too. He could feel stitches, so he tried to keep his hands off the wound to minimize the chances of an infection.

Eventually his bladder forced him to choose between placing his feet in his waste or sitting in it. He chose his feet. The fetid odor filled the tiny chamber. At one point he heaved from the stench, but there was nothing left in his stomach to vomit, not even water.

Yoshida had no idea how long he had been in the concrete closet. It could have been days. Judging from his hunger, it had been at least twenty-four hours.

He had read how the Viet Cong used discomfort and sensory deprivation to break down the resistance of American POWs. The SLA terrorist group had used the same approach on Patty Hearst back in the seventies. No wonder she had ended up toting a machine gun alongside her "comrades." Eventually a person would do anything to escape the dark, smelly hole.

Knowing his captors' objective gave Yoshida the will to resist. He kept his mind busy reliving every slope he had ever skied, recalling each snowy, sunlit detail to keep his mind from swirling down into the abyss of desperation.

There was a heavy click, then light flooded the cell. Yoshida wrapped his arms over his eyes.

"Get out!" a voice shouted. His tormentor punctuated the order with a cattle prod thrust.

His limbs were even more useless than after the van ride. He rolled more than crawled from the hole. A bucket of cold water was shoved against his side.

"Clean up your mess!" the voice shouted.

There was no brush or sponge in the icy water. Yoshida was forced to use his hands to wash his cell and scoop up the waste. He cleaned the enclosure thoroughly, to avoid any more attacks with the prod.

"That's good enough," another voice soothed. "Here, let me help you up."

Yoshida's head snapped around like a caged animal's. A friendly voice was even more of a surprise than another jab with the shock stick.

A paunchy middle-aged man in an orange jumpsuit reached down. "Think you can stand? Easy, now. Go slow."

Yoshida struggled to his feet. His legs still felt a long way away. He was forced to lean on his new benefactor. The guards had backed off, no longer poised to strike.

The other prisoner urged him along. "Can you walk? There you go, look at your feet if you need to. Let's get you cleaned up. My name's Bob Pittman, what's yours?"

His voice was raspy from thirst. "Ken. Ken Yoshida. How long..."

"A couple of days, I think," Pittman said. "You're lucky. SOP for new arrivals is almost a week in the box."

They turned right and into a shower room. Only one guard followed them. "Why less?" Ken choked out. The feeling in his legs was coming back, but he was glad to have Pittman's steadying arm.

"I think you have a talent we need," Pittman replied. Pittman stripped off his orange suit and helped Yoshida to one of the nozzles lining the wall.

"Oh God," Yoshida breathed. The lukewarm flow was one of the most wonderful sensations he had ever experienced. He gulped down some of the water. It tasted metallic, but he didn't care. Washing the filth from his body was like being reborn.

Pittman edged closer to him, close enough that Yoshida began to feel very uncomfortable. He started to move away.

"Don't move!" Pittman said in a harsh whisper. "Here's the deal. You're about to be given a jumpsuit like mine. On the back of the collar there's a plastic disk, like a shoplifting tag. If you tamper with it, they put you back in the box for five days. We think it functions as a bug, so this is the only safe place to talk." Pittman glanced over his shoulder. "The guards don't want to stand any closer to naked men than you do."

"Okay," Yoshida replied.

"I've been here a while, so they give me some leeway. Stick close to me, keep your mouth shut, do what I do, and I'll keep you out of the box, okay?"

Staying out of the box sounded like an excellent plan. "Got it."

Pittman cranked his shower valve closed. "Okay, let's wire you for sound." They grabbed towels from a stack. An orange jumpsuit was folded next to them. "That's yours," he said.

There were also orange underwear, socks, and sandals, the kind you couldn't run in if your life depended on it. The number 36 was stenciled front, back, and on both arms of the jumpsuit,

along with FEDERAL PRISONER. Yoshida fingered the collar
tag gingerly. He zipped up the suit. Even prison coveralls were
better than going naked. He posed. "How do I look?" His relief
of being out of the box was making him giddy, he realized,
which was probably part of his captors' plan.

Pittman frowned. "Not what your mother had in mind for
you, I'll bet."

Yoshida noticed Pittman's jumpsuit had 13 stenciled on all
sides. A loud horn blared.

"Perfect timing," Pittman said. "Lunch."

* * *

The food was surprisingly good, but anything would taste
wonderful after fasting for days. Pittman introduced him to several of the two dozen or so men in the cafeteria. Rumor had it
that some of the hackers present had fled to Central America a
few years ago to avoid prosecution. Yoshida wondered if those
rumors had been spread by their captors to explain the disappearances.

Derek Friedman, who went by the online alias "Dark
Bloodhand," was one of the hacker legends who had reputedly
fled when the feds closed in. He was in his mid-twenties with
glasses and frizzy blond hair.

Friedman bent forward in feigned worship, his hands out-
stretched. "Hallelujah! The great Ken Yoshida himself! We're
not worthy! We're not worthy!"

Pittman rolled his eyes. "Stop being an asshole, Derek. Ken
just got out of the box."

Friedman wasn't impressed. "Yeah, I heard they let you out
early. Maybe they went easy 'cause they actually believe that
shit you spew about being a white hat hacker. So how did they
bust you?"

Yoshida refused to be baited, but decided being truthful
would be the fastest way to shut Friedman up. "MINTNET," he
admitted. "I cracked the firewall and was downloading files
when the SWAT team came through the door."

If he had hoped going after MINTNET would at least earn
him grudging respect from Friedman, he was disappointed. The
younger hacker sneered.

"Probably just a bait file they left out for you. I'm really looking forward to this. Now I'll finally get to see if the all-knowing Kentaro Yoshida really has Kung Fu or just good PR."

"Drop dead, Derek," Pittman groused, moving to the next seat. "Ken, Paul Malechek."

Yoshida had met Malechek at the H2K hackers' convention in New York. Malechek had entertained one seminar audience by describing how he had burrowed deep inside the network of the MegaComp Corporation and skimmed confidential memos outlining MegaComp's plans to drive their competitors out of business. MegaComp denied Malechek's penetration of its system and claimed the documents were fakes. MegaComp sued Malechek for libel and won by default when the hacker failed to show up to defend himself.

"Hey," Malechek mumbled, extending his hand only after Yoshida offered his.

Now Yoshida knew why Malechek had missed his day in court. Not that showing up would have guaranteed him justice, as Yoshida knew from experience. But Malechek bore little resemblance to the flamboyant, outspoken hacker Yoshida had met at the conference. Malechek's unwashed hair was matted to his skull like black seaweed. His dark Slavic eyes were flat and emotionless, revealing nothing.

Pittman moved on to a pair of young black men seated apart from the others. "Ken, I'm sure you know the Taylor twins, by reputation at least."

Yoshida could scarcely believe the cowering pair were the same cocky teenaged troublemakers he had frequently sparred with online. Julius and Demetrius Taylor were notorious electronic vandals, kept out of jail only because of their status as juveniles and their powerful Los Angeles attorney father.

Known online as Romulus and Remus, they had perpetrated their most famous hack against StrataPlay Games, makers of the Roman Empire Simulator, a favorite of the Taylor twins. They managed to smuggle a virus onto StrataPlay's production computer, which burned it onto the game CDs. When a customer won the game, the screen would flash, "YOUR GAME TIME WAS ___, WE DID IT IN TWO HOURS! BOW BEFORE ROMULUS AND REMUS!"

But if the player beat the Taylor twins' time, the virus would reformat the host computer's hard drive, along with any other computers on its network. The entire advanced design department of one aerospace company was wiped out when an engineer on the evening shift was playing Roman Empire Simulator instead of designing airliners. The twins hated Ken Yoshida, starting flame wars against him on any hacker forum they visited.

Any fight the Taylor twins had possessed was entirely gone now. They looked years older than their early twenties and gazed up at Yoshida without raising their heads. Julius actually flinched when Yoshida tried to shake his hand. Pittman urged Yoshida on to the next table.

"That's the first time I've ever seen Romulus and Remus at a loss for words," Yoshida whispered.

"The twins were never the same after their time in the box," Pittman confided. "But they do good work."

And so it went with the rest of the hackers. Some were surprisingly upbeat, most were quietly resigned to their fate, and a few cringed like abused animals. The group was mostly young men, with a scattering of middle-agers like Pittman.

Yoshida mentally compared his recollection of hackers who had recently dropped off the map to those present. "So where are Vic Flavio and Arturo Gonzales? Second shift?"

Pittman's head dropped. "They didn't make it. Vic locked horns with Colonel Richter, and Art just wouldn't get with the program. You only have to screw up once around here, then it's off to the big house. Remember that."

That explained the difference between the number of hackers present and the number on his own jumpsuit. It also gave him an idea of the failure rate in the Snake Pit.

Yoshida had never met Gonzales, but Yoshida and Vic Flavio had kept in regular touch until Flavio's disappearance. That wasn't an unusual event in hacker society. But when Flavio didn't resurface, Yoshida repeatedly searched government records and criminal databases, just in case his friend had been snared in a legal net. Nothing.

With some inside help, Yoshida had even hacked into the FBI's NCIC computer in an attempt to learn Flavio's whereabouts. If Flavio *had* been bounced out of the Snake Pit and back into federal court, Yoshida's searches would have caught it. An alarm bell began ringing in the back of his head.

Yoshida noticed something else unusual. "No women?"

"I guess they didn't want the hassle of dealing with both sexes in such cramped quarters," Pittman offered.

That made sense. "Either that or the girls are better at not getting caught."

Pittman winced. "Let's not go there."

He gave Yoshida a brief tour of the bunker. Across from the showers was a TV room and a small gym. Next came a large area full of computers and worktables. Opposite the computer area, the stairs to the bunker's upper level were blocked by a raised guard stand. The cafeteria was the next room on the left.

Yoshida decided to risk the monitoring tag and ask a more sensitive question. "I'm surprised the morale is as good as it is."

Pittman shrugged. "Look at the alternative. We get first-class equipment, we hack all day long, nobody has to worry about being rear-ended in the shower, and as long as we only hack where they tell us to, we get out in three years. Here's your stall."

Closely spaced, narrow doors lined the hallway beyond the cafeteria. Pittman opened a metal door into a small room. It was more like a deep walk-in closet, barely big enough for a cot and a small desk, but it didn't look like any prison cell he had ever seen.

Pittman anticipated his question. "This place used to be a doomsday bunker. This was where tech folks were supposed to sleep." He pointed with his thumb. "Officers slept one floor up."

Yoshida stepped inside and gasped. Filling one wall were bookshelves. *His* bookshelves. Filled with books. *His* books. Even his beloved Japanese comics were here. Long fascinated by the futuristic artwork and concepts of their artists, he had taught himself how to read and speak Japanese as a teenager. Some of the books had been roughly handled, but they were all here, along with the reference books he used in his hacking. He sat on the cot, stunned. This certainly wasn't like any prison *he* had heard of.

Pittman examined one of the comic books. "Can you *read* this?" Yoshida nodded.

"Hoo boy! Are *you* gonna have some fun!"

Yoshida's guard went up. "What kind of fun?"

The horn blared again.

"C'mon, I'll show you," Pittman said. "Time to hack for your supper."

PROVERBS

Kentaro Yoshida came by his hacking skills naturally. Indeed, it was his father who had taught him that creative bending of the rules was sometimes necessary for survival. Ikaro Yoshida had been a sixteen-year-old boy in Sacramento when the Japanese bombed Pearl Harbor. Given the choice between joining the army or rotting in an internment camp for the rest of the war, Ikaro lied about his age and signed up for duty. He was assigned to the all Japanese-American 442nd Infantry Regiment and sent to Europe.

On the front line during the invasion of Italy, the 442nd was used repeatedly as cannon fodder, to punch holes in the enemy lines for the all-white units behind them. Their regimental motto was, "Go For Broke!" But after watching a unit in his regiment suffer almost one hundred percent casualties storming a German strongpoint, Yoshida realized that devotion to country had its limits.

From that day, Ikaro Yoshida became a master of survival. Knowing his regiment had last priority for air strikes, Yoshida learned the callsigns and accents of nearby white radio operators. When pinned down by enemy fire, Yoshida would masquerade as the "talker" for an all-white unit and call in the air support they needed.

Even with tricks like these, survival was far from assured. Of the six young men from the internment camp who had signed up with him, Ikaro Yoshida was the only one to survive the war. Going on to become a successful research chemist in New Jersey, Ikaro passed these lessons on to his son. Kentaro Yoshida lived by the proverbs his father taught him, but one would prove to be particularly applicable to his career as a hacker: When the game is rigged against you, cheating is what you do to stay alive.

* * *

Ken Yoshida had started hacking out of curiosity, for the challenge. He never destroyed or stole anything while inside other people's computers. He was only exploring. His explorations taught him two things. First, the potential of the Internet, then just in its infancy, would be limited only by the imagination of its users. Second, the dangers to those users would be just as numerous as the benefits unless robust security measures were put in place.

The list of those potential dangers grew longer every time he visited with his hacker friends. Data and identity theft, digital vandalism, and invasions of privacy were routinely practiced by the unscrupulous members of his underground community. Pleas from Yoshida that they should be a part of the solution and not the problem were ignored by the pirate branch of the hackers, who saw the Internet mainly as a tool for revenge against a society that judged them as misfits.

Yoshida knew that before average computer users could take advantage of the Internet, they would have to be protected from his "friends." He was somewhat relieved when he learned that MegaComp, the largest PC software company in the US, was about to release a program called Watchdog, designed to protect users from hacking attacks while online. Yoshida resolved to help MegaComp produce the best online protection possible.

It took a little social engineering to get himself placed on the list of beta-testers, but soon Yoshida was busy trying to punch holes through Watchdog's protective filters. He knew if he didn't find the security loopholes while the program was in testing, the pirate hackers would find them once the product was released.

At first, the engineers at MegaComp gratefully accepted Yoshida's assistance. The early security flaws were things like debugging modes and test passwords left activated. These were embarrassing but easily fixed. But Yoshida knew his hacker friends would not be deterred when their newbie hacker tricks failed to penetrate Watchdog's protection. When he delved into Watchdog's inner workings, however, the reactions of the MegaComp engineers changed.

The beta-tester's agreement he had signed with MegaComp included a clause against de-compiling the program's code. But Yoshida knew this was the *first* thing a hacker would do when trying to crack the software for real. So he turned Watchdog over to his decryption program and left for the weekend. When he returned, he was shocked to find his computer had cracked Watchdog's protection after only twenty minutes of random attempts. MegaComp had used a ridiculously antiquated encryption program to protect its code, probably to avoid hassles with the government when Watchdog was exported overseas.

Yoshida was now free to study every line of the Watchdog program, looking for avenues of attack. He found several. The most disturbing was a command with the comment "NSA KEY." Yoshida used his decryption program again, eventually finding over a hundred solutions which activated the NSA key. Plugging in a password bypassed every one of Watchdog's safeguards. MegaComp was preparing to sell an Internet protection program the NSA could defeat at will.

Yoshida called the MegaComp software engineer with whom he was on the most friendly terms. When Yoshida recounted his discovery of the NSA key, the engineer asked hesitantly, "Uh, Ken, did you de-compile the program?" After a number of justifications, Yoshida answered in the affirmative. "Okay, let me put Mr. Arbuckle on the line," the engineer replied.

From his arrogance and lack of technical knowledge, Yoshida guessed Mr. Arbuckle was a suit. Probably a corporate lawyer. Arbuckle was blunt and confrontational, rebuffing Yoshida's explanations with a curt, "Just answer the question!" After two minutes of cross-examination, Yoshida hung up on him.

Three days later, the FBI broke down Yoshida's door, seizing his computer equipment and throwing him in jail. Instead of being charged with the relatively minor infractions he had committed against MegaComp, Yoshida was arraigned on multiple counts of interstate computer fraud. He was accused of committing the very crimes he had begged his compatriots not to indulge in, against a list of high-profile targets that would make even the most accomplished hacker proud.

Not surprisingly, the "evidence" extracted from Yoshida's computer entirely supported the government's charges. Yoshida's father was sympathetic, remembering his ill-treatment at the hands of the US government as a young man. He raided his retirement account to obtain the services of the best defense lawyer in Newark for his son.

But even the expensive and self-assured lawyer representing Yoshida was deflated when he saw the weight of evidence heaped against his client. With slumped shoulders, he counseled Ken to accept the plea agreement the US Attorney was offering.

Yoshida protested his innocence and recounted the tale of the Watchdog program and MegaComp's NSA key. His lawyer shrugged and suggested that Yoshida's story must be true or the government wouldn't have gone to such lengths to send an innocent man to prison. Forced to choose between a guilty plea and a five-year sentence or a rigged trial and up to twenty-five years in prison, Yoshida pleaded guilty.

Shortly before Yoshida was transferred to a federal medium-security prison, a Justice Department official paid him a visit. The official said he knew about the NSA key, and that Yoshida had been framed to discredit his story. Keep silent, the official advised. If Yoshida refrained from disclosing the truth about MegaComp and the NSA, the official would do his best to have Yoshida released early for good behavior. And after his release, the official hinted, he would give Yoshida a chance to expose the men who had put him behind bars.

So Yoshida stayed quiet. After three years, the man from the Justice Department kept his promise and Yoshida was paroled. During those three years, MegaComp's Watchdog Internet protection software became one of the hottest-selling programs MegaComp ever produced. A ringing endorsement from the director of the NSA resulted in a large purchase of the program for government PCs, which also helped sales figures. "At last," the director of the NSA declared, "average citizens are able to purchase a level of protection previously available only to the US government."

ACCEPTABLE LOSSES

Stoyer forced himself to relax during the limousine ride back to NSA headquarters. His plan was going forward, although certainly not as he had anticipated. Casualties for the Nebraska attack had been much higher than expected. But that mistake had guaranteed the President latching forcibly onto any solution Stoyer proposed. And latch on he did. The expansion of the DATASHARK mission against Japan would stretch his team to their limits, but it would also fully demonstrate the threat information warfare posed.

And that was Stoyer's true mission, to increase the national security of his country, as the moniker for his agency suggested. It had long been known that the United States had no coherent infowar strategy. Some had even been bold enough to suggest that a small-scale infowar attack against the US would actually work to the nation's long-term benefit, to shake the complacent from their stupor.

But none of these political fortune-tellers had the boldness to carry out the attack themselves. Only *he* was willing to take that kind of risk for his country's welfare.

Risk was something that came naturally to Jonathan Stoyer. He was living proof that fortune favored the bold. Late in the Vietnam war, *Captain* Stoyer had piloted an aging EC-121 electronic surveillance aircraft over Laos, gathering signals intelligence for the NSA.

Purposefully flying the propeller-driven plane over a known anti-aircraft site, three of his four engines were shot away, "forcing" him to ditch the aircraft in a rice paddy. He and his surviving crew members were taken prisoner. The code-books and classified mission orders were also seized, which revealed Stoyer's orders to gather transmissions of a new Soviet code called SNOWBLOWER that had defied all NSA attempts to break it.

Only Stoyer and his case officer at the NSA knew Stoyer's real mission. The rarely used SNOWBLOWER code actually contained a fault that allowed it to be broken with ease. But Russian analysis of Stoyer's captured documents caused SNOWBLOWER traffic to increase dramatically.

For the next six years, the NSA had a unique window into Soviet operations at the highest levels. Analysis of SNOWBLOWER transmissions helped avoid world-wide nuclear conflict during the Yom Kippur War in 1973. It also spurred US diplomatic intervention to avert a Soviet nuclear first strike against China in 1978.

Captain Stoyer was released in a little over a year, to be met by his case officer in Hawaii and flown straight to NSA headquarters. *Major* Stoyer then assumed control of the SNOWBLOWER project, which resulted in his promotion to Colonel then to Brigadier General as SNOWBLOWER bore ever more fruit.

In Stoyer's eyes, the year in captivity, the three men killed in the crash, and the additional man tortured to death as a POW were acceptable losses. He even had fruit baskets delivered to each of his former crew members or their survivors every Christmas. Not that he ever told them the truth behind their sacrifices. They didn't have a need to know.

BOXES

"They want us to do *what?*" Yoshida protested.

Pittman frantically motioned for Yoshida to be silent. "Okay guys, here's our briefing packages. Look them over and we'll meet again in two hours to discuss your ideas. Remember, we're on a short fuse."

Friedman, Malechek, and the Taylor twins each took one of the sealed envelopes and returned to their desks. They were in a large room filled with computer workstations. Shotgun-toting guards prowled a catwalk ringing the chamber. Yoshida's outburst had drawn their attention. One of the guards spoke quietly into his headphone.

Pittman glared at him, wide-eyed with fear. He leaned close. "I'm only going to say this one time, Kentaro, because next time the guards will say it for me. If you want to stay in the program, produce. Don't ask questions, just *produce*. If you don't, you're going to get another close-up look at the box. And I don't want that to happen to you."

Pittman pushed the tan envelope toward Yoshida. "Briefing package. Two hours. *Produce.*"

Pittman's terminal was next to his. He rolled the chair back to his station, broke the seals on the envelope and spread its contents over the large work table beside his computer.

The alarm bells in his head went off like a firing squad. Everything inside the envelope was stamped TOP SECRET/HEADSHOT. He had never possessed a security clearance, but he knew the government wouldn't just hand out classified documents to a pack of federal prisoners. Unless the prisoners would never get a chance to divulge what they had learned.

The first item in the stack was a large city map of Nagoya, Japan. Yellow dots marked numerous utility targets: electrical substations, telephone relays, and the water plant. The map's legend indicated these were targets already selected for attack. Orange dots tagged hospitals, emergency dispatch transmitters, and the Kasugai nuclear power plant just outside Nagoya. The legend labeled them as "Possible HEADSHOT candidates."

Next were several photographs. They were fuzzy, probably satellite photos. Included were shots of different Mitsusui Corporation facilities, the Kasugai nuclear plant, and the main rail station.

Last was a map of the computer networks in Nagoya. Unfolded, the diagram covered his station's entire work table. It was incredibly detailed, showing how the computer facilities were interconnected and the level of security protecting each system.

"Pretty amazing, isn't it?" Pittman said.

Yoshida had to agree. It would take months to discern the architecture of a network like this, especially if the builders took measures to keep out intruders. "How long did it take to put this together?"

"A couple of weeks. There were several guys working on it, of course, but most of the credit goes to Derek. His RAPIDMAP program felt out the boundaries of the network and saved us a lot of fruitless snooping."

Yoshida glanced over at Friedman, who worked a few terminals away. He had apparently given himself over totally to "the program." He displayed frenzied enthusiasm, laughing frequently as he bantered with the other hackers.

Pittman traced the boundary of a red box labeled "KASUGAI NETWORK SECURITY" with his finger. Lines connected this box to the others, but the box itself was empty. "This is where you come in," he said. "A few of the networks have us stumped. Your language ability should give you an advantage in getting through their defenses. Tell me what's inside those boxes."

Yoshida shook his head. "Well, I had written a few programs that might help me, but..."

Pittman tapped Yoshida's terminal, a Sun Blade 2000 workstation. "Everything that was on your laptops and your diskettes has already been loaded onto this computer."

Yoshida briefly contemplated the damage he could inflict on the Sun Fire servers to which this terminal was hooked. Penetrating UltraSPARC systems was one of his specialties. "You guys think of everything, don't you?"

"Just remember," Pittman cautioned, "they always watch the new arrivals pretty closely. Don't try to upload one of your pet viruses to the mainframe or you'll have another appointment with the box."

* * *

Pittman's group was again circled around his table to discuss their plans for operation HEADSHOT. All except Derek Friedman were quiet and sober about the assignment they had been given.

Friedman was full of ideas on how to wreak destruction on the city of Nagoya. He marked targets on the system map. "Now, all five major hospitals have back-up power and water systems that are primarily mechanical and beyond our reach." He held up a triumphant finger. "*But*, their heating, cooling, and fire systems are computerized..."

Pittman interrupted. "Derek, our goal here..."

Friedman waved. "Wait, wait, wait! What if at two AM the sprinklers go off and the air conditioning comes on full blast? They'll have no choice but to move those cold wet sick people out into the parking lot. Don't tell me we won't croak off a few people, in addition to denying the hospital to any other casualties we create."

"Okay," Pittman allowed, "I'll submit it. Next?"

Paul Malechek poked at the empty Kasugai box on the diagram. "I really need to know what's going on in there. There may be so many safeties it's not worth screwing with. But I have to get inside to find out either way."

"That's what Ken is going to tell us," Pittman said. "Right Ken?"

Yoshida stiffened as five pairs of eyes fastened on him. "Yeah, I can do that."

Julius Taylor pushed an overhead picture of the main rail station to the center of the table. There was one rail line set apart from the others. "Anybody know what travels on these tracks? Looks like a dedicated line. None of the other rails cross it."

Pittman passed the photograph to Yoshida. "Let's ask our resident Japanophile."

"That's probably the *Shinkansen* line," Yoshida offered. "It's a high-speed commuter train that runs up the whole east coast of Japan. They want to keep other traffic away because it goes over a hundred miles an hour. They call it the Bullet Train."

Derek Friedman's eyes lit up. "The Bullet Train!" He snatched the photograph and stared at it with the excitement of a fourteen-year-old gaping at a centerfold. "The *Bullet* Train!" he whispered hungrily.

Yoshida cringed. He had always detested electronic vandals like Friedman and the Taylor twins. They hacked not to explore or to learn more about computers, but only to destroy what others had worked hard to create. And now he was handing them the weapons to cause even more destruction.

Yoshida knew he was facing a hard choice. If he did the right thing and refused to participate, the very least he could expect was more time in the box. Or worse. He knew this "prison" had nothing to do with the criminal justice system. The odds that they would really follow through on their threat and ship him to a federal prison were slim. A different kind of box was a more likely fate.

Or he could go along, do the minimum required, and look for his chance to pass a message to the outside. After all, his assignment for the Resistance had been to use his hacking skills to uncover government abuse of power. He had certainly achieved that goal, but now he had to live long enough to report what he had learned.

Yoshida fixed his mind on the hope that someone had noticed his disappearance and had already started looking for him.

SECURITY MEASURES

"I'm sorry," the recorded voice said, "the cellular customer you are trying to reach is not available at this time or is outside the range of the system."

Yoshida's supervisor swore. Yoshida was supposed to keep this phone nearby and turned on at all times. Maybe he had rolled over to his next cloned phone number ahead of schedule. That would be a good idea if he suspected he was being monitored.

The Crown Victoria was circling the block only a few hundred feet from a cell tower. If someone tried to track him, his proximity to the tower and his constantly-changing bearing around it would confuse them long enough for him to complete his business. He consulted the handwritten list in his Daytimer. No dates, no names, just ten-digit numbers. He placed his finger on the line below the number he had just called, mentally subtracting two from each digit as he dialed.

"I'm sorry, the number you have reached is out of service or has been disconnected..."

Yoshida's supervisor swore again. There was only one other possibility for reaching his subordinate. But it was risky, and it would have to be the last call he made on this phone. After a moment's consideration, he decided this qualified as an emergency and dialed the number from memory.

It was to Ken Yoshida's personal phone. Not at his hacker's post, which changed every few weeks, but at the apartment where he actually slept. Even people living undercover needed a public number, one they could give to the mechanic at the garage or the comely young lady at the gym. But Resistance business was never to be conducted over this line. With one exception.

The phone rang five times. He tapped his foot nervously, stopping when he heard Ken Yoshida's voice.

"Hi, I can't take your call right now..."

Yoshida's supervisor spat a profanity he reserved for special occasions. *Out of pocket! You're supposed to say you're out of pocket!* That was the code phrase for *surveillance spotted. Leaving for designated safe house. Will call when satisfied my trail is cold.*

No such luck. He thumped the steering wheel with a balled fist. One of his agents had missed his call-in, wasn't answering his direct line, and had disappeared without even leaving a distress message. That meant he was either dead, incapacitated, or worse.

Yoshida's supervisor needed to know which, and damn fast. His life might very well depend on it. He leaned back slightly, feeling the Glock 23 pistol press comfortingly between his back and the seat. He wouldn't be taken alive if *his* turn came. That was a decision he had already made.

He was too high profile to investigate Yoshida's disappearance directly. That job would fall to Yoshida's subordinates, who were now equally at risk. Unfortunately, he didn't know Yoshida's subordinates. That was yet another layer in their security. But he knew someone who did.

CHAPTER 4

"The evils of tyranny are rarely seen but by him who resists it." -John Hay

HAWTHORNE

FBI Special Agent Ben Hawthorne was beat. He had been in the office for almost two days straight and was glad to finally be getting home. He circled his Brooklyn neighborhood in a mental fog, searching for a parking spot. He finally found one, two blocks from his apartment building. He had just wedged the government-issue Ford into a spot when his cell phone rang.

It was his boss, the Special-Agent-in-Charge, or SAC, of the New York Field Office. "Ben! Bill Jeffries. I hope I caught you before you got home. We just received an updated hacker list. I need you back here to start chasing these names down."

"Can it wait, sir? I'm practically asleep at the wheel as it is."

Hawthorne ran a thick brown hand over his close-cropped hair. To his chagrin, the first spirals of gray had started to appear, although most men in his family didn't turn gray until well into their forties. *It must be the job*, he concluded.

"Sorry, Ben, this came straight from the top. The Director wants to be able to tell the President we've checked out every hacker the Bureau's run across in the last five years, even the low-threats and inactives. Probably a dry hole, but we need to say we did our part."

Hawthorne watched the muscles in his prominent jaw flex and relax in the rearview mirror. "At least let me get something to eat. If I eat any more fast food, I'm going to turn into a French fry."

"Have Felicia make you a sandwich. Give her my best. See you shortly."

Ben Hawthorne was a deeply religious man. At that moment, only his religious discipline restrained him from smacking his cell phone against the dashboard. *The anger of man does not achieve the purposes of God*, his father often recited from the pulpit. Hawthorne shoved the phone deep into a coat pocket.

And preachers thought *televisions* were an invention of the Devil.

He hauled his short, powerful frame out of the car and trudged to his apartment. Felicia would probably be in a foul mood after watching the kids for two days by herself.

He was right. Felicia was having it out with Vanessa, their seven-year-old. Hawthorne tried to close the door silently and slip behind them. No such luck. Felicia whirled about, shaking her hips in what Hawthorne called "the wiggle of wrath."

"About time you showed up!" she scolded.

"Honey," he said quietly, "please don't start. I'm really tired."

"You're telling me! Those two have been like wild squirrels the last two days!"

"I'm just doing my job, sweetheart," he reasoned. "Everybody at the Bureau is working long hours since the Nebraska attack. Nobody gets a day off when Americans have been killed. You know that."

That comment deflected but did not extinguish Felicia's anger. "If the FBI keeps this up, you're going be the next victim. Look at you, Ben, you're a zombie!" She sighed. "Well, you're home now. Dinner's in the fridge. Go wash up, I'll throw it in the microwave."

Hawthorne retreated to a safe distance before dropping his next bomb. "Hon, I have to go out again. I'll just take it with me and nuke it at the office."

"*What?*"

"Bill Jeffries just called me. More hacker intel came down the pipe. Bill says he needs all hands on deck to chase down the leads."

Hawthorne knew this hacker chase was busy work. The FBI wanted to show Washington it was all over the Nebraska case. The way to do that was to turn in lots of full timesheets, which the SAC of every field office around the world would be trying to do right now. And you couldn't do that with your agents at home in bed. The scuttlebutt going around that the CIA had already pegged the attack on a group outside the US didn't change things a whit.

The fire was back in Felicia's eyes. "Oh no, you don't! You've been gone since two AM Wednesday morning! You call Bill Jeffries back and tell him you'll be in after you get some sleep!"

Hawthorne changed the subject in the sweetest voice he could muster. "Hon, could you wrap up dinner for me before I go? I'm starving."

"Sure, sweetheart," she said, mocking his tender tone. "But *you* have to explain to Vanessa why you'll be at the office instead of attending her play."

"Oh *no*, that's tonight, isn't it?" Hawthorne hung his head and shuffled to his daughter's room.

TURNCOAT

Ken Yoshida's skills had advanced the Snake Pit's technology by months, if not years. His custom-built hacking programs had been designed to find weaknesses in his clients' security, so they could shore up their defenses. Stolen by Richter and his goons, Yoshida's software was now a vital part of the current campaign against Japan.

The most damaging program Yoshida had written was called CSERPENT. Written in the C programming language, CSERPENT tested one fault in a mainframe code after another until a security gap was found. Unless the computer administrators had been extremely vigilant in upgrading their systems when manufacturers found a flaw, CSERPENT would punch right through. None of the system administrators in Nagoya had proven very vigilant.

Every time Yoshida opened a hole in a network's security, one of the other hackers would take over, executing the Snake Pit's plan for death and destruction. It made Yoshida sick. He was dragging his heels in breaking the security at the Kasugai nuclear plant. This system had several unique security features, and Yoshida wasted as much time as he dared in cracking each of them.

Many of the security programs were written in a strange Japanese variation of C, which helped him delay things. But Pittman was right there, looking over his shoulder. He would point out defects in the code Yoshida was trying to overlook. It was only a matter of time before operation HEADSHOT would be complete, and there wasn't a damned thing Yoshida could do to stop it.

APPOINTMENTS

Hawthorne was almost back to his car when his cell phone rang again. He had shoved it through the lining of his trench coat, which made it difficult to fish out.

"Hawthorne," he snapped. Unless Bill Jeffries was calling to tell him to take the evening off, he didn't want to hear it.

"Uh, Ben? This is Tony Broadman. Bad timing?"

"Nah. Just long hours." He had recently revived his friendship with Broadman after running into him at a New York State University alumni reunion. Since then, their wives had become closer friends than even the two old college roommates.

"This Nebraska deal got you hopping?"

A tired moan. "You could say that. I think half the hackers in America live in or around New York City. If this is an invite to another jazz concert, I'll have to pass."

"No, this is work. You near a pay phone?"

There was one twenty paces ahead. Broadman was a smart guy. He knew never to discuss anything of consequence over a cell phone. There were too many people with lots of equipment and no life waiting to listen in. Hawthorne wondered how many phone phreaks were monitoring this conversation right now.

"What number are you calling from?" Hawthorne asked, dropping coins into the slot. "Okay, I'm switching over."

A few seconds later they were safe from casual eavesdroppers, although Hawthorne knew that privacy was always a matter of degree. If the conversation was important enough, *somebody* could always find a way to listen in.

"Ben, you ever heard of Ken Yoshida?"

A jolt of adrenaline burned away Hawthorne's fatigue. "Ken Yoshida the *hacker*? Only by reputation."

"Well, I sourced him for one of my stories. He was supposed to contact me again, but he's gone missing."

Hawthorne measured his words carefully. "I wouldn't worry about it. We've been questioning a lot of hackers about Nebraska, and they're all pretty tight with each other. Yoshida probably just decided to take a vacation until the heat dies down."

"He didn't take a vacation," Broadman insisted. "At least not at any resort you'd want to visit. His landlady said some guys in plainclothes who looked like Marines hauled off his stuff. And Ben, there was blood on his carpet. At least I think it was blood. Are you sure somebody in your department didn't, ah, detain him for questioning?"

Hawthorne sagged against the pay phone. He felt faint. "No...no, we don't have him. I'd know about that."

"Ben, you okay?"

Pull it together, Hawthorne! "Yeah, Just thinking."

"It's the story he was telling me that's got me worried, something about..."

"Stop, stop, stop!" Hawthorne chastised. "Not even over a landline!"

"Okay, I was just..."

Hawthorne quickly worked through the possibilities. If someone had taken Yoshida, they might also have tapped the phones of his recent contacts. Or added his name to the NSA's ECHELON watch list. Either way, this conversation was over. "Listen, we need to talk in person. I'll call you later to set it up."

"Ah, Sure, great," Broadman stammered. "I'll be waiting."

Hawthorne didn't remember the rest of his walk. Just that he was inside his car when his cellular went off again.

"Hawthorne!"

There was no answer, just a long, steady tone. He swallowed, then pressed the SECURE button. The tone changed in pitch, then ended.

"Hello?" he probed.

"So, are the Yankees going all the way this year?"

Hawthorne didn't recognize the voice, although the digital encryption distorted any voice to some extent. *Of course,* would have been his automatic reply, but that wasn't the correct response.

"I think it's the Mets turn, don't you?"

A moment's silence.

"I'm a friend of Ken's," the unfamiliar voice said. "Have you talked to him recently?"

"No, why?" he asked warily.

"I've been having trouble reaching him by my usual channels. Could you assist me in contacting him?"

A deep breath. "I was just speaking with a...business associate of Ken's. He had a similar problem. I'm afraid Ken may have taken an unscheduled vacation."

Another pause. "I'm sorry to hear that. In that case I'll need to discuss my business with you. In person."

Hawthorne hesitated. This was outside normal procedures, procedures set up to keep people like him alive. "My schedule is very full."

"Clear it."

The line went dead.

ANCESTRY

No one could accuse the members of the Hawthorne family of backing away from a fight. An escaped slave, Benjamin's great-great grandfather Rufus fought with the Union Army during the Civil War. His grandfather Marcus was a Tuskegee airman, racking up three German aircraft and numerous decorations as a "red-tailed angel."

Ben's father, the Reverend Franklin Hawthorne, was an activist throughout the Civil Rights movement. He had the scars from police dogs and thrown bricks to prove it. Now that it was popular among politicians to claim, "I marched with Dr. Martin Luther King, Jr.," Hawthorne's father often deflated their boasts by exposing his scars and asking the politicians to show him theirs. One former presidential candidate owed his return to private life in part to a televised confrontation with Franklin Hawthorne on the campaign trail.

It was no surprise then that Ben Hawthorne's choice of careers would include both public service and personal sacrifice. His father would have preferred Ben follow him into the ministry, but Ben reminded his father that a minister's job was easier when people saw wrongdoers face the consequences of their actions.

Ben Hawthorne had been a wrestler and football player in high school, and the idea of knocking down criminals and slapping handcuffs on them also appealed to him. But that was before Ben's idealistic views of administering justice collided with the realities of federal law enforcement.

* * *

Two years previously, Evergreen Air had been a small commuter airline, providing regional transport for business travelers between cities in the Northeast. The "hot and low" flight profiles of Evergreen's regional jets on their short flights also made them ideal training aids for Air Force F-16s in the area.

Every few days an Evergreen flight was selected as a target, to be located and intercepted by the fighters. A "kill" would be scored when the F-16s closed from behind and snapped a picture of the distinctive pine tree on the airliner's tail. This practice had gone on for many months, despite the protests of the airline after several "near misses" in flight. The Air Force countered that the training missions were "vital to national security," and since no one had been harmed, Air Force officials insisted, there was no foul.

Evergreen 331 had taken off from Albany for Buffalo with twenty-three passengers and a crew of two. Twenty minutes later Flight 331 hit heavy weather. The pilot reported a loud noise in the tail section of the aircraft during his final distress calls. Flight 331 crashed southeast of Syracuse, killing all aboard. To assist the NTSB, a team from the FBI was ordered to investigate the possibility of a bomb.

Arriving in Syracuse, Ben Hawthorne was driven not to the crash site but to a farm almost ten miles away. There he and his supervisor were greeted by machine-gun-toting Air Force security police. Wreckage from an F-16 fighter was being loaded onto a flatbed trailer.

Another twisted piece of metal sat by itself, covered with a tarp. Hawthorne looked under the tarp and saw the vertical tail of an Evergreen Air jet, sporting the same pine tree logo as the aircraft that had carried him from New York City to Syracuse. It didn't take a seasoned investigator to figure this one out. No wonder the Air Force personnel looked so grim. There would be hell to pay when this hit the press.

Hawthorne and his supervisor took the statement of the farmer. The man said he had rushed outside at the sound of the fighter crash, to watch the tail of the civilian jet flutter onto his front yard like a leaf. The farmer correctly concluded the F-16 pilot had "swapped paint" with the civilian jet before crashing.

Hawthorne's supervisor warned the farmer that his testimony was now part of an ongoing investigation. He should discuss the incident with no one until called upon to testify in court.

The farmer was never summoned. The tail of the Evergreen Jet was "found" a few days later, showing evidence of a structural failure rather than a collision. The National Transportation

Safety Board concluded the Evergreen flight was brought down by an embedded thunderstorm, the same storm that had caused an Air Force F-16 to crash on the same day.

In closing out the paperwork for the case, Hawthorne discovered that the farmer's witness statement had been altered--all reference to the Evergreen wreckage had been deleted. Hawthorne confronted his supervisor with the doctored form and was told there was no way the Air Force and the government were going to expose themselves to liability, even if it *was* their fault.

"Ben, the FBI is part of the government," the older agent explained. "Your responsibility is to buttress the government's case, period. If you value your career, you'll leave your signature on that form and push it through." Hawthorne didn't see he had much choice. He stuffed the Flight 331 file and the commendation he received for it in a drawer and never looked at it again.

Evergreen Air didn't fare as well. After strongly disputing portions of the NTSB report, Evergreen was hit with a multi-million-dollar fine for shoddy maintenance, which led to a flurry of lawsuits from victim's families and a substantial loss of market share. Evergreen Air filed for bankruptcy on the second anniversary of Flight 331 and never flew again.

The farmer suffered the worst fate of all. Frustrated that his testimony was ignored in the final NTSB report, he went directly to the media, who painted him as a conspiracy monger. The IRS visited the farmer a week later, having found large errors in his returns for several previous years. After a lengthy legal battle, the farmer hanged himself, the night before his farm was to be auctioned off to pay his back taxes.

Although tormented by his conscience, Hawthorne knew that one man standing up against a corrupt federal bureaucracy would be like trying to stop a speeding locomotive bare-handed. He prayed that someday he would have a chance to right the wrongs he had ignored.

A month later Hawthorne received a telephone call. The caller seemed to know every detail of Flight 331, including the cover-up. The caller advised him not to contradict the official story, but to wait for further instructions. He later met his mystery contact, a young man named Ken Yoshida. If Hawthorne joined his "cell," Yoshida promised to pass Hawthorne's information about future FBI corruption to the media in an untraceable manner. Ben Hawthorne had been introduced to the Resistance.

Some might have questioned Hawthorne's decision to risk a promising career and possibly his safety in what could be considered a disloyal act. But no one in the Hawthorne family had ever been dealt a fair hand. That didn't stop his ancestors from showing their courage when it counted. Ben Hawthorne would have been disappointed had he not been afforded a similar opportunity.

SCAPEGOAT

Stoyer never tired of the view from the raised walkway inside the NSA Tordella Supercomputer Facility. Before him opened ECHELON Center, more than two football fields of networked CRAY Y-MPs, IBM RS/6000s, and Silicon Graphics Power Challenge supercomputers. The supercomputers ran day and night, greedily feeding on the data from every microwave and satellite link the NSA could tap, both domestic and international.

The engineers called ECHELON the "vacuum cleaner" approach, meaning suck it all in and let the computers sort it out. And sort they did, executing keyword searches in dozens of languages from millions of purloined transmissions each hour, culling out the interesting intercepts for human review later. ECHELON could even pick out a designated voice print, no matter where in the world the target picked up a phone. More than one terrorist had discovered this particular ECHELON capability the hard way.

Constitutional scholars would scream at the invasions of privacy carried out here. But Stoyer reasoned that most constitutional scholars had smoked pot at some point in their lives and hence would never possess a clearance high enough to review ECHELON's methods.

A door opened behind him.

Jeff Archer emerged with a knowing smile, joining Stoyer at the rail. "I figured I might find you here, sir."

Stoyer eyed the rows of supercomputers, butte-like cylinders in the vast pit below. "I like to come here to think. It kind of reminds me of the Grand Canyon for some reason," he said idly.

"I can see it," Archer agreed. "Gives a whole new defini-
tion to the Silicon Valley, doesn't it?"

Stoyer rested his elbows on the railing. "The air in here is
cleaner than Arizona's, too. But you're not here for the fresh air,
are you?"

"No, sir. I have a question about project DATASHARK."

Stoyer's mental guard went up. "Shoot."

"Sir, until the day we briefed the President, I had never
even heard of DATASHARK. As Deputy Director, that's just
not right."

He tried to maintain his casual tone. "Some projects are too
sensitive even for the DD, Jeff, you know that." That was a lie.
While the NSA's military-rank Director typically only served
three or four years before moving on to his next assignment, the
civilian Deputy Director often served much longer. The name-
sake of this computing facility, Lou Tordella, served as Deputy
Director for over fifteen years. Because of that, the Deputy Director often "shielded" the Director from the most sensitive or
potentially embarrassing NSA projects, but not the other way
around.

"Yes, sir, but DATASHARK doesn't seem to fall in that
category. Actually, General, it's in *conflict* with some of the
information warfare technology projects which report directly to
me."

Stoyer saw his opening. "Those are *technology* projects,
Jeff. Research and development. DATASHARK is a *weapon*. It
takes the output of your projects and merges them into a tool
warfighters can use." He tapped the stars on his shoulder. "And
that makes DATASHARK *my* responsibility, not yours."

Archer studied him. Stoyer could almost see the wheels
turning in the younger man's head. Archer correctly concluded
it was time to back off. "You're keeping DATASHARK to
yourself because you think it's *cool*, aren't you?"

Stoyer faked a chuckle. "Guilty as charged! DATASHARK
is sexy as hell, and I want that fourth star as much as any other
candidate for the Joint Chiefs. You nailed me there."

Archer continued his retreat. "Okay, but if DATASHARK
stumbles, you won't have me as your convenient scapegoat."

Stoyer's smile was genuine this time. "Don't kid yourself,
Jeff. I can still pin anything that happens around here on you.
Everybody knows you run the NSA. You just keep me around
for a pretty face."

Archer straightened. "Very well. Thank you, sir."

He clapped Archer on the back. "Well, I guess I'd better get back to work."

* * *

Archer hadn't seen that many teeth since *Jaws*. Appropriate. Like a Great White, Stoyer only smiled when he was about to bite.

DATASHARK. That had really pushed a hot button. The last time Archer had seen Stoyer lay on the charm that thick was when the Senate oversight committee had proposed cutting the NSA's budget. Shortly thereafter, taped phone conversations between Chairman Halton and his mistress surfaced. The budget cuts were quietly swept aside.

Luckily Archer was able to make a joke about DATASHARK and back away. If he had pushed it, he would be swept aside as well. In that respect Stoyer was completely truthful. He would not hesitate to put the blame for any failing of the NSA on Archer's shoulders, regardless of fault. A general doesn't get to three stars unless he's learned how to make other people take the fall for his mistakes.

And that bit about the Deputy Director not being privy to some NSA projects was just plain bogus. The Director didn't even have *time* to be cleared into the dozens of codeword compartments the Deputy Director was expected to manage daily. And those compartments held *the* crown jewels of the American intelligence community--things exceeding even the wildest Internet rumors about the NSA's secrets. Just because a project was ready to be deployed as an information warfare weapon wouldn't keep him out of the loop, either.

Something was dirty about DATASHARK. Archer didn't know what, but his instincts told him it wasn't something he could ignore.

PATIENT ZERO

In most respects, Dr. Ravi Prakash's windowless office at CIA headquarters was unremarkable. As a department head his office was slightly more spacious than most, decorated with pictures of India from a recent trip home. The volume of classified material he had archived required three of the ugly gray Mosler four-drawer safes found in every CIA office. But it was what he could do from this office that made it extraordinary.

On the other side of his wall sat a group of computers his employees referred to collectively as the Beast, from the all-knowing world ruler in a Christian book of prophecy he had never gotten around to reading. The Beast had servant computers operating in plausibly deniable locations all over the world. These could all be controlled from the Beast, allowing CIA experts to hack into foreign computers without fear of their actions being traced. Such tracing was possible, of course, but few entities other than the US government had the necessary computing horsepower.

As Head of Information Security, he was one of the few agency employees with blanket authorization to use the full capabilities of the Beast. That was why his office was its own level four secure area, TEMPEST protected and with both electronic locks and a combination wheel on the door like a bank vault.

Prakash was trying to carry out Director Walsh's orders, verifying the origin of the Nebraska attack. It was turning out to be a bigger job than he thought. The "cornhackers," as Prakash called them, had covered their tracks well.

Their attack programs threaded through multiple secure networks, making it necessary to break the encryption on each system to retrace even a single turn in the maze. Prakash had to use every power in the Beast's arsenal to get past the security of the Mitsusui servers, especially since he didn't speak Japanese. But the Beast did, and it could shoulder aside any job on the Agency's supercomputers to ensure that Prakash never had to wait more than a few minutes to crack the firewall on any system.

* * *

Derek Friedman was the "tunneler" for operation HEADSHOT. Since the computer system at Mitsusui had been thoroughly compromised in preparation for the Nebraska attack, it was being used as the point of entry for the attack on Nagoya.

When one of the hackers finished an attack program against a city system, Friedman "tunneled" a connection between the target and the supercomputers at Mitsusui. Any postmortem investigation of the attack would then show the Mitsusui Corporation as the source. And Friedman had a very special fate in store for Mitsusui's computers, to prevent any backtracking past that point.

* * *

Once Prakash got inside the Mitsusui system, his problems only compounded. There he expected to find the origin server-- one computer to which all the attack programs could be traced. Instead, Mitsusui seemed to be just another conduit for the hackers, albeit one through which *all* their attack programs had passed. After leaving Mitsusui, each of the trails separated again, heading all over Asia. He met more brick walls at every turn.

* * *

"Pittman!" Derek Friedman shouted. "We are not alone, and I ain't talking about aliens!"

Pittman hustled over to Friedman's station, along with one of the guards. "For crying out loud, Derek! What's the problem?" Avoiding attention from the guards was one of Pittman's primary survival goals.

"I was tunneling out from Mitsusui's supercomputer, and look what I just found!"

Pittman and the guard leaned in, watching text scroll on Friedman's screen.

Friedman was wide-eyed. "Look familiar?"

The guard was more puzzled than alarmed.

"Somebody's found our code on Mitsusui's system," Pittman explained.

The guard keyed his radio. "Colonel Richter to the programming bay, ASAP."

* * *

Prakash stroked his beard. The attack programs seemed to have passed *through* Mitsusui's system--they certainly didn't originate there. If they had, Prakash should have found a network of terminals feeding diseased code into one virus-laden server. A "Patient Zero," as the epidemiologists liked to call it. Instead, Mitsusui was just a carrier, not the source.

* * *

Richter trotted to Pittman's side. "Report!"

"Somebody backtracked the Nebraska attack to Mitsusui's system," Pittman said.

"Who? Mitsusui Security?" Richter asked. Discovery by the corporation itself had always been one of Richter's secret fears.

"Unknown," Pittman replied. "We're trying to trace it now."

"Leave that to me," Richter said. "Just tell me what they're doing." He changed frequencies on his radio. "Watchers, lock onto terminal...six. Call ECHELON Center and have them do a global track." He leaned over Friedman's shoulder. "Talk to me."

Friedman fixed an unblinking stare on his terminal. "He's outside Mitsusui's domain now, continuing his backtrack. Man, is he driving some kind of kick-ass system! If he keeps this up, he's gonna land on our doorstep eventually."

"Time?" Richter demanded.

"I don't know how long he's been at it. He may reach us in a couple of hours. Maybe never. Depends on how persistent he is. If Mitsusui's Security department latches onto this..."

"Where is he now?"

Friedman pushed his glasses up on his nose. "He's trying to crack our conduit through the Hong Kong Stock Exchange. That'll take a while."

Richter took a deep breath. "Okay, there are two more jumps after that before he hits our satellite. Keep an eye on him and let's see if the folks at ECHELON Center are as good as they say they are."

* * *

Prakash rubbed his eyes. He checked his watch. *Oh hell*, he thought. He had been working for almost twelve hours non-stop. He pushed away from the terminal. He certainly wasn't getting any farther tonight. But he *had* answered one question. The NSA had pegged the Nebraska attack on the wrong party. The Director would want to know right away.

* * *

Four terminals on the upper level of the Snake Pit were dedicated to monitoring the hacker's activities. Air Force specialists trained at the hacker's art "mirrored" terminals at random from the pit below, making sure the prisoners were doing exactly what they had been tasked to do. But the hackers would never know who was being watched or how many watchers there were.

Two terminals were manned at the moment. Senior Airman Dave Jackson spent most of his time monitoring the new prisoner, Yoshida. Senior Airman Tim Feldman was mirroring Friedman's computer. Feldman called ECHELON Center, giving them the address of his terminal to begin the trace.

With the link to ECHELON established, every line of text Friedman intercepted was dumped into the array of supercomputers at the Tordella facility. The supercomputers searched international traffic for signals matching the C code slithering through Mitsusui's computers. The ECHELON software started with transoceanic satellite links, finding a match almost immediately.

"We have a hit!" the ECHELON technician declared. "Satellite uplink station, Sugar Grove, West Virginia. Still searching."

Feldman keyed his radio. "Colonel Richter, ECHELON Center says it's domestic."

* * *

Prakash found the card Walsh had given him and called the Director's private line. It was already early evening and the call rang over to the Operations center. The watch officer gave him the option of calling the Director at home, but Prakash declined. Instead, he left a voice mail message with Walsh's secretary requesting an appointment for tomorrow morning. This kind of hot potato was best handled after a good night's sleep.

* * *

The discomfort was evident in the voice of the ECHELON technician. "Okay, we've completed the trace."

"Ready to copy," Feldman replied.

"Government Secure Node Seventy-Six, Falls Church, Virginia."

Feldman's shoulders dropped. "*CIA*," he said under his breath, as if the acronym was a profanity.

The ECHELON technician was apologetic. "I can't pursue this any further without authorization from the Deputy Director. Do you want me to call him?"

Feldman passed the question on to Richter.

"No, we'll take it from here," Richter said.

* * *

Prakash secured his computer. He toyed with the idea of handing the problem over to one of the analysts on the night shift, but stopped short. The Director was better known for burying problems than solving them. Prakash didn't want to drag an innocent member of his staff into a cover-up if that was the course Walsh decided to take.

* * *

Richter's nostrils flared. "Get me inside Government Secure Node Seventy-Six, right now!"

Yoshida watched the other hackers carry out a practiced drill, activating programs and typing commands. He had no idea what he was supposed to do.

Friedman cracked his knuckles. "Okay, spooks, here we come! God, I love pulling the CIA's shorts over their heads!"

"Pipe down, people!" Richter ordered. "Pittman, plan of attack?"

"There's forty users logged on to Node Seventy-Six right now," Pittman said.

"Damn! We'll take the whole system down if we have to."

Friedman's head popped up. "He broke the trace! Looks like he's just packed it in for the night!"

"How far did he get?" Richter asked.

"He made it through Hong Kong, then he hit the Singapore Defense Ministry and gave up."

A cruel smile. "Mr. Pittman, can you tell me who just logged off Node Seventy-Six?"

Pittman typed. "Prakash, Ravi, Department 992."

"What's Department 992?"

More typing. "Information Security Center. Dr. Ravi Prakash is listed as the department head."

Even Yoshida felt the chill that passed through the Snake Pit.

"*Walsh*," Richter hissed. "Get me Prakash's phone number. We might just get lucky again."

* * *

Dr. Prakash called his wife, who chided him for missing dinner. His penance was a short list of groceries and bath duty for all three of their children tonight. He accepted his reproof and told his wife he would make a brief stop before heading home. Prakash waved farewell to the night shift on his way out.

RENDEZVOUS

It had been a long day. Broadman trudged into the parking garage, stopping short of his space. A rusty brown van was parked inches from the driver's side of his Jeep. Hell, doesn't anybody in this city know how to park? He had to turn sideways to wriggle between the vehicles. The van's side door slid open, bumping him against the Cherokee.

"Tony! Get in!" a voice commanded.

Broadman whirled, his finger on the "panic button" of his remote.

Ben Hawthorne was inside the van, his face tense. "Come on, we gotta move!" He extended a hand.

Broadman reluctantly accepted the offered grasp. He was hauled brusquely into the van, the door slamming shut behind him. He felt his way into a chair as the van began moving.

Broadman's eyes adjusted to the darkened interior. A partition walled off the driver from his view. A heavily tinted side window was just behind that partition. Passing street lamps cast the only light into the van's interior. A man was seated in the captain's chair facing Broadman. The man wore a suit. He also wore a ski mask.

Somehow the suit made Broadman more afraid than the ski mask. What kind of people was Ben Hawthorne mixed up with? Were they involved in the disappearance of Ken Yoshida, despite Hawthorne's denials? A chill ran up Broadman's spine. Were they about to make him disappear, too?

The van stopped a few minutes later. The side door slid open. A muscle-bound young man in a denim jacket jumped inside. Broadman saw a glint of the Hudson River before the door slammed shut. He prayed not to receive a closer, more permanent view of the water. Even with Hawthorne here, this abrupt meeting and its cast of characters reminded him more of a gangland kidnapping than a friendly rendezvous.

A ship's horn in the distance amplified the silence in the van's tomb-like interior. Despite the chill air off the water, sweat broke out on Broadman's forehead. The man in the denim jacket and the man in the suit stared at him. Hawthorne finally spoke.

"Tony, we need to talk with you about Ken Yoshida."

FREE DONUTS

The convenience store wasn't convenient to Prakash's suburban home, but it was the only way for Ravi to see Sunil.

"Greetings, little brother!" Prakash called out in Hindi. "Working late, are you?"

Sunil wagged a finger at Prakash's shirt pocket. The CIA badge was clearly visible through the fabric. "I could ask you the same question."

Prakash reversed the badge. "Just picking up a few things. Working alone tonight?"

Sunil scowled. "The evening shift girl says she's sick. Bullshit! The spoiled little American bitch is just lazy."

"If Mother heard you curse like that, she'd beat you with a stick."

Sunil shrugged. "Mother is in India. Besides, even Mother would swear if she worked here."

Prakash selected the items on his list. "You know, Sunil, my offer to help you still stands. You could dump this place and come work at the agency."

Sunil laughed. "Like they would hire me! Sorry, brother, I got the good looks, but you got the brains! And I'm managing four stores now. Even Mother is proud of that."

Prakash placed his groceries on the counter. "Come on, Sunil. India is a nuclear power now. We can always use more translators. You don't have to be a rocket scientist for that. And we all worry about you working nights at these stores. You might not get lucky twice."

Sunil waved off his brother's concerns. "I was working a lot closer to DC then. Besides..."

Both brothers turned when the front doors swung open. Two men rushed into the store, wearing ski masks and brandishing pistols. The Prakash brothers instinctively raised their hands.

A gun was leveled at each brother's face. "Put the money in a bag! Hurry!" the lead robber yelled.

Sunil had learned his lesson in the last robbery. He had no desire to take another bullet for revenue's sake. "You got it, sir! You are in charge!" Sunil worked quickly, throwing cash on top of the groceries he had started to place in Ravi's sack. He emptied the register of bills, then held out the bag with shaking hands.

"Here you go! You got a good haul!"

"Thanks!" the lead robber said. "Oh, one more thing."

Sunil kept his hands up. "Anything you want."

"No witnesses," the robber said.

Both gunmen fired twice and ran from the store.

* * *

The black Ford Expedition started moving as soon as the doors slammed shut. "How did it go?" Richter asked.

Kramp tugged off his ski mask. "Slick as a deer's gut."

Womack rummaged through the bag, sorting the bills. "Looks like about two hundred and eighty bucks. Three-way split?"

Richter glared in the rearview mirror. "What are you talking about?"

"We had to make it look like a robbery, sir," Kramp said. "Do you want to split the money three ways?"

Richter glowered at his subordinate. "Keep your damned money! Do you have any idea how lucky we just got? If he hadn't told his wife where he was going, we'd be wasting his whole family at home right now. Even you wouldn't be mister glib-ass after a wet job like that."

The two men in the back seat shrugged and divided the cash. Kramp reached in the bag again, pulling out a small package of powdered-sugar donuts. "Hey, talk about lucky! Look what *we* got!" He ripped open the cellophane and popped one in his mouth. He tossed the package to Womack.

Richter cringed. "Idiot! Don't get that all over the seats!"

"Mmm! Love these things!" Womack mumbled, spraying white powder.

"You two should have been cops," Richter growled.

"Either way, free donuts!" Kramp declared.

CHAPTER 5

*"A little rebellion now and then is a good thing, as neces-
sary in the political world as storms are in the physical."*
- Thomas Jefferson

LEVERAGE

In the darkened van, Broadman felt more than saw the gaze
of the three men boring into him. Hawthorne, the man in the
denim jacket, and the man in the suit were sizing him up. Only
the presence of his friend stood between Broadman and abject
panic. This was too much like a gangland drama, and he was the
character who wasn't going to be around for the next episode.

Hawthorne continued. "Tony, I apologize for the dramatics,
but our reasons will be clear soon enough. You understand that
everything we discuss here is completely off the record, right?"

Broadman was torn between trust in his old roommate and
fear for his own safety. "Sure. Of course."

"Ken was a key member of our organization. We're very
concerned about his disappearance. At your meeting he dis-
cussed the release of information pertaining to MINTNET, correct?"

Did Yoshida really work for them, or were they just finding
out how much he knew? "MINTNET? Doesn't ring a bell."

"Come on. *I* was the one who gave Ken your name. Quit
playing games. He proposed releasing the MINTNET data to
you, and you said you had to think about it, right?"

Could Ben Hawthorne and Ken Yoshida really be on the
same team? Why would an FBI agent be involved in leaking
government secrets? "Actually, it was my editor who had to
make the call."

"And?"

"She killed the story. Said I should leave the investigative
reporting to the guys who are getting paid for it." Broadman
could feel his mouth bending into a scowl.

Even the man in the ski mask gave Broadman a sympathetic nod.

"So what are you going to do now?" Hawthorne prompted.

"Well, I..." Broadman stopped short.

"Go on. We're all on the same side here."

God, I hope so, because it looks like you're about to rob a bank. "I was thinking about pursuing the story on my own time, maybe write a book about it. That's why I went to Yoshida's apartment, to see if Ken would still work with me as a free-lancer."

"You took a real operational risk going back there, Mr. Broadman," the muscle man in the denim jacket interjected. "Ken's security measures were as much for your protection as his. You should have waited for him to call. If the people who took Ken had been watching his place, we might not be having this conversation right now."

"If I hadn't gone back, we *definitely* wouldn't be having this conversation." A dark thought crossed his mind. "By the way, you don't think they..."

Hawthorne jerked his thumb at the muscle man. "If they did, they lost interest pretty quick. Eric followed you from your house this morning. No one else was tailing you. So what did you find at Ken's apartment?"

"Other than the bloodstain, not much," Broadman mumbled, unnerved that he hadn't noticed the tail. He described his questioning of Yoshida's landlady and his collection of the blood-stained strands.

"Where are those carpet fibers now?"

Broadman hesitated. Those tufts of evidence were his only leverage. He wanted to be on neutral ground when he made the exchange, just in case Hawthorne's friends turned out to be as dangerous as they looked. "They're in a safe place. I can deliver them to you tomorrow."

"You'll give them to us tonight," Eric demanded.

Okay, let's both be blunt. "I need a guarantee of my safety."

The man in the ski mask finally spoke. His voice was deep, his diction precise. It was a voice used to giving orders and being obeyed. "We have no intention of harming you, Mr. Broadman. Actually, we need your help."

Broadman blinked. "Help? Help with what?"

"To finish the job you started. To find Ken Yoshida."

THUMBPRINTS

Operation HEADSHOT was almost complete. It would only be a matter of hours until the Snake Pit's attack programs were ready to execute. The best Yoshida could do was delay the inevitable. But with a team of hackers working against him and Pittman watching his every move, there could only be one outcome.

Yoshida yearned for some way he could put himself in the path of HEADSHOT's bullet, to exchange his life for the innocent civilians who were about to be killed. Some of those Japanese citizens might be distant relatives of his, after all. But even that consolation was denied him. If he tried to stop HEADSHOT, his death would be as meaningless as it would be immediate.

Adding to Yoshida's dejection, his CSERPENT program had been key to HEADSHOT's rapid completion. But Yoshida's intimate knowledge of his program had allowed him to leave something behind.

The final routine in the CSERPENT program was a clean-up line, which erased all traces of his code from the target computer. In his security business, the clean-up line was simply to protect the proprietary elements of his program. Now the hackers in the Snake Pit were using it to cover their tracks.

But Yoshida had been able to make a subtle change. Instead of erasing all traces of the CSERPENT code, the clean-up line would now leave a few scattered clues behind. Hopefully not so many that the watchers in the Snake Pit would notice, but enough to be detected in a postmortem analysis by the victims. And once detected, Yoshida's code might be distinctive enough to be linked directly to him.

It would be like leaving a bloody thumbprint behind at a murder scene. He couldn't stop the murder, but he could implicate himself in the crime. And right now, having every law enforcement agency on the planet after his head would be a step in the right direction.

THE RESISTANCE

"Me?" Broadman protested. "How am *I* supposed to find Ken Yoshida?"

"By doing the same things you did before," the man in the ski mask said. "Look around. Ask questions. Dig. Because of our positions, the members of my organization can't carry out an open investigation, but as a journalist you can. You have the perfect 'cover,' if you will."

Broadman considered his ex-roommate. Ben Hawthorne had never even bent the rules back in college, much less broken them. Surely *Ben* wasn't involved in some sort of criminal enterprise. But Hawthorne and his friends were certainly acting like criminals.

"What kind of *organization* are we talking about?" Broadman probed. "Is this a 'family' problem?"

A smile was evident even under the ski mask. "If you're talking about the *five* families, no. This isn't organized crime. It's more dangerous than that. And much less profitable."

Broadman was really confused now, but his professional curiosity overcame his fear. "Who *are* you people?"

The masked leader looked to Hawthorne, as if to offer him a chance to explain the situation, but Hawthorne remained silent.

"Do you trust the government, Mr. Broadman?" the leader finally asked.

"As long as I can keep both eyes on it, I suppose."

The leader seemed encouraged by Broadman's answer. "And *that's* the problem! No one can look over the government's shoulder all the time, particularly if it's *trying* to avoid scrutiny. Fortunately, most people in the government are like you and me. They just go to work every day and try to do the right thing.

"But a growing number of government employees, particularly in federal law enforcement, view the citizens as career fodder. They wouldn't hesitate to put the wrong person in jail just to get a quick conviction. Or destroy evidence that would set an innocent person free. Power is a narcotic, just like heroin or cocaine. If a power addict is in charge, the Constitution becomes irrelevant."

"Yeah, I know things like that happen," Broadman interrupted. "But what can you *do* about it?"

"We *resist*. We work within the system when possible. When the system is unresponsive or corrupt, we take more direct action."

Broadman's panicky feeling was back. "Oh god, you guys don't blow up federal buildings, do you?"

Everyone but Broadman laughed.

"Mr. Broadman," the leader chided, "if I blew up a federal building, I would be killing my own people."

Now Broadman was totally confused.

"We're not a bunch of right-wing fanatics. My people are professionals. Government employees, law enforcement, military...hell, we even have a judge on the team. We place the Constitution above anyone's career or any administration's agenda. When we find evidence of abuse, we expose it. That's what Ken Yoshida was trying to do with MINTNET. It must have been even more important than we suspected. That's why you have to find him."

"What if it *was* the NSA or some other secret agency that took him? What can you do about it?"

There was deadly confidence in the leader's voice. "Leave that to us. Just find out who took him and where."

Oh, is that all? Why didn't you say so? "What if the people who took Yoshida hear that I'm digging around and decide I need to disappear, too?"

"That's where Eric comes in. He'll watch your back and keep an eye out for surveillance. Ben will be your contact back to me."

Broadman avoided eye contact with the dissidents, even the one he considered a friend. Their offer held a certain visceral appeal, but the chances of success were minimal.

"You know," the leader cajoled, "every successful reporter launched their career with one big story. Until then, they were just another struggling journalist. If you can break the story of MINTNET *and* the kidnapping of Ken Yoshida, even Woodward and Bernstein will know your name."

Now he had Broadman's full attention.

"And if this leads to important people going to jail," Hawthorne assured him, "I *promise* you you'll be there to see it. And write about it."

Broadman thought about all the ways this adventure could go sour. "I can't believe *Ben Hawthorne* is asking me to do this."

Hawthorne flashed his choir boy's smile. "I never steered you wrong back in college, did I?"

He had to grant Hawthorne that one. Hawthorne was always the one goading him to start his term papers earlier and to stop bringing beer into the dorm. "Yeah," Broadman countered, "but you were always trying to keep me *out* of trouble, not get me into it!"

The leader locked eyes with him. "The most important qualification you bring to this task is integrity. If you weren't a person of integrity, we wouldn't have considered handing over the results of Ken's investigation to you. We trust you. Now I'm asking you to prove yourself worthy of that trust."

Broadman's heart pounded. He *wanted* to do this, but the risks were sobering. Hawthorne was the only one here he even *knew*, much less trusted. But Ben had never lied to him--about anything. He had earned Broadman's trust many times over.

What was it his father had said about his old Vietnam War buddies? *Trust isn't really trust until you've placed your life into someone else's hands. That's when you find out who your friends really are.* A moment of mental clarity drifted by, and Broadman seized upon it.

"Okay, I'll do it."

Hawthorne looked as if a weight had been lifted from his shoulders. It occurred to Broadman that his friend may have placed himself at great personal risk just arranging this meeting. But what could Broadman possibly bring to the table that justified taking that kind of chance?

The leader shook Broadman's hand with a firm but warm grip. "Welcome to the Resistance, Tony!"

With that simple handshake, Broadman realized his status had changed. Hawthorne's friends were so dangerous that secret government agencies hunted them like terrorists. Yoshida's capture or murder had pushed them all underground, forcing them to hide like common criminals. And now he was one of them.

What the hell have I just done?

FINAL THOUGHTS

The evening meeting of the National Security Council was somber. No assistants were present, and the door to the Situation Room was closed and locked. Jeff Archer had not been invited. Stoyer had just finished his briefing, the NSC receiving an abbreviated version of operation HEADSHOT. The President had been privately briefed on the more lethal details of the mission. Stoyer assumed a formal but relaxed stance to one side.

"Thank you, General," the President said. "Good work."

"My pleasure, sir." Stoyer wondered if his Commander-in-Chief had any idea the amount of whip-cracking that had been necessary to make the secret additions to operation HEADSHOT. Probably not.

"Very well. Final thoughts?" Knowing that his National Security Advisor would be one of the few dissenting voices, Adams motioned for Cynthia Hale to comment first.

"Mr. President," Hale said, "we are about to exact revenge against innocent civilians for an act their government may or may not have initiated. If we are correct, we are punishing everyone *but* the responsible persons. If we are wrong, we're committing terrorism. I *beg* you to reconsider this!"

Hale rested her clasped hands on the table, the closest thing to a gesture of supplication her pride would permit. "Mr. President, *please* allow Director Walsh's people to verify the NSA's conclusions. Ask General Stoyer for an attack plan which targets only the Japanese government and the Mitsusui Corporation. *Anything* but declaring war on innocent civilians! It's just *wrong*, sir."

Adams made a show of thoughtfully considering Hale's objections. *He hides his fury well*, Stoyer realized. That quality alone would make Adams dangerous to his adversaries.

"Thank you, Cynthia. I appreciate your candor. Admiral?"

"Ms. Hale," Holland rumbled, "everyone in this room respects your abilities and your viewpoint, myself included. But in this case I have to disagree. I have been a warrior my entire adult life. There is nothing more abhorrent to me than waging war on civilians. But in my experience, there is nothing that ends wars faster than taking the fight to the people. And we *are* at war, Ms. Hale. The weapons may be unfamiliar, but the coffins look just the same.

"General Stoyer's plan will attempt to avoid civilian casualties," Holland lectured. "The NSA is being a hell of a lot more careful with Japanese civilians than the hackers at Mitsusui were with ours. And DATASHARK is more precise than I could be with Tomahawk missiles. Count your blessings."

Hale frowned but remained silent.

It was time for Stoyer to cover himself. "There will be casualties," he cautioned. "No weapon is perfect. There will *always* be collateral damage."

Adams watched the council's response to Stoyer's statement, but said nothing.

The comments continued around the table, most closer to Holland's opinion than Hale's. Finally all the members had expressed their viewpoints.

"Ladies and gentlemen," Adams pronounced, "thank you for your advice. I have made my decision. Operation HEADSHOT will go forward as planned. General Stoyer, timing for the strike?"

Stoyer had already preset his watch to Tokyo time. "The morning rush hour is about to begin there, sir. We can attack at any time."

Stoyer watched Adams's eyes become distant for a few seconds, then quickly snap back to the present. It further increased Stoyer's admiration for his president. The man had just looked Death in the face and didn't even flinch.

"Very well, General, proceed. And may God be with us."

EVIL SPIRITS

Mitsusui's Computer Research Center in Nagoya was in chaos. The center's Systems Operator hated *nothing* more than chaos. Shuji Takagi wanted the neat rows of terminals and quietly humming servers in his control room to mirror the harmony and tranquility of his meditation garden at home. Everything in its proper place, perfectly in order. If words were spoken at all, they were to be few and in hushed tones.

There would be no meditation in the control room today. Yesterday's routine back-up had discovered a large number of hidden files on the system. The files were encrypted and had defied every attempt to access or delete them. Attempts to track their source were also fruitless. The files slipped like ghosts through every gateway Mitsusui possessed. And their number was still growing.

Strangely, though, the mysterious additions had done no harm, at least not that Takagi or his team could find. They were a small drain on network resources and took up some storage capacity, but not enough to hinder system efficiency. The mere fact that they were *there* was affront enough to Takagi.

The files *did* show a special affinity for the supercomputer's data storage units. On the other side of a glass partition, the high-powered and expensive Hitachis continued to function normally, processing a huge batch job for the Thermodynamics group. Takagi regarded this as one of the few favors his ancestors had granted him this day.

The only way he could stop the enigmatic intruders would be to cut the system off completely from the outside world. Then he would have to restore the entire system from last week's back up, losing thousands of hours of employee research. He was reluctant to take such a drastic step without further provocation.

Takagi and his team had worked on the problem until a late night became an early morning, but they were no closer to a resolution. The only intrusion they had been able to trace back to its source had originated from a United States government computer in Virginia. That trespasser had left nothing behind on Mitsusui's system but had also shown a curiosity about the cryptic files. It was alarming enough for Takagi to warn his management, who had alerted the Trade Ministry, who in turn would be lodging a formal protest with the US government later today.

Oh, my, a *formal* protest! That would be no help to Takagi. He needed an answer *now*. Like he often did before the prayer shrine in his garden, Takagi clapped his hands together once, as if to summon a Shinto spirit of system salvation. His team nodded in grim agreement. Prayer was the only sensible course of action remaining. The digital clock on the wall rolled over to "05:00:00."

The first alarm buzzed in the supercomputer bay. The batch job that had been quietly churning for the last two hours had come to an abrupt stop. A quick check of his terminal told Takagi that another program had bumped ahead of every job in the schedule. Cursing, he attempted to override the interloper but was rebuffed. The insurgent program had used his own command code to jump the queue and refused to relinquish control of the system.

Ignoring Takagi's frantic orders, the runaway supercomputer dispatched jobs over Mitsusui's entire network. In seconds, every server in the center became fully dedicated to whatever agenda the alien program in the supercomputer was executing.

His team simultaneously winced at their terminals. "I'm locked up!" they exclaimed in unison.

Takagi's ulcer jabbed a red-hot poker into the pit of his stomach. He had only one option left to regain control of his hijacked system. He would have to cut power to both the supercomputers and the mainframes, then reload the entire system with clean boot programs. He ran for the master power controls, hoping this disaster wouldn't cost him his career.

Then the fire alarm sounded.

Streams of Halon gas erupted from the ceiling. Takagi briefly contemplated continuing his task, but remembered the fate of Yakushi-san. The aged professor had been his mentor at Tokyo University. He was asphyxiated by staying a few seconds too long during a computer room fire. The old man didn't realize the Halon would snuff out his life as quickly as it did a fire.

Takagi waved toward the door. "Get out! Stop your work! Get out now!"

Takagi and his team ran cursing through the empty halls under a steady torrent from the fire sprinklers. Outside, they huddled in a cold drizzle and waited for the fire department to arrive. And waited.

"Call 110! Find out what's going on!" Takagi ordered after several minutes had passed.

One of his workers flipped open a cell phone and dialed Nagoya's emergency dispatch number. He examined his phone with a confused look. "There's no answer."

"Your phone's just wet!"

The rest flipped open their cell phones like a synchronized drill team, then stared at the displays. "Mine's working, but it says 'No Service,'" one finally said.

Having exhausted his list of familiar curses, Takagi began experimenting with original combinations. He plucked his badge from a drenched shirt pocket and ran it through the door lock. Maybe he could find a phone inside that hadn't been ruined yet. He tugged at the door. Locked.

He tried again. Nothing. Each of his subordinates ran their badge through the reader in turn. The security system rejected them all.

"I'm open to suggestions," Takagi said to his team. Then something caught his eye.

The Mitsusui complex was perched on a hillside overlooking Nagoya. The city filled the wide Nobi valley below, sloping down toward Ise Bay. Like a lighted checkerboard, sections of Nagoya went dark, one after another. The blackout worked its way up the valley like an advancing army of darkness. Finally the lights in the parking lot went out with a pop, leaving a fading orange glow.

"I have a really bad feeling about this," Takagi muttered.

* * *

The computers inside the Mitsusui building continued to run on their independent power supplies, but their work was completed. The supercomputers executed their final commands. The fire alarms ceased and ventilation fans pushed fresh air into the computer room, purging out the Halon gas.

Like the American CRAYs, the supercomputers used liquid nitrogen to cool their circuits. Coolant flow was carefully regulated according to the Hitachi's workload. Without this coolant, their wiring would melt and pour out like mercury in less than ten seconds.

With the final commands completed, coolant flow ceased. A real fire now spread through the computer room, and the Halon bottles were already empty.

HONORABLE DEATHS

Chief Engineer Takeo Hirosawa stretched and stifled a yawn. He poured himself another glass of his wife's strong tea. Hopefully it would keep him alert through the last hour of his shift. Hirosawa and the staff on duty at the Kasugai nuclear plant northeast of Nagoya were like third shift workers everywhere. They toiled through the night while others slept, the struggle against mind-numbing boredom more challenging than any other task they faced.

Hirosawa studied the status screens wrapping around the front wall of the control room. A product of the local Mitsusui Corporation, the huge color displays were almost identical to the flat wall-sized HDTV screens Mitsusui was using to dominate the worldwide HDTV market. Fine products, to be sure. Mitsusui even wrote the control software that managed the Kasugai plant's operations.

A flash of red on one of the screens drew Hirosawa's attention. An electrical generator had gone off-line. Before he determine the reason for the failure, another generator symbol turned red, then another. All six of the station's generators dropped off-line in sequence. When the last generator failed, the screens and everything else in the control room went black.

For a few harrowing seconds, battery-powered emergency lights provided the only illumination in Kasugai's control room until the back-up diesel generators kicked in. The status screens winked back on, their computers protected by emergency power systems. Only then did Hirosawa and the operators he supervised exhale their collective gasp.

Even Kasugai's veteran Chief Engineer had never experienced a "station blackout." The Kasugai plant used a substantial portion of its output to power the pumps, valves, and motors necessary for its operation. Without that power, the plant had to borrow electricity from the national grid or rely on its back-up generators to continue safe operation.

Hirosawa broke the silence. "Why aren't we receiving power from the grid?"

The lead reactor technician, Hitoshi Izumi, stabbed at his terminal, to no effect. "Power-sharing controls are off-line!"

"Then call Kyoto and have them shunt the power to us manually!" Hirosawa ordered. *Youngsters! Take away their computers and they act like you've cut off their arms!*

"Phones are down too!" Izumi reported a few seconds later.

What the hell is going on? "Then we'll have to make do with the diesels!"

The diesel back-up generators only provided enough power to run the reactor's emergency cooling systems, a tenth of what was needed for normal operation. To prevent a catastrophic core meltdown, the operators now had only a few minutes to reduce the output of the nuclear reactor, in addition to scrambling to find the reason the main generators were off-line. The fact that the Chernobyl disaster had occurred during a station blackout wasn't far from anyone's mind.

Hirosawa flipped to the emergency procedures section of the station manual, a manual he had helped write. "Execute emergency reactor shutdown!" he recited, checking off the steps on the laminated pages with a grease pencil he carried just for that purpose.

"Executing shutdown!" was the immediate response.

The computer normally handled the power management at Kasugai. Operators told the computer the necessary power output, and it manipulated the valves, pumps and turbines until the desired result was achieved. This arrangement cut the number of personnel required to run the Kasugai plant by half. It also made manual operation something of a lost art.

"Confirm reactor scram," Hirosawa ordered.

The computer also governed the control rods for the nuclear reactor. Manipulating the number and position of the control rods could reduce or stop the atomic reaction in the reactor core. When the generators stopped producing electricity, the computer was programmed to immediately "scram" the reactor, fully inserting every control rod into the core. This would slow the reactor as decisively as slamming on the brakes of a car.

Izumi checked his terminal. "Reactor scram confirmed."

Izumi's display lied. The computer had not done as instructed. Instead of scramming the reactor, the control rods were being removed. The atomic reaction accelerated. Heat in the core increased, demanding more coolant water for the reactor. Coolant flow increased, forcing the pumps to demand more power from the already-limited amount available. The lights in the control room dimmed.

Hirosawa stood at his station. "What the hell is going on? I need information!"

"The computers say everything is normal!" Izumi responded. The rest were too confused or too frightened to reply.

Hirosawa growled in disgust. These children didn't run the power plant, the power plant ran *them*. He hurried to the back-up gauges in the old control room across the hall. The mechanical devices there dated back to when *men* ran the station, not computers. What he saw made him clutch his chest. "The control rods are fully retracted!" he shouted through the doorway. "Scram the reactor, *now!*"

Izumi firmly and carefully reentered the appropriate commands. Nothing happened. "The computer must be malfunctioning!"

The computer ignored Izumi. It dutifully followed its new programming and carefully monitored the systems at the plant, making adjustments to ensure that a point of no return was reached as quickly as possible. Temperature and pressure in the coolant system rocketed upward. Paint on pumps and pipes smoked. Valves sang as flow rates reached design limits.

Hirosawa watched the needles on the back-up gauges climb higher into the danger zone. This wasn't even like the worst-case emergency drills he used to train new technicians. This was a nightmare. He reached for the manual controls. "I'm cutting the power to the control rod assembly! Emergency scram!"

As a fail-safe measure, the control rods were held above the reactor by magnetic clamps. If all power was cut, the clamps would open and gravity would cause the control rods to fall into place. But the computer routed emergency power to the clamps, making sure the control rods stayed where they were.

The ventilating fans had been one of the first systems the computer had shut down to conserve power. The control room was now a sweat box, the heat stretching frayed nerves even further.

Izumi slapped his computer. "It didn't work! It won't respond, damn it!"

Hirosawa knew what he had to do. "Then we'll have to cut the power manually. At the reactor." He pointed at Izumi. "You're with me! Grab some flashlights and a toolbox!"

All traces of color drained from Izumi's face. "*Hai!*" he shouted, scurrying to obtain the required items before he went to what would probably be his death.

The first inevitable failure occurred in the containment building. The huge concrete enclosure was designed to keep radiation from escaping to the environment. A rupture plate in the high-pressure coolant line gave way with a deafening roar. The radioactive coolant water instantly flashed into steam, rushing out in a jet that shook the entire facility. But even this failure was a safety measure, assuring the first break in the system occurred inside the containment building and not in the unshielded generator plant.

The failure should have lasted only a few seconds. As pressure in the coolant system dropped, the computer had originally been programmed to scram the reactor and add more water to the reactor at low pressure only. A pool of contaminated water might collect in the containment building, but the spill would end there.

The computer's new programming had a different plan. High-pressure water continued to rush into the overheated reactor, scouring uranium from the fuel rods and blasting it into a cloud of steam that filled the containment building.

Hirosawa and Izumi were halfway to the power controls when the rupture plate burst. Radiation alarms rang out almost immediately. Izumi froze. A bank of contaminated steam rolled across their path. Izumi was a civil servant--suicide was not part of his job description. He dropped his toolbox and ran from the deadly cloud, leaving Hirosawa alone.

Hirosawa watched Izumi's back recede. He lifted the toolbox with a grunt and continued toward the reactor. He mentally rechecked the readiness of his life insurance policy and his will, an ancient samurai farewell ringing in his head:

May the gods grant you an honorable death!

The heat was almost unbearable in the containment building. Hirosawa was sure he had absorbed a lethal dose of radiation simply by entering the chamber. No matter. Unlike Izumi, Hirosawa had more than enough reasons to sacrifice his life. His wife, two children and three grandchildren lived in the valley below the plant. He closed the airtight door to the containment building behind him and headed for the core.

The power switches for the control assembly were on top of the reactor core. The core towered above him, a fifteen-meter-high pressure vessel with a ladder up the side. The ladder was already too hot to touch. He found a pair of heavy gloves in the toolbox and started climbing. A pain shot from his chest down his left arm, almost causing him to lose his grip on the toolbox. He gritted his teeth and blinked sweat from his eyes.

May the gods grant you an honorable death!

Hirosawa finally struggled to the top of the core. There were twelve large knife switches routing power to the control rods. As he had suspected, the switches hadn't been thrown since the plant's certification. They were almost immovable. He clamped an insulated wrench onto the first switch and pulled on it with his full body weight. It opened with a high-voltage crackle. The first set of control rods plunged into the reactor with a landslide crash. The control rods displaced superheated water in the core, blasting steam from the ruptured pipes with volcanic force.

Hirosawa ignored the heat roasting his skin and lungs. *A dead man feels no pain*, he kept telling himself. He fastened the wrench to the second switch and pulled. Another outburst of steam lashed at him.

May the gods grant you an honorable death!

Soon the task was done. There was no change in the hellish environment of the containment building, but Hirosawa knew the atomic fire driving the inferno had been quenched. Short of breath, he shuffled to the ladder and began climbing down. He had survived.

No, that wasn't right, he reminded himself. With the radioactive clouds swirling in the containment building, he had doubtlessly received a lethal dose before he even reached the top of the core. But how long did he have? Days? Hours? He noticed the blisters on his arms. Were they from the heat or the radiation? From the heat, he decided. The first sign of radiation poisoning was nausea. He steeled his mind for the slow, painful death that awaited him.

A fire even hotter than the steam swirling around him lanced down his left arm. He cried out, sagging against the ladder. A crushing pain seized his chest. Hirosawa felt a vague sensation of falling, but mercifully not the impact when he struck the concrete floor below.

The gods had granted Chief Engineer Hirosawa's request.

* * *

The Kasugai computer had one more step in its malevolent agenda. It monitored the radiation accumulating in the containment building. Numerous safeguards were in place to prevent a radiation leak from escaping. The last of these barriers, heavy steel shutters, closed over the ventilating fans. At the computer's signal, the status of the fans was changed from LOCK DOWN to FULL ON.

Like the breath of an angry dragon, plumes of contaminated steam spewed from the containment building, merged with the low overcast, then rolled down the valley toward Nagoya.

SHINKANSEN

The morning began much the same way all over the city. Without electricity to power their alarm clocks, many Nagoyans awoke with a start only when dawn's light crept into their windows. Frantic activity followed, the tardy workers struggling to reclaim their schedules without artificial lights or electrical appliances. Telephone calls to their supervisors to beg forgiveness were attempted without success. Dutiful wives located battery-powered radios and monitored reports of the city-wide blackout on the few radio stations still transmitting. Consternation mounted when water pressure dribbled away, making even personal hygiene impossible.

Corporate employees tucked shaving and make-up kits under their arms, hoping to complete those tasks in their lighted bathrooms at work. They found the buses running late and traffic snarled at every darkened intersection.

Trying to catch the subway was even worse. The crowds had already spilled out onto street level. The commuters unlucky enough to arrive first found the tunnels dark, but were unable to exit. A continual flow of ill-tempered riders pushed into the stations from above, forcing helpless passengers deeper into the darkness. People fell from the darkened platforms onto the tracks, their faint screams echoing up from below. But the crush continued, like a pack of human lemmings rushing to the sea.

The most frustrated of all were the businessmen and women struggling to catch a train out of town. With the subways out of service, the most convenient route to the main station was blocked. But Japanese business travelers are a determined and resourceful lot. Many hopped overflowing buses or flagged taxis in hopes of meeting the ruthlessly efficient departure times stamped on their tickets. Motor scooter owners were making a windfall, the salarymen flagging them down with wads of cash.

The travelers fortunate enough to arrive at the station found the electrically-powered intercity trains shut down. Crowds gathered on the outside platforms, no one wanting to wait inside the darkened station. Soon the train platforms paralleling the station resembled the subways. Newly-arriving passengers pushed and shoved the others against the stalled train cars.

There was little complaining, the Japanese having long ago sacrificed the concept of personal space on the altar of necessity.

"Listen!" one of them shouted.

A familiar whooshing sound in the distance signaled the arrival of the *Shinkansen*, the "bullet train" from Tokyo. Expectant travelers craned their necks and stood on tiptoes, straining to see their arriving deliverance from the crush.

This *Shinkansen* would not stop. It was the Tokyo-to-Osaka express, scheduled to blast through Nagoya at full speed enroute to its destination. The train's driver was aware of the blackout in Nagoya, but he had radioed ahead. The power supply for the express line was miraculously untouched. He was grateful Nagoya's misfortune would not affect his exemplary on-time record. Rounding a curve, he saw the idled main station, its disabled trains cluttering the yard.

The driver saw the green light at the station. His track was clear. He pushed the power lever full forward. The *Shinkansen* accelerated toward its top speed of two hundred-fifty kilometers per hour. Seconds before the train passed the turn-off into Nagoya station, the horrified driver watched the signal change from straight to turn. The switch was about to direct him into the crowded train yard.

The driver yanked the power lever back into full reverse and screamed into the radio for the switch to be changed, but it was too late. The bullet train rammed into the turn at over two hundred kilometers per hour. The locomotive rolled over on its side, immediately striking a stalled passenger train. The rounded nose of the *Shinkansen* rode over the crumpled coach, causing the locomotive to go airborne.

The sixteen cars of the *Shinkansen* were permanently linked for safety at high speeds. The lofting locomotive yanked the passenger cars into the air, arcing over the rail yard like an enormous steel snake. The twisting assembly was still airborne when it slammed into a packed platform, flattening a parked train and blasting like a battering ram through the station's exterior wall.

The bullet train then broke apart, each piece following a separate trajectory through the crowded station. The mangled cars rolled and tumbled several times before stopping, pulverizing everyone and everything in their paths. Finally an awful silence filled the station.

The rescue operation was the only thing in Nagoya that worked as planned. A policeman standing outside the station radioed in a general alarm. Dozens of fire and ambulance units, shut down by the failure of the phone dispatch system, responded immediately. In minutes over a hundred firefighters and paramedics were picking through the carnage, frantically sorting the living from the dead.

In the chaos few noticed the rain beginning to fall on Nagoya in heavy, gray drops.

CHAPTER 6

"The secrets of government, like the secrets of men, are always their defects." - Thomas Paine

MOTIVATIONS

Broadman briefly considered not even telling Christina about his meeting with Hawthorne's associates. What she didn't know she couldn't worry about. The knock on the door late that night removed that option. It was Eric, there to retrieve the bloody carpet fibers. Christina immediately insisted on a full recounting of the tale, with almost the same intensity Hawthorne and his companions had shown.

She handled the news remarkably well. She knew confrontations with the government were an occupational hazard of any determined journalist. But usually reporters could call on their publisher for back-up in such situations. In this case Broadman was on his own.

Christina had moved the discussion to the kitchen table, meaning no one was going back to bed until all questions had been answered to her satisfaction.

"So why can't Ben just take this to the FBI himself?" she demanded. "Aren't missing persons *their* problem?"

"Not this time. Ben and his friends think some rogue faction of law enforcement took Yoshida. If they go to the FBI, those same people may come after *them*."

A look of genuine fear flashed across her face. "So what are *you* supposed to do?"

"They think someone like me poking around won't raise the same red flags as an official inquest. Hopefully I can figure out who took Yoshida and let Hawthorne's friends take it from there." It didn't sound as convincing coming out of his mouth as it did from the Resistance leader's.

Christina's rare frown mirrored the uneasiness he was feeling. "Somehow, I have a feeling it's not going to be that easy."

AFTERMATH

Stoyer had never visited the Roosevelt Room before, an intimate conference room directly across from the Oval Office. Decorated to resemble a family dining room, Teddy Roosevelt's portrait in his Rough Rider uniform hung over the fireplace. At the opposite end of the table, a false china cabinet concealed the television and associated teleconference equipment.

Stoyer's seat faced a Remington bronze sculpture of a mother buffalo defending its calf from a pack of wolves. He was immediately attracted to the dramatic statue, although in his current role he realized he was more like the marauding wolf pack than the protective buffalo.

He was surprised a meeting of the National Security Council had been called for a simple raid assessment. He took it as an indication of the President's emotional stake in the HEADSHOT strike. That kind of emotional involvement from a leader usually disturbed him, but Stoyer *did* have his own place at the NSC table now, seated directly across from the President. The senior NSC members were leafing through the purple-and-white-striped folders the NSA had supplied, the top and bottom of each page stamped in glaring red letters: TOP SECRET/DATASHARK.

"The majority of our information," Stoyer reported, "has come from intercepts of the three radio stations in Nagoya which had back-up generators. One of those has subsequently stopped transmitting for unknown reasons. Analysis of those intercepts has shown the interruption of services caused by the HEADSHOT strike were near total. Electrical power, water, conventional and wireless phone service were all successfully curtailed, and should remain so for several days."

"Casualties?" Hale asked.

"There was mention of an accident at the main rail station, but..."

"I don't recall their rail systems being targeted," Hale interrupted.

Stoyer had a cover story prepared. "Train service in the city of Nagoya was shut down without incident when electrical power failed," he insisted. "However, a high-speed train entering the city apparently lost control and derailed when it entered the blackout zone. It was unforeseen collateral damage, I assure you."

Hale's voice dripped with contempt. "Is there any other 'unforeseen collateral damage' we should be made aware of, General?"

This next bullet was going to be a lot harder to dodge. He cleared his throat, turning to the appropriate page in the binder. "There was also a small release of radiation from the nuclear power plant on the outskirts of Nagoya..."

Hale's eyes blazed. "A nuclear release?"

"Cynthia," Adams cautioned.

"In my consultation with a senior member of the Energy Department," Stoyer continued, "I was assured that a lapse in electrical power would not in itself cause an accident. Apparently Japanese nuclear plants do not have the same level of safeguards we possess."

Stoyer's deception was interrupted by a knock at the conference room door. Classified folders closed all around the table.

"Enter," Adams called.

A young man leaned into the doorway, holding up a video-cassette. He nodded toward the National Security Advisor.

"Mr. President," Hale said, "we have the first video from the target area, if you're interested."

Adams pointed to the television cabinet. "Go!"

The aide cued the tape. "This is a report from an ITN correspondent," he said. "CNN picked it up a few minutes ago."

The voice-over narrated in a clipped British accent. "What began as coverage of a consumer electronics show has now placed this reporter in the center of a disaster of national proportions here in Nagoya, Japan. It started as a pre-dawn electrical failure which stalled trains and subways. It ended with a horrific accident, one of the famed Japanese 'bullet trains' losing control and plowing into a crowd at the main rail station."

The video showed the dimly-lit terminal, its interior littered with crumpled sections of the *Shinkansen* cars. CNN had obviously edited the ITN footage to remove the worst of the gory close-ups, but puddles of blood and mangled bodies were evident even in the wide pan shots. Shocked and bleeding victims were being escorted out by rescue crews, who outnumbered survivors two to one.

"But even this carnage was not the most ominous development in the Nagoya disaster. Shortly after our crew arrived at the rail accident, police ordered the streets cleared because of radioactive fallout from the nearby Kasugai nuclear power plant.

"Residents have been ordered to remain inside and seal windows and doors against nuclear contamination. However, the power failure has also affected the water supply, and without water it is not known how long citizens will be able to remain indoors."

The video showed army trucks rolling on the streets. "The Japanese government, criticized for its slow response to previous atomic accidents, has been totally overwhelmed by the disaster in Nagoya. Officials have not yet decided whether the contamination will decay to safe levels on its own in a few days, or whether a massive evacuation will be necessary to protect the citizens of this city of more than two million people."

A shot from an upper floor window showed soldiers in protective suits and masks patrolling the streets. "The fear and frustration are mounting, and the citizens are left to fend for themselves, without information or assistance from their government. Christopher Devon, reporting for International Television News from Nagoya, Japan."

Hale's aide stopped the tape.

Admiral Holland's command of a nuclear-powered carrier had made him an expert in nuclear science. "Mr. President, if the Japanese suffered an uncontrolled release of radiation, it's going to be weeks or months before Nagoya will be habitable again. They're probably just stalling while they get an evacuation plan together. The situation is going to get a lot worse."

"It already has," the Secretary of State lamented. "The Japanese knew about our penetrations of Mitsusui's system six hours *before* the attack. The shit is about to well and truly hit the fan."

Even without looking, Stoyer felt every eye in the room fix on him.

"General?" Adams asked.

What the hell? Stoyer didn't have a cover story for *this* development. "I was assured by my people the attack would be untraceable," was the best he could improvise.

Cynthia Hale suppressed a smile, but the delight was obvious in her voice. "Well, General, as you told us a few days ago, there's no such thing as a perfect crime."

CODEWORDS

The bumper-to-bumper traffic heading into the NSA complex told Archer he wasn't the only one who decided to get an early start after hearing about the attack on Nagoya last night. The watch officer at the NICC had called him at home with regular updates, and Archer called in again shortly before he left for work.

He pulled his Volvo S80 into the Deputy Director's reserved parking space, which spared him the quarter-mile walk most employees endured. Like the Director, Archer was entitled to an official car, a driver, and even bodyguards if he desired. But he wasn't as fixated on the trappings of rank as General Stoyer. Archer only used his perks when they helped him get his job done.

The main entrance to the NSA complex was through the Access Control Center, a pentagonal concrete structure with two-story mirrored windows ringing the outside. It was meant to intimidate, and it succeeded. Upon entering, visitors and employees faced a six-foot-high plaque with the NSA eagle grasping a skeleton key beyond the ten access-control turnstiles.

Archer slid his blue NSA badge with the gold Director's border through the turnstile's reader and punched in his access number, watched by an armed guard from a bulletproof control booth to one side. The turnstile unlocked with a click and a green light, signaling Archer through.

A harried woman with a bulging purse followed close behind him. Her turnstile stopped after half a turn, trapping her inside. The turnstile beeped loudly. Three guards emerged from behind the control booth to free the woman, escort her to a side room and close the door. She had won the NSA "door prize," a random and thorough search of employees' belongings to make sure they weren't bringing in cameras, recorders, or other subversive devices.

Archer tried not to show his relief. A few seconds later and the door prize would have been his, his title notwithstanding. He had nothing to hide, at least nothing that would show up in a physical search. But he knew too much about searches and interrogations to accept one casually.

Beyond the Visitor Control Center was the Red Corridor, where contractors staffed the NSA cafeteria, drugstore, bank, travel office, and other services, their uncleared status marked

by a red badge. After the employees complained about the cafeteria fare, the NSA opened a Taco Bell and a Pizza Hut here as
well. Archer was currently in negotiations with the state of
Maryland to set up a DMV office in the Red Corridor, much
like Virginia had in the Pentagon. Anything that kept his workers happy, productive, and continuing in government service
couldn't be overlooked.

Several escalators led from the Red Corridor up to first
Blue Level. A pair of guards waited at the top, making sure everyone coming up displayed the blue badge of a cleared NSA
employee or the green badge of a cleared contractor. The nearest guard greeted him with a smile.

"Good morning, Mr. Archer!"

"Good morning, Bill!" he replied. Archer tried to get to
know as many of the guards as he could. If there was a recur-
ring security problem, the guards usually spotted it first. And
Security *was* his agency's middle name.

"Did you get caught in that mess coming in today?" the
guard asked.

"Yeah, I did. What was the deal?"

"Same thing it usually is. Somebody's car crapped out, and
we had to wait an hour for a tow truck. Traffic flow went
straight to hell."

"Does that happen often?" Archer asked.

"Only every day or two. You know, if we had our own tow
trucks, we could get those hulks out of the way and get things
moving again."

The NSA already had their own fire department, medical
center and SWAT team. They also had a budget which had been
cut every year since the Cold War ended. Throwing money at
problems wasn't an option anymore.

"We might try contracting with a local garage to have a tow
truck on site for a month to see if it helps," Archer offered. "Is
there any pattern to the breakdowns?"

"Yeah, it's usually a single mom or some food service
worker who can't afford to keep their car up."

An idea sparked in Archer's mind. "Bill, are you handy
with a wrench?"

A shrug. "I can change my own oil, if that's what you
mean."

The spark flared brighter. "Yeah, that's what I mean. What
if we had a car clinic for employees some Saturday? Have all

our shade tree mechanics volunteer to do routine maintenance work for these people who can't afford it. Then we could pass the hat among the rest of the staff for oil and parts, and tell them the more they give, the less we'll all sit in traffic."

The guard's eyes brightened. "That's a great idea!"

Archer pulled out a business card. "No, it's *your* idea." He wrote on the back, "I LIKE BILL'S IDEA. LET HIM RUN WITH IT--J.A." He handed over the card. "Give this to your boss and keep me posted."

The guard straightened and blinked. Archer called it "the shock of empowerment." Like rats in a maze, some NSA employees got so used to being trapped in the bureaucracy that they didn't know what to do when liberated. "Oh, okay, I'll...I'll do that," he stammered.

"Let me know once you set a date," Archer said as he walked on. "I'll bring the coffee and donuts!"

The elevators for the OPS 1A building were near the escalators. Archer went down two floors and past another checkpoint to the NICC entrance, a double set of glass doors, the letters "NICC" inlaid in the floor. The outer set of doors closed behind him. His badge and access code were again required to open the inner set.

The NICC's morning shift watch officer, Army Colonel Joe Morris, gave Archer a quick and clinical rundown of the situation in Nagoya, including satellite data on the current dispersal of radiation from the Kasugai plant. This didn't look anything like the limited information warfare attack General Stoyer had proposed.

Archer spent a lot of time in the NICC, and had developed a cordial relationship with Morris. "Dear God!" Archer whispered. "Did we do this?"

Morris said, "Not to my knowledge, sir," along with an almost imperceptible nod.

Why am I being shut out? Archer's mind shouted. Morris was obviously in the dark as well, but he apparently knew something Archer didn't. "Was this a DATASHARK attack?" he asked, hoping the correct codeword might pry loose more information.

"I don't know, sir. Honest." Morris tried his best to maintain a stone face at the mention of DATASHARK, but the reflexive widening of his eyes told Archer he had hit paydirt.

"Walk with me," Archer said, leading Morris toward the stairs. The glassed-in balcony at the rear of the NICC was unoccupied. General Stoyer was the only one who *really* enjoyed being up here. But it did offer privacy.

"C'mon, Joe, level with me," Archer said in a low voice. "I'm flying blind here. If *anybody* at the NSA has a need to know, it's me!"

Morris frowned. "As far as Nagoya is concerned, I really don't know who did it. But somebody uploaded a shitload of encrypted data to one of our satellites last night just before Nagoya went dark."

"Who somebody? DATASHARK?"

"I don't know," Morris insisted. "It went through one of our satellites, but it didn't come up through our ground network. We started to investigate last night, but I got a call from General Stoyer himself telling me that the upload was valid NSA traffic and to drop it. I dropped it."

So the General had his own satellite ground station, isolated from the rest of the NSA network. That meant DATASHARK was located offsite from NSA headquarters. But where?

"Understood," Archer said. "But why am *I* being cut out of the loop?"

Morris lowered his voice another notch. "Because DATASHARK is a military *only* operation, sir. No civilian staff *at all*. That much I know. I also know if DATASHARK calls the NICC, I jump. It reports directly to General Stoyer and acts with his authority."

There had always been friction between the military and civilian staffs here at the NSA, each camp thinking it was more important than the other. But this went way beyond rivalry. Archer knew Morris was violating his orders by even telling him this much, but decided to push his friendship a little further. "So you have *no* idea why the General is holding this project so close to the vest?"

"Just rumors," Morris offered. "Most information warfare programs have an offensive *and* a defensive side. I've heard that DATASHARK is totally offensive. It's an ax, meant for cracking heads. Scuttlebutt is Stoyer's got some tiger team of hackers offsite he doesn't want to share with anybody else."

That didn't make sense. "But why?" Archer pressed. He wondered why Stoyer had even exposed him to the codeword in the first place. Stoyer probably thought he was irrelevant, like a fly on the wall. That was Stoyer's first mistake, and Archer was grateful for it.

Morris's voice hardened. "Hey, *I don't know*. What I *do* know is that when I see a sign that says, 'There be dragons,' *I don't go there*. And you shouldn't either, or Stoyer might wonder if you taste good with ketchup."

The sharp buzz of a phone cut off Archer's response. Morris answered, then stiffened. He held out the receiver like a poisonous serpent. "Mr. Archer, the General would like to speak with you."

CURRENT EVENTS

Television in the Snake Pit was a very structured affair. Each shift was allowed one hour of TV each day, generally sitcoms, and one sporting event each week. Even the commercials were edited out to prevent the residents of the Snake Pit from lusting after a product or service they were missing. News programs were also forbidden--knowledge of the outside world came only through Colonel Richter.

But not today. To give the hackers a chance to survey their handiwork, a series of tapes from the Nagoya area were broadcast to the Snake Pit. A congratulatory statement from General Stoyer was read, then the hacker team was given the rest of the day off. The television room would be open all day, and each inmate would be allowed two hours in the fenced compound outside the bunker--a rare treat.

Derek Friedman reveled in the destruction he caused in Nagoya. Every time a distant shot of the Kasugai plant was shown, he began chanting, "Meltdown! Meltdown! Meltdown!" Even the citizens of Nagoya were not beyond his derision. When an elderly man with radiation poisoning was carried away on a stretcher, Friedman railed, "Hey! Look at that old bastard puke!"

Malechek and the Taylor twins had an initial euphoric reaction to their success, but it faded to stunned silence as the casualties mounted. One shot repeated by all the networks was a bloodied child weeping over his dead mother at the Nagoya train station. After the third repetition of the heart-wrenching scene, Demetrius Taylor went ashen and ran for the bathroom.

Yoshida left the television room, feeling ill himself. Pittman followed. Yoshida collapsed on his cot, burying his face in his hands.

Pittman leaned against the doorway. "Hey Ken, how did these Japanese comics help you hack their code?"

Yoshida stared, startled by the stupidity of the question. Pittman made a rolling motion with his hand. He reached for one of Yoshida's notebooks.

Yoshida played along. "Well, even though C and UNIX and assembler languages are the same all over the world, the programmers still write comments and mark their subroutines in their native tongue."

Pittman borrowed the single ball-point pen each prisoner was allowed from Yoshida's desk. He began writing in the notebook.

Yoshida continued. "Since I'd learned Japanese, I could read their comment lines instead of having to figure out what every piece of software did from the code."

Pittman held out the notebook. "No wonder you ran circles around everybody in that last attack! How long do you think it would take me to pick up Japanese?" Scrawled in the corner of a blank page was a note. "I DON'T THINK ANY OF US ARE GETTING OUT OF HERE ALIVE! DO YOU AGREE?"

Finally someone was catching on. Yoshida nodded ruefully. "Oh, it took me a couple of years," he said. "But I can give you some pointers." He made hard eye contact with Pittman. "We'll make it a *team* project."

Pittman tore off the corner of the sheet. "That sounds good. Can I borrow one of your Japanese comics?"

"Sure."

Pittman rolled the paper into a tiny ball. "Great! See you later!" He popped the wad into his mouth and chewed.

"Yeah, see you outside," Yoshida agreed.

MARKING TERRITORY

After the NSC meeting, Cynthia Hale felt both depressed and relieved. She waved the CIA Director into her office and closed the door. While her three assistants outside were jammed into a space little larger than a walk-in closet, the square footage she was afforded broadcast her status in the White House hierarchy. Besides a large desk with a built-in computer work-station, an elegantly carved conference table took up a third of the cream-colored carpet. A powder-blue couch with matching wing-back chairs occupied the remaining floor space.

Hale motioned her guest to the couch, indicating this to be an informal meeting. She settled into the nearest chair with a sigh. "Well, that should be the end of that loose cannon. I just hope we can clean up the mess he's made."

"Pardon?" he asked.

Barton Walsh was wearing the overtly-blank expression he had developed during his twenty-plus years in the intelligence business. Hale had once worked under Walsh in the CIA's Inspector General's office, investigating CIA wrongdoing. Or covering it up. She knew Walsh only used that face when he was about to stonewall or tell an outright lie to someone. It damn well better not be her.

"Stoyer!" she snapped. "Marshall gave him a mile of rope and Stoyer made a noose for himself with it."

Walsh maintained his studiously non-expressive face. "He made a noose all right, but not for himself."

Hale knew her former mentor had caught something she had missed. As she had fresh out of law school, Hale again assumed the role of student under Walsh's guidance. "Okay Bart, what am I missing here?"

"Did you notice the President didn't ream out the General for flubbing the HEADSHOT mission? Marshall just sat there like a potted plant through the whole meeting."

"He called Stoyer and Holland into his office afterward," Hale insisted. "Don't you think that's what's going on right now?"

Walsh admonished her with a look. "When's the last time Marshall was reluctant to chew on someone's ass in a staff meeting? If the door's closed, he considers it private, no matter how many other people are in the room."

Hale had seen Adams's temper often enough to know staff members seldom got the chance to provoke him twice. "That's true. So what do you think's going on in there?"

"Oh, possibly a commendation for a job well done?"

The suggestion hit her like a slap. "No!"

Walsh regarded her like an inattentive student. "You saw the damage HEADSHOT did to Nagoya. Did that look accidental to you? And what kind of code name is HEADSHOT? Does that sound like a non-lethal strike? My guess is Marshall amended the NSC's plan so he could take a little personal revenge."

"For Nebraska?"

"It *is* his home state. And they *did* kill sixty-one people."

It all seemed so improbable to her. "But why would he keep it secret from the NSC?" she wondered aloud. "Was he afraid we wouldn't back his decision?"

"Maybe he wanted to keep the blood off our hands. Or keep DATASHARK for himself as a personal vengeance weapon."

Hale couldn't bring herself to believe *that*. She had left her cushy position at Stanford *because* of Adams's character. If there was *anyone* she believed would do the right thing, for the right reasons, it was this President. "That's not the Marshall Adams I know."

Walsh patiently helped his slow pupil along. "Do you remember the old Star Trek episode where the evil twin of Kirk had a weapon that could make his enemies disappear with the touch of a button?"

Hale was too grounded in the present to waste time with science fiction. "Sorry, not a Trekkie."

"The point was that even good people can be tempted by evil weapons. And this DATASHARK thing scares the hell out of me. It's like Chet Holland said, there's really no defense against it. The only thing you can do is demonstrate to your enemy that they're as vulnerable as you are."

"Just like nuclear weapons."

"Exactly. Except if your enemy strikes first with a DATASHARK weapon, your systems may be so beaten up you *can't* strike back."

Great, Hale thought. That's just what the world needed--another weapon of mass destruction, one anybody with a computer could duplicate. "At least we know Stoyer's claim about DATASHARK being untraceable is false."

Walsh's stone mask was back in place. "Why do you say that?"

"You heard what Harry Abramson said! Mitsusui caught the NSA digging around in their computers *before* the attack. It won't take Tokyo long to start laying dead children on our doorstep." Just the thought of it sucked the life out of her. Hale rested her head on her hands. "What a god-forsaken mess!"

Walsh's voice was almost inaudible. "More than you know."

Hale felt her stomach sink. "What?"

"Take a close look at that Japanese protest letter. Mitsusui traced the intruder to a secure server in Virginia. We go to a lot of trouble to hide any ties from that server to the CIA, but the point is it's one of ours. We use it as a jumping-off point for illegal computer activity."

That didn't make any sense. "What would *your* people be doing digging around in Mitsusui's computers?"

"I ordered one of my department heads to verify the source of the Nebraska attack," Walsh admitted. "*He* was the one they detected, not Stoyer's people."

Like they had during the bureaucratic trench fights in the IG's office, Hale's loyalty instincts revved to full speed. "Don't worry, Bart, I'll back you up on this one! We need to challenge that bastard Stoyer in front of the Council, before he gets us into a shooting war!"

Walsh refused to pick up the gauntlet she had thrown down. "Count me out, Cynthia," he murmured.

Hale had never seen her former boss so cowed. "For god's sake, what did your man *find?*"

Walsh opened his briefcase. "I don't know. Had a little trouble getting a straight answer from him." He tossed two black-and-white photos onto the coffee table.

The first photo showed two men lying on their backs. The second showed a close-up of a middle-eastern man. His sightless eyes stared past the camera, two bullet holes in his forehead. She cringed.

"Meet Dr. Ravi Prakash," Walsh explained, "my former head of information security. He was gunned down in a convenience store the night before last."

What damned luck. "A robbery?"

Walsh snorted. "That's what it was supposed to look like. Bullshit! Both of them were double-tapped between the eyes with a nine-millimeter. *My* people couldn't have done it any better. Look at these pictures! Hell, the holes even *overlap.*"

Hale pushed the photographs away. Walsh had a fascination with the morbid aspects of intelligence she didn't share. "Thank you for sharing *that* with me!"

"Well, before he had his rendezvous with destiny, Ravi left a message in my secretary's voice mail that he had found something important. He needed to set up a meeting with me first thing in the morning. He missed his appointment."

"Did you find anything on his computer?"

"Yep, there was one program left in active memory, feverishly writing random ones and zeroes on every sector of his hard drive, over and over. His damned computer had practically melted itself by the time we shut it down."

The room suddenly seemed colder to Hale.

Walsh fished another photograph from his briefcase. "Of course, I threw every guy on Ravi's team at the problem, trying to duplicate his results. But DATASHARK got to Mitsusui's computers before we did." He tossed the photo next to the others. "That's a satphoto of Mitsusui's computer research facility at HEADSHOT plus four hours."

The overhead picture showed an ordinary two-story office building. A square section of the roof had collapsed, smoke pouring from the cavity. "That smoking hole is where their mainframes used to live," Walsh explained. "Nobody's going to be getting information from those computers again, covertly or otherwise."

Hale gaped. "DATASHARK did this?"

"Pretty damned scary, isn't it? The fact that Stoyer can do this with a keyboard makes you want to go back to an abacus and counting sticks."

"But what about your man, Dr....Prakash?" In the IG's office, Hale had once participated in the investigation of a CIA officer's murder. The operatives she worked with had used the term "asset nullification" to describe the motivation for that killing. In the intelligence community it was the gravest of crimes, inviting certain retribution.

Walsh spoke with complete dispassion, as if giving a lecture. "My guys call it 'marking territory.' If you have someplace you *really* want free of enemy activity, you mark the boundaries and kill the first bad guy you catch inside. Then you put his head on a stick to tell his buddies that you really mean it. That's the message Stoyer was sending via Dr. Prakash. Leave DATASHARK alone, or else."

Hale blanched. Her specialty at the CIA had been international law, the sometimes vague but always present boundaries between right and wrong in international relations. The gritty realities of the operations side of the CIA had always seemed alien to her. "But what are we going to *do*?"

Walsh gazed at the ceiling. "Well, first I'll grab my ankles and take the blame for the Mitsusui intrusion. I'll admit fault and say that, yes, we did it, but it had nothing to do with the disaster in Nagoya. The intrusion was the work of a lone CIA employee, acting without orders. Of course I'd fire him, but he's already dead. If it really gets bad, I'll blame Prakash for the whole HEADSHOT fiasco. Sound like a plan?"

Hale was shocked. "I can't believe you're just rolling over like this, Bart."

He held up the photo of Mitsusui's building. "Sorry, I don't want this happening to *my* computer facility."

Even if Adams didn't realize the kind of monster he had just gotten in bed with, Hale did. She had to take action. "But what do we tell the President?" she challenged. "He has a *right* to know."

Walsh lifted an eyebrow at his former apprentice. "I'd think twice about that, Cynthia. Stoyer's just done a *big* favor for Marshall. And I'd rather not get between the President and the man who slays his enemies with the touch of a button."

NECESSARY SACRIFICES

Stoyer was on the limousine's secure phone. He fed a document into the encrypted fax machine.

"Archer," he heard.

"Jeff, we have a crisis on our hands. I'm sending you a diplomatic letter right now. Investigate the particulars and make sure it wasn't us. Put your findings in a letter to the President and have it ready for signature when I get back. I'll be there within the hour."

"I'm on it, sir!" was the terse reply.

"I'm counting on you. This one's going to get nasty real fast."

"Understood."

Stoyer leaned back into the leather seat. That Archer had nothing to do with DATASHARK or HEADSHOT would make his findings even more convincing, which is why Stoyer selected him for the task.

It wasn't that Stoyer was without guilt, or even remorse. He had seen the single column story at the bottom of the front page. Murdered convenience store owner and his brother, the latter a husband and father of three young children. Not to mention the dozens killed in the first DATASHARK attack, then the hundreds or even thousands who had died or would die from the second. The first set of casualties due mostly to an accident, the second set inflicted by the wrath of a deceived President. Stoyer sighed. He knew this kind of inner conflict would destroy most men.

But General Stoyer answered to a higher standard, the National Security of the United States. By this standard, the protection of the whole was paramount. The death of an individual, even many individuals, was insignificant. Some lives *had* to be sacrificed for freedom to continue.

One hundred fifty-two such lives were remembered at the National Cryptologic Memorial Wall. Located in a passageway between the new and old sections of NSA headquarters, Stoyer visited the eight-foot-high triangle of black granite often. Under the gold letters THEY SERVED IN SILENCE were carved the names of the men and women of the NSA who had died in the line of duty.

Most had perished on long-range ferret flights, probing the electronic borders of Communist countries during the Cold War. Some were covert operators killed while planting eavesdropping equipment on hostile soil. Many of their deaths would *never* be acknowledged, except here, where only employees of the NSA were allowed to honor their sacrifices.

The four men under Stoyer's command who died during operation SNOWBLOWER were there. When he stared at his own reflection in the mirror-polished stone, Stoyer was reminded that his name could just as easily have been carved there as well. He would not allow their sacrifices to be in vain.

Someone had to be willing to demand those sacrifices, of himself and others. Stoyer was such a man. It was a heavy responsibility, but one he had learned to shoulder from an early age. It was almost an accident of birth.

* * *

Jonathan Paul Pulchinsky, eldest son of Air Force Sergeant Paul Pulchinsky, had learned survival skills in his own home, protecting himself and his two younger brothers from the violent tirades of his alcoholic father. His abused and passive mother was of little or no help in sheltering the boys, and she later developed an alcohol dependency of her own to escape the bleakness of her life.

At the age of ten, Jonathan made a decision. While the families surrounding the Pulchinskys in the base non-com housing were hardly idyllic, Jonathan realized that in any of those homes at least he would not be in fear for his life. A sacrifice was necessary to preserve his life and those of his brothers.

A bottle of Wild Turkey stolen from the PX was the first element of his plan. He opened it and took a swallow. He gagged. It tasted like gasoline and burned his throat like fire. He wondered how his father could even drink it, much less crave it. For a moment Jonathan thought he was going to throw up. He left the bottle open and in plain sight.

He took a deep breath when the back door slammed shut. His father would be in a foul mood, having gone without alcohol since he left the house that morning. But Jonathan knew the sacrifice was necessary.

His father held up the bottle. "What the hell is this?" Paul Pulchinsky growled.

Jonathan stepped forward. "It's mine!"

"Where'd you get it?"

"I stole it!" Jonathan said, as if expecting a medal.

Pulchinsky's eyes widened with fury. "You did *what*? Did you drink this? Come here!" He seized Jonathan by the shirt and bent to smell his son's breath. He thrust Jonathan away in disgust. "Why'd you do this?"

Jonathan stood and approached his father again. "'Cause I want to be a drunk, just like you!"

Jonathan felt the first blow loosen two teeth on the left side of his jaw. His whole skull rang like a bell.

"I didn't raise you to be a thief, you little bastard!"

Jonathan forced himself to stand. "Yes you did! I've watched you lift cigarettes from the PX every week! And I want to be just like you!"

There was nothing more infuriating to a failure like Pulchinsky than to see his children following in his footsteps. More blows pounded down on Jonathan. When they slowed, Jonathan would hurl an obscenity he had learned from his father to keep the blows coming. Then he began borrowing his mother's taunts, like how Pulchinsky would have made Master Sergeant by now if he hadn't been a lush. That did the job almost too well. A torrent of kicks followed, one striking him in the face and another in his stomach. Jonathan could rise no longer.

Paul Pulchinsky grabbed his son and dragged him to his room. He hurled Jonathan through the doorway. Jonathan struck the opposite wall and slid down. Jonathan's brothers cowered in a corner.

"You stay in this room, you little son of a bitch!" Pulchinsky screamed. "I don't want to even see your face until tomorrow!" He slammed the door behind him.

One of Jonathan's eyes was swelling shut and his nose was about to explode. He also felt a stabbing pain in his left side when he breathed, but this was all part of his plan. It just hurt a lot more than he thought it would.

As Jonathan had foreseen, by that evening the bottle of Wild Turkey was empty. The slaps and the sound of his mother's crying were evidence of that. When all was quiet again, Jonathan continued with his plan.

Jonathan knew his mother slept on the couch on the nights his father drank. After his father passed out, she usually followed up with a drinking bout of her own, so both would be sleeping soundly. His brothers would stay in their beds no matter what, for fear of their father's wrath.

Jonathan crept into his father's room. He was lying face down, one leg hanging off the bed. His clothes were piled on the floor. By feel, Jonathan found his father's fatigue shirt and buttoned it on.

He crept past his mother into the garage. He located a pair of work gloves and one of his father's largest hammers. Returning to the den, he stood over his mother for a long time. There would be no going back after this. His hands shook. But the sacrifice was necessary. He whispered "I love you, Mom" one last time, then raised the hammer.

Jonathan made sure to strike the first blow with all of his might, and not to stop until the job was done. His mother groaned once, but that was all. He kept pounding until he felt warm liquid strike his face. He was glad the room was dark. Just the sharp coppery smell almost made him vomit. He stepped away, forcing himself to take deep breaths, even though it hurt his ribs.

He dropped the bloodied hammer and gloves at the foot of his father's bed. Removing the tent-like shirt, he wiped his face on the unsoiled back and threw it beside his father's unconscious form.

He walked to the front door, his eyes avoiding the darkened den. He leaned against the wall and tried to calm his adrenaline-charged nerves. The next step in a way would be the most difficult, because it would force him to muster emotions he did not feel.

Master Sergeant Michael Stoyer lived across the street from the Pulchinskys. He worked beside the younger man and kept Pulchinsky's alcohol problems out of sight of their superiors for the sake of Pulchinsky's children.

Sergeant Stoyer's heart ached for the Pulchinsky boys, especially the oldest boy Jonathan. He was bright and friendly, but just old enough to understand the tragedy unfolding around him. Stoyer tried to help when he could, like when he took the boys on an unscheduled camping trip, which was really to get them away from one of Paul Pulchinsky's weekend benders.

Sergeant Stoyer was awakened by a pounding at his front door. He pulled on his bathrobe and grabbed his .45 from the bedstand drawer. He jerked open the front door to find Jonathan Pulchinsky weeping uncontrollably.

"Please help me! Daddy killed her!" he cried.

Stoyer gasped. The little boy's nose was broken, one eye was swollen shut, and he was holding his side gingerly. Stoyer exhaled heavily. "Oh Paul, you son of a bitch." He yelled back to the bedroom. "Janet, I need you!"

Janet Stoyer stumbled to the entryway, gathering her robe. "For the love of Pete, what's...oh my God! *Jonathan*, what happened?"

Jonathan Pulchinsky just pointed across the street. "He, he...*Momma!*" His voice broke down into sobs.

Michael Stoyer pulled Jonathan inside. "Janet, call the MPs!" he said, his eyes blazing. He chambered a round in the pistol and padded in his houseshoes across the street.

Janet pulled Jonathan to her. "Michael! What are you going to do?"

"What I should have done three years ago," he called over his shoulder. "I'm gonna get those boys out of there!"

Despite his pleas of innocence, the jury convicted Paul Pulchinsky of murdering his wife after only a two-hour deliberation. There were some inconsistencies in the evidence, but Pulchinsky's history of violence and the severe beating of his son Jonathan weighed heavily in the jury's decision. Pulchinsky was sentenced to twenty-five years in prison. He died there twenty years later.

A childless couple, Michael and Janet Stoyer adopted all three Pulchinsky boys. At his request, Jonathan also had his middle name changed from Paul to Michael. The Stoyer boys went on to be successful in life. The youngest, Timothy, became a police officer. Steve started his own business. But retired Chief Master Sergeant Stoyer's secret favorite would always be Jonathan. Sergeant Stoyer lived long enough to help pin the second star on his oldest son. That photograph was one of the few things that could bring tears to the eyes of the stoic General Stoyer.

* * *

General Stoyer swallowed hard and rubbed his eyes. So many sacrifices had been made just to reach this point. Surely DATASHARK was the most audacious gamble of his already risk-filled life. But the national security of the United States demanded it. And if there was one thing Stoyer was certain of, there would be more sacrifices to be made in the future.

CHAPTER 7

"It doesn't take a majority to make a rebellion. It only takes a few determined leaders and a sound cause."
-H.L. Mencken

DOUBLE LIVES

The Resistance leader blinked and shook his head vigorously at the stoplight. That was the problem with leading two lives. Neither one got a chance to sleep. Going to New York on short notice was hassle enough. Doing so without the knowledge of his coworkers or superiors was a bigger feat. But losing a cell leader was critical, especially since Yoshida knew his identity. If Broadman could help track down Yoshida, the trip had been worth the risk.

He pulled into his reserved spot in the underground garage. After taking the elevator to the lobby, he flashed the ID that allowed him to bypass the metal detector. "Good morning, George," he said to the security guard.

"Good morning, Mr. Patrick. Not going to let the promotion keep you from carrying a piece, huh?"

"It reminds me that my real job isn't just pushing paper."

"That it does, sir," the guard agreed, waving him through.

Jeremy "Paddy" Patrick was an Irish cop, the son of an Irish cop. In his mid-forties, his reddish-brown hair was turning a steely gray, which he kept neatly trimmed in what his stylist assured him was the latest "executive" hairstyle. In his new position, image *was* important, even if damned time-consuming. His most prominent feature was his pale blue eyes. His ex-wife had called them "Husky-dog eyes"--cold, piercing, and hungry.

Patrick was glad the regulations still allowed officials at his level to carry a personal weapon. Most of the bureaucrats in the offices adjacent to his were happy to hang up their holsters. In his official duties he was more likely to be struck by a meteor than to use his pistol, but his second life was another story.

Patrick still visited the range every week. His coworkers seldom challenged him to a match, unless it was for a chance to learn from an expert marksman. He also kept his shorter-than-

average physique in shape with regular Judo workouts. Prominently displaying trophies from both sports in his new office
helped earn respect from subordinates and kept brown-nosers at
a respectful distance.

Patrick's secretary had beat him into work this morning.
That alone would be unusual enough to arouse her curiosity, but
it couldn't be helped. "Good morning, Diane," he said.

"Good morning, Mr. Patrick." Her smile was brief but
genuine. "The Director wants you to call him first thing. He said
he tried to reach you at home last night, without success. Hot
date?"

Patrick's two lives were colliding again. "Yeah, I was out
last night."

The stocky black woman clicked her maroon-painted fingernails. "*Really*? Sit down and tell Momma all about it!" Diane
envisioned herself as the den mother for everyone on the floor.
"Was it that new technician from Forensics? I saw your pretty
blue eyes follow her out the door the other day!"

Patrick was the world's most eligible bachelor, from
Diane's point of view. But it was his devotion to the job that
had doomed his marriage, and that was before he had added his
second life to the mix. Besides, he already had a love interest
who serviced his needs in *both* lives. He tried to look guilty for
Diane's sake.

"I'm sorry, Diane, that's classified."

Diane made a face and rocked her head from side to side.
"Uh-*huh*! So you could tell me but you'd have to kill me, right?
My son's tried that before. Didn't work with him, either."

No, Diane, I really would have to kill you.

She crossed her arms. "And where was your cell phone
during this night of passion?"

Patrick lifted one eyebrow. "It was on vibrate. She *begged*
me to let it keep ringing."

"Mmm, *child!* I hope you have a better explanation than
that for the Director!"

Patrick started to close his door. "*Thank* you, Diane!" He
pulled back slightly at the smell of fresh glue. "Hey! They finally got my sign up!"

Diane was smiling again. "Yes, sir, they did it right after
you left last night. Congratulations again!"

"Thank you!" He allowed himself a long look before closing the door:

JEREMY PATRICK
ASSISTANT DIRECTOR FOR SPECIAL OPERATIONS
FEDERAL BUREAU OF INVESTIGATION

DIPLOMACY

President Adams rubbed his temples, willing his coffee to kick in. He hadn't slept well, and the news video flooding in from Nagoya wasn't making him feel any better. When Abramson entered the Oval Office, Adams reached into his bottom drawer and placed the bottle of Tums on the desk.

"Okay Harry, how many am I going to need?"

Secretary of State Harold Abramson sat down heavily. "I suggest we split the bottle fifty-fifty. Deal?"

Adams knew it took a lot to put his long-time friend in a negative mood. "It can't be *that* bad."

The impish old man ran a hand through his unruly gray hair. "Judge for yourself. I visited the Japanese Embassy this morning. Per your instructions, I extended a public offer of disaster assistance and a private olive branch. I expressed regret that relations had degraded to this point and suggested immediate negotiations to resolve our differences and prevent any further hostilities."

"Nobody's better at talking people away from the ledge than you, Harry."

Abramson reached for the bottle of Tums, shaking out a few into his hand. "Well, if there had been a ledge close by, their ambassador would have tossed me over it. He said, 'So it *was* you! Our intelligence people were right!' Then he started reading me the latest casualty reports and called you a baby killer and some other epithets that lost something in the translation." Abramson extended the bottle.

Adams waved it away. "If the Nebraska attack was an undeclared action on their part, there's no reason their ambassador would be briefed. Once he passes our olive branch up to Prime Minister Noguri, I think you'll see a different reaction from the Japanese government."

The intercom buzzed. "Mr. President," his secretary said, "Admiral Holland on line one, he says it's urgent."

"Thank you, Elaine." Adams punched the speakerphone button. "Hello Chet, Harry Abramson is here with me, go ahead."

The speakerphone made Holland's voice seem even more gruff. "Mr. President, Mr. Secretary, I just received a call from Yokasuka Naval Base in Japan. The admiral has been handed a diplomatic letter informing him that all US bases in Japan are now under quarantine. Nothing goes in or out. They've parked three destroyers outside our dock facilities to let us know they're serious."

Adams's stomach reminded him that black coffee made a poor breakfast. "What about our Air Force base?"

"I just got off the phone with Misawa. The Japanese 'requested' we cease all air activity immediately. They say if we comply, they won't cut off water and electricity to the base."

"Sweet of them," Abramson groused.

"Same story at Sasebo, our naval base at the southern tip of Japan. There aren't any picket ships in the harbor yet, but I'll bet they're on their way."

Harry Abramson had warned Adams when he took office. *A president makes no small mistakes.* "And the million-dollar question, where are the carriers?" Adams asked.

The Admiral's sigh was audible. "Not in port, thank God. *Kitty Hawk* and *Carl Vinson* are exercising south of Japan with, of all people, the Japanese Navy. *Nimitz* is in the Indian Ocean. *Lincoln* and *Stennis* are docked at Pearl. The only assets trapped outright are some fleet supply ships and a destroyer that was alongside for repairs anyway."

The tactical section of Adams's brain refused to function this morning, despite his caffeine intake. "What do you recommend, Admiral?"

"Unless you're ready to start shooting bullets instead of electrons, Mr. President, I recommend we bow respectfully to our Japanese hosts and comply. We should also politely conclude our FleetEx with their navy and put some space between our forces and theirs, just in case."

Adams was grateful for the cool hands and clear heads assisting him. "Agreed, Admiral. What immediate problems will losing those bases cause you?"

Another sigh. "The oilers and replenishment ships in Yokasuka were taking on supplies for the fleet. If they can't sail, those carriers will need to take on fuel and supplies somewhere else, and soon."

Adams mentally called up a Pacific map. "Nearest base?"

"Guam, about a thousand miles south of their current location."

Adams had passed through that snake-infested rock as a twenty-two-year-old second lieutenant on his way to Vietnam. He thanked God for it now. "Sounds like a good fallback plan, Admiral."

"Very well, sir, I'll give the orders. Let's pray no one decides to cause trouble while we retreat our fleet."

"Thank you, Chet." Adams reached across the desk toward Abramson. "I'll take those Tums now."

* * *

News of the rift between the United States and Japan spread quickly, and one of America's enemies was not about to let such an opportunity pass. Orders were given, ships left port, aircraft were manned, and missiles were trained toward their targets. Finally, a diplomatic cable was transmitted, a fig leaf of propriety to cover what would be an overtly hostile act.

PRIVATE LINE

Jeff Archer took the diplomatic letter to the ECHELON desk in the NICC. "I need to know about a server in Virginia called Secure Node Seventy-Six," he asked the technician, whose blue NSA badge indicated his name as WATSON, STEVE. "It may be a government system of some kind."

Watson smiled knowingly. "So Colonel Richter decided to complete the trace after all, huh?"

"Who's Colonel Richter?"

"His people called us a couple of nights ago. Had us run an international trace on a signal that led to Node Seventy-Six. It's a CIA system. When I told them we couldn't trace it any further without your authorization, they got shy and hung up. So what made them change their minds?"

"I've never heard of Colonel Richter. But you say this is a CIA system?"

"Oh yeah." Watson called up a network map on his screen. "The CIA buried Seventy-Six in the middle of a bunch of federal secure networks in Falls Church. They belong to Social Security, FDA, and a bunch of other bureaucracies that need secure data transmission but aren't national security targets."

"Hide in plain sight. I'm with you. But what does the CIA do with those computers?"

"Anything they don't want tied to the CIA. Say we suspect the Mossad isn't telling us everything they know about some terrorist group. The CIA can use Seventy-Six to hack into their computers and see for themselves. If somebody tries a backtrack, the trace disappears into the federal bureaucracy and hits a dead end."

Archer checked his watch, mindful of Stoyer's imminent arrival. "So bottom line, it's *not* an NSA system?"

"Absolutely not. We just watch their back door. If someone overseas tries to hack into Seventy-Six, we run a trace and pass the results upstairs. After that...." The watch officer shrugged and raised his hands in a gesture of feigned ignorance.

"Understood." Unlike the CIA, the NSA operated almost totally free of legal strictures, especially abroad. Archer knew that many of the crimes blamed on the CIA over the years had actually been the work of NSA operatives, keeping the world safe for American eavesdropping.

He handed Watson the diplomatic letter. "Do you have any idea why someone from the CIA would be using Seventy-Six to hack into the Mitsusui corporation?"

"Well, sir, *everybody's* heard the Japs were behind the infowar attack in Nebraska. But tracking that down would seem to fall in our bailiwick, not the CIA's." One of the TV screens at the front of the NICC showed news video of crying Japanese schoolchildren being scrubbed down by soldiers in decontamination gear.

Watson jerked a thumb toward the image. "Sir, I heard Nagoya was an infowar attack, too. We didn't have anything to do with *that*, did we?"

Archer matched Watson's ambiguous shrug with one of his own. "Not that I've heard."

"Sorry, sir, shouldn't have asked. But if the CIA was digging around in Mitsusui's system, it was unprovoked. The Japs have never tried to get inside the CIA's system. *That* I would know about."

It wouldn't take long to draft General Stoyer's letter. Archer decided he had time to satisfy his curiosity. "Okay, what can you tell me about this Colonel Richter?"

Watson typed a command into his terminal. "Let me pull up the trace record. Hmmm, that's strange."

Archer leaned closer. "What?"

"The log shows the terminal number of the guy from Richter's group who requested the trace, but when I searched for the location of the terminal, I pulled a blank. It just says "secure remote terminal.""

Archer knew that would be standard procedure for any off-site computer used in a codeword or compartmented program. "So we're SOL?"

"Not hardly, sir." Watson pulled up another window with his mouse, then poised his hands over the keyboard. "This will cause a message box to pop up on that terminal. I can order him to call you at my phone number right the hell now. Then you can get the answer straight from the horse's mouth."

"No, I'm pressed for time," Archer dodged. "Can you print out that trace report? Have a courier take it up to my office."

"Yes, sir, I'll deliver it myself."

Archer thought for a moment, then reached inside his jacket. He wrote on the back of his business card and handed it to the younger man. "Listen, Steve, contrary to what you might think, people *don't* tell me everything just because I'm Deputy Director. Maybe *because* I'm Deputy Director. But my private line is on the back of that card. If you hear something I should know, but you think it might not make it up the ladder, call me. That line and its voice mail system are both secure, so don't be afraid to use them."

Watson's eyes brightened. "Yes, *sir!*"

Archer thanked Watson and jogged upstairs to dictate his report. Apart from his duties to General Stoyer, it had been a very productive meeting. He had an interesting lead to investigate and had met a promising candidate. After all, recruiting was one of his many duties.

FINDINGS

After a full day at work and the hour-plus commute home, Tony Broadman was usually good for nothing but a soak in the hot tub or dozing in front of the TV. Not tonight. Tonight Broadman began his search for Ken Yoshida.

He started with Lexis-Nexis, a nationwide search engine almost frightening in its speed and depth of resources. He blessed Christina's employment with the Newburgh library system. Her position as a senior librarian gave her access to the library's Lexis-Nexis account from home, which would have cost him several hundred dollars a month to purchase on his own.

The Lexis system searched nationwide for criminal and civil proceedings involving Kentaro Yoshida. He might have made powerful enemies long before he began knocking at MINTNET's front door.

After the record of his arrest and plea bargain for multiple hacking-related offenses five years ago, Yoshida's slate was clean. He had served his time, was paroled early for good behavior, and had stayed out of trouble since then. He had no other arrests, nor had he sued or been sued by anyone since he had started his security business.

The Nexis system searched newspapers and magazines nationwide for stories about Ken Yoshida. The first hit turned up stories in a local New Jersey paper about his arrest, then a follow-up when Yoshida entered the computer security field. He had also been quoted as an expert by the Los Angeles *Times* and the *Wall Street Journal*. But the majority of the references were in something called *2600: The Hacker Quarterly*. Broadman pulled up a score of articles in *2600* mentioning Yoshida.

Yoshida was something of a folk hero in the hacker underworld, both for his hacking exploits and his ability to make money from the same corporate interests he had once victimized. From the range of favorable and hostile articles, the hackers seemed split on whether Yoshida was a sell-out or a modern-day Robin Hood. Jumping to *2600*'s website, Broadman scanned for any recent developments in the hacker community that might aid him in his search. One online article seized his attention: "Where Have All the Hackers Gone: the Search for the Missing Many."

"Well, what do we have here?" Broadman whispered.

FEAR AND HOPE

Senior Airmen Dave Jackson and Tim Feldman were alone in the monitoring room on the upper level of the Snake Pit. With the lull in activity following the Nagoya strike, only one of the four stations was manned per shift. Jackson had just arrived to relieve his fellow watcher. Tomorrow they would both be with Richter's go-team in California. No watchers would be monitoring the hackers at all for a day or two, although the hackers certainly wouldn't know that.

Jackson was horrified. "Richter? Why the hell did you get Richter involved with this?"

Feldman gave his partner a puzzled look. "Because he's the *boss*, that's why. Why shouldn't he know about it?"

Jackson measured his words carefully. He was definitely in the minority around here. "You just never know how Richter's gonna react. The guy spooks me sometimes. His idea of raising morale might be to stage a crucifixion."

Feldman laughed. "Nah, a gladiator fight would be more like it. Hey, that might work! How about Kramp getting medieval with that new guy Yoshida. He looks pretty buff. Might even know some karate shit. I'd pay money to see that fight!"

What really frightened Jackson was that Richter might take Feldman's suggestion seriously. Working here at the Snake Pit was like stepping through the looking glass. Once inside the bunker, the rules of the outside world just didn't apply anymore.

Now he realized what a trap General Stoyer's sponsorship had been. When Colonel Richter had offered him a spot on the General's personal staff, Jackson felt rescued. He had been fixing computers at Cheyenne Mountain for a pin-headed CO who hated his guts. When he found out he was transferring to the NSA to do information warfare, it was like a one-way ticket to Valhalla.

Even when Richter put him on the go-team that roped the hackers, Jackson still thought he was performing some kind of legitimate security function. Now he was in too deep to back out. Richter had made that very clear. Even though he went home to Ft. Meade's base housing every night, Jackson was beginning to feel as trapped as the hackers he watched. He just tried to keep his contact with Richter to a minimum. That guy scared the hell out of him.

* * *

Colonel Richter entered the monitoring room. "You wanted to see me?"

Feldman motioned Richter to his terminal. "Yes, sir. Since the prisoners aren't doing any hacking today, I've spent more time listening in. They apparently know how the monitoring tags work and stay pretty tight-lipped. But some of them let their discipline slip on their day off."

Richter never passed up a chance to get inside his prisoners' heads. "So what are they saying?"

"The Nagoya attack really shook them up. They rationalized the Nebraska deaths as accidents. But now they've spilled a lot of blood--on purpose. Besides that, several of them think we're going to kill them to make sure the real story never gets out."

Richter's eyebrows rose. "They *said* that?" *So they finally figured it out. It took them long enough.*

"Yeah, one of them said, 'I wonder if there's going to be a slit trench waiting for us when we go outside.' His buddy replied, 'Hell no, they'll make us dig our own graves.'"

Wrong. That would leave bodies behind. "Well, it's a good thing you told me," Richter said.

Jackson was troubled. "So what do you want us to do?"

Unlike Jackson, Richter was no longer burdened by his conscience. He had learned if he quit answering that phone eventually it stopped ringing. It made his job much easier. "Operations like the Snake Pit have to be managed with a balance of fear and hope," Richter explained. "We obviously have the fear side licked. I think it's time we inject a little hope into the equation."

Jackson eyed him skeptically but said nothing.

HISTORY

Stoyer hung up the phone after approving Richter's plan. He gazed out the window of his top floor office. Carl always was a clever son of a bitch. That's why Stoyer had picked him

for a member of his inner circle even before operation
SNOWBLOWER, when Richter was just an Airman back in
Vietnam. Stoyer's inner circle were officers and men as loyal to
him as they were to the Air Force and their country.

Securing such loyalty was not that difficult. The first step
was to find good men whose service careers had landed on the
rocks through bad luck, bad habits, or bad superiors. Some had
made the mistake of being smarter than their commanding officers, a mortal sin for those in uniform. Others drank, gambled or
fought too much. Some, like Richter, had failed to keep their
homosexuality under wraps in a military that was even more
homophobic than American society at large.

Whatever the reason, these men were on their way to
stunted careers or dishonorable discharges when Stoyer took up
their cases. After using his rank and connections to make their
problems go away, Stoyer transferred them to his command,
slowly building a cadre of soldiers and officers who owed their
careers to him and him alone.

This inner circle formed the core of the Snake Pit team. After demonstrating the threat hackers posed to their country in
general and their benefactor in particular, few of his men ob-
jected when Stoyer proposed the Snake Pit plan. They *urged*
Stoyer to proceed.

Stoyer then reinforced this group with soldiers like Kramp
and Womack, whose problems indicated a cruel or violent bent,
to make sure none of the guards developed sympathies for their
captives. The officers and men with less steely resolve were
kept at the fringes of the program, where loyalty at least assured
their silence, if not their complicity.

Carl Richter served as the enforcer of that loyalty. Those
whose careers had been saved were reminded often of whose
hand had snatched them from the fire. Those with behavioral
problems were warned that further missteps would have far
worse penalties than the courts martial General Stoyer had
helped them avoid. The few who didn't straighten out learned
that Carl Richter never made idle threats.

Good old Carl, Stoyer thought. Now *there* was a man you
could count on. Stoyer had recruited Richter into the NSA after
Vietnam, then encouraged him to join the Special Collection
Service, a joint CIA/NSA project. The SCS broke into embas-
sies and communications centers around the world, stealing en-

cryption material or planting eavesdropping devices. The SCS was a major player at the NSA.

Richter excelled at the SCS's black bag jobs, so much so he was recruited into an even more sensitive compartment of the SCS called Buyout. Buyout terminated foreign security officials who refused bribes or had become too efficient in blocking SCS operations. Richter excelled in these assignments as well, becoming an even more valuable asset to Stoyer's team.

It was a pity the Air Force hadn't seen his potential. Or maybe they just couldn't see past his personal preferences. Richter's mistake had been in not getting married, even if just for show. Once you became an officer, it was more or less expected.

Stoyer toyed with the gold band on his left ring finger. Sally had been dead for what, ten years now? But he still wore the ring, and not even his fellow general officers questioned it, out of concern for his feelings.

Part of that had to do with the way Sally died, he was sure. Gunned down in the parking lot of a Colorado Springs mall, her empty purse and wallet found near a homeless shelter downtown. No fingerprints, no witnesses, and no one ever prosecuted for the crime. Tragic, but still better than a messy divorce, which usually doomed a senior officer's career. Especially so considering the secrets of his inner circle Sally carried with her to the grave.

In a way, it was very similar to the demise of that CIA computer expert, Dr. Prakash. Stoyer felt a small flush of satisfaction. It was uncanny how history repeated itself.

INDULGENCE

The vinyl cover on the couch yielded with a flatulent burp when Broadman's full weight settled onto it. A clock in the shape of a cat gazed down from the pastel green wall, its eyes swinging to and fro in opposition to its pendulum tail. The clutter of ceramic figurines on every horizontal surface gave the room a claustrophobic feel.

Cheaply-framed pictures on the wall showed a pimpled youth in progressive stages of development. As the school portraits became more recent, the young man's complexion grew worse and the smile shrank to a surly challenge of its earlier innocence. Broadman assumed this was Derek Friedman.

"Derek was always such a *smart* boy," Dorothy Masterson bubbled, returning with iced tea for her guest. It was served in a plastic cup, its earth-tone colors matching the couch. "Why, when he was just seven, my adorable little cat clock stopped working for some reason..."

"Maybe because it was a cheap Chinese piece of crap?" Derek's stepfather Don Masterson grumbled.

Dorothy ignored him. "I gave it to Derek because he loved to take broken things apart. He had the pieces scattered all over the kitchen table, but in an hour he had it back together and working just fine!"

"Of course, she's not telling you about all the things that worked just fine *until* he disassembled them," Don said.

"I understand your son was very good with computers," Broadman said. He knew that was an understatement. Derek Friedman had been one of the most prolific contributors to *2600* magazine, including several articles that had landed the publication in legal hot water.

Dorothy beamed. "Oh, he could just do *amazing* things with that little computer! I could have spent hours watching him, but I never really understood much of it, and Derek didn't like me looking over his shoulder."

"Especially when he was stealing people's credit card numbers over the Internet," Don added.

Dorothy made a swatting motion at her third husband. "He said he wouldn't do that again! And I was just trying to encourage him in something he was good at! He was such a bright boy, I just trusted him to find his own way."

Don rolled his eyes. "You mean you let him sit around on his ass, pecking on that damned keyboard at all hours instead of going out and getting a job."

Dorothy changed the subject. "It's so good to see someone in the news media finally taking an interest in Derek's disappearance."

"Disappearance my ass!" Don scoffed. "The little freeloader just figured I was about to make him pay rent and took a hike!"

"Don, please!" Dorothy pleaded. "This man is trying to help."

"Actually, Mrs. Masterson, I'm just a freelance journalist," Broadman cautioned. "I don't have the pull to launch a major investigation. And your husband raises a good point. Are you sure Derek didn't just move out on his own? Young people don't always check in regularly when they first leave the nest."

Especially when the family lives at dysfunction junction.

"Wouldn't that be the day!" Don said.

"But Derek and I were always so close," Dorothy protested. "To not even *call* is so unlike him."

"Yeah," Don said, "and for him not to drop in for a free meal was a real red flag, too."

"And what about the van, Don?" Dorothy insisted.

Broadman's ears twitched. "The van?"

"Don took me out to dinner for our anniversary. When we got back, Derek had just *vanished*. All his things were gone, even the posters on his walls. He didn't even leave a note to say where he was going. But our neighbors across the street said a white moving van had been in front of the house, with several men going in and out."

"Any descriptions?"

"No, and that was the strange part! Our neighbors said all the lights in the neighborhood were out. When the lights came back on, the van was gone. How did they see to work?"

"That's probably why they didn't look to wipe their feet," Don grumbled.

"Pardon?"

"Boot prints!" Don huffed. "It had rained that night, and Derek's friends were all wearing army boots. Had a hell of a time getting that crap out of the carpet!"

"Did you file a missing persons report?"

Dorothy made a throwing motion. "Oh, the police were no help at all! They said the moving van was proof he had left by choice. Even after he had been missing for a year they refused to lift a finger. Can you believe it?"

"Believe it, Dot," Don said. "They still remembered Derek from that credit card thing. They just figured he had done something even worse and was trying to stay one step ahead of the law."

"Are you sure that's *not* what happened, Mrs. Masterson?"

"If his 'friends' had helped him move, then why did they keep calling the house, asking if I knew where he was?"

Broadman's hands hovered over his laptop. "What were their names, if you can remember?"

Dorothy placed a finger to her chin. "Well, Crash, and Vandal, and I think Mutant called too."

Don groaned. "Worthless little punks! What was it Derek called himself? Darth Bloodhound?"

"Dark Bloodhand!" Dorothy snapped. "And if you had gone two steps out of your way to be more involved in Derek's life, he might have made better friends!"

"Yeah, like I was gonna take that smart-ass little geek with me to the VFW..."

Broadman cut him off. "Mrs. Masterson, do you know the kind of things Derek was doing on his computer before he disappeared? It could be important."

She thought for a moment. "It involved something called firewalls. Do you know what those are?"

"They're programs that keep unauthorized people out of computer systems."

"*That's* right," she recalled. "Derek said he was going to make a lot of money showing the government all the holes in their firewalls. One time I was bringing up his laundry and he said, 'Look, Mom! I'm inside the Pentagon!'"

Don Masterson cringed. "I'm surprised the government didn't just tear gas us and burn the house down!"

"I *told* Derek to stay away from the military computers after that, and he promised he would," Dorothy said. "The last thing he was working on was called the National Safety Administration, or something like that."

Broadman's ears twitched again. "National *Safety* Administration?"

"Yes, but Derek just called it the NSA. He said it was something horribly dull, communications and data networks and things like that."

Don gave Broadman a sour look. "Well, that just gives *me* a warm feeling all over, how about you?"

REWARDS

Sunshine. Ken Yoshida had never seen anything so beautiful in his entire life, especially since he thought he would never live to see it again. In small groups, the hackers were taken to the corridor where Yoshida had been initiated into the Snake Pit. He wondered if there were any new prisoners stuffed into those concrete closets right now.

Yoshida shuddered. No wonder the hackers around him were so cowed. His two days in the box had left a fearful and lasting impression on him. He could only imagine what a week in that hole had done to the men around him.

But he didn't have time to focus on that. At the end of the corridor was the heavy roll-up door through which he had entered the bunker. Jackhammer marks on the walls told Yoshida that this door had been recently added, probably to bring in the hacker's heavy computing equipment. Beyond that was a garage area with four bay doors. One of those bay doors was open, the early morning sunshine streaming in.

It took all of Yoshida's Resistance training not to fixate on the sunshine. His attention was on the exit doors. With furtive glances he memorized locks, switches, and alarm systems, all with an eye to escape if the opportunity presented itself.

But the sunshine drew him like a magnet. Yoshida lifted his face and savored the distant warmth soaking into his skin. The air was so fresh it smelled alive.

Yoshida's group was herded onto the blacktop driveway wrapping around the back of the bunker. They were inside a double-fenced compound, razor wire topping both fences. A guard tugged a large and aggressive German Shepherd between the fences. The dog had a strong reaction to the orange jumpsuits and kept lunging at the inner fence. Towers loomed at each corner of the yard. The watchmen standing outside held their shotguns at the ready.

"All right!" the guard escorting them shouted. Yoshida had learned his name was Kramp. "You are free to move about inside the compound. Stay ten feet away from the fences at all times. Use the opportunity to get some exercise. We'll bring out something to drink in a few minutes."

Some of the hackers were jogging in a ragged oval around the inside of the fence. Yoshida joined them, doffing his orange slippers and socks so he could run more easily. Paul Malechek and the Taylor twins were trying to run with their ridiculous inmate's slippers, which were designed to prevent just that. Malechek took Yoshida's lead, but Julius and Demetrius gave up and sat on the blacktop road, avoiding the dew-soaked grass. From their physiques, he could see that few of the hackers were used to physical exertion.

Yoshida kept running, using the opportunity to take a good look around. The woods were thick on all four sides of the compound, and no other structures were visible. The poor condition of the lone road leading away suggested they could be miles from civilization. But the number and low altitude of the jet airliners overhead indicated a large city to the west.

What city could it be? Colonel Richter had mentioned ECHELON when they were tracking down the CIA security guy inside Mitsusui's system. That would make the Snake Pit an NSA operation, which was logical. Yoshida had been caught trying to get inside an NSA network. But the NSA had facilities all over the world. Would they have the brass to imprison the hackers at NSA headquarters itself?

Yoshida knew that NSA headquarters was at Ft. Meade, Maryland. That might make Washington, D.C., the city to the west. That fit too. No truck noise offered a gauge to the direction of the nearest highway, but the access road ran toward the faint sound of a factory or power plant.

This was all interesting but useless information. The security, by his estimate, was airtight. But anything man could make was subject to human error. He would keep his eyes open and his mind working. And his legs running. Yoshida was surprised at how quickly he tired. His muscles had atrophied after only...how many days had he been here? He needed to start making marks on the wall or something.

Kramp and another guard named Womack lugged coolers out of the garage. The pair appeared to be Richter's chief lieutenants. Both definitely possessed Richter's mean streak. Like Pittman, Yoshida had learned to keep as much distance from them as possible. Kramp summoned the hackers together. Yoshida slowed to a walk and joined the others. He blinked in amazement.

It was beer. Coolers full of it. Nothing expensive and nothing in bottles, Yoshida noticed. But the hackers didn't care. They dove on the coolers like hungry dogs on a piece of meat. Yoshida hung back from the grasping mob.

"Everybody gets one beer!" Kramp shouted. "Anyone taking more will be punished!"

Yoshida waited until last. Sure enough, there was one beer
left at the bottom of the chest.

"Not a beer drinker?" Kramp asked.

"Hey, if you're giving it away, I'll take it."

"There's soda and Gatorade in the other cooler, if you'd
prefer that." He almost sounded friendly.

What the hell is going on here? Yoshida took his beer anyway, then grabbed a Gatorade from the other cooler. He found
Pittman, who had already downed his ration. Yoshida handed
Pittman his can. "Here, thirsty guy, you look like you need this
worse than I do."

"Oh God, thanks!" Pittman said, accepting the beer with a
shaky hand.

Yoshida drank his Gatorade. He watched Pittman cradle the
second beer with both hands, like a lost treasure. Probably an
alcoholic, Yoshida thought. The Snake Pit's regimen was likely
the only reason for Pittman's current sobriety. Take away the
guards and the barbed wire and he would quickly become a
drunk again. Yoshida wasn't surprised. Many of his hacker
friends had substance abuse problems of one kind or another. It
was just a part of the subculture.

Yoshida lay back in the cool, wet grass and watched a jet
pass overhead. He remembered how he used to hate airports.
The crowds, the delays, the lousy chairs, the greasy food. He
would give one of his kidneys to be stuck in an airport right
now.

Yoshida spent several minutes considering whether the
monitoring tags worked in the yard. "Hell of a change in strategy," he finally said.

Pittman stood his cans in the grass and stared at them, as if
trying to refill them by mental concentration. "Yeah. Makes you
wonder what they're up to."

After a couple of hours the day grew muggy and Kramp
whistled, waving the group in. "Lunch!" he called.

The hackers reluctantly obeyed, trudging inside with long-
ing glances at the sky. They headed for the mess hall, but the
guards motioned the group into the computer bay. Colonel
Richter was standing at the balcony rail, waiting to address
them. The hackers shifted nervously, uncertain whether the next
surprise would be a pleasant one or not.

Richter smiled broadly. "Good afternoon, gentlemen! I hope you enjoyed your time outside. I have some very special news. Since the Snake Pit has been in operation less than three years, we have never had a graduate from our rehabilitation program. Until today. General Stoyer and I have agreed that your performance during operation HEADSHOT was so outstanding that an exception needed to be made. Derek Friedman, front and center!"

Friedman cautiously stepped forward. "Y-yes sir?"

"Mr. Friedman, without your creation of the RAPIDMAP program, operation HEADSHOT would not have been possible. Your hard work and enthusiasm have been an example to the team, and demonstrates that you are ready to return to society as a productive member."

Friedman blinked, not sure whether to believe what he was hearing or not.

Richter grinned. "That is, unless you just want to hang around the Snake Pit for the companionship. Do you, Mr. Friedman?"

"Hell no!" Friedman shouted. "I mean, no, *sir!*"

"Well then, after you've packed your things and said your good-byes, you can be on your way."

CHAPTER 8

"Tyranny, like Hell, is not easily conquered."
-Thomas Paine

LAB RESULTS

Jeremy Patrick pushed away from his desk. The day was half gone already. By his estimate, the paperwork was winning. Patrick thought being Special-Agent-in-Charge of the Philadelphia Field Office would have prepared him for anything, but he was wrong.

As Assistant Director for Special Operations, Patrick was responsible for the FBI's quick reaction teams. The Crisis Response Team saw the most action. The CRT provided agents and equipment to supplement the field offices during emergencies, major cases, and special events. Patrick was gearing up the team to support an international economic summit in Atlanta next week.

Then a Pacific Air jet went down in Idaho. Now the entire CRT was in the field assisting with the recovery and identification of bodies. But the summit deadline was still bearing down on him, and he was left to do most of the work by himself.

The pride of the Special Operations Division was the Hostage Rescue Team. An elite SWAT team, the HRT was the civilian equivalent of the Army's anti-terrorist Delta Force. Having TV cameras cover the arrival of the HRT at an armed standoff was an excellent way of communicating to the bad guys that the FBI was deadly serious.

Commanding the HRT was the main reason Patrick had pursued this position. The HRT was the muscle of the FBI. With him in command and two Resistance cell members on the team, the HRT was now muscle for the Resistance as well.

His cell phone rang. He checked the ID display. His second life was calling. "Diane, could you get my door, please?"

"Certainly, Mr. Patrick."

With the door closed, Patrick pressed the SECURE key. "How are the Yankees doing?" he asked.

"I prefer the Mets," Eric answered. "Rooting for the underdog builds character."

"What's the latest?"

"I ran the fibers through the lab. As our new friend suspected, it *is* blood. The blood type matches, too. Do you want me to try to find a DNA sample for comparison?"

While the FBI might demand a DNA test, the lower profile required for his Resistance work often meant going more on instincts than lab results. "No, that's an unnecessary risk. I think the results are fairly conclusive, don't you?"

"Maybe I just didn't want to believe it."

"I hear you," Patrick agreed. "Is our initiate making any progress on that front?"

"That's what he tells Ben. Of course, he would probably say anything to keep me from showing up at his house in the middle of the night again."

Patrick smiled. In Eric's "real life," presenting an intimidating physical presence was a necessary job skill. "Keep the pressure up. We need to get this fixed quickly."

"It'll be my pleasure," Eric agreed.

STREET SMARTS

The smoke and gloom in Goalies Bar made it difficult to see the hockey mementos covering the walls of the Paramus, New Jersey, tavern. But they appeared to be from losing seasons, when scavenging for souvenirs was easier.

"The government took Bob, sure as hell. No two ways about it," Lucy Pittman rasped, shoving a mug in Broadman's direction. She took a deep drag on her cigarette, adding to the room's roiling haze. Her thick makeup merely drew attention to her acne scars and age lines, rather than covering them.

Lucy leaned her heavy frame against the server's side of the bar. "Nobody ever said Bob was a saint, least of all me. But there's one thing for damn sure, my brother wasn't no criminal!"

Broadman had a harder time tracing Bob Pittman's relatives than he did with Derek Friedman. Pittman's parents were deceased, and the most recent records Broadman could access on the man were cold by at least three years. With the records his Lexis search *had* uncovered, he doubted Bob Pittman could have stayed out of trouble that long, regardless of his sister's contentions.

Bob Pittman's legal record included several DWIs, a suspended driver's license, and a divorce. An assault on a software company coworker occurred within days of the divorce proceedings. That had been pleaded down to a suspended sentence and enrollment into a substance abuse program. But not one entry in the public record since then, not even an attempt to regain his license at the local DMV.

If it hadn't been for Lucy, Broadman would have skipped Pittman and gone to the next name. But apparently she had complained to a reporter at the Newark *Post*, who had written an article about Lucy's search for her brother and her unorthodox theories about his disappearance. It was a clumsy piece, probably written by a journalism intern. *Let's all have a laugh at the crazy lady who says the government took her brother*, the little putz might as well have written.

But it had mentioned the name of Robert Pittman, which caught the piece in the fine mesh of Broadman's Nexis search. That gave him Lucy's name, which led--through a few more hoops--to her less than auspicious bartending job. The real trick to his search had been staying productive at the *Times*. The last thing he needed was to arouse Janet Randall's suspicions about his second job.

Broadman took a swallow of his beer. "The article mentioned that your brother had stumbled onto a secret government project, but it didn't say anything more."

"It was some kind of Big Brother monitoring system called ECHELON. Ever heard of it?"

"It's a National Security Agency program. Sixty Minutes did a story on it. Scary stuff."

Lucy held her cigarette at an indignant angle. "Well, Bob was way ahead of Sixty Minutes! He actually hacked into the NSA and pulled out some of their data files."

Broadman pushed his drink aside. "What kind of data?"

Her voice was full of sibling pride. "How about a list of the politicians the NSA was keeping an eye on and a record of how many intercepts they had for each one?"

Holy shit! Broadman forced himself to maintain a skeptical detachment. "So you think the NSA took him?"

"Pretty safe bet. I don't think even Bob expected to get inside their system. But he was really freaked out by what he found. Came over to my apartment all shaky and paranoid, waving this diskette around, saying they'd kill him for what was on it."

Broadman remembered Yoshida's similar warnings about the MINTNET data. "So what happened to that diskette?"

"I told him to calm down and stay with me for a week or two in case somebody busted down his door. He left the diskette with me and went back to his apartment to pack some clothes. I never saw him again."

"*Please* tell me you still have that diskette."

Lucy aimed her cigarette like a weapon. "Listen, I didn't ask for any of this shit, and that damned disk has bought me a lot more trouble than it was worth!"

"I'll take that as a no."

She vented smoke. "Let me tell you a story. When that snot-nosed college kid interviewed me, I gave him a copy of the disk. He said it was all gibberish."

"Maybe your brother encrypted the data."

She nodded. "That sounds like Bob. Only he never gave me the secret decoder ring to unsnarl it. But that didn't stop somebody from ransacking my apartment. That happened right after the little shit made fun of me in the paper."

"So they stole your original?"

She gave him a street-smart smile. "I didn't say that. But it pissed me off, so I took another copy to a computer store and told them my story. They couldn't read it either. But they were real nice. They made a website for me to tell about Bob's disappearance and posted the gibberish file on it. They challenged every hacker who logged on to crack the file themselves."

"That was a good idea!"

Lucy stubbed out her old cigarette, promptly lighting a new one. "That's what *they* thought. Until a week later when somebody crawled in from the Internet and trashed their computers. Really hosed them good. Scared that computer guy shitless. Needless to say, that was the end of my website.

"About a week after that, some guy in a suit showed up and said Bob had joined the Witness Protection Program. Said I was endangering Bob and myself by publicizing his story. I told him that was bullshit. So the guy gave me a letter in Bob's handwriting that said he was okay and he should be able to come home in about three years."

That was certainly a new angle. "How long ago was that?"

"About three years. So pardon me if I don't want to stir up the hornet's nest again. The only reason I'm telling you this is because you said a friend of yours went missing too. But do yourself a favor and leave it alone. These guys play rough."

"I'll watch my step."

ILLEGAL ENTRY

Hawthorne waited until most of the other agents were at lunch. For added safety, he used one of the visitor's terminals in the office common area. He took a deep breath, then logged in using Bill Jeffries' ID number. He typed with one handkerchief-covered finger. The computer accepted the login and asked for his password.

Hawthorne was only trying this because he had helped his boss set up the NCIC 2000 account. The SAC was a notoriously reluctant computer user and only opened an account on the NCIC 2000 system when he received a letter from the Director's office ordering him to do so.

The successor to the thirty-year-old National Crime Information Center program, NCIC 2000 helped carry the information revolution down to the local police squad car. Using a handheld fingerprint scanner, a cop anywhere in the country could scan a suspect's right index finger, submit it to NCIC 2000, and have a match against warrants nationwide before he and the perp had returned to the station house.

A federal officer could also receive notice if a suspect he or she was tracking received so much as a speeding ticket anywhere in the country, even if an arrest warrant had not been issued. That was the kind of data Hawthorne was hoping to obtain.

Perhaps Yoshida had been caught in a legitimate hacker sting operation by another federal agency. His MINTNET search had been for a good cause, but it was still illegal. If another agency like Secret Service had made an arrest, it should show up on the computer. But Hawthorne had to exercise caution, since the system kept records of every request for information.

Jeffries had whined at length about the NCIC 2000 password system. To thwart unauthorized users, every password had to include two words, a control character, and a number. No one could remember all that, the SAC insisted, given the prohibition against writing down passwords, even in one's personal memo book.

It was all in choosing the right combination, Hawthorne had countered. He illustrated by typing: "BREAD&BUTTER1." He challenged Jeffries to come up with a similar construction, but the SAC just entered Hawthorne's example and hit RETURN. The system demanded a new password every ninety days, but Hawthorne was sure Jeffries would bend that rule. It had been about a year since Jeffries had opened his account, so Hawthorne typed:

BREAD&BUTTER4

WELCOME SPECIAL AGENT JEFFRIES the system replied.

Hawthorne restrained himself from smirking. Openings like these were gifts from God, nothing less. He typed into the ALL AGENCY search window:

SEARCH PARAMETERS: YOSHIDA, KENTARO

The computer sat idle for several agonizing seconds before spewing:

SECURITY VIOLATION: ALL RECORDS SEALED

Hawthorne hit ENTER, but the system rejected it. The terminal was locked up, the incriminating data there for everyone to see. He reached under the desk, grasped the power cord with his handkerchief and yanked. After a few seconds he plugged it back in. The computer rebooted, ignorant of its previous connection.

Hawthorne jumped from the chair. He grabbed his coat and hurried to join his fellow agents for lunch. Bill Jeffries' phone was ringing before he even reached the office door.

FAREWELLS

Lunch was steak and potatoes. And another beer. Yoshida had to admit that good food even took the edge off a hellhole like the Snake Pit. He wondered whether the food and sunshine and beer were really a reward or just an enticement for an even more distasteful task ahead. Yoshida had just pushed away from the table when Friedman reappeared, carrying a fat three-ring binder.

"Here," Friedman said brusquely, "Richter wants you to take over the RAPIDMAP program. These are my notes. The rest of the stuff is on my terminal." He reached over the table to shake hands with Pittman. "Hey, old man, see you in a few months! You know where to find me!"

Yoshida noticed something odd about the handshake, but the guards were close by. He kept his eyes on Friedman.

"Sure," Pittman replied uneasily, "I guess my sentence will be up in another six months or so. Good luck!"

"Yeah, same to ya!" Friedman then addressed the group. "Well guys, it's been real! I won't say real what!"

Yoshida noticed Pittman moving his clenched hand under the table, but averted his eyes quickly.

With two guards in tow, Friedman left the mess hall. Passing through the doorway, he tossed a final insult over his shoulder. "See ya later, losers!" he shouted.

REACTIONS

The National Security Council had been summoned to the White House so many times one member suggested they assume permanent residence in the Situation Room. Cynthia Hale took the lectern at the far end of the table from the President.

The last few hours had been a frantic dash of activity. Immediately after the diplomatic cable from China, the entire US intelligence machine began spewing reams of photographic and signals data on the actions of the Chinese military. Her job had been to dip the cup of *essential* information from the flood that had landed on her desk.

Despite her earlier disagreements with Admiral Holland, Chet had been indispensable in preparing the brief for the President. It puzzled her why Holland hadn't been given the task instead of her. Most of the decisions requiring the President's attention would be military in nature. But Adams had specified that she conduct the briefing, perhaps as peace offering for ignoring her advice on the Nagoya strike. Hale accepted it as the olive branch she hoped it was.

"Mr. President," she began, "It didn't take long for the Chinese to capitalize on our difficulties with Japan. Less than two hours after the news of our diplomatic row hit the newswires,

China announced the beginning of their annual summer fleet exercises in the Taiwan Straits."

"What are they up to?" Adams asked.

A large map of Taiwan and coastal China replaced the introductory slide bearing the presidential seal. "Every year the Chinese stage exercises in the Taiwan Straits, usually coinciding with Taiwanese elections or important votes in their Congress. The Chinese shell one of their coastal islands and release the footage to remind Taiwan, or the Republic of China, that they're still just a 'rebel province' as far as Beijing is concerned. It also frightens foreign investors away from the ROC, which is a secondary objective."

Hale's laser pointer dotted three red-tinted wedges to the west, east, and north of Taiwan. "But at least once every American presidency they really step up the pressure. In the past, they've launched cruise and ballistic missiles into the waters around Taiwan, right over highly populated areas in some cases. Since the Chinese consider Taiwan their property, they don't give a damn about diplomatic protests. They've already issued Airman and Mariner notices to stay clear of these designated missile impact zones."

"Which just happen to be the areas we would want to maneuver our fleet to protect Taiwan," Admiral Holland interjected.

"Then they mobilize all their amphibious ships and act like they're about to invade Taiwanese territory," she said.

Hale could read the worry on Adams's face. He had already been forced into one act of war this week. "Could the Chinese actually pull off an invasion of Taiwan?"

"Not a chance," Hale assured him. "The ROC navy is almost as big as China's and of better quality."

Admiral Holland had included an order of battle for both navies in her briefing package. The Chinese Navy was basically a coastal enterprise--twenty destroyers and thirty or so frigates, all with 1970s-vintage weapons systems. Their submarine force was even worse, with forty ex-Russian subs so decrepit they spent most of the time tied at pier.

The only bright stars in China's lineup were two *Sovremenny*-class missile cruisers, bought brand-new from the Russians. Their electronics were equal to all but the newest US warships, and they carried Russian Sunburn anti-ship missiles. A handwritten note from Holland pointed out that the Sunburn had about the same range and warhead as an American Harpoon missile but traveled at Mach 2.5. Each cruiser could fire eight missiles at a time, at single or multiple targets. It was a good thing the Chinese only had two of those monsters.

"China doesn't have enough amphibious capability to invade the main island," Hale went on, "but they could easily invade Quemoy or Matsu. As long as they were willing to go to war over it."

Although rarely sympathetic to China's viewpoint, Hale wondered whether the US would have the patience to tolerate a hostile power holding islands just outside its territorial waters, as China did with Quemoy and Matsu. It would be like Cuba holding the Florida Keys. Fortunately, the Chinese took a very long view in foreign relations. If an objective was denied them today, there would always be next year. Or next decade. Or even next century.

But Quemoy and Matsu were where President Eisenhower had drawn the line, and if the US wavered there, the Chinese would inevitably wonder about American resolve elsewhere. Quemoy and Matsu were also floating antenna farms for the NSA. From there, the US could monitor Chinese military activity for hundreds of miles inland. Losing those listening posts would be as bad as losing Taiwan itself, from an intelligence point of view.

Adams scowled. "So, since I'm the new guy in the hot seat, they want to try me on for size."

Hale suppressed a smile. Adams had always impressed her with his ability to grasp the big picture from just a few disjointed facts. "Since we have no formal relations with Taiwan, the Chinese feel they have to test every president and see if we still care about the Republic of China."

To cover her bases, Hale had pulled a copy of Public Law 96-8, the Taiwan Relations Act. It bound the president by law to arm and protect Taiwan as a vital national interest. She doubted her boss would need to be reminded of that.

Adams rubbed his eyes. "Okay, how do I show I still care?"

"Two carriers and a dozen roses," Holland deadpanned. "The problem is that the carriers are fifteen hundred miles east of Taiwan, and they're already in need of resupply. Without those supply ships that are locked up in Japan, the fuel bunkers in the task force are going to be damned near empty when they reach Taiwan. And a potential battle zone is a lousy place to run out of gas. But if they continue their retreat to Guam for resupply, the Chinese may see a window to make a *real* military move, not just one for show."

"Which is exactly why the Chinese are making their move now," Hale added.

"Attack when your enemy's options are the most limited," Adams grumbled. "Sounds like something straight out of Sun Tzu, doesn't it?"

"That it does, Mr. President," Holland agreed.

Adams was massaging his chin, which always made Hale nervous. The Boss was about to display his famous unpredictability. "Admiral," he pondered aloud, "perhaps we can use China's fixation on our carriers to our advantage. Has General Stoyer been tasked to provide a DATASHARK option for our dilemma?"

Hale felt a flash of panic. She spoke before Holland could respond. "Mr. President, DATASHARK is why we're *in* this current crisis! General Stoyer's wonder weapon isn't nearly as precise or predictable as he led us to believe."

"I understand that," Adams said. "But as Commander-in-Chief, I need all my options on the table, even the less desirable ones. Have General Stoyer draw up a plan for my consideration, please."

When Hale and Holland shared dumbfounded looks, Adams added, "*Now* was what I had in mind, people!"

PERKS

"Certainly, Admiral," Stoyer acknowledged. "That won't be a problem, sir." He hung up the phone and checked the time. After a moment's reflection, Stoyer grabbed his dress cap from the credenza and left his office. "Barbara, call my car," he told his secretary.

"Sir, you have a one o'clock with the Chairman of the House Intelligence Committee," she reminded him.

"Can't be helped. Admiral Holland just gave me an emergency tasking. I have to handle it offsite," he lied. "Pull Jeff Archer off what he's doing and have him give the Chairman and his staff a tour of the NICC. That always wows them. I'll be back before two."

His secretary accepted the burden of entertaining a dozen pompous and impatient bureaucrats with her usual long-suffering grace. "Yes, sir."

Stoyer turned the key to his private elevator in the corner of the executive suite. "Oh, and have the kitchen send up a couple dozen cinnamon rolls to my conference room." Congressman Carsten had a notorious sweet tooth, and a girth to match. "They can't bitch with their mouths full."

Barbara rewarded his rare display of humor with a broad smile. "Good point, sir. I'll take care of it."

The narrow doors opened. Stoyer hated small enclosed spaces, but this little lift was a real time saver. With all the drones returning from lunch, it would take forever just to go down eight floors in the regular elevators.

Since the Deputy Director's office was in the same suite, Stoyer often wondered why Archer never used *his* key. Maybe he wanted to show that he identified with the little people by jamming elbow-to-elbow with them in the same elevator. The thought disgusted him, but Stoyer realized it was just his military training. He was taught to never socialize with people he might have to order to their deaths.

Stoyer debated his decision while he waited for his car. He could have handled this task just as easily with a phone call. But no, he *wanted* to do this himself. Like his private elevator, it was just another perk of his position.

THE DRAGON

With more than four hundred worldwide intercept stations monitored by twenty-five thousand personnel, one of the most difficult problems the NSA faced was, strangely enough, paper. Whole buildings had to be built to warehouse the truckloads of blank paper used daily, and then to store the highly classified intercepts which were eventually printed on them. The Government Accounting Office estimated that the NSA produced over a hundred million classified documents a year--more secrets than all four armed forces, the CIA, and every other government agency combined.

Getting rid of that paper was a different problem. Even intercepts regarded as inconsequential could not be cast off like yesterday's newspaper. Each discarded document revealed closely-guarded capabilities of the spy agency. Despite the efforts to create a "paperless" organization, the NSA was creating forty tons of classified waste every day, burying itself under a mountain of secret garbage. Another solution had to be found.

With trademark ingenuity, the NSA turned to Disney World for help. To prevent the magic of the Magic Kingdom from being marred by the sight of workers hauling away truckloads of trash through Fantasyland, Disney constructed a system of underground conveyor belts to transport the garbage from each of the parks to a central waste disposal facility. The NSA copied this concept with a two-million-dollar system which trundled burn bags of classified waste from all over the NSA complex to a central incinerator.

The incinerator was a story in itself. Initially dubbed White Elephant One, the "classified waste destructor" used jets of natural gas to create a swirling inferno that consumed the NSA's secret trash at 3,400 degrees Fahrenheit. Except when too much trash was dumped in at one time. Then bits of sensitive intercepts and classified computer printouts spewed out the stack, the top-secret tidbits fluttering downwind over miles of Maryland countryside.

Eventually the NSA built their own paper recycling plant. Instead of burning them, they turned the country's deepest secrets into pizza boxes. The incinerator was saved for magnetic tapes, computer diskettes, and the like. NSA employees now nicknamed it "The Dragon" for its low, throaty roar, which was audible from every part of the NSA complex.

* * *

The van carrying Friedman pulled out of the bunker's garage. He had been allowed to change into civilian clothes and carried a small bag containing the few possessions he had accumulated during his stay in the Snake Pit. Richter sat next to him on the bench seat. Kramp and Womack faced him on the opposite side.

"So, Mr. Friedman," Richter asked. "What are you going to do now?"

"I'm gonna get laid and I'm gonna get wasted and I don't care which happens first!" Friedman effused.

Kramp and Womack laughed.

The driver pushed a button on what looked like a garage door opener. Ahead, a washed-out bridge blocking the road to the Snake Pit rose up from the stream on hydraulic cylinders. After the van crossed, the bridge returned to a state of collapse. Driving out of the woods, the van turned right and headed toward a large white building.

The farther Friedman traveled from the Snake Pit, the more giddy he became. His natural skepticism gave way to the euphoria of actually regaining his freedom. "Hey man!" he bubbled. "Once I start my own Internet company and become a millionaire, you'll have to look me up! I'll have more naked women at my parties than you can shake your stick at!"

Richter's smile never wavered. The poor bastard had been in the hole so long he didn't even know that most of the people who had started dot-com firms were broke now. "I'll do that!" he assured Friedman.

Friedman's eyes darted around the windowless interior. "Hey! Why are we stopping?"

"We're at the main gate. We'll change vehicles here."

Kramp and Womack slid open the side door and stepped out. Friedman followed. Richter brought up the rear, reaching under the seat for an object.

Friedman's head swiveled. They were out of the woods, but the only sign of civilization was a large white building with a smokestack. His gaze traveled up the length of the flue. "Hey! Where are we?" he shouted over the jet-engine roar. "What the hell is this thing?"

Friedman's upturned chin offered a perfect target. Richter raised his baton and slammed it end-first into Friedman's exposed throat.

Friedman collapsed backward, clawing at his crushed larynx. He tried to scream, but only a high-pitched wheeze came out.

"Bag him!" Richter shouted over the Dragon's thunder.

Kramp and Womack rolled out a body bag and wrestled Friedman into it. The skinny hacker was no match for the burly security men, especially since he was unable to breathe. The struggle caused his face to turn pale blue. His eyes were wide with surprise and terror. Friedman was still mouthing "*No!*" as the guards zipped the bag over his head.

Richter led the way to a side entrance of the incinerator building. He punched in a security code, then held open the door for Kramp and Womack, who lugged their cargo inside.

The heat inside the building was withering. Richter was reminded of a Bible story he had heard as a child. Three Israeli prisoners of war were cast by the order of an evil king into a furnace so hot it killed their tormentors who threw them in. Nice story, but nobody was walking out of the fiery furnace today, Richter concluded.

A metal ramp protruded from an opening in the wall opposite the incinerator. Every few seconds, a canvas bag rolled off the end. A shaker table below funneled the burn bags one at a time onto a conveyor belt leading up to the incinerator.

Richter saw General Stoyer standing in the control booth. The operator was evidently waiting outside. Although Richter had asked for Stoyer's help to minimize the number of witnesses, he hadn't expected the General's personal participation. Stoyer stood with his arms folded, his eyes fixed on Kramp and Womack's burden.

Waiting for a gap between the bags, Kramp and Womack threw Friedman's body onto the conveyor belt below. The final step before the incinerator was a shredder. Adapted from a commercial wood chipper, it could reduce bags of twelve-inch magnetic tape reels to confetti in seconds.

The body bag inched closer to the shredder. Friedman still writhed inside it, like a butterfly struggling in vain to free itself from a cocoon. The wriggling grew violent as the sound of the thrashing blades drew closer. Guardrails on each side held him captive to the belt's inexorable progress. One of the cutters caught a strap and yanked the body bag violently inward. There was a long grinding wail as the shredder slowly ingested Derek Friedman into the Dragon.

Richter shouted at his subordinates over the roar of the incinerator. "Did you bastards put him in feet first on purpose?"

CHAPTER 9

"In God we trust, all others we monitor."
-NSA intercept operator's motto

YIN-YANG

Stoyer watched Admiral Holland rise to address the National Security Council. Today the meeting was being held in the Cabinet Room to accommodate the additional military officers present. The sunlight streaming in from the Rose Garden was a welcome contrast to the gloom of the Situation Room downstairs. Holland's adjutant had updated the ship positions on the map of the western Pacific just before the meeting.

"Good morning, ladies and gentlemen," Holland rumbled, "things look a hell of a lot better now than they did a few days ago." He tapped his pointer on the aircraft carrier symbol near Guam. "Admiral Meacham pulled a maneuver that surprised even me. Using his fleet oilers, he transferred fuel from the *Kitty Hawk* and some of the task force's older escorts into their fastest ships."

He traced a line westward. "Those ships and the nuclear carrier *Carl Vinson* then made a speed run for Taiwan, where they'll arrive shortly. The *Kitty Hawk* and her escorts are proceeding at best economy toward Guam. They will arrive later today. After refueling, they'll join the fleet at Taiwan in a few days."

Holland circled the submarine symbols in the Taiwan Strait. "We have four attack subs on station now, and two more will arrive with the *Vinson* task force. With six nuclear attack boats we could turn the China Sea into a shooting gallery and let the Taiwanese navy sit back and enjoy the show."

Holland wagged a thumb at a large formation southwest of Taiwan. "The Chinese navy apparently wasn't planning on us arriving at the party so quickly. They staged a massive task force out of Guangzhou, equal to about half of their total fleet. But that took time, and they aren't in position yet. If our ships join up with the Taiwanese before the Chinese enter the straits, this game will be over. That's the good news."

He thumped the missile impact zones north, south and east of Taiwan with a weathered finger. "But these are our problem. We can't put our ships in these areas with Chinese cruise missiles dropping in at random. It's too damned dangerous. And we can't stage effective blocking maneuvers with our fleet except from these zones."

The days of continual stress were beginning to show on President Adams's face. "So the Chinese still have us by the yin-yang?"

A rare smile lifted one side of the Admiral's mouth. "Not quite, Mr. President. General Stoyer has an interesting option he'd like to present."

MEN IN BLACK

The security goons were waiting when Hawthorne returned from lunch. Two grilled Bill Jeffries in his office and another checked terminal numbers in the common area.

One federal agent in a suit might seem indistinguishable from another, but Hawthorne's trained eye noticed a difference. For one thing, FBI agents were usually sharp dressers. The black suits these men wore looked like they came from a discount outlet. The jackets had not been tailored, riding tight on one man and slightly baggy on another. And their haircuts were even shorter than the conservative norm for FBI agents.

"I've got a match!" the terminal tracker called out.

The two men in Jeffries's office rose, signaling for the SAC to follow them. Hawthorne ducked around a cubicle, taking the long way around to his office.

"Hawthorne!" Jeffries shouted. "Get your butt over here!"

His heart leapt into his throat. *Stay calm, Ben!* He commanded himself. *You covered your tracks.*

"Yes sir?" he asked innocently.

Jeffries's face was flushed. "Some asshole broke into NCIC using my password! Tell these guys I wasn't even here!"

"I just got back from lunch myself. Special Agent Jeffries wasn't here when I left," Hawthorne said, leaving a seed of doubt in his voice. "Could it have been a hacker?"

"Not unless he was sitting right *here*," the terminal tracker snapped.

Hawthorne kept his face impassive. "Origination codes can be faked, you know."

"Then how did a hacker get the ID number for this terminal?" *Smart ass*, the tracker's tone added for him.

"This computer is used by visiting agents from other field offices. If any of those agents carried out a nonsecure Internet transaction from this terminal, the ID number might have been picked off by a skilled hacker."

"Not damned likely," the tracker insisted.

Hawthorne ignored the barb and addressed the older suit, obviously the leader. "If I may ask, what information was stolen in the break-in?"

"Nothing, luckily. Someone tried to access the NCIC file on a hacker, but the transaction was blocked."

Hawthorne feigned surprise. "A *hacker*, you say?"

"Is that significant?" the leader asked.

Hawthorne forced his body language to display a confidence he didn't really feel. "Well, sir, hackers sometimes go to *extreme* lengths to play dirty tricks on each other. Imagine the mischief you could make if you had access to a rival hacker's NCIC file!"

The leader cocked his head at the tracker. "Kaminski?"

The younger man poked the terminal Hawthorne had used with his finger. "It came from *right here*, I'm telling you!"

The leader shrugged. "This hardly seems a likely spot for a security leak, Kaminski. I'm more inclined to accept the theory of Agent...I'm sorry, what was your name?"

"Special Agent Hawthorne, sir," he said, producing a business card.

The leader gave the card a cursory look before pocketing it. He extended a hand to the SAC. "Special Agent Jeffries, sorry to have bothered you. After that deal in Nebraska, the hackers have all of us a little on edge. Looks like you were the butt of one of their practical jokes."

Jeffries started to breathe again. "Okay, no harm done, I suppose."

"You damned well better change your password," Kaminski prodded. His eyes were fixed on Hawthorne. He knew something was wrong with Hawthorne's story, but he couldn't prove it.

"I'll assist Agent Jeffries with the latest password protocols," Hawthorne assured the group.

"Looks like you're in good hands, Mr. Jeffries," the leader said. "Thanks for your time, gentlemen."

"Yeah, sure," Jeffries mumbled.

The trio in black left the office, Kaminski giving Hawthorne a steely gaze before exiting. Hawthorne smiled back politely.

Jeffries exhaled, deflating like a Macy's parade balloon. "Thanks, Ben! Those guys gave me the creeps!"

Hawthorne had little sympathy for Jeffries. The worst he could have received was a written security violation. But if it endangered his next promotion, that was hazard enough for the Special-Agent-in-Charge.

Hawthorne needed to visit a restroom. Immediately. He was about to lose the lunch he had just eaten. "No problem, sir. I'll help you change that password in a minute."

"Thanks, Ben, you're a lifesaver!" Jeffries said to Hawthorne's rapidly receding back.

CHIP SHOT

General Stoyer's first slide showed a large winged missile. "This is a Russian SS-N-19 anti-ship cruise missile, NATO codenamed Shipwreck. It's the size of a fighter jet and packs a warhead big enough to snap the keel of an aircraft carrier. It flies at thirteen hundred miles per hour at medium altitude, then makes a final dive at about Mach four." He lifted an eyebrow. "The Chinese have purchased over a hundred of these."

There was a collective groan from the council.

"The Chinese have designated the missile XH-1 for *Xiangyang Hong*, which translates roughly as 'Red Sky at Morning.'"

"Sailor take warning," Adams observed.

"That's the idea. Satellite photos show at least five launchers operational on the Chinese coast. With these, they can shoot *over* Taiwan and hit targets a hundred miles at sea to the east. They did just that two days ago. The intel plane we had in the area said the missile's seeker was fully active when it hit the water."

"Meaning what?" Cynthia Hale asked.

Admiral Holland's face was grim. "Meaning when it nosed over on its final dive, it was looking for a target. If one of our ships had been in the area, their missile might have locked on and sunk it. That's why we can't risk operating in one of their target zones. And they've designated half of the ocean around Taiwan as a target zone."

Adams's eyes blazed. "That's damned near an act of war."

"Not from the Chinese point of view," Harry Abramson reminded the President. "They view Taiwan as *their* property, regardless of world opinion. It would be like us shooting missiles over Catalina Island. We'll do it whenever we please, thank you very much!"

"So you have another option for us, General?"

"Are you familiar with the concept of 'chipping,' Mr. President?" Stoyer asked.

"Not unless you're talking about golf."

Stoyer gave Adams the chuckle he expected. "No sir. The instructions modern weapon systems use to operate come in two forms, hardware and software. Software is computer code. That can be sabotaged, but it can also be inspected for tampering. Hardware instructions are commands burned right into the computer chips. Unless you designed the chips yourself, there's no way to decode *all* the commands that reside on a chip.

"The Chinese purchased the XH-1 missiles from the Russians for two million apiece. The Russians are very hard up for cash. So we paid them double that amount per missile to let us install a few *custom* computer chips the NSA designed before the missiles were delivered."

"You're joking," Adams countered.

"No sir. The XH-1 has a command update guidance system. It can be fired in the general direction of a target, then given the final coordinates by a friendly ship or aircraft possessing the correct command code. A self-destruct order can also be sent, in case a missile is fired in error. The chips we installed assure that the NSA *always* possesses the correct command code, regardless of what the Chinese select."

Adams straightened. "We *own* their missiles."

"Yes, sir. After all, we *paid* for them."

Adams gaped. "Is this done *often?*"

Possessing secret knowledge was always gratifying, especially when it was very secret, very useful knowledge like this. "Oh, yes, sir. That's why we try to sell weapons to both sides in trouble spots around the world. It drives some members of Congress crazy, but they don't understand the big picture. In the event of a conflict, chipping gives us the ability to pick which side we want to win and simply turn off the other side's weapons."

"I had no idea," Adams whispered.

Stoyer's expression hardened. "It's a capability we keep very close to the vest, sir. Everyone understands, of course, the discussion of this subject does not leave this room."

Adams scanned the group. "Everyone *does* understand that, correct?"

There were affirmative nods around the table.

"So," Adams proposed, "We sail into their test zones, and if they fire on us, we send their missile a self-destruct command?"

"We can do even better than that, Mr. President. Do you recall the satellite technology that was illegally sold to the Chinese by your predecessor?"

Adams's face reddened. "That bastard! I still don't understand why his ass isn't rotting in a federal prison right now! Of course I remember!"

Stoyer had to work hard to keep his expression serious. "I wouldn't take it so hard, Mr. President. Because of the technology that made its way illegally into their satellites, we are now *intimately* familiar with how they work. That would not be the case if the Chinese had developed the technology independently."

"Are you saying we own their *satellites*, too?"

The temptation to gloat was almost irresistible. "Yes, sir, we do."

The next image was of a spacecraft in a clean room. "This is their *Lianhua* 'Earth resources orbiter,'" Stoyer explained. "It's supposed to image Chinese agricultural areas and use the data to help boost food production. The system can also be used as a primitive sea surveillance satellite. On clear days, it can locate the heat plumes of surface ships and pass on the information for targeting the XH-1 missiles. Mid-course corrections can even be sent to the missiles directly from the satellite."

A photo of a featureless black cone appeared. "This is a *Sky Trash II* shadow satellite," Stoyer said. "It's designed to look like a discarded launch fairing to satellite tracking telescopes and is officially listed by NORAD as 'orbital debris.' It's also in a matching orbit with the Chinese *Lianhua* satellite and hears every signal beamed up to it from the ground. Because of *Sky Trash*, we know the Chinese send a signal to the *Lianhua* before every XH-1 launch. The *Lianhua* sends an update of the target area, and only then is a missile fired."

"So not only do we own their missiles, we have advance warning when they're about to launch," Adams said.

"Exactly."

The stress and fatigue visibly lifted from the President. "This gets better and better. What are you proposing, General?"

"We believe the Chinese are waiting for us to challenge their test zones before they launch their next missiles. When our task force nears Taiwan, we should split into two elements. The first would be two *Ticonderoga*-class cruisers and their escorts. The Ticos have the AEGIS radar systems and are the best air defense ships in the fleet."

Stoyer traced on the map. "They would steam through the northern impact zone and take up station off the western coast of Taiwan. The *Vinson* and the remaining escorts would position themselves on the other side of the island, in the eastern impact zone."

Stoyer tapped the launch sites on the Chinese coast. "If the Chinese launch one or more missiles, we'll have advance warning and broadcast a destruct signal from the *Sky Trash* satellite the second the missiles leave the launcher.

"If we're lucky, the missiles will damage their launchers when they blow up and the missile threat will be over for the near term. If not, they'll likely interpret the explosions as a defect in the XH-1 and will be unlikely to shoot any more for a while. Failing that, we'll then have an impenetrable air defense screen in place. If they *insist* on launching more missiles, we can shoot them down before they reach Taiwan, and long before they endanger our fleet. That should send a clear enough message, Mr. President."

"Well, Harry," Adams asked his Secretary of State, "will this send a message, or get us into a war?"

The wizened old man cocked an eyebrow at his younger boss. "They're getting pretty damned bold, Mr. President. If we tolerate missile overflights this time, what will they do next? No, sometimes a blunt instrument is the *best* tool for diplomacy. If they start a war, they'll lose. They know that. Which means if we push them hard, they'll retreat."

Stoyer saw Adams relax at the approval of his trusted friend and advisor. This mission would be a go.

"Mr. President!" Cynthia Hale stammered. "After the *disaster* in Nagoya, why are we even *considering* another NSA solution to our problem?"

Stoyer watched Adams closely, wondering how he would answer the question without admitting the devastation inflicted by HEADSHOT had been entirely his idea.

"Admiral Holland," Adams asked, "it's your men and women who will be going into harm's way if this operation... General, does this operation have a codename yet?"

"PUZZLE BOX, sir," Stoyer said.

"Admiral," Adams continued, "are you confident enough in PUZZLE BOX to risk the lives of the men and women under your command?"

Holland also knew the truth behind the "disaster" in Nagoya. "Yes, Mr. President," he said after a moment's reflection. "PUZZLE BOX is a completely different operation from HEADSHOT. I believe it will work as advertised."

Stoyer felt Hale's eyes boring through him. He didn't make eye contact. There was only one opinion in this room that counted, and it wasn't hers. His eyes remained fixed on the President.

"General Stoyer," Adams said after a long silence, "if you can pull this one off, you're back on my Christmas card list."

Stoyer had never been off the President's list, but the performance was required. "Nothing would give me greater pleasure, sir."

LAND MINES

Broadman answered Hawthorne's summons immediately but wondered what he was going to tell Janet Randall upon his return. It was well after lunch, so the only excuse he had for leaving the office before press time was to meet with a source. He hoped Hawthorne could give him something for a story in addition to their Resistance business.

Broadman had not seen Eric the Viking, as he had nicknamed him, all day. He wondered if the Resistance had meant what they said about watching his back. But when he crossed the street, he saw a rusty brown van pull into a parking space half a block away. So Eric *was* watching. Whether he was watching Broadman's back remained to be seen.

The quality of the deli assured that business was brisk even at an off hour, but Hawthorne had found a table with some privacy. He was already seated, working on a bowl of soup. Broadman bought a soft drink and joined him. Hawthorne was noticeably ashen, and the hand holding his spoon shook slightly.

"Whoa, Ben! You look like you saw a ghost!"

Hawthorne swallowed another spoonful before answering. "Not a ghost, Tony. A spook. Three of them."

Broadman made sure there was no one in earshot. "Okay, I'll bite. What happened?"

Hawthorne recounted his hacking of the NCIC database, and the security response that resulted. "They were definitely military intelligence of some kind," he explained. "They looked downright uncomfortable in civilian clothes. And they had been watching Ken Yoshida's file like a hawk. Got there in less than an hour after I hit their firewall. If I hadn't been able to convince them it was an outside hacker attack, I might not be here right now."

Now it was Broadman's chance to turn pale. "I guess that shows how important Ken Yoshida is to them."

Hawthorne worked the soup around in his mouth, like he was trying to wash out a bad taste. "Yeah, but it also rules out legitimate law enforcement. Whatever took Ken was something dirty, something secret, and probably something military. What did *you* find out?"

"That Ken was just the latest in a long string of hackers who went missing under similar circumstances."

Hawthorne's eyes rose. "How similar?"

"All of them had been trying to hack into the NSA when they vanished. And the circumstances surrounding their disappearances mirrored Ken's pretty closely. The MO of the guys who do the abductions is fairly consistent. Almost military precision, if you know what I mean."

Hawthorne set down his spoon. "Yeah, that makes sense. Electronic security *is* the NSA's mission. So they've taken it upon themselves to rid the world of hackers. Sweet. The only question is whether they imprison them or dump their bodies in a river."

Broadman told Hawthorne about Pittman's message to his sister. "If the note was authentic, then they're alive. The NSA might even release them, eventually."

Hawthorne finished his soup with difficulty. "Yeah, right. And Santa Claus eats the milk and cookies my kids leave out for him every Christmas."

"But wouldn't the FBI hear about it if the NSA was making dozens of people disappear all over the country? That's got to show up on somebody's radar."

"These aren't missing *persons*, Tony. They're missing *hackers*. There's a difference. When a six-year-old goes missing, people care. But a hacker? The only good thing these guys ever did was stop people from wasting their money on eBay for a few hours. To the FBI, it's kind of like the disappearance of your mother-in-law. If you're smart, you don't ask too many questions."

Broadman worked up a wry smile. "Benjamin Hawthorne, cynic. Never thought I'd see the day. So what's next?"

Hawthorne compressed his trash into a ball. "We have enough information for me to make a report. After that, we'll see what the boss wants to do."

"It doesn't feel like I've done much. Certainly not enough to get Ken back."

Hawthorne's color and composure were returning. "You found out who took Ken and why. That's all we asked. Getting him out isn't your job. And unlike yours truly, you didn't set off any land mines in the process. You did fine."

Broadman checked his watch. He had less than an hour until deadline, and the story back at his desk wasn't finished. Iron Jan was going to skin him alive. "Ben, I need a favor. Have you heard any juicy computer-related stories at the Bureau lately?"

"Ever heard of NCIC 2000?"

"Your new criminal database program? Sure."

"It has some features they'd rather the public never find out about. Let's take a walk."

Maybe Iron Jan wouldn't be displaying his hide after all. "Thanks, buddy. I owe you one."

UPLINK

If releasing Friedman and giving the hackers the day off had been designed as a morale builder, it worked. The mood had lightened considerably in the Snake Pit, with friendly banter being the rule rather than the exception. It was noticeably quieter without Derek Friedman's cutting humor, but his influence lingered. "I wonder what Derek is doing now" was the Taylor twins' favorite topic of conversation. The normally-silent Paul Malechek openly debated what he would do when his own sentence expired.

Pittman didn't join in. He had persisted in an ambivalent funk, which deepened each day. Yoshida had tried to joke with him, but was rebuffed. Yoshida assumed Pittman was in mourning after enjoying alcohol and then having it denied again. And their idleness wasn't doing anything but allowing Pittman to fixate on his problems.

Yoshida was relieved when the Snake Pit received another assignment. China was stirring up trouble with Taiwan. The hackers were now probing for weaknesses in any Chinese network with a military connection. The prisoners worked with new-found enthusiasm, hoping exemplary work would earn their own early release.

But Pittman and Yoshida were assigned to a different task. Richter gave them their briefing personally, explaining that they would be hacking into a Chinese satellite called the *Lianhua* and preventing it from guiding Chinese cruise missiles toward the approaching American fleet. At least they wouldn't be killing anyone on this assignment. They might even be saving American lives. It made Yoshida feel better, anyway.

The mission seemed to lift Pittman's spirits as well. He could hardly wait for the *Lianhua* to pass over the US so he could probe its inner workings. Soon he was picking through the satellite's control menus with ease.

"Damn, you're fast!" Yoshida observed.

"The *Lianhua* was one of my first assignments here in the Snake Pit," Pittman said. "I had no idea we'd ever go operational with it. Lucky for us they used a Chinese translation of an American satellite control program, or we'd be screwed. I just hacked their missile control subroutine and added it to the American software."

"But how do we control the satellite when it's over China?"

"We must have a satellite dish in the area," Pittman explained. "They just don't want to risk giving away its position until they have to. It's probably on Taiwan or on a ship. But if our uplink transmitter has more power than theirs, their satellite will ignore the Chinese signal and do anything we ask it to."

Yoshida could see Richter scurrying about, talking with the watchers on the upper level. They were definitely getting ready for action of some kind.

Pittman opened a window on his computer and began entering code as fast as he could type.

"Pittman, what are you doing?" Yoshida whispered.

"Now that I know the plan, I'm making an enhancement to the missile destruct code. I know a lot more tricks than I did then. I'm just making sure it works."

Yoshida tried to follow Pittman's entries, but he was unfamiliar with the program. He decided just to watch and learn.

Twenty minutes later Richter leaned over the rail. "Headsets, gentlemen! Signal coming in."

Pittman and Yoshida donned the Telex headsets they were given. Yoshida flexed the thin boom mike, positioning it in front of his mouth. Soon a message box popped up on their screens. "It's a tasking order," Pittman announced. "The ground station is asking for a series of images."

Richter's voice crackled over their headsets. "What are those numbers following the latitude and longitude?"

"Zoom factor and spectrum frequency," Pittman answered. "Looks like wide angle shots in the infrared band."

"That's ocean surveillance," Richter concluded.

Soon images were feeding onto their screens. Other than the coast of Taiwan, the images of the ocean were meaningless to Yoshida. Just clusters of various-sized white dots. Richter used his link with their screens to draw a red circle around one group. "See that?" he asked. "That's the Chinese fleet."

He snapped a latitude and longitude grid on another image and drew a large red wedge. "That's where they've told us not to go because of their missile shots." He drew a red circle around another group of white dots in the upper-right corner. "That's our fleet, headed straight for the impact zone."

"Meaning what?" Yoshida asked.

"Meaning things are about to get very interesting," Richter said.

FINAL REPORT

Patrick placed his cell phone in secure mode. "How are the Yankees doing?"

"I prefer the Mets," Hawthorne replied.

"What's up?"

"Tony just gave me his final report."

"That was fast."

"It doesn't take long to hit a brick wall," Hawthorne admitted. "Short version--Ken wasn't the only one to go missing. Several other men in his line of work disappeared under very similar circumstances. What little evidence there is points to a large bureaucracy outside of Baltimore. Digging any further would involve significant risk."

Hawthorne explained in generic terms his run-in with the NSA security types. "I'm open to suggestions on our next move."

Patrick noted how carefully Hawthorne guarded his words, even on a scrambled line. He had been trained well. So was the National Security Agency making hackers disappear? He pictured Ken Yoshida with a bullet in his head, but pushed the image away. The government usually left the body behind when they killed someone, with the cause of death easily labeled as suicide or accident. A disappearance meant Yoshida was probably being held somewhere, alive. And Patrick would die before he left one of his own behind.

"I have some ideas on where to go next," Patrick answered. "Let me make some phone calls." He thought for a moment. "In the meantime, I want you to prep Tony for a trip to see Liberty."

There was a moment of stunned silence. "Sir," Hawthorne replied, "with all due respect, do you really think he's a suitable candidate for Liberty?"

He chuckled. "I didn't say we were going to let him *join* Liberty, I said we're going to *show* it to him."

"But sir, what about *security?*"

Patrick's voice remained friendly, but firm. "Let *me* worry about the security angle, Ben."

Hawthorne knew an order when he heard one. "Yes, sir! Did you have a time in mind for the trip?"

"Immediately. Trust me on this one, Ben. I have a plan."

"Then I'll make the arrangements."

TRACKING

Jeff Archer hated these kinds of crises. He was trying to split his very finite number of Mandarin Chinese-speaking translators among the infinite number of tasking requests coming in from the Taiwan theater. His doctorate in math would be of no help with this problem. It was almost a relief when his private line rang.

"Archer."

The voice on the other end was hesitant. "Uh, Mr. Archer? This is Steve Watson, from, ah, the ECHELON desk?"

"Oh yes, Steve, I remember. What can I do for you?"

"Well, uh, sir, are you familiar with the Hacker Tracking Project?"

Archer closed his eyes. One of his mental skills was the ability to pull up any NSA organizational chart on demand. "HTP? That's Amanda Tonini's project, isn't it?"

"Yes, sir. She's figured out how to tag an intruder with an ID number they can't erase. We can use the ID tag to follow the hacker all the way back to their home computer. It's pretty cool."

"But?"

"Well, sir, last night I was helping her track a hacker back to his home in Fresno. I asked her how long it would be until the FBI was busting down this guy's door. She said they just pass their findings off to a guy in Security named Colonel Richter. He takes it from there."

Well, isn't that *interesting.* "Colonel Richter, huh? She didn't have any idea which law enforcement agency Richter would contact?"

"No, sir, but she said the hackers usually dropped off her screens after that point. Since you had asked about Colonel Richter I thought you'd want to know. I hope I haven't bothered you, sir."

"Absolutely not! This is good information. You keep that ear to the ground, okay?"

Watson's confidence buoyed. "Will do, Mr. Archer!"

KILL BOX

General Stoyer had a spring in his step on his way to the NICC. DATASHARK was finally going to be used as he had originally envisioned, to grab an enemy by the jaws and yank out their fangs. And he was the man holding the pliers. It just didn't get any better than this.

The Marine guard standing watch inside the NICC snapped to attention. "Ten-hut!" he shouted.

Stoyer signaled for Archer to follow him up to the balcony. "Report!"

Jeff Archer wore a harried expression. Stoyer's concerns for security were such that he had only brought his deputy in on PUZZLE BOX a few hours ago. Archer could handle it even on short notice, Stoyer had concluded.

"All units are in place, General. I think."

Stoyer took his seat in the command chair. "I'm sure you have everything well in hand, Jeff. Admiral Holland?"

"His limousine just entered the main gate."

"Very good. Cheer up, Jeff. This should be a very eventful evening for the NSA." Especially with the Chairman of the Joint Chiefs here to watch.

"If you don't mind, sir, I'll leave the champagne corked for the moment. A lot of things have to work together just right to pull this off."

Stoyer was in an expansive mood. "That's why I put you in charge, Jeff."

"Thank you, sir," Archer said, without much enthusiasm.

A few minutes later the Marine guard escorted Holland up to the balcony. "Admiral on deck!" he announced.

After saluting, Stoyer joined Admiral Holland at the windows. Holland gawked at the high-tech wizardry below.

"Damn, John!" Holland breathed. "You get all the best toys! I always thought Momma liked you best!"

Stoyer motioned to the command chair. "Was there any doubt, sir? Please, Admiral, have a seat."

Holland shrank back from the button-festooned throne. "No thanks, John. I was never any good at video games. You drive." He took a slightly lower chair at Stoyer's side.

Stoyer restrained himself from smiling. He didn't like the idea of someone else sitting in his chair, even if it was the

Chairman of the Joint Chiefs. "Very well, Admiral. Let me show you why I enjoy my job so much."

Stoyer deftly spun the trackball on the chair arm, highlighting the symbols on the main display screen in sequence. The map was centered on the Taiwan Straits. "Most of this data comes from the Lacrosse radar satellites," he explained. "It can spot anything that moves on the ocean, so the Chinese fleet has nowhere to hide. We get a pass every few hours, and this was just updated fifteen minutes ago."

Stoyer circled the Chinese Fleet, which was hugging the line dividing the Chinese and Taiwanese sides of the strait. "Normally the Chinese stay well away from this boundary, especially with a fleet this large. It just makes the chance of an accidental conflict greater. The Chinese are *looking* for trouble."

"They're sure as hell going to find it," Holland predicted. "What's the makeup of that task force?"

The Chinese formation resembled a thick red arrow, with their largest ships forming the head. Two lines of frigates formed the shaft, and a cluster of amphibious assault ships filled the protected center. Stoyer placed a crosshair on the arrow's tip. "Their two *Sovremenny* cruisers are leading the pack, with three destroyers on each flank. There are six frigates on each side of their amphibious group, which numbers about thirty ships."

"Some of those frigates carry French anti-submarine helos," Holland remarked. "They were also refitted with French electronics and Crotale SAMs. Nothing you'd want to turn your back on, that's for sure. Any idea how many troops are in that amphib group?"

When Stoyer paused, Archer held up a classified folder. "General, the analysis you requested just arrived. The CIA estimates those ships are carrying about 2,400 troops, plus tanks and artillery."

Bless you, Jeff! Stoyer had requested no such analysis. Archer was thinking ahead of him.

"That's equivalent to a Marine Amphibious Unit," Holland offered. "Plenty big enough to take and hold a small island. Intentions?"

Stoyer highlighted a small island group to Taiwan's north. "They might be able to take Matsu, but why come so far out? I would keep that fleet close to the coast and under ground-based air cover."

"It's a shit-disturbing operation," Holland concluded. "The People's Republic wants to show the Republic of China what they can do."

A mass of green symbols swarmed like angry hornets off Taiwan's west coast. "If they meant to get Taiwan's attention, they succeeded," Stoyer said. "The ROC has every ship in their navy working the fence. Ten destroyers, twenty frigates, and a Hawkeye radar bird on continuous station. The PRC Navy won't be able to throw their trash overboard without the Taiwanese knowing about it."

"And our ships?"

Four blue submarine symbols moved slowly east, away from the demarcation line. "These LA-class subs are closest to the action. We didn't think the PRC navy would rush the border like this. And they're pounding away with their active sonars in every direction. Our guys had to retreat under Taiwan's picket ships, but they have an instant firing solution on every escort in the Chinese task force."

"Let's hope it doesn't come to that. Surface ships?"

Stoyer zoomed out the map to show the missile test areas. "The *Vinson* task force entered the eastern zone about an hour ago. The AEGIS group cut across the northern zone at about the same time. They'll be through the test area and join up with the Taiwanese navy in about four hours."

"How much warning will we have if the Chinese decide to cut loose with a missile?"

Stoyer highlighted five rocket symbols on the Chinese coast. A yellow circle overlaid all of them. "These are their known XH-1 launch sites. We have a DSP missile warning satellite staring down on them continuously. We'll be able to spot the launch plume and give an almost instant warning to every ship in the area."

An orange symbol designated "LHST" was moving at high speed toward Taiwan. "What's that one?" Holland demanded.

"That's the *Lianhua* satellite and the *Sky Trash* shadow. They made a pass about three hours ago, just before our ships entered the danger zones."

Archer's head came up while Stoyer was talking. Data scrolled down one of the smaller display screens. "*Sky Trash* reports the *Lianhua* has just been given a surveillance tasking order," he said to the flag officers.

* * *

The hackers in the Snake Pit were locked in a battle with their Communist Chinese counterparts. The previous year, Taiwan had suffered an island-wide electrical blackout after an anti-reunification vote in its congress. The blackout was strongly suspected of being a Chinese infowar attack. The PRC was now staging a repeat performance.

ECHELON had detected several feelers reaching out from the Communist side of the straits, and the hackers were busy trying to block their efforts. But instead of defensive measures, DATASHARK was taking the fight to the enemy, assaulting the "Great Firewall of China."

Once a feeler was traced back to its origin, the Snake Pit unleashed every tool at its disposal, overloading satellite links, crashing communications nodes, and cutting electrical power to the servers the Chinese infowarriors were using. If the feelers could not be localized closer than a city, its entire power grid was shut down.

The hackers in the Snake Pit were also locked in an internal contest, each trying to outdo the others with the speed and ferocity of his attacks. Yoshida saw the bravado resurface that the hackers had exhibited when free.

"This is like hunting moles with a bazooka!" Paul Malechek exclaimed.

"More moles!" the Taylor twins chanted. "Give us more moles!"

Yoshida and Pittman were not allowed to participate in the digital combat. They sat waiting for the Chinese to make a different kind of move. Yoshida returned from the bathroom to find Pittman surfing a hacker tools web page, one of the few Internet sites the Snake Pit hackers were allowed to visit.

"Hell of a time to be surfing the net, Bob," Yoshida needled.

Pittman quickly closed the window. "Just checking for a program that might be helpful."

"I thought you had this Chinese satellite all figured out."

Pittman tapped his headset. "Richter says there's a signal coming in. Let's get to work."

* * *

Holland and Stoyer watched the stolen images from the *Lianhua* fill the display screen. Holland could see the distinctive constellation of the American carrier group even without Stoyer's help. He could guess the smaller formation to Taiwan's north was the cruiser phalanx. Archer snapped on the test zone grid. Both squadrons were well inside the threatened areas.

"Predictions, General?" Holland asked.

"If I were them," Stoyer said, "I'd put a missile or two in the water right ahead of both task forces. Not close enough to risk a response, but close enough to show that they know where we are and they could hit us if they wanted to."

Holland's face showed the weight of the lives that hung on this gamble. "We'll find out soon enough. They know we're in the kill box."

CHAPTER 10

"The public has a duty to watch its Government closely and keep it on the right track."
-Lieutenant General Kenneth A. Minihan, USAF
Director, National Security Agency, 1996-1999

SURPRISES

Tony Broadman felt like celebrating. He had completed his assignment for the Resistance. As far as Ken Yoshida's fate was concerned, he had done his part. Hawthorne had assured him that rescuing Yoshida wasn't his job. His chance at writing a book about the MINTNET story had vanished along with Yoshida, but *he* would live to write another day. After hearing about Hawthorne's close call, Broadman decided that was accomplishment enough.

Broadman hoped he would hear nothing more from the Resistance. Let Hawthorne take on the world of rogue agencies and hidden agendas. Broadman would be content to live out his days quietly as the Gadget Guy, his dreams of investigating government corruption relegated to the list of dangerous hobbies he had decided to forego like rock climbing and bungee jumping.

While Christina was in the shower, Broadman got things ready outside. He lit several Citronella candles on the deck to keep the bugs at bay, then lit a few scented candles by the hot tub. He poured two glasses of wine and set them by the towels. He loaded one of Christina's favorite CDs in the boom box and set it by the tub as well. He flicked off the motion light over the deck and left a note on the kitchen table for her to join him.

Anticipation had him more than ready by the time the back door cracked open. Christina had exchanged her worn but comfortable purple terry cloth bathrobe for the short, sheer wrap he had given her on their honeymoon. The white satin shimmered in the moonlight as she came to him, her cat-like steps slow and teasing. His readiness grew more insistent.

Stopping just out of his reach, she hugged the robe close to her body, swaying sensuously to the saxophone lilting softly from the boom box. The candlelight flickered off her shapely leg muscles as they flexed for his benefit. Facing away from him, she stood on her toes and worked her hips in a circle, the round firmness of her bottom peeking out from under the taut satin. Broadman resisted the temptation to stroke himself as she gyrated. "You're gonna get raped if you keep that up," he warned.

"Promises, promises," she said. Continuing her dance, she eased the sheath off her shoulders, slipping it lower at a maddeningly slow rate. When the white fabric finally fluttered to the deck at her feet, she stepped into the water and slid into his arms in one smooth motion. Her kisses were hot and passionate as she moved over him, wrapping her legs around his waist, pulling him closer.

His lips delighted in the slick softness of her breasts as she raised up, guiding him inside. Their lovemaking had always been delicious, but tonight was something special, the relief at his escape from danger mixed with their passionate joining to create a third life, a blending of themselves. It was a rapture Broadman had never experienced.

They had just begun making love in earnest when a bright light stabbed over them from the side. Broadman had turned off the motion-triggered light over the deck, but the one beside house was still on. A man stood at the back corner of the house, caught in harsh silhouette by the quartz lamps.

Christina screamed, pulling away from him and submerging to her chin in the sheltering swirl of the hot tub. She let out a shriek she hoped would be loud enough to carry to their neighbors.

Broadman rose up slightly, preparing to jump from the tub if necessary to defend himself. When he did, he saw the New York State Highway Patrolman's uniform.

"Sorry to interrupt," the patrolman said, without the slightest tinge of embarrassment. "There was no answer at the front door, and this is kind of urgent. Can we talk, Tony?"

It was Eric.

Broadman wasn't in a position to offer much protest. "You have a hell of a sense of timing, do you know that?"

"I'll wait out front," Eric said, a trace of amusement creeping into his voice.

After Broadman explained to Christina that Eric was a member of the Resistance, she wrapped herself in a towel and dashed inside. Broadman sat in the tub for another minute or two, contemplating how quickly his celebration had turned sour and why Eric would be showing up on his doorstep again. He couldn't think of any reason that wasn't bad news.

Once he had recovered enough to dash inside, he was greeted with the unmistakable *shuck-shuck* of their twelve-gauge shotgun from the bedroom. *"Tony?"* a frightened and angry voice called.

"It's me, honey," he said. "Eric's still outside."

"Lock the doors and leave him there!" she shouted.

Broadman knew he couldn't do that. He wrapped himself in a bathrobe and went to the front. He took a deep breath and unlocked the door.

"Good news," Eric announced. "The boss was impressed with your report." He gave no explanation for his uniform, as if Broadman had known his true position all along.

So for that you come and interrupt us in the middle of making love. Lucky me. "Other than the fact that Ken wasn't the only hacker to go missing, I didn't find jack," Broadman retorted. "What was it your boss liked?"

"You may have confirmed something he was already suspecting. Whatever it was, he has something he wants to show you."

All Broadman wanted to see was Eric gone and his wife back in the hot tub. "What is it?"

"Pack an overnight bag and you'll find out. He's asked to meet with you immediately."

For the first time, Broadman's heart started thumping from something other than surprise or anger. "One question."

"Okay."

"Will I be allowed to write about it?"

"I think that's my boss's intention, yeah." What he thought of that idea was evident in his tone.

Broadman's ears twitched at the story that might be waiting. "Back in five."

Christina did not take the news well. Pulling on the sweats she wore for her women's self-defense class, she charged the front door like a tigress protecting her cubs. "Listen to me!" she snapped at Eric. "What gives you the *right* to barge in here unannounced, snatch up my husband, and whisk him off to God knows where? I don't even *know* you!"

Eric put his hands on his pistol belt, speaking with a practiced voice of command. "That's right, you don't. And that's just as much for your protection as it is for mine." He paused for effect. "My boss wants to speak to your husband, *now*. I can either take Tony to him, or he can come *here*. But my boss will be in a lot better mood if we do things my way, and you've just found out that our visits can come as something of a surprise. But if you *insist* on another late-night visit, I can arrange it."

Christina looked over her shoulder for back-up, but Broadman was already in the bedroom packing his bag.

Eric waited outside in his van. He had used the interval to change into civilian clothes. He slid open the van's side door. "Look familiar?"

"Can't say it's a pleasant memory."

"Don't worry, no interrogations tonight. Have a cell phone or pager with you?"

"No."

"Good. They can give away your position, even if you're not using them. You knew that, didn't you?"

"Yep."

Eric waved him into the back of the van. There was a piece of cardboard taped over the rear compartment's only window. "Have a seat. You brought something to read, didn't you?"

Broadman patted his bag. "Always."

"Then keep your nose in it. Not knowing our destination is as much for your protection as ours. We'll be on the road most of the night. If I catch you trying to look outside I'll have to blindfold you, and that'll make the trip much longer for you."

"Understood."

Eric slid the side door shut.

ROLL CALL

Stoyer's enthusiasm grew along with the tension in the command center. Victory was in the air. He could smell it. "It won't be long now," he declared. "Jeff, call the roll."

Archer pressed several buttons on his console. "This is Archer-NSA at the National Information Command Center.

Intelligence reports a Chinese missile launch may be imminent. All PUZZLE BOX units report status."

"This is the Missile Warning Center at Cheyenne Mountain," a woman's voice said over the speaker. "Space Command reports DSP satellites in position and nominal."

"This is NSA Quemoy station," the next voice said. "Satellite uplink is online and nominal."

"This is Admiral Meacham on the *Bunker Hill*. All ships are armed and ready for air action. I'll pass the warning on to the subs."

"This is Colonel Richter for DATASHARK. All systems are manned and online."

Stoyer noticed Archer startle for some reason at the mention of Richter's name, but he didn't have time to dwell on it.

Holland retrieved the headset hanging from the arm of his chair. He spoke into the mike without donning the headphones. "All right people, this is Admiral Holland at the NICC. All of you are professionals, so I know you give your best every day. But lives are at stake on this one. Those of you not in harm's way, remember the men and women who are. They're counting on you not to let them down. Holland out!"

"Well said, Admiral," Stoyer observed.

Holland ignored the flattery. "What now?"

"Now we wait. And see if the Chinese have the brass to show us their guns."

* * *

Pittman was poring over the latest images from the *Lianhua*, zooming in on the individual ship formations.

"What's up?" Yoshida asked.

Pittman zoomed the image further. "I'm trying to see just how good their resolution is." The white dots enlarged into elongated blobs. "See? You can't make out any detail, but you can tell the big ships from the little ones."

"Is that important?"

Pittman placed his cursor over one. "It is if you're targeting. Watch." He clicked on the lead ship in the Chinese formation. A set of coordinates appeared. "Now you have the exact location of that ship." He repeated the process for several other ships in the Chinese task force. "See how easy it is? They could do the same thing to us."

Richter's voice cut in on their headphones. "Pittman, what are you doing?"

"I'm demonstrating the targeting software to Yoshida, sir. You said to bring him up to speed as quick as possible."

"Well, quit jacking around. We could get a missile warning any second."

Pittman closed the targeting menu. "Yes, sir, standing by."

Yoshida covered his mike. "Think they'll shoot?"

"If they're going to do it, it'll be soon. They won't let this targeting info get cold."

BEST LAID PLANS

The Defense Support Program satellites were relics of the Cold War, designed to provide early warning of Soviet ICBM launches. Parked in geosynchronous orbit, the DSP satellites stared down with sensitive infrared sensors, waiting for the first flash that accompanied a missile launch. During the first Gulf War, the DSPs provided early warning of Scud missile launches by Iraq. Their sensitivity was such that fighters in afterburners could be tracked from 22,300 miles above.

Four XH-1 missiles were launched in unison, two each targeted at the northern and eastern missile test zones. Solid rockets blasted the missiles skyward and to supersonic speeds, where the missiles' ramjet engines ignited. The robot aircraft leveled out at 10,000 feet and began their short cruise toward their targets.

The DSP satellites detected the launches and passed the alert to Space Command headquarters inside Cheyenne Mountain. The warning was on its way to NSA headquarters a few seconds later.

* * *

Even though it was expected, the alert startled like a gunshot inside the National Information Command Center.

"This is Space Command with a missile warning!" the woman's strident voice announced. "Four, repeat, four missile launches have been detected by DSP satellites. Analysis confirms XH-1 signature."

"DATASHARK, acknowledge!" Stoyer ordered.

"Acknowledged, sending destruct codes now," Richter confirmed.

* * *

With nothing to do but watch an empty screen, Yoshida slouched at his terminal and fought drowsiness. He envied the other hackers, who at least had a real enemy to fight. Richter's voice in his headset jolted him awake.

"Pittman! Four missiles have been launched! Send the destruct code!"

"Standby," was Pittman's cool response.

"Standby for *what?*"

"I'm still waiting for missile telemetry."

"Those missiles are *airborne*, Pittman! How long is this going to take?"

"I can't send a destruct code until the *Lianhua* receives telemetry from those missiles," Pittman said. "It doesn't even know they exist yet. Okay, there they are."

Four yellow crosses appeared off the Chinese coast on their displays. Yoshida watched Pittman highlight the crosses, then pull down a menu option which read "MISSILE ABORT." Pittman picked it. A warning box popped up on the screen: CONFIRM MISSILE ABORT!

Pittman confirmed the order. The crosses turned from yellow to orange. "Destruct code sent!"

* * *

"Destruct code has been transmitted!" Richter reported.

Stoyer took a deep breath. "Space Command, can you confirm missile detonation?"

There were several seconds of chilled silence. "Negative, DATASHARK," Space Command finally replied. "DSP reports missiles continuing, same speed and heading."

Stoyer gripped the arms of his chair. "DATASHARK, resend the destruct code, *now!*"

* * *

Richter passed the order to the Snake Pit. "Pittman! It didn't work! Resend the destruct code!"

Pittman picked the missiles and selected "MISSILE ABORT." A warning box popped up:
ERROR 404: ABORT ALREADY SELECTED!
COMMAND REJECTED!
"It's says they've already aborted!"
"They have *not* aborted!" Richter insisted. "Resend the code!"
Pittman tried to pick the missiles again, but nothing happened. They refused even to be selected by the mouse. "I'm locked out! They must be overriding our signal!"
"*What?* I thought you had that satellite under control!"
Pittman was sweating now. "I did! They must have detected us!"
"You're the hacker, dammit! Get it back!"
"Yes, sir, I'll try!"
Yoshida watched in horror as Pittman tried to modify his program on the fly. He was wiping out whole sections of code, trying to find the commands that had wrested control from him.
"Talk to me, Bob," Yoshida pleaded. "What are we looking for?"
"Back off! I'll fix it!"
Yoshida was forced to sit back and watch. The orange crosses marched eastward toward their targets.

* * *

"Sir, something went wrong!" Richter stammered. "DATASHARK no longer has control over the missiles!"
Stoyer felt a moment of free fall, as if the balcony had given way underneath him. "Don't tell me that, Carl!"
Holland snatched up his headset. "*Bunker Hill*, this is Holland! You have missiles inbound, repeat missiles inbound! Acknowledge!"
"This is *Bunker Hill*," came the calm reply. "Missile warning acknowledged."

* * *

Admiral Meacham was seated in the Combat Information Center aboard the cruiser *Bunker Hill*. "Look sharp, people! We're about to have uninvited guests! Report combat status!"
"Radar is up, no new contacts!"

"Sonar is up, no submerged contacts!"

"Signals are up, no new contacts!"

"Comms are up, datalink is nominal!"

"Weapons are up, one hundred twenty-two SAMS ready for launch!"

"Bridge reports deck secure for weapons launch!"

"Very good," Meacham acknowledged. He waited for the Chinese missiles to appear on the "video game" display at the front of the CIC. Radar information from all six ships in his formation were datalinked together on his screen. The data from the Taiwanese Hawkeye radar plane and a few newer ships in the Taiwanese fleet were also shown.

Meacham allowed himself a satisfied smirk. Privately, he had placed little faith in the NSA's "hex the missiles" plan. Besides, it was rare enough that an AEGIS ship got to engage a real threat with real missiles. Nothing was going to slip past his net, even if it was going supersonic. It didn't take long.

"Radar contact! Missiles inbound!" the technician shouted.

"Weapons?" Meacham asked.

"Unable to engage!" the weapons officer reported. "Current track will take all missiles well south."

"What? They're not shooting at *us?*"

"No, sir," the radar technician affirmed. "The missiles appear to be heading for the Taiwanese fleet."

"Comms!" Meacham ordered. "Make sure they get that warning!" *Sail a hard target into the crosshairs and they decide to shoot at someone else*, Meacham brooded.

"Their flagship just acknowledged," the communications technician reported.

"Course change!" Radar said. "Missiles are nosing over!"

"Their seekers are going active!" Signals warned.

"Are they coming down on the Taiwanese?" Meacham asked.

"Negative, sir!" Radar said. "They're going down on the Chinese side of the strait. Confirm terminal dive on all missiles. Okay, that's it. They've dropped below the horizon."

"The Hawkeye confirms missile splashdowns," Comms relayed a few seconds later. "No friendlies hit."

Meacham took a deep breath and let it out slowly. "Thank God." He punched the button that connected him with the NICC.

* * *

"This is the *Bunker Hill*," the voice said over the speaker in the NICC. "The Chinese missiles went into the water well clear of our forces. Give your team a pat on the back for me, General!"

Relief and confusion wrestled in Stoyer's head. "The missiles weren't supposed to splash down, Admiral. They were supposed to *blow up!*"

Meacham sounded neither surprised nor disappointed. "Either way, General, they didn't hurt anybody, so I'm not choosy."

Before Stoyer could respond, another voice broke in.

"This is Space Command. DSP reports multiple fires and secondary explosions in the XH-1 impact zone. NICC, are you sure that area was clear?"

* * *

"Wow!" the *Bunker Hill* sonar operator exclaimed. "Those missiles must have packed a hell of a warhead! They landed over sixty miles away and I'm still picking up echoes!"

"The shock waves must be bouncing against the coastline," Meacham theorized. An alarm bell inside his head told him that wasn't the correct answer.

"Admiral!" Comms said. "I just received a priority message from the *Tucson*. They report secondary explosions and break-up noises from the vicinity of the Chinese fleet. They request permission to investigate."

Meacham compared the position of the submarine *Tucson* to the impact area of the XH-1 missiles. He shook his head in disbelief. "They couldn't have been *that* stupid, could they?"

The radar operator interrupted his contemplation.

"Radar contacts!" he shouted. "*Multiple* missiles in the air bearing two-two-zero!"

* * *

Barely after reaching their cruise altitudes, the XH-1 missiles received the command to descend and begin looking for targets. A ship was waiting for each of them, right where the command signal said they should be. The missiles continued until they were directly over their targets, then dove vertically, to maximize their impact velocity.

The two *Sovremenny*-class cruisers leading the Chinese formation each took a missile. The first cruiser took the hit in the forward magazine and disappeared in an enormous fireball. The second took the missile straight down the funnel. The missile passed completely through the hull, detonating under the keel. The massive warship was lifted from the water, snapping in two like a piece of driftwood. The forward half, top-heavy with weapons and sensors, rolled over and sank immediately. The aft section of the cruiser remained upright, to burn and sink independently.

The two *Luda*-class destroyers flanking the cruisers suffered similar fates, each taking a missile. Half of the Chinese squadron's spearhead, its flag officers, and most of its firepower was wiped from the sea in less than a minute.

The Chinese formation was in crisis. They were already on edge after being ordered to sail so close to the provoked rebel fleet. Then they received a notice that the Coastal Defense Force would soon be taking action to keep the American imperialist navy at bay.

Suddenly their lead ships disappeared in a series of thunderous explosions. They were under attack. There had been no warning, but there was only one enemy close enough to cause such destruction. The senior surviving officer, a destroyer skipper, ordered the formation to turn east and fire on Taiwan's navy with every available weapon.

* * *

The Taiwanese Hawkeye warned the fleet that thirty-six HY-2 missiles were airborne. Roughly equivalent to the American Harpoon missile, the HY-2 was subsonic. But the forty-mile separation between the Chinese and Taiwanese fleets would be covered in just over four minutes.

The lead air defense ship for the Taiwanese navy was the *Tien Tan*, a Japanese hull design with the American AEGIS radar system. Instead of the standard twin rail naval SAM launcher, the *Tien Tan* used the Vertical Launch System, with its forty-eight SAMs clustered in silos just forward of the bridge. Like an enormous Roman candle, the *Tien Tan* ripple-fired eighteen of its SAMs, the maximum number the AEGIS radar could control simultaneously.

Trailing thick columns of white smoke, each Standard missile tipped smartly toward the horizon and accelerated to two and a half times the speed of sound, seeking a target. When a Standard found its mark, another was launched to take its place. The *Tien Tan* was striking over half its targets, but time and distance were working against them. Twelve Chinese missiles would still reach the Taiwanese fleet.

The second line of defense for the Taiwanese navy was six *Kang Ding* frigates. Based on the futuristic French *LaFayette* design, the ships carried modern electronics and Crotale SAMs. The *Kang Dings* heeled sharply to face the threats, loosing fusillades of SAMs from the Crotale's eight-tube launcher at the "leakers." Although short-ranged, the Crotales traveled at Mach 3.5, turning the airspace around the *Kang Dings* into a combination fireworks show and skeet shoot.

The Chinese missiles were fired "in the blind," lobbed in the direction of Taiwan without specific targets. At a preset distance, the HY-2 missiles activated their radars and veered toward the largest ship in view. The more modern Taiwanese ships automatically fired off chaff and electronic countermeasures to spoof the incoming missiles. But this served only to deflect the weapons toward the fleet's older ships. Of the three remaining HY-2s, one went wild and fell into the sea. The last two anti-ship missiles each found an elderly *Knox*-class frigate, handed down from the US in the 1970s.

The first frigate took a missile in the superstructure, killing the captain and the bridge crew. The second was hit amidships, knocking out the engines. Both frigates burned furiously, and would require assistance from the fleet if they were to be saved.

* * *

Admiral Meacham swore. He was a helpless spectator in this deadly drama, his squadron too far away to help the Taiwanese navy. The casualties could have been far worse, but an ally's blood had just been shed, in an unprovoked attack.

"Signal from the Hawkeye, sir," Comms reported. "The Chinese fleet is turning hard about."

"Are they retreating?"

The Weapons officer shook his head. "Repositioning, sir. Their missile launchers fire salvos abeam in opposite directions. They could be turning to hit the Taiwanese again."

Meacham's jaw flexed. There wasn't time to pass the problem up the chain of command. He guessed the Taiwanese had fired most of their SAMs blunting the first wave. The second wave would be far more deadly.

"Comms!" Meacham ordered. "Dial up the subs!"

* * *

General Stoyer had the same data as Admiral Meacham, but still couldn't comprehend the failure of his plan. As a naval officer, Holland had a better grasp of the tactical situation, but he mostly cursed under his breath. Meacham was just a spoken command away, but Holland knew better than to interfere with the commander on the scene.

"Sirs?" Archer said. "Signals reports the *Bunker Hill* is transmitting an ELF message."

"ELF?" Stoyer asked.

"Extremely Low Frequency," Holland explained. "We use it to communicate with submerged submarines. What does it say, Mr. Archer?"

Archer shook his head. "I'm not sure, sir. It's in the clear, but it just says 'GO FISH.'"

Holland's face turned florid. "Oh my God," he breathed. He peeled off the headset and cast it to the floor. "Well, thanks for the entertainment, John!" Holland stood and reached for his gold-leafed cap. "If you'll excuse me, I'm going back to the Pentagon. It looks like we have a real war to fight now!"

* * *

In the Taiwan Straits, four *Los Angeles*-class submarines rose to periscope depth. They each ran a thin antenna above the surface, pulling in the datalink signals from the Hawkeye and the *Tien Tan* and passing them to the subs' fire control centers. After a short radio consultation between the sub captains, targets were selected and orders were given.

Seconds later, four Tomahawk anti-ship cruise missiles burst from each submerged submarine's vertical launch tubes. Two Harpoon missiles each followed, launched from the subs' torpedo tubes. One Tomahawk was aimed at each Chinese warship, with an additional Harpoon slated for the vessels with advanced SAM capability.

Without overhead radar coverage, the Chinese had less than a minute to react when the sea-skimming American missiles popped over the horizon. Only four ships in the flotilla avoided a catastrophic missile hit from the first wave, but the information on these survivors was relayed immediately to the submarines by the Hawkeye. A follow-on strike with eight more Harpoons solved that problem. Soon, the only members of the Chinese task force not sunk or burning out of control were the amphibious ships, but the submarines would not attack the lightly-armed transports without further authorization.

The wounded Taiwanese force had no such inhibitions. The sight of the American cruise missiles arcing toward the Chinese fleet was like a bugle call. The Taiwanese warships charged toward the demarcation line in unison. They loosed their own short-ranged cruise missiles toward the fleeing amphibious assault group, then closed to finish off the surviving transports with cannons and torpedoes. By nightfall, the only Chinese naval vessels remaining in the Taiwan Straits were lifeboats.

CHAPTER 11

"Tyrant's fears decrease not, but grow faster than the years." - Shakespeare, *Pericles*

TOOLS OF FATE

As usual, Cynthia Hale was the President's first appointment, to give Adams his daily intelligence briefing at seven A.M. The lines in his face had visibly deepened, and his eyes were dull from too many days of running on adrenaline and caffeine. His mouth was turned down in the dour expectation of more bad news. He waved her toward a chair with the enthusiasm of a patient waiting for root canal. "What's the latest, Cynthia?"

Hale was also haggard but fully alert, for reasons that had nothing to do with the crisis. "The situation is surprisingly calm, considering there's a war on."

She repeated the information she had gleaned from a series of pre-dawn telephone calls. China was still breathing threats and violence against Taiwan, but the CIA said China wasn't gearing up for any serious retaliation. The Chinese were also hampered by power failures at their largest military bases, which would have made mobilization difficult. The Taiwanese were telling everyone who would listen that the Chinese shot first, and everyone who counted believed the ROC version of events. A few of America's allies privately expressed glee that the Chinese had fired first and still lost.

Adams focused his bloodshot eyes. "What are the Chinese saying to us?"

"Nothing, really. Their news release blamed us for interposing ourselves into an internal Chinese matter, but that's it. No statements to our ambassador at all, not even veiled threats."

Adams blinked. "How is that possible? We fired, what was it, upwards of fifty missiles at them?"

She consulted her notes. "Thirty-two. Sixteen Tomahawks and sixteen Harpoons. But I don't think they know that, sir."

"How could they *not* know that?"

"Fog of war, sir." She related the call she had made to the NSA's Deputy Director. The Chinese had been in complete confusion, not realizing their lead ships had been taken out by their own missiles until *after* the survivors had opened fire on the ROC fleet. Archer had said the admirals on shore and the surviving Chinese ship captains were in a screaming match when the American missiles ended their conversation. In the NSA's opinion, the Chinese leadership thought the missiles were simply a Taiwanese counterstrike and had no clue America was involved.

Adams leaned back in his chair. "Damn! We may have just avoided World War III." He stared at the ceiling for a few seconds, until clarity suddenly pierced his contemplation. "No wonder they're laying low! They think the Taiwanese did this all by themselves!"

Hale managed a smile, despite the tension. "Three cheers for the underdog, huh?"

Adams's lethargy melted away. "There won't be any cheering if the Chinese find out the truth! We have to bury our involvement in this, Cynthia. Make sure everyone on our side knows--no gloating allowed. The Taiwanese will have to stick with the story, too. I'm sure they won't mind taking credit for single-handedly defeating the PRC navy."

"Yes, Mr. President. I'll see to it immediately."

"What about prisoners?"

Hale consulted her notes for the figure, which was running at about two thousand so far. A lot of the Chinese had been badly burned. Taiwan was doing a great spin job, showing the PRC sailors receiving the same care as their own casualties. Harry Abramson had suggested that Taiwan tell the Chinese to back down and stay down or the ROC would start offering asylum to the prisoners. It was unlikely China would risk a propaganda disaster of that magnitude.

"Good. I like that," Adams agreed. "How badly was the ROC hurt?"

"Forty-five confirmed dead so far, sir. About three times that many wounded. They saved the two ships that were hit, but Admiral Holland doubts they'll be useful for anything but torpedo practice."

"Well, I don't think we'll have to worry about Taiwan reuniting with the mainland any time soon," Adams concluded.

"Does that Archer fellow have any idea why the Chinese missiles didn't self-destruct like they were supposed to?"

Hale related Archer's theories on why PUZZLE BOX had failed, including a possible misconception about the destruct mode for the XH-1. When she heard 'self-destruct,' she thought of an explosion. But Archer had explained that the Russians might have programmed the missiles to self-destruct by nosing over and diving into the ocean.

Adams squinted. "But scoring a bull's-eye on four ships with four missiles? They wouldn't do *that* in self-destruct mode!"

"Archer is still looking into it. He admitted up front he was just guessing."

Hale watched Adams's worry lines fade as the specter of war receded. "Okay, we got lucky this time," he said. "It could have been a lot worse. Anything else?"

Hale paused for a moment. She didn't have to go through with this. But she couldn't ignore her conscience any longer. She laid a single sheet of paper on his desk. "Yes sir, there is."

Adams drew back. "What's this?"

Hale charged into her rehearsed speech, knowing there was no going back. "My resignation, sir. There's no point in continuing as your National Security Advisor if my advice is going to be routinely ignored. I might as well be your fashion consultant. Like you said, we were lucky this time. When our luck runs out, which it will, Americans are going to die. And I don't want to be around when that happens."

Adams donned his glasses and read the letter carefully. "It's Stoyer, isn't it?"

"Sir, I'd be lying to you if I said he wasn't a factor in my decision. He has no personal loyalty to you. I do. He didn't quit a good job to join your team before you were even elected. I did. He isn't even a member of the NSC. I am. All those factors should weigh into your decisions when the NSC meets. But my opinion hasn't even been respected lately. And yes, I do resent that."

Adams removed his glasses. "Cynthia, you *know* I respect your opinion. But you also know I don't listen to *any* of my advisors all the time. Just ask poor Harry Abramson. He's been with me longer than anyone. He'll tell you *I* gave him half his gray hair from not listening to him when I should have. I'm an intuitive leader, not an analytical one. That's why I need *you*, to

lay out the facts for me. But sometimes I have to listen to what
my gut tells me, the facts be damned. And I wouldn't be here if
I was wrong more times than I was right, would I?"

Hale had always admired Adams's instincts. She studied
the carpet. "No, Mr. President."

"Drop the 'Mr. President' crap, Cynthia. We're friends. But
face it, you got *used* to being listened to, and I can't promise
that to *anybody* on my staff. I suspect General Stoyer got used
to that over the last few days, too. You don't need to be a palm
reader to figure out his winning streak with me just came to an
end."

Had she read her boss that badly? Maybe she didn't know
him as well as she had believed. "I just thought you didn't value
my opinion anymore, sir."

He winced. "Oh, Cynthia! Stop it! If I didn't value your
opinion, I'd show you the door myself. That hasn't happened,
has it?"

Her indignation turned into embarrassment. "No, sir."

Sensing her discomfort, Adams tried to change the subject.
"Do you believe in fate, Cynthia?"

"Fate, sir?"

Adams toyed with his bifocals. "Fate. The idea that things
turn out the way they're supposed to in the end, even through
what seems to be happenstance or accident."

"No, sir. I've never considered accidents fortunate."

Adams leaned forward, as if sharing a confidence. "Maybe
you should. Take China and Japan. Both countries have two
guiding moral principles in foreign relations." He counted with
his fingers. "Is it good for us, and can we get away with it?
That's it. We've catered to them both like youthful royalty
when we should have spanked them like the spoiled brats they
are. General Stoyer may have screwed up big time, but he *did*
deliver two needed spankings. I think both countries will think
long and hard before they throw trash on our yard again."

Hale thought she had missed his point. "Are you saying it
was *supposed* to turn out this way, sir?"

Adams opened his hands dramatically. "*We* certainly didn't
plan it that way! But fate sometimes has her own plans. Sometimes she even uses arrogant fools like General Stoyer to do her
bidding. Just as often, she uses them and throws them away.
Time wounds all heels, as they say."

Hale could never follow Adams when he waxed philoso-
phical.

Adams checked his watch. "General Stoyer should be waiting outside for his personal ass-chewing by now. Still want to
quit the team?"

She extended a sheepish hand. "I'll take back that letter,
sir."

In one smooth motion, Adams grasped the letter, pivoted in
his chair, and fed it through the shredder beside his desk. The
high-quality machine devoured the memo with a barely audible
whine.

"What letter?" he said.

She nodded deferentially. "Thank you, Marshall." She
wasn't sure Stanford would want her back under these circumstances anyway.

Adams gave her a fatherly smile. "You just keep telling me
what you think, Cynthia. If I don't listen, then it's my damned
fault, not yours." His smile turned mischievous. "And show the
General in, would you please?"

Hale felt a weight lift from her. "Certainly, sir."

THE ROAD TO NOWHERE

With General Stoyer away, Jeff Archer had a few minutes
to deal with a personal matter. Meeting with the President was a
heady experience, but he was glad to have missed this particular
trip. He didn't think the Commander-in-Chief had summoned
Stoyer to the White House to inquire about the General's health.
The data Archer had requested appeared on his screen.

NAME: RICHTER, CARL A.
DEPARTMENT: 069E
TITLE: COLONEL-USAF
LOCATION: SAB4
PHONE: x29361

Archer drummed his fingers on the keyboard. This was the
only information readily accessible about the mysterious Colonel Richter. Department 069E was External Security, but that
didn't refer to fences and guards. External in this case meant
dealing with threats outside the fence, which ES took very seri-

ously. This included "black bag jobs," to bug the homes of NSA employees suspected of espionage. ES also ran a fleet of TEMPEST vans, which could read the screen of a specific TV or PC inside a locked building from up to a mile away.

The NSA had helped the FBI nail the spy Aldridge Ames using a TEMPEST van. Instead of trying to find and decrypt the diskettes Ames dropped off to his Russian case officer, the NSA simply read his dispatches as he typed them on his home PC. Perhaps that was what Richter was doing with the hackers fingered by ECHELON.

But Richter's military status hinted at a darker purpose. His title indicated that he was still active duty Air Force. While that was normal in the intelligence units of the NSA, to be active duty military in the Security department was unusual indeed. It also made Richter's personnel documents unavailable to Archer without a special request to the Pentagon, which was tidy.

A phone call to one of his contacts verified that Richter did indeed occupy an office in Security Annex Building 4. But his contact also informed him that Richter only stopped by his office twice a week to pick up his mail, frequently wearing a black paramilitary jumpsuit. Where he spent the rest of his time was a mystery. So were his ties to the DATASHARK project. Archer's private line rang.

"Mr. Archer, this is Sergeant Townsend," his contact reported.

"Hi Stan, what's up?"

"Sir, you asked about Colonel Richter. Well, he just drove through the Ream Road gate."

After construction of the Tordella Supercomputer Center, Ream Road was sealed off to most NSA traffic. Only delivery trucks were supposed to come through the Ream Road gate. Ream Road was also lined with warehouses and support buildings, but even the personnel who worked in those buildings were required to enter through the main gate off Savage Road.

"The Ream Road gate?"

"Yes, sir," Townsend answered. "His SUV has an all-gates-all-times pass on the mirror."

Archer spun around in his chair. From his office on the top floor of the OPS 2B building, Archer had a clear view of Ream Road. "A black Ford Expedition?"

"That's the one. Do you want the tag number?"

"Just a second." The Expedition continued past the support buildings and turned left onto a gravel road leading into the woods behind the NSA complex. "Hey Stan, where does that gravel road past the Dragon lead?"

"Nowhere, sir."

"What do you mean, nowhere?"

"Well, that road used to lead to the CCC, but it's been closed for years."

"The CCC?" It wasn't often Archer was confronted with an unfamiliar NSA abbreviation.

"It was before your time, sir. If I remember right, it stood for the Contingency Codebreaking Center," Townsend explained. "It was a doomsday bunker. They built a newer one under a golf course near here during the eighties. You can't even get to the old CCC anymore. The bridge over Savage Creek washed out a few years ago."

Archer watched the dust cloud from Richter's passage dissipate. "Well, they must have fixed it, because that's where he went. Will you do me a favor, Stan?"

"Name it, sir," was the immediate response. Archer had pushed through a paid leave of absence for Townsend to care for his ailing wife two years previously. Townsend had been a dependable source of information since his return.

"Keep a watch on the Ream Road gate and that path into the woods. If you see anything unusual, call me. I'm ready for that tag number now."

COMMENDATIONS

Colonel Richter delivered the good news personally. Even the prisoners in the Snake Pit needed positive reinforcement. He stepped to the rail overlooking the computer bay. The thirty or so faces peering up at him looked tired and apprehensive.

"Men," he called out, "I've just returned from the Pentagon. Although operation PUZZLE BOX had a much different outcome than we had planned, recent reports from the area are very positive. We appear to have inflicted a humiliating defeat on the Chinese military, with minimal casualties on our side.

"We also turned back numerous attempts to carry out cyberattacks on the island of Taiwan, which was a real demonstration of your skills. The Snake Pit has become a potent asset in our nation's defense. I told General Stoyer how hard each of you worked on this operation and he wanted me to pass on his personal thanks."

Ken Yoshida allowed himself to exhale. After last night's disaster, he half-expected to be marched out and shot. That their screw-up hadn't started a world war was also a relief.

"In recognition of your hard work," Richter continued, "I've had a special breakfast trucked in and everyone gets an extra hour in the exercise yard." Faces brightened. *Like a pack of damned dogs. Throw them a bone now and then, and they'll jump through any hoop you put in front of them.*

Richter sighed. "However, men, I do have one bit of bad news to share with you. I know we work you men hard here in the Snake Pit, but we also offer some unique opportunities. All we ask in return is that you cooperate with the program. However, two members of our team actually tried to sabotage our hard work on operation PUZZLE BOX last night. I'm sorry when that happens, but I'm sure it won't be repeated, will it, Mr. Pittman and Mr. Yoshida?"

Richter watched the color drain from the pair's faces. He had to restrain himself from laughing. That would be bad for the performance.

Yoshida gaped like a landed fish.

"N-n-no, sir!" Pittman finally stammered. "It won't happen again!"

Richter nodded. "That's right, gentlemen, it won't." Guards rushed forward on cue to drag away Pittman and Yoshida. The other prisoners averted their eyes.

"Now that we've taken care of that," Richter said, "I'd like to thank the rest of you again for a job well done. Breakfast will be served in a few minutes, and enjoy your time outside. That is all!"

After the hackers had shuffled off to the mess hall, Richter turned to Kramp and Womack. "Find out how they did it and why. I want answers!"

Kramp smiled. He liked getting answers. "And after that?" he asked hopefully.

Richter gave the pair a dismissive flip of his hand. "Feed 'em to the Dragon!"

REDEMPTION

General Stoyer gazed out the window of his limousine with an unfocused stare. His stomach felt like he had taken a sucker punch from a prize fighter. He almost ordered the driver to pull over so he could vomit.

In a way, the dressing down he had just received from President Adams was worse than the inquisitions of his North Vietnamese captors. They were the enemy. Adams was his Commander-in-Chief. As a POW, Stoyer had nothing left to lose but his life, which he had already offered up willingly for his country. Now he had much more to lose.

Director of the NSA was once the last post a general officer would hold before retirement. It was a command from which none returned. But the computer revolution created an explosion of new capabilities at the NSA. Becoming DIRNSA was now a pathway to the highest levels of military power. Stoyer's predecessor had gone on to become a full admiral and commanded all naval forces in the Pacific from his headquarters in Hawaii. Stoyer's sights were set on his fourth star and appointment as Chief of Staff of the Air Force, a member of the Joint Chiefs of Staff.

But that was shattered now. The President had all but fired him in their meeting, saying his incompetence had endangered American lives and nearly sparked a war between the US and China. Firing Stoyer now would invite difficult questions from the world intelligence community, possibly exposing the NSA's involvement in the conflict between China and Taiwan. So Stoyer would remain, for the moment, until an officer with the proper qualifications became available to take his place.

It had all come apart so quickly. His stomach spasmed again, almost forcing the churning bile into his mouth. Stoyer clenched his teeth and willed his agitated body back into submission. The question of *why* still gnawed at the back of his skull. Why had such a carefully crafted operation gone so desperately wrong? What could he have overlooked? A phone call interrupted his deliberations. He had to swallow twice before he found his voice.

"Stoyer," he finally choked out.

"Richter, sir. I think I found the reason for our difficulties last night." He paused.

"*Well?*"

"Pittman sabotaged the code, sir. We're not sure how he did it. But when he transmitted the destruct signal, instead it redirected the missiles to the targets of his choosing, which happened to be the lead Chinese ships. Thank God he didn't have the urge to take out an aircraft carrier."

"Why didn't your watchers catch it?" Stoyer fumed.

"Well, sir, we're still investigating, but we think he may have planted the bug in the software over two years ago, when he wrote the original program. Everyone was learning back then, sir, even the watchers. Since the program worked flawlessly ever since, it didn't occur to them that the code might have a logic bomb inside."

The plastic handset creaked under Stoyer's grip. "*Why* did he do it, Carl?"

"My men are, uh...*eliciting* that information from Pittman and Yoshida as we speak."

"Yoshida?"

"Yes, sir. He and Pittman were working as a team. Perhaps Yoshida talked Pittman into it, or maybe he found the bug and exploited it himself. But if he had a hand in it, we'll find out."

"What are we going to do with them now?"

A dry sound that was probably a chuckle came through from Richter's end. "I thought we'd hold a cooking class, then give them a tour of our waste disposal facility."

Stoyer's nostrils flared. "Don't burn the meat. And don't feed the Dragon until I get there."

"Understood."

Stoyer set the phone down with a shaking, white-knuckled hand. A hacker. A stinking, good-for-nothing hacker had shattered his entire career. It couldn't end like this. He wouldn't *allow* it to end like this. Another stab of nausea pierced his gut. He had sworn he would never die a failure like his biological father. Yet that fate now stared him in the face. It pounded on him like one of his father's beatings.

No. Too many sacrifices had been made for it to end like this. He would redeem himself. There was one more operation he had held in reserve, just for a situation like this. It was an operation so vital to national security that President Adams would be forced to reconsider his decision to end Stoyer's career. He took a deep breath.

Slowly, his stomach settled. With a goal once again ahead of him, his focus returned. He had once won over his adoptive father, and now he would win back the approval of his Commander-in-Chief. He would do it. No matter who he had to sacrifice in the process.

ASSOCIATIONS

Archer was almost out of his office when his private line rang again. Stoyer was still at the White House, so Archer was about to fill in for him at a staff meeting. He almost kept walking and let the call go into voice mail, but something changed his mind. He snatched the phone on the fourth ring.

It was Sergeant Townsend. "Sir, you said to let you know if anything unusual came through the Ream Road gate? Would General Stoyer's limousine qualify?"

Archer spun to face the window. "Not necessarily. Sometimes he likes to hang out at the Supercomputer Center to clear his mind."

The limousine followed Ream Road at a rapid clip. Instead of proceeding to the supercomputing facility, the limousine reached the Dragon, then slowed and turned onto the gravel road into the woods. Archer kept staring at the woods, even after Stoyer's limo disappeared. How many times had he looked out this window and never even noticed that gravel track, much less the vehicles traveling on it? It made him wonder what else he was missing.

"Hail, hail, the gang's all here," Archer said quietly.

THE VISITOR

Jeremy Patrick started his journey well before dawn. He drove west from Washington, D.C., to the horse country of northern Virginia, down successively smaller roads until he reached his destination. He pulled up slowly to the ornate iron gate, where a guard with night-vision goggles was unobtrusively waiting. Patrick lowered his window so the guard could see his face clearly. The gate began to retract.

"Good morning, sir," a voice said out of the darkness. "You haven't stopped by in a long time."

"Too long," Patrick agreed. "Any word on our visitor?"

"He should be here in about twenty minutes."

Patrick nodded his acknowledgment and drove through the gateway. The ornate arch overhead read, "JEFFERSON STABLES," but training horses and riders had not been the primary activity here for some time. The driveway meandered through the forest around landscaped berms, some of which doubled as hidden observation posts. Finally the red brick Colonial mansion came into view, its three-story white columns reflecting the early dawn light.

Patrick remembered the first time he came to Jefferson Stables. He had just served as pallbearer for a fellow agent in the FBI's Phoenix office. His friend was working undercover on an anti-drug task force when he "committed suicide" with his service weapon. An "unforeseeable tragedy," the Agent-in-Charge had said at the funeral. Except that the dead agent had called Patrick the week before to say his operation had uncovered something dirty. He had warned Patrick that if he was found dead, especially by suicide, not to buy the official story.

So Patrick didn't. He kept digging quietly, trying to piece together his fellow agent's last days. He found nothing but uncooperative bureaucrats and evasive law enforcement officials at every turn, until a knock came at his hotel room door late one night. A kindly older man introduced himself to Patrick as a retired CIA officer who was there to keep Patrick from getting himself killed.

The polite gentleman explained that Patrick's friend had blundered into a joint drug-smuggling operation between corrupt Drug Enforcement Agency and Immigration and Naturalization Service agents guarding the Mexican border. Using illegal immigrants as "mules," the INS border guards took receipt of hundreds of pounds of cocaine monthly, then handed the drugs over to the DEA for distribution. The illegals were then returned to Mexico by the INS with a fatter wallet and the process started again.

The retired CIA officer said DEA officials were already aware of Patrick's informal investigation. Further probing would do nothing but earn Patrick a fate similar to his friend's. But there was another way to avenge his comrade's death, the intelligence officer hinted, if Patrick was willing to take a trip with him.

Two days later Patrick was standing in front of these same columns, although he had no idea where or what Jefferson Stables really was. Later he received a tour very similar to what he was about to grant to their guest.

A guard met Patrick and moved his government car out of sight. Patrick went inside the mansion to greet his old friends and bring them up to speed on his plan. Some had reservations, but Patrick's track record in Resistance operations was persuasive. Neither could they think of another way to achieve their goal. A few minutes later the guard at the front gate called. Their guest had arrived.

Patrick and the reception committee moved to the front steps. There were no guns in evidence, but the postures of Patrick's companions left no doubt they were armed. Eric's van wound along the tree-lined path.

"Masks," Patrick called out.

Patrick and his compatriots donned black balaclavas, leaving only their eyes visible. The van stopped at the front steps. A tired Eric emerged.

"Smooth trip?" Patrick asked.

"He didn't whine much," Eric said. "Are we ready?"

Patrick nodded. "Let's do it."

Eric slid open the side door and a stiff Tony Broadman appeared, visibly nervous at being among the ranks of the hooded again.

Patrick shook Broadman's hand with both of his. "Good morning, Tony," he said warmly. "I'm sorry for all the security arrangements. You'll understand their necessity in a few minutes. Welcome to Liberty."

CHAPTER 12

"If this be treason, make the most of it." - Patrick Henry

EXECUTION MODE

Ken Yoshida panted in spasms. He heaved, although his stomach had already been emptied. He sucked in a gasping breath, aspirating some of his vomit. He gagged, his ragged coughs making his whole body ache.

He was strapped face down on a gurney, his face protruding through a hole. Two buckets had been placed under the stretcher, one below his head and another at waist level. Richter shifted his attention to Pittman, who was screaming like a wounded animal. Every question was accompanied by an electronic whine, like a flash unit charging, followed by more shrieks. The smell of human waste verified that one or both of them had lost control of their bodily functions in the process.

The interrogation was taking place in the concrete entry hallway, too far for the hackers in their cells to hear the questions, but close enough to hear the screaming. Richter seemed most concerned *how* Pittman had sabotaged the satellite control program, not why he had done it. Pittman admitted he had rigged the code to accept any mouse picks as targeting inputs when he originally wrote the program. He claimed the only change he made during PUZZLE BOX was to transmit the targeting data when the abort order was selected.

Yoshida had repeatedly maintained his ignorance of the sabotage during his torture. If Richter had questioned him about the Resistance, he might have broken. Even his interrogation training hadn't prepared him for this level of agony. Yoshida couldn't see what Richter was using, but when he pressed the machine against different parts of their spines, rivers of electric torment coursed through their bodies.

When Richter placed the device against the back of Yoshida's skull, it felt like daggers stabbing out his eyes from behind. Richter seemed satisfied with Yoshida's pleas of innocence. He may have been abusing Yoshida just to give Pittman a chance to hear someone else wailing before the attention returned to him. It seemed to go on for hours.

"Well, that pretty much answers my questions," Richter said calmly. "There's only one thing left to do." He held the torture device below the gurney so Yoshida could see it. It resembled a radar gun with a white point the size of a golf ball. A black rubber cone surrounded the point. There was a large red knob beside the trigger.

"You know, this device has an interesting history," Richter expounded. "It was developed by the CIA in cooperation with one of our Mideast allies, who wanted a truly frightening torture device to keep dissidents in line. It causes pain by radio frequency nerve induction. There's no tissue damage like if you used a raw electrical current. I could torture you for days without killing you."

Pittman whimpered weakly in the background.

Richter toyed with the red knob. "One feature our ally wanted was an execution mode, where the power could be turned up so high it would cause death by neural shock or cerebral hemorrhage, without leaving any marks on the body. Funny thing was, it never quite worked. Oh, it could fry somebody's brain like they'd been on a month-long acid trip, but it wouldn't kill them. Very disappointing to our ally, but just fine for my purposes."

Richter placed a cold hand on Yoshida's bare back. "You see, I can't think of anything more fitting than turning you two into vegetables. Death would be too quick. But the thought of you two stuck in the corner of some nursing home sucking baby food through a straw until you die of natural causes, now *that* warms my heart!"

Richter placed the device against the base of his skull. "Let's start with you, Mr. Yoshida!"

"What?" Yoshida howled. "But I didn't *do* anything! Why are you doing this to *me?*" He kicked and rolled against the straps, to no avail.

Richter lifted the torture gun from his skin. "Why? Because *I can!* You hackers are a dime a dozen. I can replace both of you tomorrow." He placed the device against Yoshida's neck again. "This will take a little while, but the results are worth it!" The gun began to charge, its buzz growing louder and louder.

"Any last words?" Richter needled.

Yoshida started screaming before Richter even pulled the trigger, trying to roll his head away from the point of the gun. Kramp's gloved hands clasped his head, holding it fast. The point bore down again on his neck. Yoshida heard the trigger click.

The impact of the charge hit the back of Yoshida's skull like a baseball bat. His eyes bugged and his tongue flew out. A white sheet of flame blanked out his vision, then stopped just as suddenly. He gasped convulsively, too stunned to even scream.

"How did you like that, Mr. Yoshida?" Richter whispered in his ear. "You ever cross me and I'll finish the job. That's a promise."

Before Yoshida had recovered enough to speak, Richter moved to Pittman's gurney and repeated the process. Pittman screamed in terror, thinking he was about to become a vegetable. The gun discharged.

Pittman's screaming stopped a few seconds later, replaced with a gagging sound.

"Clean them up and take them upstairs," Richter ordered Kramp and Womack, the disappointment evident in his voice. "The General has plans for these two."

LIBERTY

Patrick gestured toward the mansion. "Tony, I'm sure you're hungry. Let's go inside."

Broadman gawked as he was ushered through the foyer. The house was richly decorated with hunting scenes and riding tack, in keeping with the stated equestrian purpose of Jefferson Stables. While the Resistance was well equipped to stave off unwelcome intruders, innocent visitors like utility workers and veterinarians caring for the horses needed to see exactly what they expected and nothing more.

Thomas Jefferson himself would have been pleased to serve visitors in the dining room. A fire roared in the marble-trimmed fireplace and pictures of several early presidents adorned the pale blue walls. Broadman ate enthusiastically when breakfast was set before him.

Since the balaclavas made joining Broadman impractical, Patrick used the opportunity to give his guest an introduction to his visit. "As I told you in our previous meeting, the only purpose of the Resistance is to stop the abuse of power by the government. Whenever the Constitution is circumvented or ignored, we take action. Simply exposing these abuses stops most of them. Even the most entrenched bureaucrats recognize that if they draw bad press, their gravy train may be cut off.

"As you know from experience, the major media have so cozied up to the government that investigative journalism is almost dead. But no reporter can resist a juicy story that's dropped in their lap. Since many members of the Resistance are inside the government already, it's very difficult to keep secrets from us. Most of the time we simply deliver the evidence and let the media do the rest."

"Most of the time?" Broadman asked.

Patrick lowered his gaze. "The weakness of the media is that they're no longer independent. They've all been gobbled up by huge corporations, and their reporters like going to cocktail parties too much. They like hanging around powerful people. It makes them feel powerful too. If they uncover a story that will make their parent corporation uncomfortable or get them crossed off an invite list, they might bury it. In those cases the Resistance will take more direct action."

"What kind of action?"

Patrick smiled underneath his mask. "I'll let our training speak for itself. We teach our members everything an undercover agent for the CIA would learn before working in a hostile country. Except the hostile country in this case is the United States."

Broadman eyed Patrick and the two men seated beside him. "I don't mean this as an insult, but if I hadn't investigated Ken Yoshida's disappearance myself, I'd think you guys were in need of some serious therapy."

All three Resistance members chuckled.

"You don't know how much I wish a therapist could tell me the government was working exactly as the Constitution had ordained and this was all in my head. I'd pay big money for that to be true. But you and I both know it isn't. *We* know something needs to be done, but by the time John and Jane Q. Public figure it out, it may be too late."

Broadman finished his meal. "So you want me to warn them?"

"That's part of it," Patrick agreed. "There *is* something very wrong inside the government. Even we're not sure what it is.

But an agenda is being pursued, at a very high level. And I don't think it's to the benefit of the United States or its citizens."

Broadman pushed his plate away. "Please tell me this isn't about black helicopters and the New World Order."

Patrick shrugged. "Not that I know of. But assume for a moment that the New World Order story *was* true. If you were in charge of the secret, what better way of keeping it than to find the biggest, most loudmouth wacko around, feed him the real plan until he was good and frothed, then turn him loose?"

Broadman completed the thought for him. "If anyone happened across the truth after that, they wouldn't dare reveal it, or they'd be a wacko too."

A nod. "And wackos don't get invited to cocktail parties."

Broadman wondered how many people he had considered nut cases were actually telling the truth. "Shit."

"Welcome to Proactive Propaganda 101. But the other audience for your story is the government itself."

"You *want* them to know about you?"

Patrick's eyes glinted. "Let's say you ran a cheating ring in college. But one day the professor announced that he knew the cheating was going on, and several students in the class were actually informants for the university. How would that modify your behavior?"

"I'd look over my shoulder a lot more."

"You might even cheat less. But that's enough theory for now. Let me show you how we prepare our members for harsh reality."

SMOKE SIGNALS

Pittman and Yoshida were unstrapped from the gurneys and herded to the showers. Yoshida was so weak he leaned against the tile and let the water flow over him.

"Thanks a lot, Bob!" he croaked. "Why the hell did you *do* that?"

Pittman rested one hand against the wall and held his head with the other. "Trying to kill myself, I guess," he mumbled.

Yoshida would have punched him if he could have done so without falling down. "Good try! Mind not taking me with you next time?" He had to stay calm. Getting mad just made the throbbing worse.

"They're going to kill us all anyway. I just wanted to take some of them with us."

Yoshida worked his neck in a circle, moaning. "They let Friedman go, didn't they?" Not that he really believed it, but it gave the other hackers hope.

Pittman shook his head. "No. They killed him."

Yoshida squinted against the water running into his eyes. "You don't know that for sure."

"Yeah, I do. They killed him. You know that hacker's website I was surfing right before all hell broke loose? Derek passed me a note when he left. He was going to insert three specific misspellings into the subject headings on that site. Nothing most people would notice, but it would be his signal to me that they really *did* let him go."

"Maybe he hasn't gotten around to it yet. Face it, once he got out, you probably weren't at the top of his list."

Pittman was exhausted but emphatic. "The note said 'within forty-eight hours.' I gave him twice that."

"Maybe he had trouble hacking the site. Maybe they wouldn't let him near a computer as a condition of his parole." It was amazing how hard he was willing to argue against a conclusion he had reached himself days ago. Maybe this place was getting to him, too.

"That site? No way in hell! He could have cracked it while he was taking a leak! And there isn't a hacker around who couldn't have done it for him for twenty bucks. That means they probably buried him right outside the fence!"

Yoshida tried to wash the sweat out of his hair. Even his scalp hurt. "Okay, say they killed him. Why sabotage the satellite program? What did that buy you?"

Pittman finally raised his eyes. "Don't you get it? I targeted those missiles at four Chinese ships, right off the coast of Taiwan! If it worked, it should have started World War III. We're still here, so I guess it didn't. But I couldn't think of a better way of getting back at these assholes than taking a bunch of them with us!"

Yoshida had to restrain himself, keeping his voice low. "*Hello?* Does the rest of the planet have a say in this?"

Pittman scowled. "If *we're* dead, who gives a damn?"

Before Yoshida could respond, Womack shouted at them.

"All right, you maggots, if the stink ain't gone by now, it ain't coming off! Cover up those ugly asses of yours and follow me!"

TRAINING

After breakfast, Broadman was led upstairs. Here, all pretense of the estate's equestrian cover was abandoned. The second floor resembled a military barracks. Bunk beds occupied several Spartan bedrooms. The larger rooms were now classrooms, with tables and marker boards. Six students in one class were disassembling cellular phones under an instructor's guidance. Two of the hooded students were women.

"Are the ski masks part of the dress code," Broadman asked, "or do you only wear them when reporters are around?"

Patrick laughed. "They're just for you. I'm sure they'll be glad when we move along. This class is learning how to clone a cell phone. The government has become very skillful at locating people by their cellular signals. They transmit whenever they're turned on, by the way, not just when you're talking. One way around this problem is to change the ID number on the phone's chip every few days, which these students are learning how to do."

Patrick showed him another room filled with computers, radios, night-vision goggles, and other equipment whose purpose he could only guess. "In any intelligence organization, communicating without being detected is a primary concern. We teach in depth about electronics and surveillance technology."

"How many students do you train at a time?"

"Up to twelve, although the number varies. We try to train all members of a cell group together."

"Cell group? Like a *terrorist* cell?"

Being compared to a terrorist didn't sit well with Patrick. "Today's terrorist is tomorrow's patriot," he snapped. "I prefer to compare our organization to the French Resistance during World War II. The cell group members know each other, but they don't know anyone else in the organization. Only the cell group leader knows the identity of his supervisor, and no one above that. It limits the damage one member can do if captured or turned."

"How many cell groups are there?"

The question earned a raised eyebrow. "I'll let you and the government *both* wonder about that." He led Broadman further down the hallway. "But speaking of being captured, this is one of our interrogation rooms."

One side of the closet-sized booth was a one-way mirror. What appeared to be a dentist's chair with heavy straps sat beyond the glass. "This is where our students learn about government interrogation methods, both legal and illegal, and how to resist them. We also teach how to defeat polygraph and voice stress analysis tests."

Patrick did not inform Broadman that this room was also used to test the true loyalties of new members. The sodium pentothal session was very effective in screening out infiltrators.

"Our members also receive advanced self-defense and weapons training, as well as escape and evasion techniques," Patrick said. "Let me show you."

Broadman followed him down the back stairs to a large grassy field. One horse was being exercised inside a corral, and another was being led through a jumping course. Two large stables backed up to the woods.

Patrick entered the first one. "We do keep a few horses here, as you would expect on a horse farm, but a lot fewer than the stables would indicate." Horse stalls occupied only half the stable. The other half was a large gym with a padded floor. Four students were waiting there in Karate outfits.

"This is where we train our recruits to be dangerous," Patrick said. "These students are going to demonstrate a CIA move that isn't popular with the police."

Two of the students took the role of arresting officers, with the other two bent over desks, in position to be handcuffed. The "prisoners" waited until one hand was being cuffed, then quickly pushed off with the other, wrapping a leg between the "officers'" feet in the process. One of the "policemen" managed to jump clear, but the other tumbled backward. The "prisoners" pounced on them, one student even managing to deprive the "officer" of his weapon.

"It isn't a perfect tactic," Patrick said, "but it's not bad for a last resort. We teach all our recruits a variety of escape techniques. We also have a number of locks and simulated jail cells in the basement of the main house. Our members learn the weaknesses of all of them."

The next "stable" was an indoor firing range. Two men were practicing with strange-looking guns. They stopped firing when Patrick entered.

"Most people assume that once the SWAT team has shown up, the game is over," Patrick said. "But while SWAT tactics are effective, they're also predictable. The shooting house is where we teach our recruits how to take the initiative when surrounded. Set me up."

"Six rounds left," one of the shooters said. He flicked on the safety and tossed the weapon to Patrick, who caught it with one hand.

Patrick held out the weapon, a stubby submachine gun with a fat barrel. "This is a Heckler & Koch MP5 SD. The fat end here is an integral silencer, which makes it the perfect weapon for our use. Ready?"

The shooters made sure they were standing to the side. "Ready!" one acknowledged.

Patrick spun to face downrange. Three human silhouettes were spaced from twenty to thirty-five feet away. Working from closest to most distant, he fired two quick shots at each. Instead of the normal report of a gun, the weapon's loud hiss was like the air brakes on a truck.

"Time?" Patrick asked.

"Two-point-six seconds," the man who had loaned the weapon answered.

"Students are required to score one lethal hit per target in three seconds or less," Patrick said.

Broadman squinted. The bullets had all struck at center head on the targets, each hole within an inch of the other. "I'm beginning to see what you mean by dangerous. How many people have you, I mean your group...?"

Patrick safetied the weapon. "How many people have we killed? A few. Remember, we're not interested in blowing up buildings or overthrowing the government. But if some bureaucrat decides he or she is above the law, we'll be there." He motioned at the perforated targets. "Tell them that."

"That kind of talk is going to scare the hell out of a lot of people." It certainly scared the hell out of *him*.

"Government is about *power*," Patrick said. "In the right hands, power is a good thing. You *need* power to fight terrorists and organized crime. But when power falls into the wrong hands, the Resistance won't just be the *best* friends you've got."

He held up his weapon for emphasis. "We'll be the *only* friends you've got."

* * *

Eric was already sitting on the edge of his bed when Patrick entered.

"Get any sleep?"

"A little. I'll still need some coffee before I leave, though."

"I'll have them fill a Thermos for you."

One corner of Eric's mouth turned downward. "Permission to speak freely, sir?"

Patrick smiled. Eric had been an Army Ranger before joining the highway patrol. "Granted."

"Giving the government this kind of look inside our operation is only going to make the FBI double their efforts to hunt us down. I honestly don't see what allowing Broadman to write this story is going to buy us."

Patrick folded his arms. "Chances are he's not going to have time to write this story, much less get it into print."

"Sir?"

"I'm only making sure he has enough information so they'll interrogate him thoroughly, not just shoot him outright."

"Poor bastard."

* * *

Patrick said his farewells to Broadman and Eric. He and the two instructors watched the van weave down the driveway and disappear. They removed their balaclavas in unison.

Patrick checked the time while waiting for a guard to return his vehicle. To justify his day trip, he needed to visit the FBI's Quantico facility before he returned to D.C. Patrick was lost in thought for a moment, remembering his first departure from Liberty, five years ago.

* * *

Patrick had been teamed up with several senior members of the Resistance on a mission to Nogales, Mexico. Late that night they followed the same path the immigrant drug couriers used. Dressed like the couriers they had replaced, the Resistance team was met by the INS reception committee. The corrupt INS agents were surprised to learn that these couriers' knapsacks concealed automatic weapons instead of drugs.

The DEA distribution team arrived an hour later to receive the same surprise. The news media spun the affair as the "worst case of drug-related violence against federal law enforcement officers in American history." As far as Patrick knew, the bodies of the Mexican couriers were never found.

* * *

"How long till you carry out your plan, Paddy?" one of the instructors asked, jolting Patrick back to the present.

The risks involved made Patrick reconsider whether his plan should be executed at all. He stared into the woods.

"Not long," he finally replied.

SECURITY

Yoshida was counting guards. After the horror of Richter's torture session, Yoshida was surprised that any part of his brain was still functioning, much less the compartment that held his Resistance training. But his eyes were moving, recording the number and placement of guards as he and Pittman were goaded from the showers in handcuffs and ankle chains.

Richter had called out the cavalry today. His head goon Kramp had a steely grip on Yoshida's arm. Kramp's sidekick Womack was holding Pittman in an obviously painful grasp. Beyond the computing bay, two guards watched the hallway where the hackers were locked down in their cells. Four more guards with cattle prods formed a chute, channeling Pittman and Yoshida toward an open door directly opposite the computing bay.

It was the door to the upper level. A guard *always* blocked this door while the hackers worked, so Yoshida knew the upper level held more than just Richter's and the watchers' offices. He glanced at the lock as he was dragged past. A magcard swipe *and* a keypad. Yep, they were damn serious about keeping the hackers on the lower level. Just stealing a keycard from a guard wouldn't cut it.

They emerged on the upper level. Yoshida tried to look around. Kramp grabbed the back of Yoshida's head and forced it down, almost breaking his neck.

"Keep yer head down, maggot!" Kramp growled.

Yoshida still caught sight of an airlock, blocked by two more guards. That made ten so far. It was an obvious show of force, but why? Maybe to convince him and Pittman that the guards were more numerous than was actually the case. Yoshida guessed at least two guards would be manning the fence outside. That would make it an even dozen, a nice round military number. But they had guns and he didn't. Yoshida refused to let the odds demoralize him. He filed this new information away for future use.

* * *

From the doorway of Stoyer's office, Richter watched the two manacled hackers shuffle into the conference room. He gave Stoyer a nervous look. "I still think disposing of both of them would be a safer option, sir. Pittman has confessed to his sabotage, and it may have given Yoshida ideas if we allow them to continue working."

"Now that we know the problem, we can watch them more closely," Stoyer countered. "I agree we should remove them from the DATASHARK program, but those two are the most talented hackers we have. I'm going to use them on a special project."

Richter's bushy eyebrows met. "What project is that, General?"

"PANDORA," Stoyer whispered.

Richter's eyes widened. "*PANDORA?* Sir, allowing these two *hackers* access to that kind of information would be an ungodly risk! Besides, wasn't there an executive order forbidding any more work on PANDORA?"

Stoyer nodded slowly. "Yes, there was. By the previous administration. To my knowledge, President Adams hasn't been briefed on the concept. But when he is, I don't intend to hand him a concept. I intend to hand him a working key to America's future."

He locked eyes with Richter. "The President handed me my head this morning, Carl. We may have a month before I'm forced out, maybe less. And I don't have to tell you the career options of a senior Colonel who's lost his protector."

"You can hand them our resignations together, as far as I'm concerned, sir!"

"I appreciate your loyalty, Carl, but it may not come to that. One of the reasons PANDORA was never authorized was the final security that would be necessary. If even one worker on the project talked, it could be disastrous for foreign policy. No one had the guts to order the programmers killed to guarantee their silence. But if PANDORA works, it could save both of our careers. And Pittman and Yoshida will have a hard time talking with bullets in their heads."

CHAPTER 13

"Insurgents are like conquerors; they must go forward. The moment they are stopped, they are lost."
- The Duke of Wellington

INITIATION

Pittman and Yoshida sat silently in the conference room. Both were still weak and shaking from Richter's torture gun. Yoshida was grateful a chair had been offered before he fell down. But the Resistance part of his brain was still working, noting the rich wood grain of the table and the wood paneling covering the concrete walls. Only high-ranking officers rated this kind of treatment. His observations were interrupted by a sharp poke in the back.

"You two, stand up!" Kramp snarled.

Yoshida gripped the table and hauled himself to his feet. He hung onto it to stay upright. Pittman was in worse shape. Womack finally grabbed Pittman under the arms and pulled him out of his chair, holding onto Pittman's jumpsuit with both hands to keep him from falling over.

Richter and another man in uniform entered. The hard-featured officer wore three stars and a chest full of ribbons. Yoshida realized with a start that this was General Stoyer himself. It made his already-queasy stomach sink even lower. The only reason Stoyer would get involved personally was to exact vengeance. Yoshida steeled himself to face death bravely.

Stoyer and Richter stared at the wobbly hackers. Finally Stoyer spoke, his face drawn as if in pain.

"Mr. Pittman, you've known from the beginning that failure was always an option in our program. You've seen almost a dozen participants removed from the Snake Pit and sent to federal prison because of insubordination or incompetence. You've also seen hackers rewarded for good performance. Why then would you endanger your good standing and imminent release by sabotaging our work here?"

Come on, Bob, Yoshida prayed. *Don't say something that will get us both killed for sure.*

"I guess I got discouraged, sir," Pittman mumbled. "After all, I've been on the program longer than Derek Friedman, and my work was just as good as his. If anyone deserved an early release, it was me."

Yoshida took a grateful breath. Pittman hadn't lost his skills as a liar. That may have temporarily extended both their lives.

"Well, Mr. Pittman, I'm sorry you feel that way," Stoyer said. "However, I'm here to offer you a chance to redeem yourself. Colonel?"

Richter placed several fluorescent-striped binders on the table. "These are the files on project PANDORA. You will familiarize yourself with this program and draw up a plan for its immediate implementation. As of right now, you will have no contact with the other hackers. You will be moved to separate quarters and will remain there until this project is completed."

Yoshida's mental alarms blared again.

Stoyer leaned across the table. "Gentlemen, PANDORA is the most urgent project the Snake Pit has tackled to date. You will extend your very best efforts to its immediate success. Is that understood?"

Pittman and Yoshida nodded.

"Mr. Pittman," Richter said, "the only other motivation we could think of for your sabotage was some sort of death wish on your part."

Womack thrust his pistol at Pittman's temple, slowly cocking the hammer.

"If that's the case," Richter continued, "I can assure you the only person you will be killing with further vandalism is yourself."

The pistol's hammer slammed home on an empty chamber. Pittman jerked, almost toppling onto the table.

Richter's face was devoid of expression. "And Mr. Yoshida, of course. If you try something cute again and he fails to detect it, both of you will suffer a similar fate."

Womack chambered a round and returned the pistol to Pittman's head.

Richter glowered at them. "The next time he pulls the trigger it will be a lot louder. Now, follow me!"

DRAWBRIDGE

It wasn't often the Deputy Director visited the NSA's Facilities office, but the department head was delighted to receive such high-level attention. Roy Pigeon was a small man, but he was a master of NSA politics. This had allowed him to outlast his competition and seize the reins of a department most NSA managers regarded as a backwater. That didn't matter to Pigeon. What mattered was that *he* was in charge. And with Mr. Archer coming to visit *him*, Pigeon was sure his political flag would soon be flying a little higher.

"Good morning, Mr. Archer! How can I help you?" Pigeon asked. He sat a little straighter, the booster pad on his chair almost bringing him eye-to-eye with the seated Archer.

Archer slowly withdrew a folder from his briefcase. "I'd like to talk with you about your travel budget."

Pigeon blinked, but his smile was steady. "Why, certainly, Mr. Archer. Are you conducting this review with all your managers?"

Archer looked up. "No. Just you."

"Well," Pigeon said quickly, "I'm honored."

Archer leafed through the folder and stopped at a page with several highlighted entries. "You do seem to jet around a lot, for a facilities manager."

Pigeon shifted on his chair. "We have some unique facilities challenges here at the NSA! Sometimes we have to consult experts from all over the country! Why, I remember when we were trying to get the Dragon up and running..."

"In Las Vegas?" Archer interrupted.

"I'm sorry?"

"Las Vegas. Almost half your travel budget is used to take a group to Las Vegas every year."

"The National Facility Manager's Convention!" Pigeon spouted. "I tell you, I get some of my *best* ideas at that conference!"

Archer pulled a thick file from his briefcase. "You certainly should! I had my secretary pull your expense reports for the last few of your trips. Your expenses were well in excess of NSA limits, but you were still reimbursed. I wonder why no one in Travel flagged this?"

Pigeon gaped. "I have no idea."

Archer continued his examination. "Well! Mr. Gregston signed off on this expense report himself. That's odd, the department head of Travel personally signing off on your expense report?"

Pigeon swallowed. "I'm sure it's not *that* unusual, Mr. Archer."

"About as odd as the head of the Travel department attending a Facility Manager's conference in Las Vegas, wouldn't you say?"

The color drained from Pigeon's face. "I'm *sure* there's a logical explanation, Mr. Archer!"

"Yeah, there is. It's called travel fraud," he said quietly. "I fire people for that."

Pigeon's mouth moved, but no sound came out. For a moment Archer thought the man might swallow his tongue. He needed to make his move before Pigeon had a seizure.

Archer pulled a Post-It note from one of the folders. "Oh, sorry to change the subject, but I had a history question. Ever heard of the CCC?"

"Civilian Conservation Corps?"

"Huh?"

Pigeon's laughter was nervous and high-pitched. "Sorry, bad joke! Are you referring to the Contingency Codebreaking Center?"

"That's the one."

Pigeon was hyperventilating. "Oh sure, the DATASHARK bunker! I just haven't heard of it referred to as the CCC in a long time."

Archer hid his surprise. "Sorry, didn't mean to confuse you. Do you have any facility maps of that area?"

Pigeon jumped down from his seat. "I understand! You just didn't want to use the codeword! I probably shouldn't have either! Do you have your program badge? Those documents are restricted."

Archer patted his suit jacket. "No, I didn't bring it with me! That was stupid."

"That's okay! That's okay! Don't worry about it!" He dashed outside his office to a file cabinet secured with a heavy bar, then manipulated the combination lock with trembling hands.

Archer had to restrain himself from laughing. In reality there was no National Facility Manager's Conference. But the department heads' annual drunken bash in Las Vegas was the stuff of NSA folklore. Rumor had it that if you invited old man Gregston to your parties and kept the alcohol flowing, he would sign off on any expense report without question, right down to the dollar bills you stuffed into the strippers' G-strings. Archer wondered why he had never been invited on that junket.

Pigeon tucked a blueprint under his arm and darted to a drafting table. He rolled out a large drawing of the NSA complex. "This is the current facility map." He circled a blank section between the western property line and Savage Creek. "The CCC bunker is right here, but it was deleted from every NSA facility record after DATASHARK took it over."

Pigeon unfolded the restricted blueprint. Just west of Savage Creek was a blue rectangle marked "DATASHARK."

"Will this help you at all?" Pigeon asked.

"I see the bridge across Savage Creek is back up on this map," Archer hinted.

Pigeon laughed, the sweat beads on his forehead glistening under the fluorescent lights. "Are you talking about that remote control drawbridge of theirs? Isn't that a piece of work?"

Archer played along, shaking his head. "Why in the world did they put that in, anyway?"

"I guess they didn't want some uncleared security guard stumbling onto the bunker! I honestly don't know why they had to keep it so hush-hush. Everything we do here is classified in one form or another, isn't it?"

"That's a fact. How tight of a latitude and longitude fix can you get from this map?"

Pigeon, a former surveyor, snatched a ruler and began measuring. "Accurate to about thirty feet. Why, are you planning an air strike?"

Archer winked. "Something like that."

Pigeon handed over the coordinates with a shaky hand. "Is there anything else I can do for you?"

"Yeah, my secretary's office is awfully drab," Archer offered. "Think you can get some pictures to lighten it up? Something with tulips. And she would really be thrilled if I could get her a fichus tree."

Pigeon held out his hands, as if warding off an unseen attacker. "Oh, *absolutely!* By the end of the day! No problem!"

Archer glanced at his watch. "Look at the time! I have to run to a meeting!" He gathered his files. "We'll finish this some other time, Mr. Pigeon!"

Pigeon was on the verge of fainting. "Of course, sir! Come and see me anytime!"

GRADUATION

Broadman had never even visited the floor where the executives in the news department worked. The plush carpeting and mahogany furniture were in sharp contrast to the gray rows of waist-height cubicles downstairs. The cries about declining revenue used by management at raise-time every year evidently didn't pertain here. Broadman and Janet Randall sat across the table from the short bespectacled man who wore a thick cardigan over his shirt and tie.

"Holy shit." The New York *Times* national news editor regarded Broadman over his bifocals. "You swear you're not making any of this up, Broadman? I'll have your ass if you are."

Broadman knew the *Times* editors were on red alert for fiction writers posing as journalists after recent scandals. He held up three fingers. "Scout's honor, Mr. Rosenstein."

He scanned the proposed outline of Broadman's contact with the Resistance. "So how did you *find* these people?"

"They found me," Broadman said. "I made a mutual friend during my research for the hacker story."

Randall crossed her arms and legs tight enough to imitate a pretzel. Broadman hoped this would end her derogatory comments about his nose for a story.

Rosenstein shivered. "Just reading your notes gives me the chills. I can't wait to see the finished piece. This is one hell of a scoop. What's your angle going to be on these terrorists?"

"I wouldn't call them *terrorists*, sir."

"For a New Yorker, you sure have a hell of a short memory," Rosenstein snapped. "If they threaten to kill people, they're terrorists, Mr. Broadman, period. By the way, Janet, thank you for bringing this to my attention. Starting now, Tony works for me on the National desk."

Randall bristled. "I'm sorry, Al, I can't release Tony from his duties right now." As editors of the Technology and National desks, Randall and Rosenstein were on the same level of the *Times'* organizational chart. But org charts seldom told the whole story.

Rosenstein shrugged. "Then take it up with the editor-in-chief, if you feel that strongly about it."

Randall's eyes blazed. She marched from the room, the thumping of her high heels audible all the way to the elevator.

Rosenstein reached across the table. "Congratulations, Tony. You just graduated to the big leagues."

BETRAYAL

Patrick spun in his chair, looking down at the tourists and bureaucrats mingling along Pennsylvania Avenue. Now that the pieces of his plan were all in place, he was suddenly seized with hesitation. Once his plan was initiated, there would be no going back.

He had sent men to their deaths before. That wasn't the issue. The sole criteria for his decision was whether the plan would achieve its objective. At least that was what Officer Candidate School and the FBI's leadership training courses had taught. How reasonable a maxim could seem in a comfortable, well-lit classroom, and how different it looked with the dark, heavy mantle of responsibility draped over one's shoulders.

But the indecision that gripped him left just as suddenly as it had come. Yoshida was a cell group leader. If he talked, the lives of every member of his cell were already forfeit. The possible sacrifice of one Resistance agent was inconsequential if the rest were saved. As if focusing a camera lens, his decision leapt into clarity. He reached for the phone, consulting the number he had been given.

AIR STRIKE

Archer waited until the balcony of the NICC was empty. Then he called Bernie Marks at the National Reconnaissance Office, the agency responsible for the nation's spy satellites.

"Hey Bernie, this is Jeff Archer. I have a tasking for you."

The pitch of Marks' voice rose. "On *this* line?"

"This line is secure. And this is a discreet tasking."

"Meaning what?" was the suspicious reply.

"Meaning there will be no written record of the photos you're about to give me."

"Listen," Marks pleaded, "I could go to *jail* for that."

Archer checked to make sure the classification window on the secure phone read TOP SECRET. "And *I* could go to jail for giving you the intercepts of your wife's conversations with her divorce lawyer, too. Are you saying that wasn't helpful information?"

"Of course not," Marks mumbled.

"Then are you ready to copy?"

"Ready," a shaky voice replied.

Archer read off the latitude and longitude coordinates.

There was silence on the line while Marks consulted a map. "Hey, that's CONUS!" he declared, using the acronym for Continental US.

"Really? I thought it was an Al-Qaeda training camp! Now, I want several max-resolution shots of the building at those coordinates, especially of any people or vehicles present. How long will that take?"

Marks consulted a computer that traced the path of the NRO's spy satellites. "You're in luck. I've got a KH-14 bird crossing the east coast in thirty-five minutes. Its crew usually goes to lunch when it's over quiet turf. I'll try to get your shots then."

"I'll be waiting."

GHOSTS

Instead of returning downstairs, Pittman and Yoshida were ushered to a room on the bunker's upper level. They passed the balcony overlooking the computer bay.

The hackers looked up at their two disgraced comrades. Malechek and the Taylor twins regarded them as if ghosts were wafting past. It filled Yoshida with even more dread. *Want to see a dead man, folks? Take a look!*

"Lunch break!" A guard on the lower level announced. "Everyone going outside, line up at the entry corridor!"

Yoshida's shoulders dropped. Knowing the others would soon be breathing fresh air hammered home his isolation even more.

Their trip concluded at the end of the upper level hallway. The room contained two computer terminals and two cots. Richter followed them inside.

"Welcome home, gentlemen," Richter said. "This is where you'll live and work until the project is completed. A guard will be outside at all times. If you need to go to the john, you go together. Neither of you works without the other looking over his shoulder. If that's uncomfortable, let it motivate you to work faster." He placed the PANDORA binders on a table. "Start reading. I think you'll be impressed."

PAYBACK

Archer returned to the NICC at the time Bernie Marks specified. The secure photo fax started humming almost immediately.

"Come to Papa," Archer whispered, grasping the full-color fax with both hands. He held it up to the light, scrutinizing the gray concrete bunker, bedecked with antennas. He wished he had brought a magnifying glass. "What the hell?"

As if in reply, the next photograph focused on a smaller portion of the DATASHARK complex, showing details clearly. Archer let out a low whistle. "Good job, Bernie!" he whispered. "I believe we're even."

He picked up the phone. "Yes, I need Corporal Rawlins to make a classified delivery for me. What? Well, he's back on duty now. This is Deputy Director Archer. Page him at home and have him report to my office ASAP. No, I don't want another courier, I want Rawlins. And tell him to forget his uniform. Street clothes will be fine. Better, in fact."

That task done, Archer hurried back upstairs. He had an important phone call to make.

PLUGGING LEAKS

Despite his enthusiasm for the DATASHARK project, Stoyer hated visiting the bunker. Too many reminders of his POW days. The barbed wire, the shouted commands, the stern-faced guards, but most of all the smell. This place was a perfume factory compared to the Hanoi Hilton, but Stoyer could still smell the fear, even on the bunker's upper level. It was something deeply primal, and it made his stomach churn.

But some tasks could only be handled here. He had created a front corporation to handle DATASHARK's expenses, and he couldn't very well cut those checks in the Director's office back in OPS 2B. Even though his was the largest office in the bunker, it still made him claustrophobic. His motions were quick and efficient, making every second count.

His desk phone rang. Checking the display, he saw it was Archer. The comm system in his limo had automatically forwarded the call. "What is it, Jeff?" he answered gruffly.

"Sorry to bother you, sir, but I just received a very strange call from the FBI. An official there said a reporter for the New York *Times* is chasing a story trying to link the NSA to the disappearance of several computer hackers over the last three years."

Stoyer felt like someone had plugged his pen into an electrical outlet. "*What?*"

Archer chuckled. "Yeah, I know, it's crazy. The FBI thought we should take the initiative and keep the reporter from embarrassing himself. I could call the *Times* and offer this guy an on-site interview. Let him see for himself that there's no monster in the closet. But I wanted to check with you before I made any public moves."

Stoyer was only half-listening to Archer, the other half of his brain frantically devising strategies for plugging this leak. "So how did the *FBI* get wind of this reporter's story?"

"The official said the reporter was trying to pump one of his agents for information about missing hackers. He just wanted to give us a PR heads-up."

Stoyer was already scribbling several unpleasant contingencies for dealing with this crisis. "What was this FBI official's *name?*"

"Uh...Patrick, Jeremy Patrick. He's their Assistant Director for Special Operations, whatever that is."

"That's right," Stoyer recalled. "He runs the Crisis Response and Hostage Rescue teams. Good man."

"You *know* him?"

"I've worked with him on the President's Counterterrorism Task Force." Stoyer traced his pen to the line where he had written *agent provocateur* and crossed it out.

"So," Archer probed, "do you think I should give this reporter an interview? This is the New York *Times*, we're talking about, after all."

"No!" Stoyer insisted, biting off the words. "If you give one *goofball* special treatment today, tomorrow the *tabloids* will want tours of the NICC! I have contacts at the *Times*. I'm not going to coddle some grunt-level reporter when I can cut off the story from the top."

Archer measured his words carefully. "Do you think that's...*wise*, sir?"

Stoyer ignored the challenge. Now that he knew what had to be done, his temper subsided to a manageable level. "Fortunately for you, Jeff, public relations is the millstone around my neck, not yours. If the NSA gets a black eye over this, Senator Carsten won't be inviting *you* up to the Hill for a chat. I'll take care of it."

"Fair enough, sir. Anything else I can do for you?"

"Yeah, what's this so-called reporter's name?"

Archer laughed on cue. "Tony Broadman. He writes a technology column."

Stoyer wrote Broadman's name on his pad. "Got it. Thanks, Jeff." He hung up the phone.

"*CARL!*"

Richter bounded into Stoyer's office almost by the end of the shout. Stoyer explained the situation. It was a curious feeling seeing the fear on Richter's face. Stoyer realized it was an emotion he had never seen the man display until now. "How soon can you get your team together?" Stoyer asked.

"We can leave within the hour."

"Do it," Stoyer ordered. He placed his pen beside Broadman's name and crossed it out.

BACK DOORS

Richter was right about one thing, Yoshida concluded. PANDORA *was* impressive. Or at least audacious. The first binder Richter gave them bore a red-and-black-striped cover marked SENSITIVE COMPARTMENTED INFORMATION.

During the Cold War, both the Soviets and the Chinese had become master copycats, stealing superior Western weapons systems and reverse-engineering the technology. A Russian air-to-air missile purchased on the black market for CIA analysis was found to be a perfect copy of the American version, right down to the company logo stenciled on the guidance chips. The Chinese were even more prolific copy artists, willing to duplicate Soviet systems if American or European hardware was unavailable.

Analysts at the NSA saw a unique opportunity in this frenzy of replication. CIA agents had already alerted Washington that the Soviets were attempting to steal Western technology to upgrade the control computers for their nuclear forces. High-powered computers and their software were among America's most jealously-guarded secrets. But CIA and NSA operatives arranged for a sale of the restricted technology to a known front company in West Germany. The computers quickly made their way into the hands of the Soviets, where they were studied and reproduced in large numbers.

Unknown to the Russians, the NSA had tweaked the computers before delivery, inserting special software and hardware to allow American spies to enter the systems at will after they were installed. Because their copies were such faithful reproductions, duplicate computers the Soviets mass-produced for their military also reproduced the "back doors" the NSA had inserted. Soon the NSA had penetrated the computer systems installed in the most modern elements of the Soviet military, including the Strategic Rocket Forces.

Now Yoshida understood why the Russians lost the Cold War. They were an empire with transparent walls.

This was all accomplished under the aegis of the NARCISSUS project. No offensive actions were taken against Russia's computers under NARCISSUS--the NSA only listened. The Russians would certainly have found that offensive enough, had they known about it. The next binder in their stack bore glaring orange-and-yellow stripes, marked EXTREMELY

SENSITIVE INFORMATION. It directed Pittman and Yoshida to files stored in their terminals, some of which were only days old. The files were translated intercepts of Russian military communications concerning nuclear weapons. NARCISSUS had exposed the Russians' readiness reports, their operational orders, even their launch codes. It was chilling to see a simple sequence of numbers and letters and know they could be used to kill every man, woman, and child in North America and Europe.

The last binder was the most ominous. The black cover bore the NSA seal, with large crimson letters proclaiming VERY RESTRICTED KNOWLEDGE. Richter told them this level of classification had been created specifically for PANDORA. Yoshida knew opening the binder was equivalent to sticking a loaded gun in his mouth and pulling the trigger. But Richter had already pulled that trigger by giving them the files. It was only a question of when the bullet would strike.

PANDORA was an offensive program. If NARCISSUS could expose the launch codes, it might be possible to invade the Russian computers and prevent those codes from being transmitted. In concept, PANDORA could be used to pull the plug on the Russian nuclear forces.

But PANDORA was only a concept. Because an enemy could interpret interference in their nuclear command computers as preparation for a first strike, PANDORA was never allowed to become operational. Immediately following the project summary was an executive order from President Wilcox forbidding the further development of PANDORA. Yoshida wondered what had spurred President Adams to reverse Wilcox's policy. No matter, he decided. He and Pittman wouldn't live long enough to find out.

The rest of the binder outlined programming strategies that could be used to implement PANDORA. Yoshida was stunned. The mechanics of executing PANDORA were not complicated at all. The hardest part of the operation had been obtaining the permission to proceed.

Pittman broke what had been a tense and extended silence. "You know what the scariest part about this is, Ken?"

You mean other than the fact that they'll kill us the day we finish? "What's that?"

"This'll probably work."

CUSTOMER SERVICE

Tony Broadman was jubilant. Not only had Al Rosenstein delivered him permanently from Janet Randall, he had told Broadman to write his piece at home, so he could avoid distractions and finish the story more quickly. He was looking forward to sitting on the deck with his laptop and writing the story that would cement his place as a real investigative reporter at the *Times*.

A cable company truck was parked in front of his house. That was strange. He didn't even know the cable company had lines this far out in the sticks. Maybe they were expanding their territory. Two men worked beside the truck, one reeling out a long tape measure and the other taking notes on a clipboard.

Broadman felt a flash of irritation. Part of why he got a satellite system was to never have to deal with the cable company again. The thought of their trucks driving through his yard while he tried to write made his blood hot. He skidded to a stop beside the cable truck and stalked out to confront the two hard-hatted workers, both of whom looked like bodybuilding contestants.

"What the hell's going on here?" Broadman demanded.

The worker with the clipboard smiled pleasantly and walked over to meet Broadman, as if greeting an old friend. His companion worked hard to keep from scowling. Broadman noticed both had extraordinarily short haircuts, even for outside laborers. In addition to the plate-sized tape measure, the second worker had a long electrical tool Broadman didn't recognize in a holster on his tool belt.

"I hope we didn't block your drive," the man with the clipboard said. "We're just making some measurements."

"Measurements for what?" Broadman countered. "Everyone in this development has a dish! We don't need cable company trucks stringing wire back here!"

"It's just a feasibility study," the man soothed. He held out his clipboard. "Here's the permit from the county authorizing our work."

Broadman examined the sheaf of papers. It contained some maps of the development, but nothing else. "What kind of crap is this?" he argued. "There's no permit in here!" Broadman sensed more than saw the other worker casually move behind him. He turned to see what the man was doing.

It was like being struck by a lightning bolt. The blow knocked the wind from his lungs and drove Broadman down to all fours. He fought desperately to breathe but was unable. He gaped, his lungs paralyzed for several seconds.

When he was finally able to suck in a spastic breath, he heard a sharp hiss and felt a stinging prick on the side of his neck. A cool numbness flowed up and over his brain. His arms and legs suddenly felt very far away.

The pastrami-laced breath of the second worker was hot in his ear. "Now, aren't you glad we're not *really* from the cable company?" he taunted.

Broadman was conscious long enough for his anger to melt into fear before he collapsed face down in the grass.

TRUSTED FRIEND

Christina Broadman pulled her aging RX-7 next to Tony's Cherokee in front of their house. He usually wasn't home this early, but she took it as a good sign. He would have called if he was leaving work sick.

"Hi, sweetheart!" Christina called from the front door. No answer. She checked the bedroom, then the deck. No Tony. The deadbolt had been thrown and the security system was still armed, but neither his keys nor his briefcase were inside.

There was a knock at the front door.

She smiled, her momentary concern relaxing. Tony must have locked himself out and waited at the neighbors until she arrived home. She threw open the door without even checking the peephole.

She backed away with a start. Instead of Tony, it was Ben Hawthorne, Tony's old roommate. His face was grim.

Hawthorne flashed his FBI ID out of habit. "Christina, I'm afraid I have some bad news. May I come inside?"

Her trembling hands flew to her face. "Oh my God! They killed him! Oh God, no!"

Hawthorne grasped her arm. "Christina, calm down! Tony's alive!"

That bought enough stunned silence for Hawthorne to deliver his speech.

"Tony's been kidnapped. A police officer witnessed the abduction, but the men who took Tony were too heavily armed for him to intervene. We know exactly where they are, and the FBI is making preparations for a rescue right now."

Christina was holding herself together only by great effort. "Who? Who took him?"

"A corrupt element of the government, we believe. We're not positive, which is why we have to be very careful. But I wanted to give you my assurance, as a personal friend as well as an FBI agent--we *will* get Tony back safely. You have my word."

She choked back her tears, lifting her chin. "Thank you, Ben. Tony always said you were one of the few people he could really trust."

BEACON

Broadman didn't so much regain consciousness as he began sensing pain. It was too dark to see, but there were other sensations. Vibrations. Road noise. Cold metal against his cheek. A burning tension on his face. He tried to open his mouth, but duct tape was stretched tight over it. He tried to reach up, but plastic loop-ties bit into his wrists. The restraints were cinched so tight he could barely feel his fingers. A tingling in his feet told him his ankles were similarly bound.

Every muscle in his back ached from the stun weapon they had used on him. The drug that followed had given him a pounding headache. He squirmed, trying in vain to find a position that was less painful. Just the attempt made him groan. A flashlight beam stabbed him in the face, making him cry out against the gag.

The flashlight went out immediately. A voice spoke out of the darkness.

"Hello, Mr. Broadman. I apologize for our abrupt methods, but they are necessary. We believe you may have illegally come into possession of vital national security information. I promise if you cooperate fully and answer all our questions, no harm will come to you."

The man's voice was chilling in its measured calm, as if abducting people was an everyday part of his job. Maybe it was, Broadman realized. His search for the people who made Ken Yoshida disappear had finally succeeded.

"We'll be on the road for several hours, so try to..." his abductor stopped in mid-sentence.

Above the ringing in his skull, Broadman heard another slowly increasing sound.

A siren.

Eric! Broadman's heart leapt. The Resistance hadn't abandoned him after all!

"What's going on?" his abductor demanded.

"A police cruiser behind us, closing fast!" another voice answered.

"Well, pull over and let him pass!"

Broadman heard the van slowing and crunching onto the gravel shoulder.

"It's pulling in behind us!" the driver cried out.

"Kramp, you idiot! Were you speeding?"

"No, sir!"

Broadman heard the bolt on an automatic weapon being pulled back. "I can open the rear doors and hose him right now, sir!" a third voice announced.

"Stand down, both of you! It's a routine traffic stop! Just smile, take the ticket, and he'll let us go on our way!"

Broadman felt a gun barrel press against his temple. "Don't get any ideas, Mr. Broadman," the leader said. "If you so much as sneeze, I will not only kill you but that innocent police officer out there. So being stupid will get two people killed, not just one. Nod if you understand."

Broadman nodded.

A tarp was thrown over him. The leader sat on the bench seat over Broadman, shoving the gun barrel into his right side. "Get that weapon out of sight, Womack!" he snapped.

"He's not getting out of his car!" the driver protested. "What's he waiting for? Our plates are clean!"

"Pipe down, Kramp! Vans are high-risk stops! He's probably waiting for back-up! Just stay cool, damn it!"

Broadman smiled as much as the gag allowed. Eric was no doubt calling in the SWAT team right now. It was going to be fun seeing the tables turned on these bastards. As long as he didn't get shot in the process.

They waited for several minutes in anxious silence.

"There's a second patrol car pulling in," the driver announced. "Okay, the lead guy's coming out."

"There," the leader admonished, "just waiting for back-up, like I said! Now turn on the charm and agree with anything he says. I want to see teeth when you smile, damn it!"

Come on, Eric, Broadman's thoughts cried out. *Just order them out of the vehicle already!*

"He's gone behind the van," the driver whispered. "What the hell is he doing back there?"

"Anything he wants! Now shut up and stay cool!"

With his ear pressed against the van's floor, Broadman heard a metallic scratching sound. The sound stopped and the footsteps approached the driver's door. The gun pressed more firmly into his side, urging silence. His heart pounded.

"Good evening, sir," he heard Eric's voice say. "Sorry to make you wait. Did you know your license tag light is missing?"

"Uh, no, sir, I didn't," the driver stuttered.

"Yeah, first I thought it was just burned out, but I checked and the bulb is gone. Must have vibrated loose, eh?"

"What? Oh, yeah, that must be what happened."

"Are you on your way back to Maryland?" Eric asked.

"Ah, yes, sir, Maryland, that's right."

"Then you'd better get this fixed before you cross over into Jersey. License tag lights are their bullshit ticket of the month down there. They nailed my wife just last week. There's an auto parts store at the next exit that should be able to fix you up."

Come on, Eric! Broadman's mind shouted. *What are you waiting for?*

"Oh, okay, officer, I'll do that right now."

"Pardon me for asking," Eric continued, "But are you with the government?"

The driver almost choked. "Uh, why do you ask?"

"Your license tag came up as an unissued plate," Eric said in a friendly tone. "Mind if I see some ID, please?"

"Well, sir, I..."

"Show it to him!" the leader hissed.

A flashlight beam played across the interior of the van. Broadman almost screamed out, but the gun was pressed with painful urgency into one of his kidneys.

"Oh, you're not alone in there!" Eric bantered. "It's just a formality, sir, I won't report it to anyone."

What the hell are you doing, Eric?

"Well, ah, okay, here you go."

A long silence ensued. Broadman's eardrums almost split from the pounding of his heart.

Now Eric was stuttering. "Whoa, NSA! Gosh, I'm sorry to have bothered you guys! Man, it took so long, too! I had to wait until my backup came--it's procedure on all van stops."

The driver's confidence was returning. "That's no problem, officer, we just prefer to keep a low profile. Would you mind not talking about this over the radio, please?"

"Oh, absolutely! And sorry again for the delay! Have a nice evening, gentlemen!"

"Okay...thanks for the warning, officer."

No! This can't be happening! Broadman almost screamed out loud when the van pulled back onto the highway and accelerated away.

"See?" the leader lectured. "Just stay cool! You didn't even get a ticket! You're sure as hell not going to get an Oscar, either! *'Uh, uh, uh! Yessa, officer!'*" he mocked. "I'm glad you guys weren't around in the bad old days! The KGB would have eaten you two for lunch!"

Broadman's mind wailed. *Eric! Don't leave me with these bastards!*

* * *

Eric waved as his back-up pulled away. He fished the van's license tag light from his pocket and threw it into the ditch. Back in his patrol car, he reached under the seat and retrieved his laptop. He strung its antenna wire to the dashboard while the software booted. The laptop beeped.

"Tally ho," he whispered. A flashing symbol slowly pulled away from his position on the map screen. He placed the cruiser in gear and keyed his mike. "Dispatch, Patrol Six. Traffic stop completed, returning to service, southbound 87."

"Roger, Patrol Six," Dispatch replied.

Eric already had his cell phone in secure mode with the number loaded. He pressed the SEND key.

"How are the Yankees doing?" Patrick answered.

"I prefer the Mets. The pickup was completed. The cargo appears to be intact. The beacon is in place and sweet. By the way, our new friend was right about the moving company. Positive ID on one of the movers. Maryland appears to be their final destination."

"Acknowledged. I have an aircraft moving into position now. Good work, Eric."

"Thank you, sir."

CHAPTER 14

"To dare--that is the whole secret of revolutions."
- Antoine Saint-Just

ARRIVAL

The cellular phone on Archer's nightstand rang. "Hello?" he answered groggily.

"How are the Redskins going to do this year?" he heard.

The code phrase jolted him awake. "Who cares?" Archer replied. "I can't afford those tickets."

"You were right," Patrick said. "They're coming straight to you, ETA about one hour."

Archer was already pulling on his clothes. "On my way."

* * *

An hour later in his office at the NSA, Archer's private line rang.

It was Sergeant Townsend. "They've arrived."

"Read the tag number back to me."

Townsend recited the digits of the van's plates.

"That's a match," Archer agreed. Since the windows of the NSA's headquarters buildings were electronically shielded, his cell phone was useless. He used his private line to call Patrick.

"They're here. I'm signing my statement now." He placed his index finger against the imager. The laptop beeped when his authentication was accepted. He popped out the CD and handed it to a young man who looked very out of place in civilian clothes.

Corporal Rawlins nodded smartly and left the room. He even marched when out of uniform, Archer noted.

"The courier is on his way."

"I'll add your statement to my package," Patrick said. "Wish me luck."

THE DAMNED

Senior Airman Dave Jackson hurried into the Snake Pit's cramped monitoring room, throwing his jacket over a chair.

"You're late," Senior Airman Tim Feldman said without looking up.

"Sorry," Jackson said. "Didn't sleep well."

Feldman scanned him with one eye. "Then at least you have an excuse for looking like shit."

Feldman had earned his spot among Stoyer's favored few by gambling away his Air Force paycheck, then using his hacking skills to pay his debts. Jackson knew Feldman could only build himself up by tearing everyone else down, so he didn't take the barbs too seriously. "Thanks for your concern. I love you too."

Feldman had already tuned him out. "Most of the slimeballs are still working the after-action review of the China attack, trying to find stuff we can do better next time. So they don't have much opportunity to make mischief. Yoshida's loafing today. They practically had to prod him out of bed at bayonet point. For what he's got done so far, they might as well have let him sleep in. He's not the hot property Richter took him for."

Feldman changed windows on his monitor. Text was being entered at an amazing speed. "Pittman's making up for both of them, though. Be sure and keep an eye on him. It looks like he's working to the script, but I'm just waiting for him to try to pull another fast one."

"Gotcha," Jackson replied. Richter was making Pittman and Yoshida work double shifts on PANDORA, requiring Jackson and Feldman to trade off watcher duty.

Feldman walked out without making eye contact. "All the snakes in the pit are now yours to watch. Enjoy."

Jackson noticed how Feldman never referred to the prisoners even as hackers. It was always slimeballs, snakes, or scum. He guessed it was to avoid thinking of them as human beings.

Not that he faulted Feldman's reasoning. Jackson wished *he* could keep a little more emotional distance. Listening to Richter torture Pittman and Yoshida yesterday was like listening to the cries of the damned. When Jackson went home last night, he had briefly contemplated getting on the highway and driving until he saw tumbleweeds. But he had never put together a serious escape plan. And Richter was very good at finding people who didn't want to be found.

Jackson tried to follow what Pittman was doing, but Pittman kept scrolling up and down through the Russian program. It was almost like he was trying to hide what he was doing from the watchers. After a few futile minutes, Jackson gave up and instead examined Pittman's proposed changes to the Russian nuclear control program. The code was clean and straightforward.

It didn't make sense. The idea that you could take somebody like Pittman, who had already sabotaged their efforts, torture him, and then put him back to work like nothing had ever happened? No way. Jackson knew too much about the hackers he watched. Pittman would just be that much more determined to get revenge, and might even persuade Yoshida to join him. The way Stoyer and Richter were playing this didn't make sense.

Hell, PANDORA didn't make sense. It had been a long-standing NSA policy not to screw with foreign computers tied to national systems like nuclear forces and air defenses. The consequences of a mistake were just too grim. But PANDORA was going forward anyway. It was crazy.

Like anything that happened in the Snake Pit was sane. Jackson willed his eyes to focus on the screen. He needed coffee. After what little sleep he had gotten last night, he would take his coffee in an IV drip bag if he could get it.

Jackson had the same nightmare three times last night. *He* was the one strapped to the torture table, totally at Richter's mercy. When he awoke in a cold sweat the third time, Jackson had realized that for all practical purposes he was just as damned as Pittman and Yoshida. When Stoyer was finished with the hackers, Richter would clean up all evidence of the Snake Pit's existence. The hackers were dispensable. About as dispensable as a lowly Air Force E-4 Senior Airman who had outlived his usefulness.

TRAP DOOR

Bob Pittman was admiring the PANDORA program in a way only a hacker could appreciate. The elegance and subtlety of its back doors--and there were many--engendered a profound respect for the NSA computer experts who had tunneled into the very heart of the Soviet military complex. How sad they had been reined in before they could carry their hacking to its logical conclusion--taking control of Russia's nuclear arsenal.

Wait a minute, he thought.

Pittman had the unique talent of "running the code" of any program in his head before he executed it. Often he could spot logic flaws and ambiguous decision paths faster than a debugging program. That talent was scratching at the back of his mind right now. *Something's wrong, something's wrong.*

Pittman ran through the subroutine which routed nuclear attack information again. He had a duplicate of the Russian system on his workstation. But his every keystroke was being watched, if not by Yoshida, by some unseen watcher on the other side of these walls. He would have to run the code in his head, like he had done many times on the outside. Sometimes he only had one shot against a well-defended computer.

No, it couldn't be that simple.

He checked the code again just to be sure. He scrolled the screen up and down frequently, not wanting whoever was monitoring him to zero in on the section of code he was dissecting. There it was. There was no doubt. Pittman closed the window and sat back.

It was only logical, really. Eventually the Russians would figure out their systems had been penetrated. Once the CIA had acted on enough information secured by NARCISSUS, the source of the leak would be traced. In most countries, the compromised system would be ripped out and discarded.

But that would be expensive, and the Russians were broke. So they kept a system they knew was not secure--with a catch. Over a decade of experience with the CIA and NSA since the Cold War had verified America's "look but don't touch" strategy with Russia's nuclear computers.

In case the US changed that strategy, the Russians had inserted an anti-tampering subroutine, buried among a number of innocuous diagnostic programs. The diagnostic programs appeared routine, so the NSA's experts had ignored them. But if an unauthorized change was made to the system, even a minor one, the anti-tampering routine would sound the alarm. Unless the NSA tested their modifications and the diagnostic programs together, they would never see the trap waiting for them.

Pittman did not have to check the line number the anti-tampering program referenced. He had stared at it long enough before. It was the command line that released Russia's launch codes. It made sense. The only reason another nuclear power would tamper with Russia's nuclear control computers would be to paralyze their arsenal in preparation for a first strike. So the Russians had designed a "launch on tamper" command to release a preemptive nuclear strike against any aggressor.

Pittman felt a flush of satisfaction. All these smart NSA people working on PANDORA and no one had seen the snare waiting for them. But they were government types, trained to carry out their orders with drone-like efficiency. He was a hacker, taught by experience not to take a step without looking for the trap beneath his feet.

President Wilcox had either been very wise or had a source on the inside who had warned him of the danger of proceeding with PANDORA. Either way, that decision had been reversed, to their folly. All Pittman had to do to bring about a nuclear war was obey orders. It was fitting. Pittman felt a small twinge of guilt, but ignored it. What had the world ever done for him?

This would be his way of getting back at them all. Back at all the women who had ever rejected him for being fat and ugly. He would kill them *and* their precious families. Back at all the computer geeks who had passed him by and raked in their "dot-com" fortunes while he rotted in this bunker. But most of all he would get back at the men who had imprisoned him, along with everyone who had stood by and done nothing. He would die too, but that was a small price to pay for such thorough and final revenge. He suppressed a smile.

"How's it looking to you, Ken?" Pittman asked.

"I don't see any problem with PANDORA," Yoshida said. "All the hard work is already done."

"Yeah, it looks clean to me, too. Ready to take a break?"

* * *

Yoshida continued his examination of the bunker's upper level during their short trips to the bathroom. The officer's head was on the opposite end of the upper level, which gave him repeated opportunities for reconnaissance.

"Keep your head down!" the guard growled. "There's nothing to see here!"

Yoshida complied but kept scanning with the corners of his eyes. Two guards were using a magnetic card to gain access to a small room directly across the hall from their cell. One guard tucked the card back into his breast pocket. *What are they hiding in there?* Yoshida wondered.

They had barely unzipped their jumpsuits when the guard shouted at them again.

"Tuck it in, maggots! Back in your cage! Move it!"

Yoshida hastily completed his business, then shuffled back to the cell. The guards he had been watching emerged from the small room, one carrying a cattle prod, the other a shotgun, which he cocked loudly for the prisoners' benefit.

The armory! Now *that* was a useful piece of information.

Once their cell door was closed, Yoshida pressed his ear against it. Something was happening. Luckily the guard watching the door had the same question. The conversation was muffled but audible.

"Hey, what's going on?" their guard asked.

"Richter snagged some reporter who found out what we're doing with the hackers," the other responded.

Yoshida's stomach sank. Did Tony Broadman come looking for him, only to fall into the same trap? Worse, did Broadman find out about Yoshida's Resistance connections before he was captured? If he talked, it would shorten Yoshida's life even more.

The first guard chuckled. "I hope the guy's got good life insurance."

THE INTERVIEW

A boot in his side woke Broadman up. He didn't how he could have fallen asleep. Probably a combination of nervous exhaustion and the aftereffects of that knock-out drug they had used on him. He had no idea how long he had been out or how far he had traveled.

His grim-faced captors prodded him from the van. It looked like they were in a large garage, but then they ushered him up a ladder and through an airlock, like on a ship or a submarine. All around were armed guards in black jumpsuits.

What the hell was this place? Broadman was shown into a small office. A hawk-faced three-star general stood and gestured to a chair.

"Mr. Broadman? I'm General Stoyer. Please have a seat."

* * *

"I'm sorry, Mr. Broadman, I just have trouble believing that," Stoyer said.

Broadman placed his forehead against his hand. The grilling had gone on for over an hour so far. The hangover from the knock-out drug blurred his thinking. Stoyer and his brawny assistant Richter firing questions from both sides didn't make it any easier.

"Well, I'm sorry too, General, but you don't have to be a rocket scientist to figure out that somebody is making these hackers disappear. It's just a logical conclusion from the public record."

Richter leaned forward. "But accusing the National Security Agency of responsibility is a hell of leap. How did you reach that conclusion?"

Broadman glowered at Richter. He had obviously left his Constitutional rights back in New York, where the Resistance didn't even give these guys a speeding ticket when they had the chance. Spouting the First Amendment and hinting about the *Times'* excellent legal department wasn't going to get him out of this fix.

Broadman counted on his fingers. "Motive, means, and opportunity. Every law enforcement agency in the US would love to get their hands on these hackers, but no one comes close to having the equipment and security cover of the NSA. The more I dug, the more the needle swung in your direction. That's it. Tell me I'm wrong, and I'll keep digging until I get the right answer."

Stoyer's cheek twitched. "I wish I could, Mr. Broadman. But you're correct. Now I need to know your source. Someone put you onto this story, told you *where* to dig. The New York *Times* doesn't give a damn about the well-being of hackers. But you love to stick it to the government, don't you?" Stoyer's eyes bore into him. "Your *source*, Mr. Broadman."

"I wrote a piece about hackers," Broadman insisted. "Do you guys read the papers? I picked up the story from *2600* during my research. After I interviewed some of the hackers' families, it seemed interesting enough to pursue as a separate report."

Broadman was desperate enough to try a desperate lie. "The editor of the national desk green-lighted it to run just today." He glanced at his watch. "I mean yesterday. Was it in the paper this morning? I haven't read mine yet."

Stoyer regarded him like a rattlesnake eyeing a rat. "Nice try, Mr. Broadman, but we have sources, too. No such hacker story is in the works at the *Times*. You must be pursuing this on your own hook. However, we *know* you've been talking to FBI employees and enticing them to violate their security oaths. The FBI says they shared nothing with you. So who's lying, Mr. Broadman?"

Broadman swallowed. Had Hawthorne turned him in? Never. Worse, could Ben be undergoing a similar interrogation right now? It took every fragment of control Broadman had left to keep his face impassive. "Neither of us are, General. The FBI told me nothing, but I still managed to put it together on my own."

Stoyer gave him a plastic smile. "That's your story and you're sticking to it, eh?"

"I'm afraid so, General. There's really nothing else to tell."

The smile melted. "I doubt that very much, Mr. Broadman. Colonel, take this man downstairs and see if the radar gun will loosen his tongue."

THE JUDGE

Judge Norma Calloway spread the satellite photos across her desk. The drapes were closed in her paneled chamber, the gloom further lending to the conspiratorial atmosphere. The heavy oak door was locked, with strict orders given to her secretary not to allow interruptions. Calloway regarded her guest with a raised eyebrow. "You're treading on very thin ice with this one, Mr. Patrick."

The humility Patrick exhibited was entirely sincere. "I'm aware of that, your honor. I thought you should see all the evidence in my possession, admissible or not."

Judge Calloway was the first black woman appointed to the Federal Courts of Appeal. Her position in the D.C. Circuit made her indispensable to the Resistance. The three-judge panel on which she served had the authority to make immediate decisions on the constitutionality of actions taken by federal agencies inside the Beltway. Prosecution of Cabinet-level officials also fell within her purview.

Calloway had been among the founding members of the Resistance. Her son Edgar had been killed in action during a classified mission as an Army Ranger in 1986. Her repeated requests for information to the Army were stonewalled.

After consulting her network of government and intelligence contacts she finally learned the truth. Edgar's unit had stumbled onto a "weapons in, drugs out" smuggling scheme in Central America using US military aircraft, for the personal enrichment of a US general. Edgar's team was subsequently wiped out by "communist guerrillas" during a reconnaissance mission.

The fledgling Resistance movement had lacked the resources to take immediate action, but they began building a dossier against the general. At the appropriate time, the release of the files to a friendly senator torpedoed the general's nomination to chair the Joint Chiefs and forced him into early retirement. It was a small victory, but it was one Calloway still savored.

"Speaking of treading on thin ice, you say this General Stoyer snatched a reporter for the New York *Times* right off the street?" Calloway asked.

Patrick shuffled his stack of documents. "Out of his front yard, actually. I had a team member up the street watching the whole thing. Here's his statement. He had to alter his story somewhat. It wouldn't look good if they knew he was sitting there waiting for the kidnapping to occur."

"Understood," she agreed. "Still a very gutsy move on the NSA's part. So you managed to plant a beacon on their van and tracked them *here?*" she said, pointing to the photographs.

"That's right, your honor. Our contact at the NSA was alerted and matched the tag number of the van when it arrived. His statement is on this disk."

Calloway inserted the diskette into her computer. She smiled. "Ah, Mr. Archer. What would we do without him? He even authenticated the document. Very thorough."

"So," Patrick summarized, "the NSA abducted a private citizen, transported him across state lines, and is now holding him against his will on government property." He advanced a piece of paper toward the judge.

Calloway reached for the document and a pen. "Excellent casework as usual, Mr. Patrick. I hereby grant your request for a search warrant of the NSA facility in question, for immediate execution. How long until you mount your rescue?"

"After I deliver this package, I'm heading straight to Quantico."

Calloway removed her glasses. "I've given you all the legal authority you need. This next step you're planning is unnecessary. What if he says no?"

"It's not legal authority I'm concerned about, it's firepower. I don't want this thing to turn into another Waco standoff."

"I see your point. But if he refuses, you come right back here. I want you to *rescue* Mr. Broadman and your man, not just recover their bodies."

"I'm counting on him to say yes. Should I leave the satellite photos with you?"

Calloway's dark eyes narrowed. "No," she declared after a short deliberation. "There's no denying the impact of seeing it with your own eyes. Keep them with the package. Good luck, and remember to zip up that flak jacket. I couldn't stand to lose another of my boys."

Patrick gave Calloway a rare smile. "Always, your honor." He collected his documents.

"Oh, Jeremy?" Calloway called to his back.

"Yes, ma'am?"

Her expression hardened. "Nail this bastard Stoyer for me. I really have a thing about corrupt generals!"

Patrick gave the judge a grim nod. "Count on it."

FINAL OPTION

Broadman's lungs were so raw from screaming, he had trouble speaking when Kramp removed the torture device.

"So how does Ken Yoshida fit into all this?" Richter grilled. "I saw you two together with my own eyes, don't even try to deny it."

The question pushed Broadman to the edge of panic. These renegades had been watching him from the very beginning. One wrong step here would kill both him and Yoshida. "He was my source for a hacker story in the paper! You can read it right off the *Times* website! If you hadn't kidnapped him, I would have never suspected a thing!"

"And you pumped your friend Hawthorne for information, too?"

"But he didn't *tell* me anything!" Broadman gasped, desperate not to doom his friend to a similar fate.

Richter chuckled. "It's worse than that, Mr. Broadman. Not only did he not help you, he reported your questioning to his supervisor, who notified us."

Broadman still had enough strength left for a burst of anger. "You're lying, you bastard! Ben Hawthorne wouldn't do that!" Strapped to the torture gurney on his stomach, Broadman couldn't even look his accuser in the face.

Richter's voice dripped with disgust. "If you were my friend, I'd turn your ass in, too! Anyone who would ask a friend to violate his oath is no friend at all! You deserve this one, you scumbag!"

Kramp increased the power another notch.

Broadman screamed again. When the electric fire abated, he heard footsteps over his own labored breathing.

"Any progress?" Stoyer asked.

"Well," Richter said, "he admitted his contact with the FBI agent, but that's old news. I think he's telling the truth about putting it together on his own."

"So journalism isn't dead after all," Stoyer grumbled. "What's your next move?"

"I've been thinking about that. He's too high-profile to just go missing. But if we fry his brain and dump him in a cheap hotel near his house, we can make it look like he had a stroke while he was with a hooker."

What? Broadman almost screamed aloud.

"That'll work," Stoyer agreed. "Need me to pull any strings?"

"No, sir, my men and I can take care of it."

"Very well, carry on." Stoyer and Richter might have been discussing plans for dinner.

Broadman's heart and mind were racing. He was tied to the tracks and the train was closing fast.

Richter moved behind him again. Broadman heard the whine of the torture gun winding up. "Hey Kramp," Richter

said, "move that bucket. I don't want him getting it all over the
floor. There. That's good."

Broadman felt the hard point of the gun press against the
back of his neck. He had only one piece of information left to
trade for a few more minutes of life.

"Hold still, Mr. Broadman," Richter growled. "This will
only hurt worse than anything you've ever felt in your whole
life!"

"*WAIT!*" Broadman screamed. "*I can tell you about the Resistance!*"

INEVITABILITY

Jackson sat at his terminal, too terrified to move. Every
scream that echoed up from below stopped his heart in mid-
beat. He had learned from one of the guards that Richter was
interrogating a reporter who had learned about the Snake Pit. If
so, that was it. Stoyer and Richter had finally gone over the
edge. Jackson couldn't just sit here while the whole situation
spiraled out of control.

He could almost hear Richter scoff back at him. *And just
what the hell are you going to do about it, Jackson?* What could
he do? Go to the FBI? What if the FBI was *already* involved?
He was sure the FBI didn't mind a few hackers dropping off the
face of the earth. Maybe the FBI was looking the other way
while the NSA did its dirty work.

Could he escape? Just run away? With the NSA's resources, he would have to leave civilization totally behind or
Richter would hunt him down as a security threat and eliminate
him. But living an untraceable existence required cash. Jackson
had saved up about three thousand dollars, but that wouldn't
even buy Ted Kazinsky's shack in Montana.

There was one last blood-chilling scream from below, then
silence. Jackson ran to the bathroom. Whether from fear or five
cups of coffee, his bowels drained out like oil from a hot engine.
He doubled over on the toilet, suppressing the urge to vomit
until he could flush.

There, with his head in the toilet, Dave Jackson's fear left
him. One moment it clenched his knotted stomach like a vise,
and the next moment it was gone. Suddenly Jackson understood
how the doomed passengers on those hijacked planes felt. He

was dead regardless of which path he chose. He could either face certain death at a time of his own choosing, or passively allow death to take him according to its own merciless schedule.

Strangely, it was the inevitability of death that lifted the burden from Jackson's shoulders. With self-preservation no longer a concern, his few options snapped into razor-sharp focus. Now all he had to do was pick one.

OPEN DOOR

Pittman and Yoshida were supposed to be partners on PANDORA, but Yoshida was determined to be as much of a hindrance as possible. He wanted to deny Stoyer and Richter a tool they obviously needed. That a slit trench was probably waiting for them upon completion of their task was also an incentive to drag his heels.

But Pittman was obsessed with PANDORA. A few carefully passed notes warning him to slow down only fueled his enthusiasm. Maybe Pittman was truly trying to work himself into an early grave. Yoshida checked Pittman's work carefully, but the code was both clean and efficient. Pittman was striving toward a new level of hacker excellence.

Yoshida spent much of his time filtering through the NARCISSUS intercepts. "Looking for an opening" was the cover story he gave Richter. The intercepts were being relayed almost hourly now, as soon as the NSA's interpreters translated them into English. It was fascinating material and did not contribute a single command line to PANDORA, which was an added benefit.

Yoshida was having trouble concentrating even on the intercepts, though. Every few minutes another animal scream echoed up from the lower level. He couldn't tell for sure whether the voice was Broadman's, but it was a safe bet.

Yoshida didn't know which was more frightening--his recollections of what the reporter was enduring below, or whether Broadman would say something to hasten Yoshida's demise. Finally the screaming stopped. Secretly, Yoshida hoped Richter had put Broadman out of his misery, or that Broadman had unexpectedly left the Snake Pit through the only certain method of escape.

"Well, the Russians are going to launch an SS-25 tomorrow," Yoshida said absently.

Pittman stopped typing and blinked for several seconds. "What did you say?"

"I said the Russians are going to launch an SS-25 mobile ICBM tomorrow. Just a test launch, nothing important."

Pittman was up and standing at Yoshida's terminal. "Show me!"

"See? It's just a routine readiness test, to make sure the missiles still..."

Pittman went to the door and pounded. "Guard! Open up!"

"You just went to the bathroom!" was the muffled response. "Sit down and get back to work!"

"I need to speak to Richter right now!"

"Richter's busy!" the guard chuckled. "Shut up and hack!"

Pittman pounded on the door for emphasis. "Tell Richter to take a break from whoever he's torturing! The Russians just handed us the key to this whole project!"

SEXUAL FAVORS

Cynthia Hale was locking away her classified documents when Secretary of State Harry Abramson knocked on her open office door. "The President wanted to know if you could join us for lunch," he asked.

Hale flinched. "Is this business?" The last thing she wanted was to be dragged unprepared into a meeting where she would be expected to improvise foreign policy and eat without smearing her lipstick. Especially today.

"No, Marshall and I were just going to grab a sandwich before the Italian PM gets here. He asked if you wanted to join us."

It wasn't often one declined lunch with the President and the Secretary of State. But she had an even more pressing appointment. "I have to get out of this building for a while," she offered, which was true enough. "Thank Marshall for thinking of me."

Abramson drew back. Adams had sent him to offer this meeting as an olive branch. Apparently he had slighted her recently and wanted to give her more face time to make it up. Abramson certainly didn't expect to have his olive branch handed back to him. He dipped his chin slightly, regarding her from under his bushy eyebrows. "Are you two having a tiff, young lady?"

Hale reached for her purse. "Not at all," she assured him. "I just have an old girlfriend from college in town for the day. With the state dinner tonight, lunch is the only time we'll be able to get together," she lied. She gave his arm an affectionate squeeze on her way out. "That's for calling me 'young' lady, you old charmer."

Abramson grinned. "I'll give Marshall your regrets."

She marched with a purposeful step toward the East Appointments Gate.

Cynthia Hale had a secret lover. They had been seeing each other for almost six months now. Their relationship had grown more passionate with time, but both desired to avoid the Washington gossip storm a public relationship would spawn. Instead, they snuck away whenever their hectic schedules allowed. It was never even a full day together, much less a long weekend, before one of their public lives intruded and dragged one of them away. Usually the best they could hope for was a tender evening together, only to part again before dawn.

But today was an exception. An encrypted e-mail asked her to meet him at the Willard Hotel for lunch. He said it was urgent. She smiled. It was always pretty urgent when they got together. The e-mail told her to ask at the desk for a message.

Though dressed in a suit and heels, she strode the three blocks to the hotel quickly, passing a power walker in tights and sneakers like he was standing still. The tingling anticipation she felt made her cheeks hot. She was breathless when she reached the Willard's opulent gold-leaf-and-crystal lobby.

"Do you have a message for Mrs. Randolph?" she asked at the front desk, using the assumed name the e-mail had prompted.

The young Hispanic clerk smirked when he handed her the envelope. It was obvious by feel that the envelope held a key card. He lifted an eyebrow suggestively, noting with his eyes her lack of a wedding band.

Can it, Romeo! she wanted to say. Ripping the envelope open revealed "ROOM 301" on a piece of paper. Hale's heels touched the carpet infrequently in her haste to reach the elevators.

She punched the up button and tried to will the doors open. She had never acted like such a teenager before, even when she *was* a teenager. She had been so intent on her career then--her personal quest to change the world. She had even spurned a few well-meaning suitors, thinking her future too important to crowd with marriage and family. Her career would be her fulfillment, she told them.

What a joke that was, and a bad one at that.

Only now, well into her forties, did she realize that solitary success and solitary failure were equally lonely. But it had been her choice, and now she had to live with it. Her lover had made no promises for a future together, but at least he fulfilled her present.

For the moment, that was good enough.

Room 301 was directly across from the elevator. She almost broke the plastic keycard jamming it into the lock. Her lover was waiting inside, his suit already draped over one of the French Provincial chairs. He was loosely clad in one of the hotel bathrobes, the tight, smooth skin of his chest and stomach visible all the way down to his waist. Hale felt her knees weaken.

He stood, gesturing to a silver tray. "I didn't know how hungry you would be, so I ordered room service."

Hale wrapped her arms around him, kissing him firmly and deeply. When she finally allowed him to come up for air, she whispered, "The only thing I'm hungry for is you!"

Jeremy Patrick regarded her with his piercing blue eyes. "You took the words right out of my mouth."

* * *

With his passion spent and hers at least temporarily pacified, they turned their attention to more mundane appetites. Patrick laid the silver tray between them.

"Sandwiches?" Hale teased. "So much for romance!"

"I wasn't sure how long you would be able to break away. It's kind of hard to tuck duck *á l'orange* under your arm and carry it back to the office."

She laughed. "Not many men can think with their pants down. I'm impressed." She reached across the tray and stroked him gently. "Especially if your needs were so urgent that you couldn't even wait for this evening to satisfy them."

Patrick blushed and looked away.

Hale set down her sandwich. "That is, unless you had *another* reason this rendezvous was so urgent?"

His plaintive blue eyes met hers. "I need a favor. A big one."

Hale sighed and returned her attentions to her sandwich. She combined her "office voice" with a suggestive flip of her short brown hair. "Very well, Assistant Director Patrick, proceed." She winked. "Then I'll tell you how much this favor is going to cost you."

PROPOSAL

Yoshida waited in tense silence for Richter to arrive. The way Pittman avoided attention, Yoshida couldn't imagine why he would *call* for Richter, especially when Richter was in the middle of torturing someone. Pittman had gotten very motivated and very stupid at the same time. Yoshida cringed at the stomp of approaching combat boots.

Richter almost tore the knob off the cell door. "This better be good, damn it!"

If Pittman felt threatened, it didn't show. "I found a risk-free way of testing PANDORA. Interested?"

Richter calmed down only slightly. "Keep talking."

Pittman pointed at the NARCISSUS intercept on Yoshida's screen. "The Russians are about to test fire an SS-25 ICBM from Siberia at something called the Pacific Test Area. Heard of it?"

"No. Go on."

"The order instructs the missile unit to go on simulated nuclear alert. Some time tomorrow, target coordinates and a launch order will be given."

Pittman had Richter's full attention now. "Testing their ability to launch on the move?" Richter theorized.

"Ken says the SS-25 is a mobile missile. It can't be easy to hit *anything* when you're launching an ICBM off the back of a truck. They probably want to make sure they can still do it."

"So how does PANDORA fit into this?"

"The targeting coordinates will go straight through the compromised nuclear computer. What if we screwed with their targeting instructions? Nothing major, just transpose a couple of digits, make it look like an input error by the missile jockey. If

we can watch this Pacific Test Area and put the missile five or
ten miles off target, then PANDORA works. So if we need to
really screw with their missiles in the future, we'll know we can
do it."

Richter stared at Pittman for a long time. Finally his eyes
shifted to Yoshida. "Is he serious, or is he trying to blow us all
to hell?"

As much as Yoshida resisted progress on PANDORA, he
couldn't think of a less risky method to test the concept. If it
worked, nobody got hurt. Even if they were detected, it would
be unlikely to start a war. That was more than he could say
about their previous Snake Pit assignments.

"Just don't give him the coordinates of your house," Yoshida said.

Richter sneered. "Not damned likely. All right, Pittman, I'll
pass this up to the General. Get started. Yoshida, keep an eye on
him."

* * *

Kramp was waiting outside. "Sir, what do we do with
Broadman?"

Richter considered his options. The reporter had just started
spinning some tale about a resistance movement made up of
government employees when Pittman made his discovery.
Broadman's story was probably just fiction, an invention to pro-
long his life. However, if true, it would be definite cause for
alarm. Either way, it had aroused Richter's curiosity, but he had
more pressing concerns at the moment. Broadman would have
to wait.

"Put him in the box," Richter said. "We'll finish with him
later."

ETHICS TRAINING

Archer checked the NSA's Facilities office for stragglers.
There were none. He had discovered the Facilities department
was deficient in its government-required Ethics and Diversity
training classes, so he arranged for the entire department to attend a make-up session at one time. If he had to sit through

those bull sessions, so did everyone else. That it left the Facilities office empty was also an added benefit.

Corporal Rawlins, back in uniform, stood watch while Archer and Sergeant Townsend went inside.

Archer patted the top of a locked file cabinet. "This one."

Townsend opened a drawing tube and extracted a small bolt cutter. After some grunting and straining, Townsend defeated the lock guarding the DATASHARK blueprints.

Archer rifled the drawers, handing any drawings he found useful to Townsend. Soon the drawing tube was packed with classified blueprints.

Townsend held up the bolt cutters. "What do we do with these, sir?"

Archer shoved the tool and the broken lock inside one of the half-emptied drawers, then secured the cabinet with an undamaged padlock. "There, that should hold them for a while."

Townsend and Archer affixed the seals and signatures to the drawing tube that would allow Rawlins to pass unmolested through Security. "Are you sure you can find this place?" Archer asked the Marine.

"Quantico used to be my old stomping grounds, sir," Rawlins assured him. "I know right where to go."

"Carry on, then!"

Archer and Townsend watched the courier march away. "Thanks, Stan," Archer said. "That concludes our Ethics training for today."

Townsend shifted uncomfortably. "It won't take them long to find out about the missing drawings, sir. And neither of us wore gloves."

Archer was exhilarated to finally be on the offensive. "Stan, by this time tomorrow, missing drawings will be the *least* of the NSA's problems."

A SIMPLE EXERCISE

Stoyer came to the bunker immediately at the news of Pittman's discovery. Richter spread a large map of the northern Pacific over the conference room table. Stoyer, Jackson, and Feldman huddled around it.

Richter tapped a red box on the map. "This is the Russians' Pacific Test Area. It straddles the International Date Line and is almost a thousand miles from land in any direction. That's where their missile is going."

"So what exactly is Pittman proposing?" Stoyer asked.

"When the Russian nuclear command issues the targeting and launch order, Pittman wants to intercept the transmission and alter the target coordinates slightly."

Stoyer was wary of Pittman's tricks. "Define 'slightly.'"

Richter presented a photograph of a camouflaged mobile launcher. The missile tube seemed too large even for the massive fourteen-wheeled vehicle. "This is an SS-25 mobile ICBM. The Russians have built over a thousand miles of forest roads in Siberia just for these monsters to hide in. But even when launched from the field, the SS-25 can hit within a half mile of the bull's eye.

"Pittman wants to throw the targeting coordinates off by a few hundredths of a degree of latitude or longitude, which would equate to about a five-mile error. Large enough for us to detect, but small enough the Russians will probably assume someone transposed a number when they typed in the launch order. This will verify the effectiveness of PANDORA without tipping our hand too much."

"If it goes down in the ocean, how will we know whether the missile landed off target?" Stoyer asked.

"The Russians always dispatch a satellite tracking ship to the impact area before they test," Richter explained. "The Navy follows those ships as a matter of course. We can also dispatch long-range reconnaissance aircraft out of Alaska. We'll know whether it hit the mark or not."

"And how do we make sure Pittman doesn't sabotage *this* test?" Stoyer demanded. "I don't want him doing to L.A. what he did to the Chinese Navy."

Feldman took the question. "The program Pittman wrote for this test is too small to hide a virus. It just accepts the target coordinates and transposes the numbers to the right of the decimal point. But we'll rewrite the program, just to be safe. We can even source-protect the code so it could *only* be executed from one of our terminals. He won't a have chance to make any mischief. We'll be pushing all the buttons ourselves."

Stoyer locked eyes with Feldman. "Are you absolutely sure about that? I have *zero* tolerance for mistakes at this point."

Feldman paused. He knew the hackers were doomed men, and he had no desire to join them. "No doubts, sir. PANDORA will work as advertised. We'll make sure of it."

Stoyer considered the plan set before him. It wasn't a difficult decision. Compared to HEADSHOT or PUZZLE BOX, this was a simple exercise. How strange no one had tried this before, considering the rewards of success.

"Very well," Stoyer pronounced. "PANDORA is a go!"

GULAG

Cynthia Hale was waiting in the Oval Office. She stood nervously when the President bustled in.

"Okay, Cynthia, what's so urgent?" he asked cheerfully. "I don't want to leave the Prime Minister of Italy for too long. His government might fall before I get back!"

Hale opened a large envelope bearing a Department of Justice seal. She focused on the plan she and Patrick had devised. He was right about this being a big favor. "Some new satellite photos just came in, sir." She spread the photographs on the President's desk.

Hale's demeanor checked Adams's light-hearted mood. He plucked his bifocals from a pocket. "Okay, this looks like a bunker. A bunker with a lot of antennas. What exactly is this?"

Hale pushed forward one of the detail shots. "It's a bunker all right. But it's the people around the bunker that got my attention."

Adams studied the two dozen or so orange-clad men milling around inside the double-fenced compound. "Those look like prison coveralls. Where is this place?"

"It looks like a penal compound in North Korea, but it's not. It's Fort Meade, Maryland."

Adams's brow furrowed. "NSA headquarters? Are you sure this isn't just Fort Meade's stockade? The Army has prisons too, you know."

Hale laid Archer's affidavit on the desk. "This was delivered to the FBI by a whistleblower *inside* the NSA. He believes the bunker may have something to do with the DATASHARK program."

Adams scanned the document. "Archer? Stoyer's deputy?"

"That's him."

Adams read the document more carefully. Suddenly he straightened. "Detaining American citizens without due process?"

"The NSA has no law enforcement authority. None. Even the assistance they lend to the FBI is closely monitored. But they're sure as hell detaining *somebody* at that bunker."

Adams regarded her over his glasses. "What does this have to do with DATASHARK?"

"Keep reading, sir. Archer uncovered the paper trail between that bunker and DATASHARK. Stoyer went to great lengths to keep it secret, even from his right-hand man."

Adams grasped the detail photo. "But who are these prisoners?"

"Computer hackers, we think." Hale pulled Patrick's statement from the envelope. "There was a reporter for the New York *Times* who was investigating the disappearance of dozens of hackers over the last three years. Last night a group of men kidnapped the reporter in full view of a New York state trooper. The trooper had the presence of mind to keep his distance and call the FBI. The FBI put an aircraft over the suspects' vehicle and tracked it all the way to *here*." Hale tapped the satellite photo of the bunker.

Adams jerked back. "Are you saying the NSA *kidnapped* a reporter?"

"Apparently he got a little close to the truth. Archer had already been in contact with the FBI about the bunker. Kidnapping the reporter just helped the FBI put the hackers and the bunker together."

Adams reached for the phone. "That idiot Stoyer! His people are *totally* out of control!"

"Mr. President!" Hale interrupted. "If you'll finish Mr. Archer's statement, he places General Stoyer at that bunker on more than one occasion. Calling him may be the *last* thing we want to do."

Adams blinked. "Are you saying Stoyer may have *ordered* the kidnapping?"

"Stoyer's deputy certainly thinks so."

"What do you propose, then?"

Hale pulled out a copy of the search warrant. "The FBI has a valid order to enter the compound. But because of the sensitive nature of the mission, the head of the FBI's Hostage Rescue

Team asked that I brief you directly, instead of going through Justice Department channels."

"Are you saying the *Attorney General* doesn't know about this?"

Hale felt very exposed. "No, sir. Neither does the Director of the FBI."

Adams cocked his head. "And how did this package find its way to you, exactly?"

Hale felt herself blushing. What a damned time to get embarrassed! "Because of the prisoners at the NSA bunker, Mr. Archer contacted the FBI's Hostage Rescue Team directly. The head of the HRT felt the need to rescue the *Times* reporter was so urgent that he should bypass the chain of command, especially in light of some special requests he needs to make."

Like a bloodhound, Adams knew he was on the trail of something. "Then why did the head of Hostage Rescue come to *you* and not to my Chief of Staff?"

Despite her best efforts, Hale felt her blush deepen. Where the hell was her emotional detachment? "I've worked with Assistant Director Patrick on the Counterterrorism Task Force," she said quickly. "I suppose he preferred to contact someone in the White House he knew personally."

The slightest of smiles curled one corner of Adams's lips. *He knows*, Hale realized.

Adams was all business again. "Fine. I want to talk to him, though."

Hale gestured toward the blinking light on Adams's phone. "He's holding for you on line one."

Adams placed the line on speakerphone and a jumble of several men talking poured out. The call was on speakerphone on the other end as well.

He raised his voice slightly. "This is Marshall Adams. To whom am I speaking?"

The other end of the call fell silent. "Mr. President, this is Assistant Director Jeremy Patrick of the FBI," a voice finally answered. "Go ahead."

"My National Security Advisor has just briefed me on the situation at NSA headquarters," Adams said. "What's your plan, Director Patrick?"

"Sir, I have two main concerns. The first is the highly secured nature of the compound. We're studying blueprints of the facility right now, and there is just no good way of taking the bunker by force. However, if the people inside the fence decide not to open the door when we knock, I have grave concerns for the hostages inside. Especially for the reporter. A rapid resolution is vital, Mr. President."

"Agreed."

"For that reason, sir, I request that the military be allowed to assist the Hostage Rescue Team, to provide a massive show of force when we arrive. The best way to earn the respect of men with guns is to show up with bigger guns, and more of them."

It was a ballsy request, abounding with political consequences. But as a Vietnam veteran, Adams had pledged to never send men into danger without the tools necessary to win. "Fair enough. Once we get the Secretary of Defense briefed, I'll sign off on any reasonable request."

The relief on the other end was audible. "Thank you, Mr. President."

"Okay, stay on the line." Adams put Patrick on hold. "Now I need a favor from *you*, Cynthia."

Hale would be willing to take the bullet-catcher position on the Secret Service detail, as long as Adams quit pulling on the thread that led toward her personal life. "Name it, sir."

"While I respect Mr. Patrick's initiative, the AG and the FBI Director *must* be in the loop for this. It's too damned big for the HRT to run as a cowboy operation."

"Yes, sir," she said, accepting her complicity in the end run, a cardinal sin in any organization.

"Now, I've got a Prime Minister who needs to be entertained while I get the bureaucracy up to speed. Think you can handle that?"

Hale was astonished. "Me, sir?"

Adams lifted an eyebrow. "From what I understand, Prime Minister Renieri is quite taken with you."

Renieri was also the reason the evening gown Hale would be wearing tonight had a very conservative cut. "With all due respect, Mr. President, the Prime Minister is a dirty old man."

Adams laughed. "You just keep him occupied while I make sure your friend Patrick still has a job tomorrow."

The way Adams said "your friend" left no doubt he was onto her secret. She lowered her eyes. "Yes, sir."

He pressed the intercom switch. "Gloria, hook me up on a secure telecon with SecDef, the AG, and Directors Boone and Walsh, *right now,* please."

"Yes, Mr. President."

Adams reached for the phone. "And while you're charming the Prime Minister, I'll get the wheels turning to shut down General Stoyer's private little gulag."

CHAPTER 15

"Our fathers gave us Russia,
To be preserved for their grandchildren,
And we call the rocket's fierce flame,
The shield of our Motherland."
-From the anthem of the Russian Strategic Rocket Forces

NUCLEAR RESOLVE

It was a scene made for photography. That a press stand stood above the square in Siberia attested to the many times the Russian military had allowed this event to be recorded on film and videotape.

General Pavel Marenko watched his troops with a cautious eye. A Western journalist was observing today, so no incompetence or disarray would be tolerated.

So far everything he had expected of the American journalist had proven correct, including the impression she would do anything for a story. Vodka had further increased that willingness, Marenko recalled with a pleasant stirring in his loins. He would have to show special consideration to this California newswoman today. She had certainly afforded him unprecedented access the previous night.

"Do your troops do this often, General?" Joan Turner asked.

"As often as is necessary," was his noncommittal answer. As often as he could find soldiers sober enough to carry out their duties would have been a more accurate reply.

Even in the Strategic Rocket Forces, the most elite arm of the Russian military, the collapse of the old Soviet system had hit hard. Many of his junior officers went weeks without pay, which did little for morale. Marenko kept his men busy on the collective farm they had carved out of the birch and fir forests surrounding the base. They might still be poor, but at least his *roketchiki* did not go hungry, as many Russian soldiers did.

Below Marenko and Turner was a large paved square. The marshaling yard for the detachment of SS-25 mobile ICBMs was big enough to parade a battalion of tanks. Ten concrete bunkers lined one side of the yard. These were the hangars that sheltered the missiles.

At the first blare of the klaxon, the troops burst from their alert barracks and ran toward the hangars. While the security detachments opened the heavy steel hangar doors, the missile crews scrambled over their launchers, preparing them to take the field.

The launchers' diesel engines roared to life, sending smoke roiling from the hangar doors. Each security detachment formed a single file line into the square, their members holding signal flags aloft. The drivers did not bring the launchers from their concrete cocoons until all the flags were raised. The last thing the teams wanted was for one ICBM launcher to be broadsided by another in the rush to leave the alert area.

"They're so *big!*" Turner exclaimed for the cameras.

Marenko nodded at the vacuous comment. He had heard little of intellectual weight from the dyed-blonde American. She probably thought the mobile ICBMs he commanded were giant wheeled phallic symbols.

"The SS-25 has a range of over 10,000 kilometers," Marenko said. "It is large out of necessity. From here on the Kamchatka Peninsula, we can strike targets anywhere in Asia. Even parts of the United States can be reached by these missiles."

Marenko had been well briefed by his military and political superiors. Their goal for this visit was to counter the impression that Russia was a dying bear, no longer able to use its teeth. Russia's newly-elected president was very keen to communicate this point to their many enemies.

Marenko's unit was the top-performing missile detachment in the Strategic Rocket Forces and a fine demonstration of Russia's nuclear resolve, he had been told. His excellent English was also a deciding factor in selecting this unit. It was flattering to be chosen for such a visit, but he had been forced to use Stalinist tactics to make sure his soldiers would all be present and sober when the alert horn sounded.

"Where exactly are these missiles targeted, General?" Turner asked innocently.

He closed his eyes momentarily at the arrogance of the question. "I cannot discuss specifics, of course, but none of these missiles has targeting coordinates loaded. That information is relayed to us by Central Command if a launch order is given. It is one of the recent safeguards we have enacted in concert with your government."

Marenko watched the launchers clear their hangars and begin their painfully-slow turn toward the dispersal road. They would have to move faster than this under attack, but no one wanted to risk even a scratch on their precious missiles. It was like watching a school of beached whales executing a formation turn.

"So none of these missiles are targeted at America?" Turner asked, her vapid expression intact.

Only the presence of cameras prevented Marenko from throwing the woman from the press platform. "The reason we are stationed in such a remote area is the ability it gives us to strike a *variety* of targets," he patiently responded. "Yes, the United States is among those targets, but so are many other potential threats to Russia."

Americans had no concept of what it was like to be encircled with a necklace of enemies, all of whom would love to choke the life from his homeland, either independently or in concert. Marenko was even aware of a target set for his missiles designed to snuff the life out of the former Soviet republics, should they become a threat. He certainly wasn't authorized to share *that* with his visitor, but it might have helped her understand what it was like to have geography working *against* one's security, not in its favor.

Turner closed the fingers of her right hand, with the thumb over the top, in line with her forearm. Pointing with her thumb, it was a combination of a pointing finger and an offered fist, a power gesture her image coach had taught her. She practiced it often to drive home her points. "But the targeting information to point these missiles at the United States could be loaded in a matter of minutes, correct?"

Marenko wondered if she would feel better if he pointed at a missile and said, *See that one? The third missile from the left? It is the one tasked to throw you and your hometown of Los Angeles into the fires of hell. Does that answer your question?* Instead, he replied, "None of these missiles are targeted at *anyone* at this moment. If the order to launch came, loading the target coordinates must of necessity be done quickly. But that order would only come if we were already under attack, Ms. Turner."

Turner's look of disbelief had also been practiced in front
of a camera for maximum effect. "So Americans have no reason
to fear these missiles?" she prodded.

Of course you should fear them, you stupid American!
That's why we invited you here, to see the nuclear gun aimed at
your head!

Marenko sighed. "Ms. Turner, we wish to demonstrate that
these missiles are under the control of professionals, and that
while we are always vigilant, we will act only in the self-
defense of our country."

The sculpted arches of Turner's brow emphasized the skeptical look she gave him. "That, and to let the world watch you
launch one of your missiles today. Isn't that correct, General?"

Marenko's chin pivoted toward her like a howitzer sighting
on a target. "If I give the order, they *will* launch. Yes, that is a
very important message you can share with your audience."

BUYING TIME

Broadman had heard Richter being called away by someone
named Pittman. Could that have been Pittman the missing
hacker? It seemed likely. It was a small comfort, but if Pittman
was still alive, then Yoshida might be too. Any sign that these
renegades from the NSA didn't immediately kill their captives
was a welcome one.

Instead of having his brain fried, Broadman was unshackled
from the table and shoved naked into a concrete closet. It was
cold, dark, and deathly silent, but still better than being tortured
by Richter's radar gun. From his growling stomach and dry
throat he figured at least a day had passed. But without any
place to use the bathroom, he reasoned an empty stomach and
an empty bladder had their advantages.

The passage of time didn't help Broadman's conscience.
Some journalist he was. And so much for never revealing his
sources. But Woodward and Bernstein probably would have
given up Deep Throat if handed over to Colonel Richter for a
few hours. And he didn't give up Hawthorne or Yoshida, just
the organization they worked for. The organization that had left
Broadman on his own when it was time to deliver.

He was alive, but how much time had he bought? Richter
would be back eventually, and sooner or later Broadman would

run out of secrets to spill. And maybe even friends to betray. The fear that his cowardice might lead him to do just that hurt worse than anything Colonel Richter could do to him.

THE CONVOY

The helicopters were the first to arrive. Approaching from the south, two MH-60 Pave Hawk transports and an AH-64 Apache gunship skirted the treetops. The gunship and one of the transports peeled off well short of the target to orbit at a safe distance, ready to provide support if needed.

The remaining Pave Hawk throttled back, lowering even closer to the trees. The custom-built special operations helicopter normally carried a two-hundred-gallon tank under a wing-like pylon on each side of the fuselage for added range. For today's short flight from Quantico, the tanks had been left off to carry a packed load of fourteen troops and a crew chief at each of the two six-barreled miniguns pointing out behind the pilots.

Just inside Fort Meade's fence, the side door of the helicopter slid open and a rope line was thrown out. Four men with bulky knapsacks clambered onto it and "fast-roped" to the forest floor. All four men hit the ground and immediately disappeared into the underbrush.

The rope was tossed off and the Pave Hawk pulled away. The four men remained completely still until five minutes after the noise of the helicopter's engine faded. At the first rustle of their leader's movement, four spectral shapes rose from the brush. Dressed in ghillie suits of camouflage netting and small strips of green cloth, the Marine sniper team resembled moving vegetation. After a quick check of a handheld GPS unit, the leader signaled with his hand. The team moved out toward their objective.

Normally a sniper team would be inserted in darkness and crawl to their observation points, arriving well before dawn. But time was of the essence today, and the orders had come straight from National Command Authority, Pentagon jargon for the White House. They trotted rather than crawled through the forest, two men sweeping arcs in front with their M4 carbines, the other two carrying the equipment. A quarter mile short of the target, the leader signaled the split. The team divided into pairs, each slowly advancing until a suitable "hide" was located in sight of the target.

The leader pulled the cover off his weapon, a Barrett Model 82A1 fifty-caliber sniper rifle. At fifty-seven inches long and almost thirty pounds, the M82 was more like portable artillery than a rifle, firing the same bullet as a heavy machine gun. The M82 was designed for one purpose: to kill on the first shot at ranges up to a mile. The leader settled the weapon on its bipod and flipped up the covers on the telescopic sight.

His target came into sharp relief through the lens, one of the four guard towers around the NSA bunker. The lone sentry was clearly visible, wearing a black jumpsuit and cap. His back was toward the sniper, his head down. Probably reading a magazine. His shotgun was propped against the rail beside him.

"Inward focus," the man beside him observed. The second man on each team was the spotter, trained to protect and call out targets for the shooter. He was observing the same tower through a compact telescope.

The leader nodded. The guard in their sights was obviously more intent on threats *inside* the fence than outside. Maybe their intelligence that this place was a prison camp was right after all.

"Only one of the towers appears to be occupied," the spotter said.

The leader swept the compound with the more narrow focus of his rifle sight. "Agreed. At least they don't know we're coming. We'll give the other teams a few more minutes, then we'll call the roll."

* * *

On the far side of the Snake Pit, ten more men dropped from the Pave Hawk helicopter. Four were snipers, dressed identically to the first team. The other six wore gray jumpsuits and black Kevlar helmets, carrying MP5 submachine guns. All ten headed initially in the same direction, but the group in gray stopped at a squat concrete structure with a steel door.

* * *

The sniper leader keyed his radio. "Viper One in position. All Viper units report."

The other sniper pairs signaled their readiness.

The leader switched from his squad radio to his satellite transmitter, which would connect him to much higher authorities. This close to Washington he probably could have used a cell phone, but the politicians loved these satellite links, the better to meddle in a squad leader's business from any point on the globe.

"Okay," he told his spotter, "time to get this show on the road."

* * *

For the first time, Archer was able to carry out his business with Patrick through normal channels. Archer then made a lengthy call to the security department. At the proper time, he joined Sergeant Townsend at the Ream Road guard shack.

The convoy was composed of five black Chevy Suburbans, a Marine Corps semi with a flatbed trailer, and two prisoner transport buses marked "WASHINGTON D.C. POLICE." As they approached from Savage Road, Archer gave the order to open the gate. The convoy roared through without even slowing. When the dust settled, Archer and Townsend stepped outside the shack to watch. NSA security vehicles blocked the cross streets adjoining Ream Road, ensuring the convoy would complete its journey unimpeded. The vehicles passed the Dragon and turned onto the gravel track leading into the woods.

"Sir," Townsend asked, "what the hell was that all about?"

Archer smiled, clapping the security guard on the shoulder. "*That*, Stan, is what we have been working toward for a long time."

UPLOAD

Richter looked over the shoulders of Jackson and Feldman in the Snake Pit's monitoring room. "That's it?" he protested.

Feldman shrugged. "We told you it was a simple program. All we have to do now is upload it to the satellite and wait for the Russians to give the launch order."

"So how do we tell the submarine where to look for the missile impact?" Richter asked.

Jackson highlighted the appropriate line in the code. "After PANDORA fiddles with the launch order, the program will tell us what the original launch order was, and which numbers it transposed. We've tested it with over a hundred hypothetical launch orders. Works like a charm," he said, with more enthusiasm than he felt.

"Very well. Load it on the satellite."

Feldman called up the screen for SPINTCOM, the Special Intelligence Communication satellites. SPINTCOM linked the many NSA ferret satellites and remote ground stations collecting signals and communications intelligence around the globe. He loaded the PANDORA program and specified the path that would route it to the back door carved into the Russian computer network. SPINTCOM beeped its acknowledgment.

"Okay, it's loaded on the system. I'll leave this window open and we can watch the launch order come down."

SPINTCOM beeped again, and an error message flashed.

"What's that?" Richter demanded.

Feldman squinted. "That's odd. We've lost our link to the satellite."

THE BRIDGE

The convoy stopped two hundred yards short of the bridge across Savage Creek. Two teams of men dismounted from the Suburbans. The first team formed a line abreast and carefully advanced along both sides of the gravel road. The other gave the road a wide berth and approached the collapsed bridge through the woods.

A member of the first team held up a fist. He cupped his hand around a green cylinder the size of a soup can that had a short antenna protruding from its top. He carefully unscrewed the canister's lid and snipped the wire leading to the antenna.

The first team advanced again. Vehicle sensors were usually installed in pairs, to indicate the direction of travel. Another member found the second sensor a few minutes later and disabled it. The leader signaled the convoy, and it continued its advance toward the bridge.

A lone member of the second team waded into Savage Creek while his comrades covered him, their weapons sweeping the foliage. He squeezed under the collapsed bridge deck and found the box the blueprints had indicated. After removing a few screws, he yanked at two wires and twisted their ends together. Hydraulic cylinders engaged with a groan, lifting the halves of the deck from the water. The FBI agent scrambled out of the muddy creek bed. His comrades silently signaled their approval of his quick work.

While the convoy waited for the bridge to be raised, Marines climbed down from the cab of their semi. They loosed the chains securing the armored vehicle on the flatbed and started its engine. After dropping the ramps on the rear of the trailer, the LAV-25 armored car eased down to the road. Its turbo-charged diesel racing, the LAV thundered through the woods and past the head of the convoy.

Ignoring the bridge, the eight-wheeled vehicle plunged into the creek bed and clawed its way up the other side. Following the Marines' lead, the convoy crossed the bridge and headed for the Snake Pit compound.

* * *

The startled sentry in the guard tower dropped his magazine. A convoy was pulling up to the gate. He fumbled for his radio with one hand and his shotgun with the other, but both clattered to the floor. While he tried to recover them, a megaphone's message thundered across the compound.

"THIS IS THE FBI! WE HAVE A SEARCH WARRANT FOR THIS FACILITY! OPEN THE GATES *NOW!*"

* * *

At the small concrete building, a Hostage Rescue Team member set his charge against the steel door. The flexible aluminum tube was filled with plastic explosives and had a notch cut along its length in one side. He formed it into a large loop and affixed it to the door with small wads of plastic explosive. Joining the two ends with a blasting cap, he reeled out detonating wire to a safe distance.

At the first announcement from the megaphone, the agent detonated the explosives. The cutting charge sliced through the steel door with a jet of flame. The smaller wads of C4 blew the severed section inward.

Without waiting for the smoke to clear, the six HRT troopers leaped inside, their guns at the ready.

DISPERSAL

Marenko and Turner watched the SS-25 units deploy. After clearing the hangars, the missile crews and security teams mounted their trucks. Marenko was pleased by the performance of his troops so far. At least no one had been run over by a missile transporter, which was a good start.

The alert yard had been built in a natural valley to make it a more difficult target for incoming warheads. At the end of the yard the road split two ways, to provide a rapid exit for his missiles. Each launcher alternated directions leaving the square. Soon the crowded assembly area was almost empty.

Turner was choking on diesel fumes. "Which missile are you going to launch, General?" she coughed.

Marenko motioned toward the last launcher leaving the yard. "That one. It's heading to an instrumented launch area now, where we will join it shortly." He thought about telling her how the warhead had been replaced with a dummy of depleted uranium for this test, but he reasoned that "mass simulation device" would be three technical terms too many for his guest.

"How long until launch time?" Turner asked.

Marenko checked his watch. She probably believed launching an alert ICBM was accompanied by a formal countdown like a liftoff of the American Space Shuttle. Instead, it was based on the minimum time Central Command thought it should take for the launcher to reach the test site. Indeed, since his troops were a little slow on the dispersal today, the order might even arrive before they were ready to launch. That would not look good on his fitness report, Marenko mused.

"Not long, Ms. Turner," he finally replied. "You will ride with me to the launch site, yes?"

ALARM

Yoshida's ear was pressed to the door. He and Pittman had heard some sort of loudspeaker outside, then an alarm sounded inside the bunker. Was someone trying to escape?

He could hear guards shouting outside. Orders to secure the prisoners. Orders for the guards to arm themselves. Orders to lock down the bunker. It sure sounded like someone had made a break for it.

"What's going on?" the guard outside their door shouted.

"The FBI has the compound surrounded!" a second guard replied. "Leave those bastards in there! Grab an M-16 and help us hold these guys off!"

"*What?*" their guard cried. "Are you going to *shoot* at the FBI?"

"Hey, asshole, look around! Do you really want the FBI poking around in here? Not unless you think *you'd* look good in prison orange, too!"

Their guard acknowledged and sprinted off to join his companion.

Adrenaline rushed like an electric charge through Yoshida's body. Patrick. It had to be Patrick.

Part of him wanted just to sit tight and let the FBI and their commandos blast their way in to free him. He knew Paddy wouldn't enter into a fight unless he was certain he could win.

But that wasn't how Yoshida had been trained. The Resistance had a proactive philosophy, and part of being proactive was taking advantage of every opportunity. Strike when your enemy is off balance, he had been taught.

"What's going on?" Pittman asked.

Yoshida's mind had already switched gears from passive prisoner to Resistance fighter. He grabbed a notebook. "ARE YOU REALLY SERIOUS ABOUT TAKING SOME OF THESE BASTARDS WITH YOU?" he scribbled. "BECAUSE NOW'S OUR CHANCE!"

REACTIONS

The Snake Pit's armory was a vortex of activity. Richter stood at the door, yelling at the guards to speed up their already frantic actions. Individual doubts were shelved along with shotguns and cattle prods as M-16s were handed out.

"Now get out in the yard!" Richter ordered. "If any of you goes soft on me out there, I'll shoot you myself! MOVE!"

The guards did as they were ordered. For the moment, their fear of Richter was greater than their fear of the FBI.

If Dave Jackson had been armed, he might have turned the gun on himself. In contrast to the frenzy just outside his closed door, he sat motionless, silently cursing himself. If *only* he had ignored his doubts about the FBI, he wouldn't even be sitting here. He could have driven to FBI headquarters yesterday and confessed his involvement in the whole filthy mess. Then he would be *outside* the fence with the FBI instead of *inside* the fence waiting to be arrested.

The thought of going to jail with Richter and the rest of his thugs wrenched his stomach. Jackson dragged over a trash can. It was the only motion he seemed capable of mustering.

Was there *anything* he could do to lessen his complicity, now that it was too late? If anyone tried to free the hackers or mutiny against Richter, it would set off a firefight. Not that being killed was such a bad option right now.

A TV monitor had been set up to watch Pittman and Yoshida's improvised cell, which had originally been the CCC's code room. Jackson noticed that Yoshida wasn't visible on it anymore. The angle of the camera didn't look right, either.

Feldman returned from the cafeteria in a dead run. "*Jackson!* Why the hell are you just *sitting* there?" he shouted. Feldman jumped to his computer station, then threw one of the PANDORA binders in Jackson's direction. He pointed to the shredder. "C'mon! If we get rid of this shit, they'll have to take *our* word about what happened." He began typing delete commands madly.

Jackson stayed put. Destruction of evidence would only make things worse. "Think the hackers might have a thing or two to say?"

Feldman didn't look up from his task. "If I know Richter, I wouldn't worry too much about *them* taking the stand against

us. Now get your ass over here and help me, or I'll call a guard
to lock you up too."

Jackson gathered his notebooks and began shredding.

ULTIMATUM

Colonel Richter walked nonchalantly to the inner gate of
the compound. Both inner and outer gates were still closed.
Snake Pit guards armed with M-16s deployed in a wedge behind him. Patrick counted eight men, plus Richter and the guard
in the tower. The soldiers flanking Richter looked much more
prepared for a firefight than surrender.

"Can I help you?" Richter asked with a smile.

Patrick was dressed in SWAT gear identical to that of the
rest of his team. "I have a warrant to search this facility. Tell
your men to disarm and open these gates. Now!"

Richter spoke into his radio. The inner gate rolled aside.
Richter strolled up to the wire mesh separating his forces from
Patrick's.

"Open this gate!" Patrick snapped.

Richter held out his hand. "The warrant, please?"

Patrick yanked the warrant from inside his flak vest and
shoved the rolled document through the chain link.

Richter made a show of reading the warrant carefully.
When he spoke, his smile was frozen in place. "I'm sorry, sir,
but this warrant is not valid! This is a highly classified installa-
tion of the United States military. I would need authorization
from my chain of command to honor your request. I'm sorry,
but the gate stays closed!"

Patrick stepped closer. "Listen, *Colonel*, my orders come
directly from the President of the United States! If you doubt
me, call the number on that warrant! The judge will be happy to
explain it to you! But my orders are to shut down this facility,
and *I will execute that order!*"

Richter blinked in mock surprise. "Sir, I would hate for this
to turn into an *armed confrontation*, wouldn't you?"

Patrick keyed the microphone on his shoulder. "Pressure
point!" he ordered.

In unison, over a dozen heavily-armed men rose from their
cover in the woods, walked forward two steps, then disappeared
again into the underbrush. The whine of helicopter engines

swelled in the distance and the second MH-60 Pave Hawk made a low pass over the compound. The helicopter's six-barreled machine guns and the armed troops inside were clearly visible.

"Colonel Richter," Patrick announced, "in addition to the men of the FBI Hostage Rescue Team, the soldiers of SEAL Team Two are standing by for my orders to seize this facility by force. Snipers have every inch of this compound covered. There's probably more than one aiming at your head right now."

Richter glanced left and right, a crack finally forming in his plastic smile.

There was nothing like placing crosshairs over a man's skull to introduce reason into a situation, Patrick thought. He didn't turn when a whirling roar whipped the trees behind him.

Richter's eyes locked upward on the Apache gunship hovering only a hundred yards away. He watched the Apache's thirty-millimeter cannon sweep the compound in unison with the movements of the gunner's head. His smile dissolved.

"Now," Patrick shouted over the whine of the gunship, "if any of your men are *stupid* enough to fire on my teams, *no one* inside this compound will live to regret that man's mistake. You have *five minutes* to validate that warrant, then I'm coming in, whether this gate is open or not!" He pressed a button on his watch, which was already set for a five-minute countdown. He walked back to the armored car.

"Five minutes!" Patrick repeated.

* * *

Richter motioned to Kramp and Womack. "We're finished here," he whispered. "I can count on most of these men to keep their mouths shut, but I don't want those hackers blabbing what they know. Hose 'em all, then get the General out the escape tunnel. I'll join you shortly. And don't forget that bastard Broadman. He could put us all away."

"How are we going to get off the base?" Kramp asked. "You know they'll have every exit out of here sealed."

Richter thought for a moment. "Fort Meade's water treatment plant isn't too far from the tunnel exit. Find an employee there who owns a van and take them hostage. We'll use them as cover to get us out."

Kramp and Womack turned to carry out their orders.

"And use your silencers," Richter hissed. "I don't want the FBI charging the gate because they hear gunfire inside the bunker."

PATIENCE

Marenko's staff car reached the launch site before the missile crew did. He exited his vehicle and gestured to the center of the clearing. "The missile will launch from the far end of this field," he called to the American video crew, unloading their equipment from the green ZIL truck. "You may place your cameras near the telemetry shack. Just don't block their view."

The crew had just finished setting up their cameras when the launcher parted the trees. It looked like a medieval dragon, lumbering across the field and belching smoke. When it reached the designated spot, the missile crew swarmed over the massive weapon, readying it to fire. Finally the crew and the security detachment withdrew to a respectful distance, leaving two men standing anxiously beside the launcher.

"Who are they?" Turner asked. "Why are they just standing there?"

"That is the missile commander and his deputy," Marenko said. "They will input the target coordinates and verify the launch code when it is received. Then they will use their keys to launch the missile."

"Aren't they awfully *close?*" Turner exclaimed.

It took all of Marenko's military discipline not to laugh out loud. "There is a time delay. They will have sufficient time to withdraw before the missile launches."

There was an extended silence, which Marenko knew the American hated. Patience was not one of her virtues.

"So what happens now?" she asked, tapping the mossy ground with her new L.L. Bean hiking boots.

Patience was one of Marenko's strengths. One could not stay sane in Russia without it. He fished in the pocket of his greatcoat. "Now we wait for the launch order, Ms. Turner. Cigarette?"

DISCONNECTED

Stoyer finished his call with Richter. He felt numb. It was hard to think. Panic closed in around him. He had almost forgotten about the escape tunnel. Escape felt like a very desirable option to his jangled nerves.

No. There were always options. He had to turn off his emotions and think. He had no intention of calling the judge who had issued the warrant. But maybe there was someone else he could call to deflect the heat outside. He dialed a number from memory.

The call was answered on the first ring. "This is Archer."

"Oh, ah, Jeff!" Stoyer stammered. "I must have misdialed, sorry."

"No, General," Archer replied. "You were calling...Admiral Holland. I'm sorry, General, I'm not authorized to connect that call."

Stoyer was so surprised by a subordinate refusing to obey him it took a few seconds to register. "What?" he gasped. "Not *authorized?* I just *gave* you your authorization, mister! Now put me through!"

Archer was unintimidated. "I'm sorry, General. By presidential order, your phone lines have been cut and your access to the agency's satellite network has been terminated. If you attempt to shoulder your way onto a commercial satellite, that Apache gunship outside will knock your satellite dish right off the roof. You might be able to make a cell call if you go outside the bunker, but that's about it. Are you sure you wouldn't like to speak to Judge Clayton? I *am* authorized to connect that call."

His face twitched with rage. "Go to hell!"

"As you wish, General."

The line went dead.

RESOURCES

Yoshida had one factor working in his favor. The room confining them had originally been designed to restrict access, not to contain a prisoner bent on escape. Richter and his goons used fear to deter any actions along those lines. Yoshida didn't have much to work with, but a guideline from his Resistance training rang in his head--*use what you've got to get what you've not.*

The first thing he needed was a screwdriver. Praying that the watchers weren't minding the surveillance cameras too closely, he set to work. If they were paying attention, his only warning would be when the guard burst through the door.

Leaning behind his monitor, he was able to work loose a fuse cover with his ball-point pen. The cover wasn't very sturdy, but it had a thin, straight edge, which is what he needed.

The security camera had been hastily added to the chamber to convert it to a prison cell. That made his work easier. The pinhole camera was about the size of a pack of cigarettes, trained on their computers. Hopping onto one of the cots, Yoshida loosened the camera's set screw with the fuse cover. He swiveled the camera down, very slowly, making sure he never strayed into the field of view. No alarms sounded, and now the camera only covered half the room. Most importantly, it couldn't watch the door. All the while Pittman continued working, to show the watchers exactly what they expected to see.

Staying close to the wall, Yoshida moved back to the door. He stripped off his coveralls to get the monitoring tag away from his body. He examined the door lock. It was a type he had learned to defeat, but mostly from the other side. There was a safety release on the deadbolt, which had been removed. With difficulty Yoshida unscrewed the back plate from the lock, giving him access to the mechanism.

Yoshida slowly retracted the deadbolt. Easing the door open, he stayed close to the floor, watching through the crack. Only one guard was visible, pacing anxiously and staying close to the airlock.

Yoshida nodded to Pittman.

Pittman fell from his chair, clutching his chest. He screamed and writhed in pain, crying out for help. Yoshida opened the door a crack, letting light from the cell spill into the hallway. He stayed close behind the door, his heart pounding. He knew the guard faced a difficult choice. He might ignore Pittman's cries for help, but he would have to investigate the open door.

Pittman was doing a fine job of faking a heart attack. His thrashings provided just the distraction Yoshida needed. When the guard pushed the door open, his eyes were fixed on Pittman, not searching for a possible threat behind him.

Yoshida threw a loop of computer cable over the guard's head and pulled it tight. He yanked hard, pulling the guard off balance while he kicked the door shut. In a move he had practiced a hundred times back at Liberty, he held the garrote tight with one hand and reached for the man's weapon with the other. He ripped the Beretta from its holster and pistol-whipped the guard into unconsciousness.

Pittman stopped his show for a second, looking back to see who had won the struggle.

"Keep thrashing!" Yoshida hissed.

Pittman continued his performance for the camera. Yoshida prayed the sentry had never gotten far enough into the room to be visible to the watchers.

He quickly stripped the guard. The soldier was taller, but the black jumpsuit was forgiving. He felt the breast pocket for the armory card. It was there. The boots were too big, but anything was better than prison slippers in combat.

Yoshida waited till he was fully ready to move before he called to Pittman. "Okay, show's over! Let's go!"

He used the guard's knife to cut away Pittman's monitoring tag. He left plenty of fabric around the tag, to avoid setting off any anti-tamper device.

Yoshida cracked the door again. The entire upper level was empty. He motioned with his head. "Okay, I'm your guard. Do the prisoner shuffle across the hall!"

Pittman played his part again, walking with his head down. Yoshida suddenly realized why the watchers hadn't been more attentive. The sound of shredders leaked out from behind a nearby door. They were too busy destroying evidence to worry about the prisoners. Their mistake. He fished for the magnetic card, and swiped it next to the unmarked armory door.

Yoshida grabbed Pittman's jumpsuit and pulled him into the closet-like space. He closed the door behind them. One whole rack of weapons was empty, presumably the one that had contained the M-16s. There were tactical shotguns, however. He grabbed two and loaded them with buckshot shells.

"Ever used one of these?"

Pittman eyed the shotgun as if Yoshida were handing him a snake.

"You cock it like this," Yoshida said, chambering a round. "Keep the stock tucked against your shoulder, even when you're moving. Then just point and shoot. Don't fire from the hip and you should hit your target most of the time."

Yoshida readied his shotgun. "Ready?"

Pittman blinked at the transformation of his cellmate. "You seem pretty good at this."

"Oh yeah," Yoshida assured him, feigning confidence. "Just nail the guys I miss."

Pittman swallowed. "Sure, no problem."

Yoshida led him back toward the hallway. His plan was to free and arm the prisoners on the lower level, then somehow make contact with the FBI units outside. But when they stepped back into the hall, Yoshida heard a familiar voice from one of the offices. It was Stoyer.

Stoyer called Richter back to discuss their options. Richter was also out of ideas. They were cut off, their enemy possessed overwhelming force, and they had declared their intention to come through the gate in less than five minutes.

"We have to make a play for time so Kramp and Womack can clear a path for us," Stoyer insisted.

"Fine with me, sir. How do we do that?" Richter asked.

Stoyer left the speakerphone connection open. "Let me think for a second," he said. He rubbed his temples with his fingertips.

A sudden movement drew his attention. A guard stood in the doorway, with a shotgun leveled at his head. But it wasn't a guard. It was Yoshida. Pittman appeared beside him, also armed.

Yoshida grinned harshly. "Hello, General! Keep your hands right where they are, please!"

Stoyer froze.

Yoshida lowered his weapon and ordered Pittman to cover him. He entered the office and circled the desk.

"Mr. Pittman! Mr. Yoshida!" Stoyer declared for Richter's benefit. "Your guard was less than vigilant, I gather. I see you've taken the opportunity to arm yourselves."

Yoshida moved behind Stoyer's desk. He slung his shotgun over his shoulder. "Shut up! Lock your fingers behind your head!"

Stoyer complied.

Yoshida drew his pistol and grasped Stoyer's wrist with his free hand. Before he could order Stoyer to stand, he noticed the red light over the word SPEAKER on Stoyer's phone.

At the same time he heard men shouting and the clanging of the outer airlock door.

LAUNCH ORDER

In the Central Command bunker of the Strategic Rocket Forces in Moscow, Colonel General Alexi Krupkin checked his watch. He had allowed an extra five minutes for Marenko to get his missiles deployed since he had that American reporter with him. Exposing weaknesses in the system was not the mission today--it was to emphasize the strengths of the Strategic Rocket Forces.

The three-star general entered the coordinates of the Pacific Test Area into the command terminal and leaned back. The range safety officer beside him double-checked his typed entry. Although the sun was already up at the Siberian launch site, it was just after midnight here in Moscow, and Krupkin was too old to keep such late hours unaffected.

"I concur, General," the safety officer announced.

Krupkin entered the launch code and pressed the TRANSMIT key. He clicked his stopwatch. The computer system could measure reaction times down to a microsecond, but the stopwatch reminded everyone in the room that he cared about a quick response to his orders. The second hand had just swept through eight seconds when alarms hooted in the command bunker. On both sides of the giant world map, revolving red lights began to flash, as they did only during missile drills.

"What the hell is this?" Krupkin gasped.

THUNDERBOLT

Archer waited anxiously in the NICC for word on the raid. Instead of perching in the balcony, he was on the lower level, pacing behind the watch officer's console. He had always thought the Director needed to be down here on the floor, close to the people with the real expertise.

The staff was treating him with even more deference than usual. They knew Stoyer was in trouble, even if they didn't know the reason. That meant Archer was in charge, which was fine with them.

"*Sir!*" one of the technicians almost screamed.

Archer jogged to the woman's terminal. "Talk to me!"

Her eyes were fixed on the Cyrillic text scrolling on her screen. "Sir, NARCISSUS has detected a missile launch order from the Russian Central Command!"

Archer's mouth dropped open. "A launch order?"

"Yes, sir! They were supposed to test launch an SS-25 sometime today, but this is a general launch order to execute a war plan called OMEGA-1."

"Do we know what OMEGA-1 is?"

Her voice trembled slightly. "No, sir, we don't. But it doesn't sound good."

Archer shouted to the entire room. "Confirmation?"

"Confirm heavy signals traffic going out to all strategic forces by microwave and satellite links!" a Signals Intelligence technician responded.

"A low frequency transmission just started up from Murmansk," another reported. "Probably sending the order to their submarines."

Archer froze for a second. Either this was everyone's worst nightmare, an accidental launch, or Russia's new president was even more of a loose cannon than the CIA had feared.

The NSA was often the first to learn of impending threats, and had a special notification system directly to the President. Messages sent by this system were to be in the President's hands in three minutes, no matter what.

Archer turned to the watch officer. "Get a THUNDERBOLT to the President *right now!*"

CHAPTER 16

"What country can preserve its liberties if their rulers are not warned from time to time that their people preserve the spirit of resistance? Let them take arms."
- Thomas Jefferson

RAT ONE

Patrick watched the Snake Pit compound from the last Suburban in the convoy, which served as his command post. He could see the guards gathered in a huddle inside the fence, partially blocked by the bunker. Patrick hoped they were having an attack of common sense and preparing to surrender. While he and his HRT commander were trying to figure out what was happening, his radio crackled.

"Juggernaut Leader, this is Viper One," the sniper announced. "Viper Three reports Richter and several of the guards just reentered the bunker in a big hurry."

When Patrick looked again, only two guards stood watch by the gate. The rest must have gone with Richter.

The HRT commander stiffened. "Could they have detected the Rat team?"

"Acknowledged, Viper One," Patrick replied. "Rat One, report!"

A breathless voice responded. "Rat team has just reached the inner hatch. Preparing to set our charges."

"Maybe they're retreating inside the bunker to duke it out," the commander offered.

Patrick was even more pessimistic. "Or to take hostages. Rat One, listen hard at the hatch. Is there any activity inside? We think you may have been detected."

A long pause. "Negative, Juggernaut Leader. All quiet."

Patrick knew he was missing something. Something important. He pressed the button on his radio that connected him with every ground and air unit on his team.

"All units, this is Juggernaut Leader! Subjects may be attempting to harm the hostages! Prepare for RAMROD on my mark!"

AIRLOCK

Yoshida had to move fast. He wrapped his forearm around Stoyer's throat and hauled him out of his chair. He shoved his pistol against Stoyer's head and pulled him back toward the hallway.

"Pittman! Cover the airlock!" Yoshida shouted.

The inner airlock door had just cracked open when Pittman discharged his shotgun. The deafening blast almost knocked Pittman off his feet. Buckshot pellets splattered against the door, knocking it closed.

Yoshida dragged Stoyer toward the stairs to the lower level. "Reload, Pittman!" he yelled.

The concussion of his own gunshot had stunned Pittman. "What?"

"*Pump the damned gun!* And pull back!"

They had only moved a few feet when the airlock door swung open again. Pittman's second shot impacted harmlessly against the metal bulkhead. The door continued to open.

The guards were playing it smart, staying behind cover and pushing the door open from the hinge side. In seconds they would have a clear field of fire. Pittman's third shot also missed, hitting the door.

Yoshida heard the shouts of more guards echoing up the stairs. That way was covered. Even if they made it downstairs, freeing the hackers below would just increase the body count. Yoshida continued his retreat back to the armory door, which he had propped open with a box of shells. The airlock door was almost fully open now. A shape with an M-16 appeared around the bulkhead. It seemed to move in slow motion.

Pittman got lucky this time, striking his target in the upper torso. The guard's flak vest took some of the pellets, but not all. A red mist erupted, and the guard went down.

Yoshida extended his pistol and fired two quick shots into the airlock. The nine-millimeter bullets ricocheted inside the metal box. He heard a scream. Yoshida jammed the muzzle back against Stoyer before he could react. Stoyer flinched and cried out at the hot metal pressing into his neck, but Yoshida held him fast. He pulled Stoyer to the open door.

"Pittman! Inside!" Yoshida barked. He knew Pittman was on his last shell, but he doubted Pittman knew that. Pittman ducked into the closet, Yoshida pulling his prisoner in after him. He kicked the shells aside and slammed the door shut.

There was a blue plastic box on the wall, the mechanism for the access card lock. Yoshida threw Stoyer to the floor, then ripped out every wire leading in or out of the box. At least they would have to force the door now.

Pittman covered Stoyer with his shotgun. "What do we do now?" he panted.

Yoshida considered their grim tactical situation. He could only think of two options. "Reload. And pray."

THE ORDER

Marenko led Joan Turner to his command van, a nondescript military truck with a camper-like shell on the back. The camera crew was only allowed a quick shot of the general and the journalist standing in the van's narrow aisle, but Turner was allowed to stay inside while the launch order was received.

"I thought it would be more high-tech," Turner observed.

Marenko shrugged. "Our mission is not sophisticated. We receive orders from Central Command and pass them to our missile crews. The commander of a tank battalion probably requires more advanced equipment than we possess."

A nerve-jarring buzzer sounded in the van, then both printers started simultaneously. Data streamed down the monitor screens of the van's two technicians. They froze in their chairs.

"Ah, our launch orders," Marenko said, pulling the sheet from the printer. He blinked. The color drained from his face.

"What's wrong?" Turner asked.

"We have been ordered to launch our missiles," Marenko stated, his voice like a robot.

Turner's eyes brightened. Her wait to acquire the launch footage and leave this backward country was nearing an end. "Good! Isn't that what we've been waiting for?"

Marenko held out the launch order, his hand shaking. "You don't understand, woman! I've just been ordered to launch *all* our missiles!"

RAMROD

Patrick checked his watch. One minute and thirty seconds to the deadline. His radio crackled.

"Juggernaut Leader, Rat One! Shots fired inside the bunker! Repeat, shots fired inside the bunker!"

Patrick's blood turned to ice. He pressed the "all call" button on his radio. "All units, this is Juggernaut Leader! The hostages are being shot! RAMROD! RAMROD! RAMROD!"

A megaphone blared from the lead Chevy. "THIS IS THE FBI! WE ARE ENTERING THE COMPOUND BY FORCE! THROW DOWN YOUR WEAPONS OR YOU WILL BE SHOT!"

The armored car gunned its engine and smashed both gates like cardboard. The tower sentry raised his weapon, probably out of reflex. The sniper leader also acted by reflex. The fifty-caliber projectile swatted down the Snake Pit guard like a rag doll.

The two guards at the gate had no such death wish. They went further than ordered, dropping to their knees and placing their hands behind their heads, along with throwing down their M-16s. Camouflaged shapes rose from the brush. Half rushed past the battered gates to disarm the guards. The rest held back to cover their comrades.

A Pave Hawk helicopter thundered close overhead. Two lines were thrown down and twelve SEAL commandos fast-roped to the ground. They stormed around the bunker, ready to shoot any guards they found. The area behind the bunker was empty, the heavy garage doors closed and locked.

The SEAL leader called Patrick. "Juggernaut leader, we weren't fast enough. They're sealed up like a canned tuna."

Patrick had foreseen this. "Stand by, SEAL leader, I'll send you a can opener."

* * *

The cell that confined Broadman was very effective in blocking out sound. After a few hours his senses had heightened to compensate for the silence. The beat of his heart pounded in his ears like a drum. Occasionally he heard voices shouting outside, but they were always too muffled to make out the words.

But he heard the alarms. At first he thought he was imagining the sound, his mind desperate to have something to fixate on besides his heartbeat and breathing. Pressing his ear against the cold steel door, he could hear more shouting and the sound of combat boots striking concrete. After a few minutes the sounds ended and Broadman again wondered if his sensory-deprived mind was just fantasizing a rescue by the Resistance.

Broadman *knew* he wasn't imagining the gunshots. Four or five booming reports were answered by a few sharp pops like pistol fire, then silence again. His ear ached from pressing it against the door. Then he realized it was far more likely that one of the hackers had attempted to escape. He had heard nothing more than that man's noisy death. He sagged against the door, his mood even bleaker than before.

* * *

Jackson dove for cover at the sound of the gunfire. It was incredibly close.

Feldman was under his table as well. "Damn it! I'm not finished! How did the FBI get inside so *fast?*" he growled.

The gunfire ended as abruptly as it began, followed by shouts and the sounds of running men. Both watchers flinched when their door burst open.

"Come on, you heroes!" Richter shouted. "Those bastards Pittman and Yoshida are holding the General hostage! Get up!"

In the hallway, Jackson saw that Richter was down to two men. One guard dragged a body clear of the airlock, the dead man's jaw and throat pulverized by a shotgun blast. The second man supported a wounded comrade, who had taken a bullet in the back of the knee. The injured man screamed in pain with every step. Jackson had never seen so much blood.

Richter's shouted radio commands brought up two more guards from the lower level. Richter waved his remaining troops to the armory door. "You four! Room clearing formation! Kill Pittman and Yoshida, but I don't want so much as a scratch on the General!"

It was the first time Jackson had ever seen the guards hesitate in obeying Richter's orders, even for a second. Jackson still hoped he could escape the meat grinder Richter was planning.

"Move it! And I need two pistols!" Richter ordered.

The fallen guards were relieved of their sidearms, which Richter slapped into Jackson and Feldman's hands. "Which of you is a better shot?"

Jackson was not about to volunteer, regardless of his skills. Richter grabbed Feldman, pointing to the open code room door across from the armory, where Yoshida and Pittman had been held.

"If Pittman and Yoshida get out of the armory, only one of them is going to be able to take cover behind the General," Richter whispered. "Hide in their cell, turn off the light, and shoot whoever isn't holding the General. That will probably be Pittman. I'll hide one door up from the armory. When the other one turns to engage you, I'll shoot 'em in the back. Jackson, you stay here and cover me. If we triangulate our fire, they won't stand a chance. Move!"

Feldman obeyed Richter's orders with the enthusiasm of a condemned prisoner. Jackson didn't know whether Richter thought the odds against his guards were that bad or if he was just covering his bases. Richter moved into the shadows of the server room next door to the armory. Jackson took his place across the hall, in the darkened door of the watcher's room. His mind and heart raced, making it difficult to hold his pistol steady.

* * *

Yoshida and Pittman pressed themselves against the rear wall of the armory closet, waiting for the guard's assault. Yoshida kept his forearm clamped tightly around Stoyer's throat, using the General's body as a shield.

Yoshida knew Richter faced a hard choice. Richter and his goons couldn't barricade the door and leave Yoshida and Pittman trapped inside, because they had the General. But Richter's men couldn't storm in, guns blazing, because Yoshida and Pittman had the General. It seemed to take a long time for Richter to make a decision. Pittman used the delay to shove some heavy metal boxes in front of the door.

"So is the FBI really out there?" Pittman asked.

Stoyer remained silent.

"That's what the guard said," Yoshida answered.

"So...we might actually get out of this *alive?*"

"Not if my people have anything to say about it," Stoyer broke in.

Yoshida rapped the General on the skull with his pistol--hard enough to leave a knot, but not enough to render him unconscious. "If we die, you die."

Stoyer was resigned to his fate. "Fine, we all die."

"We're getting out of here, Bob," Yoshida insisted. "I haven't stayed alive this long to get killed with the cavalry right outside the door."

Horror spread across Pittman's face. "Then I have a confession to make."

CRYING WOLF

The Detroit Red Wings had captured the Stanley Cup, which meant another trip to the White House. For some team members this was their third visit and the second President to share in their glory for his own political benefit.

In the Rose Garden, President Adams had just finished his congratulatory speech and was about to receive his personal Red Wings jersey and an autographed stick. A Secret Service agent sprinted up and whispered in the President's ear. Adams looked pale when he joined the agents storming from the platform. The Secret Service also pulled the members of the National Security Council with them.

The hockey players, journalists, and remaining cabinet members eyed each other in confusion. The Red Wings's goalie leaned over to his captain and muttered in a thick French-Canadian accent.

"Man, I knew he was rooting for Colorado, but this is ridiculous!"

* * *

The Secret Service herded Adams and his inner circle to the South Lawn. Adams could already hear the Marine One helicopter approaching. The warrant officer carrying the "football," the briefcase with the nation's nuclear weapons codes, was waiting there. The young Army officer gave Adams a look that expressed perfectly what he too was feeling. *I can't believe this is really happening.*

"Where is Ms. Hale?" Adams asked the head of the Secret
Service detail. He had ordered her to monitor developments at
the NSA from the Situation Room.

"She's on her way," the agent replied.

On cue, a set of nearby doors burst open, a pair of agents
almost carrying the National Security Advisor between them.
They deposited her at Adams's side and joined the protective
circle forming around the President.

"Where's the fire?" Adams said, raising his voice over the
descending rotor noise.

"The NSA reports the Russians have just sent the 'go-to-
war' code to their nuclear forces," Hale shouted. "We don't
know who they're targeting or why, but they're getting ready to
launch on somebody."

"You're certain?" Adams shouted.

"The NSA is crying wolf at the top of their lungs, Marshall!
I think we'd better take them seriously! Harry Abramson is already sending a Hot Line message!"

That was all the conversation the President's protectors
would allow. The second the big Sikorsky VH-3 thumped
down, the Secret Service pulled and shoved their principal and
his advisors onto the helicopter and slammed the door behind
them. Without waiting for everyone to strap in, the chopper
wheeled about and raced toward Andrews Air Force Base,
barely clearing the Commerce Department roof in its haste.
They were passing the Capitol when the President's phone rang.

"Adams," he answered, trying to keep the tension he was
feeling from creeping into his voice.

"Mr. President, Harry Abramson," the Secretary of State
said. "The Russians have just responded to our Hot Line message."

Adams closed his eyes. "Okay, Harry, please tell me this
was a big false alarm."

Abramson cleared his throat. "Wish I could, sir. President
Krasalov is on the line, insisting on speaking to you personally."

"Good. Put him on!"

"I'll warn you up front, Marshall," Abramson cautioned.
"He sounds well and truly pissed."

CAN OPENER

The armored car drove behind the bunker, facing the closed garage doors. "Ram 'em!" the tank commander ordered, swinging the turret backwards to avoid damaging the cannon. The LAV's twenty-five-millimeter gun could easily puncture the garage doors, but they needed a man-sized hole, quickly. The driver picked the third of the four doors and floored the accelerator. The SEAL commandos were already advancing against the back wall, ready to storm the hole the LAV created. The armored car rolled forward.

"Hold on!" the driver warned.

The vehicle struck the door, its rear wheels lifting off the asphalt when it came to a sudden stop. The heavy bay door buckled inward to match the angled nose of the armored car, but it did not collapse.

"They must've parked a truck up against the door!" the tank commander observed. "Hit it again!"

The driver ground the transmission into reverse, backing up until he heard the smash of chain-link fence behind him. The seventeen-ton battering ram now had better than a hundred feet to accelerate before impact. They surged forward again.

"This one's gonna hurt!" the driver cried out, pressing his helmet against the padded periscope mounting. It was a good thing they weren't carrying troops, he thought.

The LAV ripped the garage door out of its tracks, carrying it and General Stoyer's limousine into the opposite wall. The collision shook the bunker like an explosion. The armored car didn't halt until the limo was compressed to half its original length.

The commander swung the turret around the garage bay, searching for a target with his coaxial machine gun.

"Clear!" he called. "I'm pulling out!"

The LAV backed out with a fanfare of falling glass and protesting metal, making room for the SEALs. The commandos poured in like ants, their weapons like deadly antennae, searching for an enemy. They swarmed the ladder to the upper level, preparing to storm the airlock door.

A SEAL twisted the wheel and pushed inward. The airtight door wouldn't budge. Several joined in the pushing and twisting, without effect. A disgusted team leader finally confessed his predicament.

"SEAL Leader to Juggernaut Leader. The garage has been seized, but the airlock doors have been dogged from the inside. They're locked up tight."

"Rig cutting charges, then!" Patrick ordered. "For God's sake, soldier, the hostages are dying in there!"

"Blow it down!" the SEAL leader ordered. He shook his head in disgust. The whole operation had been thrown together too quickly. Now the people they had been sent to rescue would probably die because of it.

* * *

The thick despair that had descended on Broadman was interrupted by one booming concussion, then another that shook even the thick walls of his cell. Someone wasn't breaking out, they were breaking *in*. Broadman had his first real flash of hope. He had let his Catholicism go slack long ago, but he decided if there was any occasion for returning to the faith of his childhood, this was it. He muttered the words quietly but fervently.

"Holy Mary, mother of God, pray for us sinners, now and at the hour of our deaths...."

* * *

Stoyer laughed harshly. "Oh, that's *rich!* You bastards really screwed yourselves this time!"

Yoshida ignored him. "Maybe they didn't upload the program yet, Bob."

Stoyer snorted. "No such luck! We loaded the PANDORA program onto the satellite right before the Feds showed up! Now they've cut our uplink and we couldn't pull it back if we wanted to! This is just *too* good!"

"If the Russians launch, you'll be just as dead as everybody else," Yoshida reminded him.

"My career isn't exactly on the upswing, asshole! But since this bunker was designed to withstand a nuclear blast, I'm in an excellent position to have the last laugh, don't you think?"

"You're sick!"

Stoyer sneered. "Don't worry, losers, even if you survive the blast, my guards will make sure you don't get out of this bunker alive!"

Yoshida's retort was interrupted by a heavy concussion.

Pittman flinched. "What was that? A bomb?"

"No. Sounded like metal on metal," Yoshida said.

"Probably a Russian ICBM knocking to see if anybody's home," Stoyer needled.

The second concussion was much louder, stirring Richter's men from their indecision.

"That's it!" Richter yelled outside. "Break it down! Get the General out of there! Now!"

OMEGA-1

"Tell the missile crews to cease dispersal and prepare for immediate launch!" Marenko ordered.

Turner was more frightened by the fear she saw in the General's face than by what was going on around her. "What are you doing?"

Marenko held up the printout, already crinkled from his grip. "Ms. Turner, I have received a valid war order from Central Command! I am preparing to launch my missiles!"

"It has to be some kind of mistake!"

Marenko's face was a stone. "Possibly. But unless I receive stand-down orders, I must assume it is not."

Marenko's deputy, Colonel Sakavin, ripped open the van's door, having come at a dead run from the telemetry shack. "What's going on?" he panted.

Marenko handed him the order. "Launch order. War plan OMEGA-1."

Sakavin recoiled in horror. "OMEGA-1?" His lip curled in disgust. "This is the KGB's doing!"

* * *

From Marenko's standpoint, Russian nuclear war plans had changed little, even after the collapse of the Soviet system. Each plan was given a codeword, followed by a number. The lower the number, the broader the scope of the plan.

ALPHA was the plan he most expected and trained to execute, a strike against the United States. The plans ranged from ALPHA-5, an extremely limited "demonstration" attack all the way to ALPHA-1, an all-out nuclear exchange.

Other plans were devised for other enemies. BETA for NATO, GAMMA for the Chinese, DELTA for a combined US and NATO strike, and so on. Marenko knew them all by heart.

OMEGA was a war plan forced on the military by the KGB, an all-out strike against every nation not allied with the then-Soviet Union. The hard-line spymasters had convinced the Politburo that if the very existence of the Soviet Union was threatened, then every enemy of Communism should die with them.

OMEGA lashed out in every direction at once. To the KGB, it was the only reasonable course of action if you were under attack and unable to identify your enemy. Although the Politburo had long since been dissolved and the KGB was replaced by the Federal Security Service, many of the same hard-liners remained in place. So did war plan OMEGA.

* * *

Marenko verified the launch order's authentication code against the sealed copy kept in the command van's safe. They matched. He grasped the shoulder of one of the technicians. "Call up the target coordinates for war plan OMEGA-1."

"Yes, sir!" the technician replied mechanically.

Colonel Sakavin charged to Marenko's side. "General! You can't be serious! OMEGA-1 is insanity!"

Turner's eyes darted from one officer to the other. Unable to speak Russian, she understood nothing of their tense exchange.

Marenko cut off his deputy. "Not if we are under attack, Sergei! Placing the missiles at readiness is the only prudent course of action!"

"Missile coordinates for war plan OMEGA-1 are ready to transmit, General," the technician said.

"*General!*" Sakavin almost shouted. He knew the Russian command and control network was in such a state of decay that even an accidental launch order was possible.

Marenko held up his hand. "Before you transmit the coordinates, inform the crews that this is an *alert*, not a launch order. Get an acknowledgment from *each* of them before you give them their targets, is that clear, Sergeant?"

"Yes, General!"

Marenko raised an eyebrow at Sakavin. "See, Sergei? I have not *completely* lost my mind."

TACTICAL EDGE

Yoshida saw shadows shift through the slit under the armory door. Confusion was slowing down the guards, and the easy duty of watching prisoners had dulled their tactical edge. He knew they would be executing "the pinch," lining up close against the hinge side of the door. The "knocker" would be on the lock side, ready to blow the door open so the others could rush in. Yoshida and the members of his cell had practiced the maneuver themselves at Liberty. They had also practiced how to counter it.

Yoshida put a "sleeper" hold on Stoyer's neck, cutting off the blood supply to his brain. The last thing Yoshida needed during a firefight was an uncooperative hostage. After a brief struggle, Stoyer went limp. Yoshida hunkered low behind the general's body.

A shotgun with slug ammo was the weapon of choice for blowing door locks, but the guards had exchanged their shotguns for M-16s. Peppering the inside of an armory with high-velocity rifle bullets probably wouldn't be an option, even if Pittman and Yoshida weren't holding a hostage.

Boots and shoulders hit the door in rapid succession. The metal ammo box Pittman had placed behind the door slowed them down more than the lock. Yoshida shot out the two fluorescent light tubes above him. In the dimly-lit space it would be harder to pick out targets.

That was Pittman's cue to open fire. Yoshida had reloaded Pittman's shotgun with slug shells. At this distance, even Pittman couldn't miss, and a slug might pass through more than one of their attackers if they were cooperative. Pittman put a slug a foot off both sides of the door frame. The kicking stopped for a moment, and Yoshida thought he heard screaming. But the blast of the shotgun was so deafening in the tiny space he wasn't sure he would ever hear anything again.

A guard finally kicked open the door, to be rewarded with both a shotgun slug and two pistol rounds for his efforts. The backward propulsion of his body staggered the soldier behind him, who took two bullets in the face while struggling to regain his balance. Only the last guard had time to take aim. But he didn't have time to pull the trigger before Yoshida fired two more shots. Richter's last soldier fell lifelessly to the floor.

Yoshida threw Stoyer's body to one side and kicked the door shut again. The lights in their old cell across the hall had been turned off. Richter himself was probably waiting there in the dark for them to emerge, so he could turn the tables on them.

Yoshida hugged the floor with his pistol pointed toward the waiting ambush. He scooted the ammo box back from the door to use as cover. "Pittman!" he whispered. "Pick up Stoyer and hold him in front of you like a shield!"

"He's out cold!" Pittman said. "Do I need to stand up?"

"No! Stay on your knees! Just make sure all of you is behind him!"

Pittman couldn't know what Yoshida was planning, but he obeyed anyway. "Okay, ready," said a shaky voice in the darkness.

Yoshida reached forward and pulled open the door. Staying below the cover of the ammo box, he waited for movement. Just when he thought the coast was clear, he caught the faint glint of polished black gun metal. Unable to discern a target, Yoshida fired three rounds above the glint, in a line from left to right. The third round connected, bringing a sharp cry of pain. It sounded a little high-pitched for Richter. Yoshida fired three more rounds into the sound. A pistol clattered on the concrete and a dark form slumped to the floor.

Time to reload.

* * *

Jackson watched the massacre from his doorway. Even though he detested Richter's men, the poor bastards hadn't had a chance. It didn't look like they had even gotten off a shot. There was no mistaking Feldman's death cry, either. It was down to him and Richter against the two hackers.

Richter was hidden in the shadows of the server room across the hall. Jackson pulled back farther into the darkness.

If he had told Richter about his pistol skills, he would have been in Feldman's spot. Jackson had enjoyed pistol practice in basic training and had bought a forty-caliber Glock for his own use. It was a deadlier pistol than the Model 92 Beretta he held now, but the principles were the same. *Aim for the head and shoot 'em twice*, his instructor had drilled.

They waited several minutes for Yoshida to emerge. Finally Jackson heard the sounds of furtive movement from the direction of the armory, although he was too far back from the door to see them himself. He watched the server room carefully, waiting for Richter to make his move. Richter raised his pistol, ready for Yoshida or Pittman to cross his line of sight. Jackson traced the arm back until he could make out Richter's head.

Jackson shot him.

He aimed again for the double-tap. The second shot was easier. Richter's eyes had gone wide in the shock and surprise of being shot, giving Jackson a clear aim point in the darkness. Richter collapsed forward, his pistol sliding into the hall.

Jackson continued to hold his pistol out for several seconds. As badly as his hands were shaking, he was surprised he had been able to hit anything.

"Ken Yoshida!" Jackson shouted into the tense silence.

No reply.

Jackson tried again. "Ken, you're clear. There's one more guard in the conference room, but he's unarmed and badly wounded."

"Who the hell are you?" Yoshida said.

Jackson de-cocked the Beretta. "Dave Jackson. I'm one of the watchers. I've been trying to get away from Richter and his henchmen. You just gave me my opening."

"Where *is* Richter?" Yoshida asked.

"Doorway to your left. I shot him." Jackson slid his pistol into the hallway. "There. I'm unarmed."

Another silence. "Okay, come on out. Lead with your hands," was Yoshida's cautious reply.

* * *

Yoshida watched the young man in short-sleeved Air Force blues emerge from the doorway. Yoshida was so wary of tricks he didn't know whether to put the gun on this new *friend* or keep it on the woozy but still dangerous Stoyer. He decided to keep the gun on Stoyer.

The guy certainly *looked* like a programmer, Yoshida decided. He was skinny and in as much need of sunlight as the hackers. He sure wasn't one of Richter's goons.

"So Richter's dead?" Yoshida asked again.

Jackson motioned, keeping his hands up. "He's right over there."

"Show me," Yoshida ordered. "Pittman, cover him."

Jackson pulled the dripping corpse from the server room and laid it on its side. The glare of the hallway lights on the fresh gore made Jackson flinch. Richter's sightless eyes stared up at Yoshida. He had one bullet wound in the neck and one squarely between the eyes.

It was as clear a loyalty test as Yoshida could devise. He gestured with his head toward Jackson's discarded pistol. "Nice shootin', Tex. You ride with us."

CHECKMATE

The Marine One helicopter was tilted forward, the pilot wringing every knot of speed from the Sikorsky for its escape from Washington. Adams carried on his telephone conversation through the Russian president's interpreter, but no translation was necessary to hear the anger in Krasalov's voice.

"What is the meaning of this attack?" Krasalov demanded.

Adams straightened. "The United States has made no attack against the Russian Federation, Mr. President."

The hostility on the other end ratcheted up a notch. "Do not play the fool with me, President Adams! Did you think you could invade our nuclear control computers without our detection?"

Adams framed his words carefully. "I authorized *no* attack on your nuclear control computers, President Krasalov."

Krasalov's ire reached such levels that his translator pleaded with him to tone down his response. Adams recalled his CIA briefing on Russia's new leader. Krasalov was the previous head of the Federal Security Service, one of the successor organizations to the KGB. The former KGB operative was an ardent Russian nationalist and probably had ties to the Russian Mafia. He was elected after the leading reform candidate died in a "plane crash" shortly before the voting.

Krasalov spewed a final string of probable profanities, then fell silent. Adams could almost hear the translator gulp before continuing.

"P-president Adams," the translator stuttered, "I know full well of your computer attacks against China and Japan. We also know you personally authorized those attacks. Did you really believe you could violate my country with the same impunity as you did your other enemies?"

Adams wished Harry Abramson was here on the helicopter. Striking deals with American politicians and business leaders was his forte, not dealing with foreign dictators. But foreign or not, he knew every leader enjoyed it when a bull's eye was confirmed by an opponent.

"President Krasalov," Adams said, "I acknowledge the effectiveness of your country's intelligence gathering in this matter. I did indeed authorize the computer attacks against Japan and China. The strike against Japan was in retaliation for an unprovoked attack that killed over sixty of my citizens. The attack against China was to protect our fleet and our ally Taiwan. However, I did *not* authorize an intrusion of *any* kind into *any* Russian computer. You must believe me in this matter."

"You do not need to justify your actions to me!" Krasalov snapped. "I shed no tears over dead Chinese sailors, or dead Japanese civilians for that matter. My people have killed their share of both races. However, I have irrefutable proof of your intrusion into our nuclear control computers. Do not attempt to deny it."

Adams cursed the fact he was not having this conversation on a speakerphone, surrounded by his advisors. He was flying blind, with the fate of the world in his hands. "President Krasalov, would you consider the possibility that this intrusion was conducted without my knowledge?"

Krasalov paused long enough for Adams to check their progress. The helicopter had just crossed the Suitland Parkway, making its final approach into Andrews.

"I would consider that possibility," Krasalov allowed. "Although it would hardly encourage my confidence in your abilities as a leader, President Adams."

Adams grimaced. *Just had to get that dig in, didn't you Vladimir?* The planet hangs on the edge of nuclear war and Krasalov makes personal insults. It told Adams a lot about the former spymaster.

Krasalov continued. "In my previous position, I personally warned your predecessor, President Wilcox, about the dangers of such actions. Do you expect me to believe that warning was not also passed on to you?"

Adams's shoulders sagged. "President Wilcox and I were not on the best of terms, sir. Apparently he neglected to inform me of your message when he left office." *Or he shredded it, like the other documents my Senate committee subpoenaed.*

"Yes, that is a possibility," Krasalov admitted.

Adams could see the white 747 aircraft looming outside the windows, the National Emergency Airborne Command Post. "President Krasalov, we must pull our nuclear forces back from the brink while I investigate this incident. I understand your forces are on a very high level alert, is that correct?"

"*Alert?*" Krasalov shouted. "If it was not for my personal intervention, the missiles would have already been launched!"

Adams exhaled. At least they had *not* been launched, not yet. The helicopter flared to land beside the President's aircraft. "That emphasizes my point, President Krasalov. I suggest we both lower our alert levels. It will reduce the risk of an accidental conflict while this matter is resolved." The helicopter settled to the ground, its engines throttling back to idle.

Krasalov exploded, his interpreter making no effort to lighten the language this time. "What kind of fool do you take me for, President Adams? I sit here in my housecoat in the basement shelter while you are on your way to safety! Do you not think I have ears? Wait, I do not hear rotors anymore! That must mean you have arrived beside your escape plane! Even now your advisors are probably urging you to end this conversation and continue it when you are safely in the air!"

The door to the helicopter flew open, Secret Service agents rushing aboard to assure his safe exit. Only the President's emphatic hand signals kept them from physically removing him from his seat.

Adams sighed. "Remind me not to play chess with you, President Krasalov. You are of course correct. Perhaps you could suggest my next move?" Adams knew the remark was a mistake even as he said it.

Krasalov seized the opening without hesitation. "I would be happy to, Mr. President! First, your nuclear forces are currently at an alert level of...DEFCON-THREE. Is that correct?"

Hale was seated beside him, on the phone with the Pentagon. Adams mouthed "DEFCON-THREE?" Hale nodded.

"That is correct, President Krasalov."

Again there was no hesitation, letting Adams know the Russian understood English perfectly, preferring to use his translator only for his responses. "Then reducing your alert status to peacetime levels of DEFCON-FIVE would be an excellent display of good faith on your part."

At last the Russian was making the situation less dangerous, not more so. "I agree. I assume your forces will also be pulled back from their alert status?"

"I said no such thing!" Krasalov fired back. "My forces will remain on alert until you pull back the computer virus you used to invade our systems."

"That's a little one-sided, Mr. President. It may take some time to..."

"This is not a negotiation!" Krasalov shouted. "You are the ones who attacked *us!* If you are truly innocent in this matter, you will comply with my terms immediately! Also, if you are not planning a nuclear attack on my country, there is no reason for you to flee in your airborne command post. We will continue this conversation once you have returned to the White House. I do not want to hear jet engines in the background when we speak again, Mr. President."

The line went dead.

Everyone on board the helicopter was staring at Adams, waiting for his orders. The phone remained at his ear. He could almost hear Harry Abramson banging his head against his desk on the other end.

"Tell NORAD to cancel the alert," Adams told Hale.

Hale almost dropped her phone. "Cancel it? Why?"

Adams slammed the phone back in its cradle, furious that he had been outmaneuvered so easily. "Because I said so!"

FREEDOM

The first thing Yoshida did was make sure all the guards, living and dead, were collected and completely disarmed. He had almost forgotten about the guard he had knocked unconscious during their initial breakout. Thankfully the man had been kind enough to moan upon regaining consciousness. He, the guard with the wounded leg, and a guard who had been knocked out by a shotgun slug into his flak vest were bound by Jackson and secured in the hackers' old cell. Yoshida thought it was fitting justice. Stoyer was tied up in the hall, with Pittman's foot on his back.

"So, this is all of them?" Yoshida asked Jackson.

Jackson examined the five dead bodies and the pile of weapons they had captured. "Well, this is all the men Richter had *with* him."

Yoshida's adrenaline letdown swept over him with a wave of fatigue. The airlock door and freedom beckoned to him. He also wanted Pittman to warn the authorities of his latest sabotage in time to avert disaster. "That's good enough for me. Let's get out of here."

"Wait a minute," Jackson cautioned. "Where are Kramp and Womack?"

Yoshida *had* noticed the absence of Richter's evil twins, but had been too tired to mention it. "Maybe they got caught outside when the FBI barged in."

Jackson shook his head. "No way. Those two are joined to Richter at the hip. They gotta be around here somewhere."

The airlock beckoned to Yoshida again. "Why don't we just let the FBI in and let *them* look for Kramp and Womack?"

"How do you *know* the FBI is on the other side of that airlock?" Jackson warned.

He had a point. Even if the FBI held the garage, putting Kramp and Womack in the airlock as a last line of defense *would* be Richter's style. "Are there any phones in here? Maybe the FBI can clear a path for us."

"In my office," Jackson said.

Jackson's phone was dead. So was the one in Stoyer's office, and the one in conference room. Maybe the FBI didn't want Stoyer launching any final DATASHARK attacks during the raid. Yoshida smacked the phone down in frustration. As much as he wanted out of the Snake Pit, he didn't want to be killed ten feet from freedom, either.

Yoshida eyed the airlock door and the pile of weapons nearby. "Let's free our friends downstairs. That way we can have a lot more people behind these guns when we crack that door." He hauled Stoyer up by his collar. "Come on, General! Time to free your prisoners!"

VIRUS

The phone call took several minutes to reach Archer in the NICC. No one in the White House even *knew* about NARCISSUS, until frantic calls to the CIA and the Pentagon lead them eventually to the NSA. The task of finding the Russian computer virus then fell to Archer, with the President's National Security Advisor holding on an open line until he did so.

Archer plugged his headset into the phone at the NICC's NARCISSUS terminal. The technician, Jessica Brickner, showed him her latest findings, with Cynthia Hale listening in.

"Wait a minute," Archer said. "You're saying *no one* ordered that launch?"

Brickner highlighted the line in question. "It was an automated attack sequence, meaning if no one at Central Command countered the order, the ICBMs would start flying. It was buried inside a diagnostic program. Even *we* didn't realize it was checking the integrity of their code every time an order passed through the network. But somebody tampered with their system, and it reacted by ordering a nuclear strike."

Hale broke into the conversation. "That's kind of a drastic response, isn't it?"

"Not if you think about it, ma'am," Brickner explained. "The only reason someone would want to sabotage their nuclear command computers would be to disable their nuclear arsenal. That way, even if the attempt was successful in cutting off the brass from their rockets, the rockets would still launch. If the attack was unsuccessful, the brass calls the missile crews and orders them to stand down."

"So have they done that yet?" Archer asked.

"Not yet. They ordered the missile crews to hold at maximum readiness until the source of the computer intrusion is dealt with."

"That's where I need the NSA's help," Hale said. "Krasalov is insisting that *we* are the source of intrusion. If that's *not* the case, we have to find hard evidence of who *is* at fault."

Brickner pointed to her screen for Archer's benefit. "We've *found* the virus itself. It invaded the system from a remote terminal in St. Petersburg, which is one of the alternate entry points for NARCISSUS. I'm having a hard time tracing it beyond that point, though. Whoever did this was a pro."

Archer's brow furrowed. "Could someone else have found one of our back doors? The Russian mob, maybe?"

"Possibly," Brickner allowed, "but why would..." Her voice trailed off when a new set of Cyrillic text filled the screen. "Oh *hell*," she whispered.

The last thing Hale wanted was more surprises. "*What? What is it?*"

Brickner squinted, as if her eyes were playing tricks on her. "There's another launch order coming down."

"Is their computer having a fit again?" Archer asked.

"No, *sir*," Brickner insisted. "This launch order came from President Krasalov *himself*."

RETARGETING

"What do you *mean* it can not be done?" Krasalov almost screamed.

General Krupkin had never personally dealt with Krasalov before. The horror stories his fellow generals told him were not exaggerated. "Mr. President, I can not alter the war plans once the launch codes are released. Neither can the units under my command. That is a safeguard to prevent a commander from altering a target set on his own authority." That precaution dated back to the days of the Soviet Union, to prevent a disgruntled *roketchiki* from targeting Moscow instead of Washington in the event of war.

"Then what war plan did that damned computer release?"

"OMEGA-1, Mr. President."

Krasalov responded with a string of expletives the likes of which Krupkin had not heard since his days in the infantry, most of it directed toward Krasalov's former superiors in the KGB. "Are you saying that I can't even target *my own* missiles, General?"

"Not at all, Mr. President. It will simply require you to enter the valid release code into your nuclear briefcase. Have you selected the war plan you wish set in readiness?"

"Yes, of course," Krasalov groused.

"Then under the war plan's title there is an authorization code. Please enter that code into your briefcase."

Krupkin pictured the process in his mind. The nuclear briefcase was a shielded computer resembling a laptop, with a

portable phone and a powerful transmitter. Krupkin had helped
write the attack binder contained in the briefcase. The thought
of that *apparatchik* even *holding* those plans for doom made his
skin crawl. That Krasalov had the authority to *carry them out*
made Krupkin fear for his grandchildren's future.

A strident beeping at Krupkin's terminal signaled the arrival of the new launch code. The computer automatically verified the order, releasing a stream of data on Krupkin's screen,
including the targets for the new war plan. Krupkin was relieved
that Krasalov had shown *some* restraint in that selection.

Krupkin spoke from the script he himself had written for
his officers. The last thing needed in a nuclear crisis was a
tongue-tied weapons officer. "Mr. President, I acknowledge
receipt of a valid launch code and of the new war plan. I will
carry out these orders immediately."

"I would love to see the American President's face in about
two minutes," Krasalov said dryly.

"Yes, Mr. President," Krupkin replied. *Unless President
Adams responds by launching a strike of his own! What would
your face look like then, you power-mad fool?* Krupkin had
spent too many years preparing to fight the Americans not to
have a healthy fear of their capabilities. He winced against a
sudden tightness in his chest as he hung up one special-use
phone and reached for another.

* * *

Marenko and his deputy joined the conference call between
General Krupkin and the generals under his command. It
sounded as if the stress of the alert had almost sent Krupkin into
cardiac arrest. Decades of heavy drinking and smoking had not
helped either.

"Gentlemen," he wheezed, "the status board shows everyone on the line now, so I will begin." An emphysemic cough
rattled their earpieces. "Ten minutes ago, an intruder attempted
to sabotage Russia's nuclear command computers. This attempt
failed, but it triggered the launch order you have just received.
You will disregard that order."

Marenko and Sakavin exchanged relieved looks.

"However," Krupkin continued, "if the intruder determines
his attack failed, he may make another attempt, possibly with
different results. Until we track down and eliminate this threat,

the Strategic Rocket Forces will remain on maximum alert. The Strategic Airborne Command Post has been launched. If the saboteur succeeds in immobilizing Central Command, my airborne counterpart will take over."

Krupkin hesitated, clearing his throat. "I have been in contact with President Krasalov, who believes the Americans are the most likely source of this attack. For this reason, your war plan is being switched from OMEGA-1 to ALPHA-2, targeting all American nuclear forces for preemptive strike. I repeat, all forces are to remain at 'ready to launch' status until further notice. That is all."

Marenko and Sakavin hung up their phones.

"What? What happened?" Turner asked.

Marenko had allowed the American to remain in the command van. The end of the world was certainly a newsworthy event. Besides, he could think of worse ways to spend the last minutes of his life than with an American woman of known willingness.

Marenko shrugged. "Good news and bad news."

Turner's hands went to her hips. "What's that supposed to mean?"

Marenko examined the orders on the technician's screen and nodded. The new targeting instructions were transmitted to his crews. "The good news is a nuclear war has not begun, just yet. The bad news is we have decided to retarget all of our missiles at your country."

HIDE AND SEEK

Yoshida goaded Stoyer down the stairs to the lower level of the Snake Pit. Passing the guard stand opposite the computer bay, Yoshida swept both directions with his pistol. It was eerily quiet. He called to Pittman and Jackson, signaling the all clear.

Yoshida pointed to the concrete cells in the entry corridor. "There's a reporter in one of those boxes. Get him out!"

"You got it!" With the prospect of rescue just outside the bunker, Pittman's surly fatalism had disappeared. Jackson followed him with an M-16. Yoshida hung back by the guard stand, in case any more guards popped up from the other direction.

* * *

Dave Jackson swept his M-16 around nervously while Pittman freed the reporter from the box. He kept an especially close eye on the entrance to the shower room, which had a direct line of sight to the stairway. Every corner and doorway held a potential ambush. It was a deadly game of hide and seek, and they were all "it."

Part of him was relieved to have finally made his break from Stoyer's Mafia. But the military part of his mind was deeply conflicted over killing a senior officer, even a bastard like Richter. A third part of him was dealing with his murder of another human being and a bad case of the shakes.

BLUEPRINTS

Against the advice of his HRT commander, Patrick had insisted on moving his command post just outside the Snake Pit's garage. He wanted to be close enough to personally breathe down the SEALs' necks until they got his men out.

The SEALs had just rigged a cutting charge around the airlock door. Because of its stout construction, the SEALs had mashed extra wads of C-4 on the bulkhead surrounding the door in the path of the cutting charge.

"Clear the garage!" the SEAL leader shouted. Normally his men would only back away six feet from a cutting charge detonation, to assure surprise when they jumped through the hole. But not with *this* much explosives.

Patrick and the SEALs retreated outside. The SEAL leader reeled out the fuse line behind him and attached it to the electrical detonator. He prepared to give it a sharp twist.

"FIRE IN THE HOLE!"

The detonation was more of a "whump" than a "bang." The SEALs poured back into the garage through the gray smoke rolling out. A few seconds later, Patrick heard shouts of protest from inside the cloud.

"The door's still here, dammit!"

The SEAL leader's shoulders dropped. "Oh, you *gotta* be shittin' me!" he cried out. Patrick followed the man inside. The frame around the airtight door glowed red and was burned through in several spots, but the door remained intact.

"They sure built things to last during the Cold War," Patrick said. The comment was a lot more glib than he felt.

The SEAL leader ignored him. "Rig it again!" he shouted. "This time use enough C-4 to take out a bridge!"

The SEALs hurried to comply, until one was overcome by the fumes. Although plastic explosives were stable enough to burn for fuel, Patrick knew they also released cyanide in the process. He had heard of a few soldiers in Vietnam learning that the hard way when they burned C-4 to warm their tents as they slept. Forever.

"Gas masks!" the SEAL leader called out.

Gas masks might slow cyanide poisoning, but they wouldn't stop it, Patrick knew. That would take oxygen tanks. This didn't bode well for the Rat Team. Their breaching charge would have to work on the first try. He keyed his radio.

"Rat Team, Juggernaut leader, status."

"Charges set, ready to blow."

"Hold on detonation, Rat Team, repeat, hold!" Patrick warned. "This bunker is built like a brick shithouse, you may need a larger charge to make a breach."

"Any larger and we'll have to evacuate the tunnel before we detonate! That won't do much for our element of surprise."

Patrick was idly examining the compacted remains of General Stoyer's limousine. What was that *behind* the car? It looked like some kind of freight door.

His radio crackled. "Juggernaut leader, Rat Team, please advise."

"Rat Team, standby."

* * *

Broadman heard another flurry of gunfire outside, followed by nerve-wracking silence. Now his biggest fear was being freed for use as a human shield by the besieged NSA guards. He couldn't help cringing when the cell door finally cracked open. He threw up his hands against the flood of light.

"Hey, buddy," a voice behind the glare said. "Ready for a change in scenery?"

Broadman squinted, trying to shield his eyes. He could make out a plump figure in an orange jumpsuit. He could also make out the shotgun the man was toting. He didn't look like one of Colonel Richter's men, but he sure didn't look like the

FBI, either. He willed his parched throat to speak. "Who...who are you?" he managed to choke out.

The man laughed and extended a hand. "What's the matter, don't you recognize a jailbreak when you..."

The man's head exploded in mid-sentence. Automatic weapons thundered right outside the cell. Multiple bullet impacts tore the man's skull apart before he collapsed heavily onto Broadman. The man's bulk shoved Broadman back against the cell wall. The dead man's heart faithfully pumped blood to his exposed brain. The warm, pulsing flow sprayed in Broadman's face.

Broadman heard a man's terrified screaming, somewhere far away. It was several seconds before he realized it was his own voice.

* * *

Patrick hopped onto the wrecked car's front fender, straining to look behind the mass of crumpled metal. It *was* a door of some kind! *This* certainly wasn't on the blueprints! It must have been added later. Part of the door was even torn out of its track. If he stretched, he might even be able to look....

A flurry of automatic gunfire rang out just beyond the rollup door. Patrick caught a glimpse of a guard with an M-16 facing away before another blocked his view and shot at Patrick's head.

Patrick was already jumping backwards, not caring how he landed. One rifle round thudded into his Kevlar helmet, knocking him for almost a full somersault. He landed hard on his shoulder, ending up on his knees. The remaining rounds missed his head and pinged off the garage's metal interior.

Oh, now that was really *smart, Patrick!*

"*Man down! Man down!*" someone shouted. SEALs rushed to his side. The rattle of gunfire on the other side of the newly-discovered door was almost constant now. Patrick struggled to his feet, thrusting the medics away.

The LAV was parked just outside the garage. He could see a braided steel tow cable bracketed to the side of the armored car. "Get this wreck out of the way!" Patrick ordered. "SEALs! We make our entry *right here!*"

* * *

Jackson was looking the other way when Kramp and
Womack opened fire. The entry corridor made a shallow "L"
turn past the box cells, a perfect hiding place for Kramp and
Womack. One of them cut loose on Pittman at full auto from
fifteen feet away. Pittman's body jerked like it was hooked to a
high-voltage line before collapsing into the box, leaving a splattered abstract painting on the wall. The reporter in the box
howled.

A fury like Dave Jackson had never known rose up and
over him. Cursing like a madman, he charged sideways to the
cell where Pittman fell. He fired off three-round bursts as fast as
he could pull the trigger. Bullets ricocheted wildly in the concrete corridor, some bouncing two or three times and flying
back in his direction. He threw himself into the box cell, curling
up into a ball to get his arms and legs under cover of the heavy
steel door.

His hopes of having nailed Kramp and Womack with indi-
rect fire were quickly dashed. One of them fired at the bottom
of the door with careful, aimed shots, trying to take Jackson's
legs out from under him. He was lying on top of Pittman's
body. One of the bullets tore into Pittman's leg, jolting the flesh
and leaving a burned hole in the orange jumpsuit.

Jackson screamed in feigned pain while he dug for Pittman's shotgun. The shooting paused. Working the weapon from
under Pittman's bulk, Jackson swung it over the top of the cell
door and fired blindly without exposing himself. He was
rewarded by a cry of pain and a full auto fusillade that ended
with the distinctive clack of an M-16 firing on an empty chamber.

Hoping that both guards would be occupied for a few seconds, Jackson pushed the door open farther and hauled Pittman's body off the reporter. Grasping his M-16 tightly in his
right hand, he grabbed the reporter with his left and hauled him
to his feet. The reporter was naked and slick with Pittman's
blood. Jackson's hand slipped right off. He grasped more tightly
and pulled with a strength he didn't know he possessed.

When Jackson came up to his feet, Kramp's weapon was
swinging toward him, reloaded and cocked. Jackson fired a one-
handed three-round burst that struck the wall, throwing up a
spray of fragments into the man's face. Kramp's shots went
wild, striking the cell door with a shower of sparks.

The reporter stumbled, almost pulling Jackson down with him. Jackson went to one knee, trying to bring his M-16 to bear. Kramp's M-16 was already sighted on his face. Jackson heard two loud pops behind him and saw a hole open up in Kramp's flak vest. The guard jerked back behind the wall.

"You're covered!" Yoshida shouted. "Come to me!"

Jackson hauled the reporter to his feet and hurled him bodily in Yoshida's direction. He backed toward the sound of Yoshida's pistol, keeping his M-16 up and ready to fire. Had he known he was capable of such feats, Jackson thought, he might not have gotten beat up so much in high school.

* * *

Broadman was having two nightmares at once. The first was the one where he was naked in the hallways of a strange school, trying to find the non-existent classroom on his schedule, unable to take shelter or cover himself until he did so. The other was of being pursued by a ravenous, bellowing monster. The closer the breath of the monster came, the slower he was able to run, until he was frozen in mid-stride, waiting for teeth to tear into his back.

Broadman's legs felt like rubber, unable to bear his weight. The hallway tilted crazily with every step. He went down more than once. A figure in a black jumpsuit beckoned him on, calling him by name and firing a pistol past him.

Broadman kept running, or at least trying to.

* * *

Yoshida was covering Stoyer and the hallway leading to the hacker cells with his pistol when Kramp and Womack opened fire. Pushing Stoyer to his knees, Yoshida edged out into the corridor, trying to get a shot. Jackson was shooting like a maniac, charging Broadman's cell to rescue a man he didn't even know.

Yoshida's stomach sank at the sight of Pittman's crumpled form, but there wasn't time to dwell on it. Kramp and Womack stayed under cover, frustrating Yoshida's attempts to provide covering fire.

But Yoshida had left his back turned for too long. Stoyer came at him from behind, kicking him in the back of the leg.

Yoshida went to his knees. Stoyer followed up with a kick to the back of his head. Yoshida was down on all fours. He rolled, bringing up his pistol.

Stoyer ran away, his hands still bound behind him. He ducked into the cafeteria.

Why the hell is he going in there? Yoshida thought. More gunfire jerked his attention back in Jackson's direction. Jackson had tried to use Kramp's reloading pause to pull Broadman to safety, and almost died for it. Yoshida fired two quick shots, catching Kramp in the chest. He could tell from the impact the guard was wearing body armor.

Yoshida kept yelling to Jackson and Broadman, urging them in his direction. Womack was next to pop out, and he took a bullet in the arm before disappearing again. Yoshida heard profanity echo down the concrete hallway.

Jackson and Broadman were almost to him. "Up the stairs!" Yoshida yelled. If he had followed his instincts they would already be outside, safe and wearing FBI ball caps by now. Damn!

Jackson swung his M-16 in Yoshida's direction. "Ken! Drop!"

More guards were coming down the stairway. Apparently knot-tying wasn't Jackson's strongest skill. He made up for it by cutting the legs out from under the first escaped guard, who rolled down the stairs, head over heels. The guard had rearmed himself, his M-16 sliding almost to Yoshida's feet. Yoshida shot the guard twice in the back of the head before he could rise.

Yoshida tried to recover the M-16, but one more guard remained and fired several bursts down the stairwell. Bullets sparked and sang off the steps and concrete floor. One bullet tore at Yoshida's jumpsuit and another snapped past his ear before he dove behind the guard stand for cover.

"We're sure as hell not going that way!" Yoshida yelled to Jackson, who was crouched by the cafeteria door.

Jackson had already shoved Broadman through the cafeteria door. "In here!" he called to Yoshida.

Kramp and Womack were pressing the attack again. One of them extended his gun and fired blindly at full auto down the corridor. Shots ricocheted wildly off the concrete walls. Yoshida lunged for the cafeteria, pulling Jackson in with him. Bullets tore apart the door frame above them.

"Where's Stoyer?" Jackson asked. A crash and the sound of rolling cans sounded from the kitchen.

Stoyer had lost his usefulness as a hostage to Yoshida. "Making a sandwich, I guess. If he comes out of the kitchen with so much as a salad fork, shoot him."

"Got it."

Broadman was huddled under a table. Shaking and covered with Pittman's blood, he looked like an escapee from hell. Yoshida moved between Broadman and the line of fire. After all they had lost in freeing him, Yoshida wasn't going to risk Broadman taking a stray round. Broadman's eyes went wide with recognition.

"K-k-ken?" he stammered.

Yoshida switched gun hands to reach back and pat Broadman's knee. "Yeah, Tony, it's me. So, how do you like the Resistance so far?"

CHAPTER 17

"The tree of Liberty must be refreshed from time to time with the blood of patriots and tyrants." - Thomas Jefferson

GAMESMANSHIP

Adams would have been more comfortable in the Situation Room, but Cynthia Hale and the Secret Service insisted they use the Presidential Emergency Operations Facility, the bunker buried two stories deep under the West Wing. With its four-foot thick concrete walls, the PEOF was more heavily fortified than Adolf Hitler's bunker, although the Secret Service always cringed at that comparison. Harry Abramson had just arrived, which made Adams more comfortable regardless of their location.

Since Cynthia Hale had been on the phone with Archer, the warning came even faster than a THUNDERBOLT message. She had only to step from the communications room to the conference room across the bomb shelter's narrow corridor.

"Mr. President! Krasalov has issued another launch order!"

Adams felt his heart skip a beat. "You *can't* be serious! Get him on the phone! Now!" Thanks to his misstep during his last conversation with Krasalov, American nuclear forces would now be fully stood down from their previous alert. The part of his mind that collected nagging doubts pointed out that this would be an excellent time for the Russians to launch a first strike.

The voice of the Chief Petty Officer in charge of the communications room came over the conference room intercom less than two minutes later. "President Krasalov on line one, sir." Apparently Krasalov was staying close to the phone. Adams hoped that was a good sign. Hale and Abramson listened in on the speakerphone.

Adams stabbed the appropriate button. "President Krasalov, are you launching a nuclear attack on the United States?" he said without preamble.

Krasalov sounded very pleased with himself. "My dear President Adams, why would you *make* such an accusation?"

Adams kept a tight rein on his temper. "Now is not the time for gamesmanship, Mr. President. I have firm intelligence that your strategic forces just received a new launch order, and that order came from you. Surely you can see how we would view this action as provocative, given the current situation."

Krasalov's was imperious. "I frankly don't care how you view it! But I am *very* interested in how you know about my private communications with my senior military staff!"

"Mr. President, you are fully aware of how closely we monitor your nuclear forces..."

"Do you also watch my wife and I while we sleep?" Krasalov seethed. "And you brand *my* actions as provocative! *You* are the ones who invaded our country's most sensitive computers! I wonder what *your* response would be, were our positions reversed?"

He knew Krasalov was pushing him, trying to get the advantage as he had earlier. Adams was determined to deny him that opportunity. "Sir, we don't *know* who launched that attack. My experts haven't been able to track the virus to its source. If you will give us a little more time..."

The LCD screen on Adams's phone had KRASALOV beside line one. Beside line two the name HOLLAND began flashing. Abramson grabbed another phone and took the call.

"I need no further proof!" Krasalov ranted. "I am convinced enough to point all my missiles at *you!* That is the reason behind the launch order. It was necessary to allow my crews to target only your nuclear forces, not every man, woman and child in your country. They will not launch without my permission, but they will *remain* at alert until this virus you spawned is eliminated or withdrawn!"

Abramson slid him a note. It read, "ADMIRAL HOLLAND RECOMMENDS RETURN TO DEFCON-3. I AGREE."

It took great effort to keep the anger out of his voice. "Mr. President, if you insist on taking such aggressive action, I will have no choice but to return our nuclear forces to alert status as well."

"You will *not!*" Krasalov decreed. "If you do so, I will *launch!* You have no choice in this matter! If you do not enjoy having a loaded gun pointed at your head, you will locate the source of this computer attack and order it withdrawn!"

Adams could feel the heat rushing up his neck. "No one dictates that kind of demand to a sovereign nation, President Krasalov. No one."

A harsh laugh. "Fine! But I will warn you, in a few minutes I will be at the General Staff Headquarters. I'm sure you have been briefed on its invincibility. If you wish to test my resolve, we will see whose bunker is more robust!" It was only then that Adams recognized the faint sound of helicopter rotors in the background.

"And since you test my patience," Krasalov continued, "I will add as a requirement the deactivation of whatever monitoring equipment you have been using to listen in on my network. I will call you if I have any further demands."

Krasalov disconnected the call, leaving only the whine of the satellite carrier wave in Adams's ear.

SURVIVABILITY

Stoyer ran through the kitchen, frantically searching for something to cut this damned phone cable off his wrists. That it was a *prison* kitchen didn't help. Richter had most of the meals trucked in, so there would be nothing more dangerous back here than serving spoons and spatulas. He tried rubbing the tough plastic against table edges and a steel door frame. No good. He kept looking, while sporadic gunfire popped just outside the cafeteria.

Kramp and Womack, Stoyer thought. They were supposed to kill the hackers, then get him out. He hadn't seen their bodies on the upper level. They must have gone down to the lower level and laid in wait, in case Richter's men failed. Somehow they knew Yoshida would be bound by his do-gooder code to free the hackers before he escaped himself.

Stoyer abandoned the kitchen and started searching the walk-in pantry. The escape tunnel was hidden in this room, behind some shelving.

The escape tunnel. Like the bunker itself, the tunnel was a throwback to the Cold War. While the Contingency Codebreaking Center was designed to withstand a direct hit on the nearby headquarters building, the engineers had predicted the ejecta from the blast crater might very well bury the bunker.

So a concrete tunnel was constructed, stretching hundreds of yards to the very edge of Fort Meade's property. This would allow the victorious codebreakers to emerge once the nuclear war was won. It was laughable, since a blast that size would fry anyone inside the bunker with the gamma rays alone. But "survivability" had been an NSA buzzword when the bunker was constructed, and it sure as hell was helpful now.

Stoyer didn't know whether Pittman's sabotage would lead to nuclear war or not, but if forced to choose between incarceration and incineration, he would take the latter. Only prison awaited him if he stayed in this bunker. That was a more terrifying prospect to him than death.

He turned around and pulled at the metal shelving with his still-bound hands and almost cut himself in the process. The cheaply made metal pieces had rough edges, sharp as knives. The shelves teetered dangerously, heavily laden with cans of foodstuffs, some dating back to the bunker's original construction. Stoyer stood to the side, propped his foot against a vertical brace and pushed hard. The shelving tipped forward with a rockslide crash, some of the older cans bursting open.

There it was.

The hatch was oblong, two feet wide by three feet tall. He was almost free. Stoyer straddled the fallen shelving and hooked his bound hands underneath. He rocked forward and back, sawing at the restraints. He could feel the cable start to yield.

TRIAD

Holland's voice had no trouble filling the conference room in the PEOF, even over the speakerphone.

"Mr. President, we *must* go to DEFCON-THREE, regardless of Krasalov's threats. Our nuclear force is vulnerable in the extreme, but the Russians are cocked and ready to fire!"

"Harry, what's your reading of Krasalov?" Adams asked his Secretary of State.

Abramson scowled. "He's a gangster. He got to the top through intimidation and brute force. If he *says* he'll pull the trigger, he'll do it. The bad thing is fellows like that are notorious for overplaying their hand. I suggest we don't push him."

Knuckling under to scum like Krasalov turned Adams's stomach, but he saw Abramson's logic. "What was that he said about relocating to a command post?"

"Probably the General Staff Command Post at Chekhov, about sixty miles south of Moscow," Holland said. "Instead of getting their leader the heck out of Dodge like we do, the Russians take him to the biggest bunker they've got."

"So he's digging in for a fight. Admiral, what do we lose if we don't go on alert and they launch?"

The heavy sigh over the speakerphone made it obvious Holland didn't even want to think about it. "The bombers, most likely. Some of the ICBMs. The Russians have a new rocket called the Topol-M. It's big enough to launch several warheads into orbit. But instead it uses that excess power to flatten out the trajectory and shorten our warning time to about ten minutes. It's an excellent first-strike weapon."

"Do they have enough of these...Topol-Ms to take out *all* of our bombers and *all* of our ICBMs?"

"No, Mr. President."

"What about our submarines?"

"They're untouchable, sir."

Adams felt a decision converging. "And could the submarines acting alone take out the Russian Federation?"

"That's the basic principle of our strategic triad, Mr. President. No one can destroy all three legs of the triad simultaneously, and any one leg could take out the enemy."

Adams didn't like leaving part of the nuclear force vulnerable any more than Holland, but one of the two countries would have to start acting like a grown-up if either were to survive. "Then our deterrence remains intact. We stay at DEFCON-FIVE, and pray that the Russians can leave their system on hair-trigger without one of their units launching their missiles by accident. Cynthia, stay on the NSA's back until they track down that damned virus!"

LAST STAND

Yoshida's tactical situation was even more grim than when he and Pittman were trapped in the armory. At least then they could reload at will. Now Kramp and Womack had that option and he didn't.

Yoshida had left his shotgun upstairs when it appeared the main threat was eliminated. Idiot. His Beretta carried fifteen rounds, but he had used at least half of those, and had no spare clips. Idiot! He had lost count of his shots, too, so he had no idea when he would run out, unless he unloaded to look, which didn't seem wise. *Idiot!*

Jackson still had his M-16, but his thirty-round magazine had to be damn near empty, and he had no spare ammo either. At least he had a nearly full pistol in his belt to fall back on.

It was a good thing the cafeteria walls were concrete, not drywall. That meant any bullets would have to come at them through the doorway, not just fired blindly through the wall. It wasn't much of an edge, but Yoshida was grateful for any tactical advantages at this point.

* * *

Kramp and Womack held their position behind the guard stand. Beck, the other guard who had escaped from upstairs, was bringing down extra ammunition. Kramp stared at Thompson's body while he waited. That SOB Yoshida had shot him in the back of the head. At least *he* had guts enough to look Pittman in the eye before he shot that fat piece of shit.

Kramp wasn't all broken up about Richter taking a bullet. Under different circumstances he might have bought Jackson a beer for that. But using General Stoyer as a human shield filled him with rage. Cowards. He'd kill them with his boot knife if he got the chance.

Beck returned and they reloaded, sticking the extra magazines into the pockets of their jumpsuits. Kramp had taken a pistol round in the chest, but it didn't go through his Kevlar vest. Womack had taken a pistol round in the arm and a shotgun slug in his flak jacket's ceramic chest plate. The flattened stump of the slug still protruded from the middle of three-inch hole it had blown in the vest's fabric. Kramp knew it had to hurt like hell, but Womack wasn't complaining.

Kramp motioned his companions in close. "Okay, I saw the General run into the cafeteria, so Yoshida and that bastard turncoat Jackson still have him. There's an escape tunnel in the kitchen we can all use to get out of here, but first we gotta bag some garbage." Kramp fingered the hole in his vest. "Beck, since you're the only one here who hasn't taken a bullet, you're on point."

Beck nodded. Since it was his actions that had allowed the hackers to get out of their cell, he was hungry for his own chance at payback.

Kramp waved his gun at the rows of terminals in the computing bay. "Womack, use those for cover and see if you can get a shot."

"Will do."

Kramp pulled back the cocking lever on his M-16. "All right. Let's kill 'em all."

FIXING BLAME

Hale and Archer were back on a conference call at Brickner's NARCISSUS terminal in the NICC.

"Mr. Archer, the President has authorized you to make entry into the Russian system to remove the virus."

Archer exchanged an incredulous look with Brickner. "Ma'am, I'm sure the Russians have *found* the virus by now. Why don't they just remove it themselves?"

"They want us to do it," Hale said. "It will give them proof that it was our fault."

"But we don't even know if we're responsible!" Archer protested.

"That's not important right now. They're refusing to rescind their last launch order until we comply."

"Ma'am, if I go inside their system from this terminal, NARCISSUS will be blown, instantly and permanently," Brickner explained.

"We believe NARCISSUS is already compromised. Just get on their system and wipe out the virus. Let me worry about fixing blame later. I'll stay on the line."

"Hasn't the virus already done its damage?" Archer asked. "It looks like it was designed to perform *one* task, and that's done."

Hale wasn't in the mood for explanations. "As far as Krasalov is concerned, it's because it's *there*. Just *do it*, please!"

Brickner gave him the look of someone who was about to destroy years of hard work with her own hands. "How do you want me to make entry, sir?"

Archer shrugged. "Just go through the same back door the hackers used."

Brickner's eyes widened. "Right off the SPINTCOM satellite?"

Archer didn't like it any more than Brickner did. "That's right. Subtlety is out the window."

Brickner entered the commands. Her voice was edged with apprehension. "Just for the record, sir, the Russians can watch every move I make from this point on."

"I understand. Get rid of that virus and get out."

"Yes, sir." Brickner worked swiftly for several seconds, then stopped.

"What's wrong?"

Brickner shook her head. "Sir, the virus won't let me delete it. It's source-protected. My guess is *that's* why the Russians haven't wiped it out themselves. They can't."

Hale broke into the conversation. "Mr. Archer?"

"I'm sorry, we've hit a roadblock. Whoever wrote this code inserted a line that plugs a numerical key from his terminal into a complex algorithm. If the answer doesn't come out right, it won't allow any changes. Unless we can find the terminal where this virus was launched from and get that key, we're locked out."

"Can you back out the key from the algorithm itself?" Hale asked.

Archer thought for a second. *That* was a heck of a leap for a foreign policy expert. "Given enough processing time, yes."

"You *do* have supercomputers there at the NSA, don't you?"

Archer felt himself blushing. "Yes, ma'am, we'll get right on it."

"How long?"

Archer looked at the multi-line puzzle the hacker had designed for only *his* key to open. "Several minutes, at least. Hours, more likely."

LEGACY

Jackson was tipping over the cafeteria tables, trying to erect a barricade of some sort. Yoshida looked back at the stainless steel serving counter near the rear wall. "Jackson," he whispered, "don't you think *that* might be a little better at stopping bullets?" Not to mention being farther from the doorway.

"Oh, yeah," Jackson admitted, embarrassed at his poor tactical judgment. He started toward the back of the room.

"Here, take Tony with you!" Yoshida said, giving Broadman a gentle push in Jackson's direction. Yoshida took his eyes off the doorway for a second.

"KEN!" Broadman shouted.

Yoshida looked back just in time to see a muzzle flash pointed directly at him. He pulled Broadman to the floor and held his pistol above the table, firing three rounds in the blind toward the shooter. Jackson whirled and fired one three-round burst before his M-16 smacked on an empty chamber.

Hearing the sound, the guard leaned back in and strafed the now-empty barricade Jackson had erected. Chips of plastic and pressed wood sprayed into the air. When he paused, Yoshida jumped to a crouch and pulled Broadman by the wrist. They used the perforated tables for what little cover they offered. Fingers of light poked through the bullet holes, creating dappled patterns on the tiled floor.

One of the guards must have hidden among the computer terminals. He was firing aimed shots through the doorway at any movement. The bullets flew murderously close, close enough for Yoshida to feel the tiny shock wave from their passage. If they kept moving he and Broadman would soon be out of the sniper's field of fire.

"Beck!" Womack shouted. "They're moving to your left!"

The guard twisted around the doorway, loosing a stream of bullets against the cafeteria wall. Jackson screamed.

"*I'm hit!*" Jackson cried. "I'm hit bad!"

Yoshida fired another three rounds toward the shooter. One hit the doorpost, inches from the man's face. He withdrew. Yoshida crawled to Jackson's side. He had a large, bloody hole torn high on the inside of his left thigh. The bullet must have severed Jackson's femoral artery. Even with his hands clamped over the wound, blood flowed freely between his fingers. He gritted his teeth against the pain.

"Oh, god, it *hurts!*"

Yoshida knew Jackson's wound was serious. If he didn't administer first aid quickly, Jackson would bleed out in a matter of minutes. But they would *all* be dead long before that if they didn't get under cover.

Yoshida had only taken his eyes off the doorway for a second, but the shooter was already back. He extended his hands around the corner to fire a blind salvo directly at Jackson. Yoshida fired two more quick shots, one of them striking the guard's hands. The M-16 was withdrawn with a yelp.

Yoshida reached around Jackson's hands and plucked the Beretta from his waistband. He made sure the safety was off and a round was in the chamber. He handed it to Broadman. "You know how to handle one of these?"

"No," Broadman answered honestly. He had never *touched* a pistol in his life, much less fired one.

Yoshida grabbed Jackson under the arms. They had to move, now. "Point it that way and pull the trigger!"

Broadman did his best to imitate Yoshida's practiced shooting stance. *Sorry, Tony,* he thought, *it just doesn't look as threatening when you're bare-ass naked.* Yoshida realized it would probably be the last humorous insight of his life.

Where the hell is Patrick? was Yoshida's next thought.

* * *

The Marines poked the LAV's tow cable through a hole in the crumpled limousine's frame. The now-compact car emerged from the garage with a long, bone-grating screech. The roll-up door was exposed, battered but still intact.

The SEAL leader looked down from airlock platform, where his men were still rigging explosives. The way this op was unfolding didn't fill him with confidence in Juggernaut leader's ideas. He wanted to keep his options open. But there was another door, made of sheet metal instead of steel plate. "I'll be damned," he muttered. "Okay, let's give his way a try."

The SEALs lined up on either side of the roll-up door in combat formation. Before the LAV could disengage itself from the tow cable outside, the sounds of another furious firefight rang out from inside the bunker.

"Juggernaut leader, Rat leader," Patrick heard over his radio. "The shooting sounds like it's right outside the hatch. Should we continue to hold?"

The LAV commander was swearing at his driver. The tow cable had become twisted during the drag and now they couldn't get it loose from either vehicle. The driver swung his hammer frantically, trying to break one of the hooks loose.

Patrick groaned. He hoped this "rescue" wouldn't earn a place beside the Iranian Hostage Rescue mission in the Counterterrorism textbooks. It was definitely not what he wanted for his legacy. He keyed his mike. "We're in the middle of a Charlie Foxtrot here, Rat Team. Give it your best shot, and good luck. Repeat, you are go for entry."

"Roger, lead, go for blow."

Patrick gave the SEAL leader a forlorn look. "Chief, you got anything that could help them with that tow cable?"

* * *

The sound of gunfire outside the Rat Team's hatch was almost constant now. "Okay, let's blow this thing! Masks!" the leader said.

The team removed their Kevlar helmets long enough to put on their gas masks. It would keep them from choking on the C-4 fumes until they cleared the hatch. The team backed up twenty feet, knowing the tunnel would channel the blast right back to them regardless of how far they retreated. Everyone but the man with the detonator jammed their fingers in their ears as hard as they could.

"Fire in the hole!" their leader announced.

The hatch was now completely obscured. The team charged into the smoke, coming to an abrupt halt.

"What's the problem?" their leader demanded.

"It's no good, sir," the point man announced. "It didn't blow through."

The Rat Team leader hesitated for a moment. The cyanide fumes were already starting to slip through their filters, a burnt almond taste lightly tickling his throat. They had gambled and lost, and it was time to admit it.

He keyed his radio. "Juggernaut leader, Rat Team. The blow was no good. Repeat, no joy on the blow. Rat Team is pulling out."

"Roger, Rat Team," was Patrick's dejected response.

* * *

Broadman's senses would still be adjusting to his release from the box even if he hadn't been subjected to gunfire and a massive overdose of adrenaline. He held the pistol with both hands, almost as afraid of the pistol itself as he was of the gunmen outside the door. He blinked to clear his vision. Between blinks, the shooter appeared again.

The guard was aiming at where Jackson had been hit. A long streak of blood led from that spot back to the serving counters. It was the only thing that saved Broadman. In the time it took the guard to shift his aimpoint, Broadman fired as fast as he could pull the trigger.

The bucking pistol, the bright flame of the muzzle blast, and an occasional glimpse of his target filled Broadman's vision. He fired spastically, not realizing he had his eyes closed for some of the shots. He stopped at seven rounds, finally realizing his target was no longer present. He lowered the pistol slightly.

No one was more surprised than Broadman to see the guard lying on his back. One round had punctured the man's leg, one tore a small hole in his flak vest, and another went through his right eye. He lay there convulsing, his injured brain still trying to issue commands to his body. Broadman's horrified reverie was broken by Kramp's war cry.

"*Yoshida!* You son of a bitch! I'm gonna rip out your heart with my bare hands!"

Broadman heard the sound of charging combat boots. He suddenly realized he had no idea how many bullets this gun carried, or how many he had left. He decided it was a question best considered behind cover.

He turned toward the counter and ran.

INTERLOPERS

The phone cable finally slipped from Stoyer's wrists. Not a second too soon. Bullets were flying everywhere, a few even finding their way into the kitchen. Tiles shattered, filling the air with dust. Stoyer felt an explosion shake the floor under his feet. He assumed his men were throwing flash-bang grenades to stun the hackers before they attacked.

Yoshida came around the serving counter in the next room, dragging that traitorous scum Jackson. Stoyer was pleased to see Kramp and Womack had put a bullet in the young man who had violated his trust.

It was time to go. His men could catch up with him after they had finished off these bastards. He undogged the escape hatch and spun the locking wheel. It was warm for some reason.

The door cracked open and smoke boiled out. Stoyer recoiled away from the heat and fumes. The door was pushed open from inside and several shapes emerged like wraiths from the noxious cloud. One leveled a submachine gun at Stoyer's head, while the others scanned the space beyond him. The leader spoke, his voice muffled by a gas mask.

"Thank you, General! You just made my whole day!" His head tilted slightly. "Going somewhere?"

* * *

A slender wire trailed from the heavy tow cable on the LAV's nose and led to a small wad of C-4 wrapped around the cable. The putty disappeared in a flash and a puff of smoke. The tow cable fell limply to the ground.

"All right, LET'S *GO!*" Patrick shouted.

The LAV lined up with the garage door again, charging through with as much speed as the driver dared. The LAV connected with a deafening crash, ripping the roll-up door from its tracks and throwing it against the entry corridor wall.

The driver put the armored car in reverse. The LAV's hull ground against the garage wall. For a moment the driver thought he was stuck. Then the LAV came loose with a jolt, lurching backwards.

"Go, GO, *GO!*" the SEAL team leader screamed. If his men got this close to a firefight without getting a piece of it, there would be hell to pay tonight.

Patrick watched the SEALs pour into the bunker, silently praying that there would still be hostages left to rescue.

* * *

Broadman ran to the far side of the cafeteria. He leaped over the serving counter, almost landing on Yoshida. A volley of M-16 bullets stitched a pattern in the wall before he hit the floor. The steps came closer.

Another gunner unleashed a stream of automatic fire at the stainless steel fixtures sheltering Yoshida, Broadman and Jackson. The rounds perforated the metal a foot from the floor, coming rapidly toward them. Yoshida and Broadman pressed themselves against the tile, feeling the bullets pass inches over their bodies.

Through a six-inch gap between the counters and the floor, Yoshida could see Womack's feet near the door. Yoshida switched the pistol to his left hand and fired three shots. One round tore through the guard's ankle, knocking him to the floor. Womack screamed in agony.

Yoshida's Beretta locked open on an empty chamber. He reached toward Broadman. "Give me your gun!"

Before Broadman could hand over the weapon, Kramp stepped around the counter. Yoshida, Broadman and Jackson stared up into the barrel of an M-16. Yoshida glared at his executioner, resolved to look death in the face.

Kramp smirked at their predicament. His finger tightened on the M-16's trigger.

Two holes opened up in Kramp's forehead. There were no gunshots, just two heavy thuds. He collapsed like a severed marionette.

Yoshida craned his neck, looking behind him. A figure in gray and black whipped his gun around the kitchen entrance and fired two more silenced shots. A rifle clattered to the floor in the cafeteria. The gun swung down and trained on Yoshida's head.

"Show me your hands!" a muffled voice ordered.

Yoshida complied, dropping Broadman's pistol. He had forgotten he was wearing a guard's uniform.

"Why were they shooting at you?" the voice demanded.

"I'm a prisoner!" Yoshida pleaded. "I stole a guard's uniform trying to escape!"

"It's true!" Broadman affirmed, his hands raised as well. "I'm Tony Broadman. Both of these men were helping me escape."

"Roll over! Keep your hands where I can see them!" the man ordered Yoshida.

Yoshida complied, examining the interloper who had saved his life. He was dressed in SWAT gear and a gas mask, toting a silenced MP5. Several more SWAT troopers stood behind him.

"Identify yourself!"

"Kentaro Yoshida! I'm a prisoner here!" he repeated.

The man lowered his gun. "I remember his picture. He's clean."

"We have wounded over here," Yoshida said.

"Make a hole!" the medic announced, shouldering his way through the SWAT team. He slung his MP5 over his back, stepping lightly over Broadman and Yoshida. He examined Jackson for a few seconds. "Got a pretty bad bleeder here, sir," he said, pulling a field dressing from a pocket on his vest. "He'll need air evac ASAP!"

The leader kept his eyes on the door to the cafeteria. "How many guards are still out there?"

"I'm not sure," Yoshida admitted. "But every time we thought we had them all, more popped up. Watch yourselves."

A metallic crash reverberated down the hallway, followed by shouts of, "Navy SEALs! Drop your weapons!"

"There's the cavalry!" The SWAT officer jerked his head at the men behind him. "You three! Link up with the SEALs and secure the bunker!"

Three troopers burst from the kitchen and hurdled the counter in a gray blur. They advanced to the hallway in a crouch, their faces never lifting from the gunsights of their weapons. "HRT holds the cafeteria!" one called out.

"SEALs have the corridor!" came the answer. "HRT, hold your position and let us advance to you!"

The SWAT officer tugged off his gas mask. "You just can't stay out of trouble, can you, Ken? Special Agent McMullin, FBI Hostage Rescue."

Yoshida exhaled heavily. "Good timing on that shot!"

Another federal agent appeared in the kitchen entrance, pushing Stoyer ahead of him. Stoyer's hands were flex-tied behind his back. "Kick off your shoes, General," the agent ordered.

Stoyer scowled, but did as he was told.

The agent grasped Stoyer's pants firmly and pulled them down around his ankles. He tossed the pants and shoes to Broadman. "Here, Mr. Broadman, he looks like he's about your size."

Broadman gratefully covered himself.

Yoshida blinked. "How did you guys get in here?"

McMullin extended a hand, helping Yoshida to his feet. "It's a long story. By the way, greetings from Liberty."

THE ENEMY

Archer turned the cracking of the virus key over to Steve Watson at the ECHELON desk. Using Archer's authority, Watson had commandeered several of the ECHELON supercomputers to work on the problem in parallel.

"Steve," Archer asked, "I need a real-life, honest-to-god estimate of how long this is going to take." He knew Hale would be calling back any minute for an update, and no answer but "right now" would be acceptable.

Watson gave him a pained look. "I can tell from the code that it's a 256-bit key. That would take most supercomputers about two years to crack. Ours are really good at spotting weak keys and data patterns, which usually cuts the time to about a week. I've got every supercomputer that plays well with the others working on this thing. That multiplies their capabilities, not just adds them together. Still, you're looking at two hours, *minimum*. Best bet would be about double that. Sorry."

Archer knew that codebreaking was mostly a matter of *very* large numbers, and math didn't lie. Watson had done a remarkable job on a near-impossible problem. "No, great work. Thank you."

Every second they delayed meant the Russians stayed at full alert, with the launch keys ready to turn. One mistake, miscommunication, or degraded safety mechanism could lead to the death of millions. And the decrepit state of Russian nuclear control hardware made four hours seem like an eternity.

There had to be another way to get at this virus. Archer consulted with an Air Force sergeant named Myers manning the SPINTCOM terminal. "Sergeant, if that virus originally came over SPINTCOM, would we know it?"

Myers frowned. "Not unless we were looking for it. But they would have to be *inside* the NSA network to access SPINTCOM."

"Could you check anyway?" Archer left to make what was sure to be a painful call to the White House.

"You got it, sir." Myers ran a search comparing the traffic that had passed through the SPINTCOM satellite network that day to an electronic copy of the virus. He straightened in his chair less than a minute later. "Ho-leeey shit!"

Archer set down his phone. "What is it?"

"Not only did it pass through SPINTCOM, it originated on an NSA terminal!" Myers's fingers flew over his keyboard, homing in on his electronic prey.

"Where?"

His shoulders slumped. "Damn. I've got the terminal ID, but it just comes up on the system as, "secure remote terminal.""

A bell of familiarity rang in Archer's head. He jogged to the SPINTCOM terminal and checked the ID number. The bell got louder. He called out to Watson.

"Steve, you remember that search Colonel Richter's guys asked for, then dropped? Secure Node Seventy-Six?"

"Sure!"

"You still have a copy of that log? Read me the terminal number they gave you."

Watson did, and they matched.

"We have met the enemy, and he is us," Archer muttered.

Myers looked up at him. "You know where this terminal is?"

Archer's mental gears churned rapidly. "Not exactly, but I have a *real* good idea where to start looking."

EVAC

"How many of the hostages have been killed?" Special Agent McMullin asked. They waited behind the serving counter until the SEALs and the HRT troopers sounded the all clear.

"Just one that I know of," Yoshida replied.

A disbelieving stare. "Then what was all that shooting about?"

"When I heard you guys were outside, I talked my cellmate into making a break for it. We ended up taking Stoyer hostage, then it all went downhill from there. My cellmate didn't make it."

A sympathetic nod. "I understand. But the rest of the prisoners are unharmed?"

"I haven't checked their cells, but they're right outside that door."

The three HRT troopers returned. "The SEALs are still working the upper level," one said, "but they've cleared a path for us. Are we ready to evac?"

"Yeah, I've packaged him as good as I can," Jackson's medic said. "Help me carry him out."

Jackson had already passed out from blood loss. His head hung back limply when the troopers and the medic linked arms under him for a stretcher carry. "Easy now," the medic cautioned. "Remember, he's one of ours. Sir, are you coming with us?" he asked McMullin.

"Not yet," McMullin answered. "When you see Assistant Director Patrick, would you ask him to send in some proper clothes for Mr. Broadman? I'm sure the General would eventually like his pants back."

"Will do."

"Well, Ken," McMullin said. "Do you want to do the honors with the hackers?"

"In a minute," Yoshida said. "But if I can borrow your radio, I need to speak with Patrick, right now."

DIEX7!PITTMAN

"So what are you going to do?" Sergeant Myers asked Archer.

"I need to get someone inside that bunker."

"I'll go, sir," Jessica Brickner offered.

"No, I need you at that terminal when we get hold of the key. Sergeant, how good of a computer jock are you?"

Myers pressed his lips together. "I'm not much of a programmer, but I can drive any system the NSA's got."

Archer tossed him the keys to his Volvo. "Get someone down here to man your terminal. I may need you to move in a hurry."

Myers reached for his phone. "Right away, sir."

Archer called Patrick's command post. "I need to bring someone through your perimeter, right now." He briefly explained the crisis.

"I was about to call you," Patrick said. "One of the hackers we freed just told me the same story. He says he was forced to help write the virus and he'll help us shut it down."

Archer cringed. The stakes were far too high to entrust this task to someone he didn't know. "I'd rather have one of my people handle it."

"We can trust *this* hacker," Patrick insisted. "He values Liberty as much as we do. Plus, he's right here. He says he needs the bunker hooked back up to the network, though. Can you take care of that?"

Archer didn't know the Resistance had an agent inside the DATASHARK bunker, but that would explain why Patrick had been so gung-ho about this mission. That was the second thing to go right today. Archer hoped they were on a roll. "Let me give you the ID of the terminal we're looking for. Tell him call me at this number when he finds it. We'll get things hooked back up for him. Ready to copy?"

* * *

The hackers were released, but remained crowded into the hallway outside their cells, bottled there by the soldiers who had freed them. Yoshida stood at the end of the corridor. Stoyer stood beside him, firmly flanked by two HRT troopers. Yoshida raised his voice over the nervously murmuring group.

"Okay, guys, we'll get out of here in a little bit, but right now we've got to undo some of *this* bastard's work." He pointed at Stoyer. "Who's with me?"

Every hand went up, along with grumblings of, "Hell, yes!" and "Damn straight!"

Yoshida jerked both thumbs over his shoulders. "Then let's go find out if those terminals still work!"

If any of the hackers were in a mood to celebrate their release, the dead bodies littering the lower level brought them back to earth in a hurry. Yoshida relieved Kramp and Beck of their radios, tossing one to Paul Malechek. About a third of the terminals had taken bullets. The hackers without a working terminal looked over the shoulders of the others. The SEALs and FBI agents fidgeted, wary of letting the hackers loose again with their computers. But Patrick's orders had been clear.

Yoshida sprinted upstairs. He found the terminal number Patrick had given him in the watchers' room. A shake of the mouse brought up a log-in screen, which rejected Yoshida's password.

ACCESS DENIED. INSUFFICIENT PRIVILEGES.

It only made sense that a hacker would be unable to access one of the watcher's terminals. He keyed his radio. "Guys, bust into the server for me. I need one of the watcher's passwords. Give CSERPENT a crack at it." This would have been a hell of a lot easier if Jackson hadn't taken a bullet.

Malechek's response was immediate. "I'd love to, Ken, but somebody's already wiped the server. All our attack programs are gone."

That made sense, too. The watchers probably didn't even *start* shredding their paper documents until they had destroyed the electronic evidence. Losing CSERPENT was an especially hard blow. It could have told him in seconds which attacks would be effective against the Snake Pit's server. Now he was reduced to educated guesswork, and making up the attack software as he went. His only hope was that certain files were beyond the watcher's access privileges. Those might have survived. He keyed his radio again.

"Paul, you still remember how to write a buffer overflow program?"

Malechek was insulted. "Only in my sleep!"

"Then get on it, and have the other guys work on the payload." He briefly considered telling them the urgency of the problem, but settled on, "Guys, we don't get out of here until we fix this, understood?"

Next he called the number Patrick gave him, reaching somebody named Archer. He sounded like he was in charge. He didn't take the news of the wiped server well. Yoshida left the phone on speaker.

Malechek radioed in a few minutes later. "Okay, I'm ready to stuff the buffer. The twins just finished the payload."

Malechek's program took advantage of a weakness in some C-programmed systems, pouring large amounts of random data into the server's temporary memory storage, or buffer. Once the buffer filled, data spilled unfiltered into the computer's RAM, taking with it the root shell program the Taylor twins had written. The root shell gave Malechek direct access to the Snake Pit's server, unfettered by password protections.

"Good news times two, Ken," Malechek said. "The overflow worked, and there's five programs left in root access. One
of them's the password file. Who's do you want?"

The watchers must not have had time or access to reformat
the entire system. It was a testimony to Richter's intimidation
skills that none of the hackers had ever tried what they had accomplished in just a few minutes.

Yoshida read off the ID number. "I need someone who has
access to this specific terminal."

"Then try this log-in," Malechek suggested. Yoshida typed
as Malechek read.

USER: TSFELDMAN

PASSWORD: DIEx7!PITTman

At least Feldman got *one* of his last wishes, Yoshida
thought angrily. Now he had access to Feldman's terminal, or
what was left of it. Not a single data file remained, but Feldman
hadn't reformatted the drive. Stoyer and Richter had been so
arrogant that they didn't plug security holes like the buffer overflow or prepare a server meltdown command. Feldman hadn't
even had time to turn off his terminal, which gave Yoshida one
last opening.

He wrote a short program in C, including an intentional error in the code. The computer immediately spewed out:

"fatal read errors (1) output to: datafile.bad"

Yoshida had tricked the computer into executing a core
dump. A legitimate tool of software developers, core dumps
allowed programmers to pick through the debris of a bad program to find their mistakes. He had used it to force the computer
to dump all the data in the terminal's RAM memory into a file.
Hopefully Feldman's last commands and passwords would be
swept into the file as well.

Yoshida opened the file, ignoring the data slurry his program had induced. Just above a series of delete commands he
found:

!cmd PANDORA1 < keyfile.dat

RUNNING

keyfile.dat: 6TRee$MatteS2783^sTilts5#TotEm56

DONE

"Mr. Archer, you still there?" he said.

"Yes!" Archer almost shouted. "What did you find?"

Yoshida was impressed that the man had kept his mouth
shut while he worked. This guy knew how things got done. He

highlighted the thirty-two-character password and saved it to a
file. "Look on my terminal for a file called key.dat. Do you see
it?"

"Yeah, we found it," Archer said a few seconds later.

"That's your baby. Give it a try."

Yoshida heard a woman shout in the background.

Archer sighed into the phone. "It worked. Thank God!" A
short pause. "Ken, you need a job?"

"Thanks, but I have a feeling Mr. Patrick will be keeping
me pretty busy for a while."

Archer laughed. "I bet he will! Thanks again."

"No charge. See ya."

Yoshida smiled. This is what separated real hackers from
the kids who downloaded hacking programs off the Internet.
His team had all their tools taken away and still got the job
done. He keyed his radio one last time.

"It worked, guys. Good hack. Let's go home."

COORDINATES

Even Krasalov was speechless.

Adams leaned toward the speakerphone. "Mr. President?"

Krasalov responded in English this time, without his interpreter. "Yes, I am here." There was a long pause. "This rogue
general...Stoyer. He nearly blows all of us to hell today, yes?"

Adams nodded grimly. "Yes. Yes he did. General Stoyer is
being placed under arrest right now, and his operation is being
shut down."

"I would like, how do you say?" A brief aside with his interpreter. "Confirmation. I would like confirmation that this is
so."

Adams rubbed his temples. "I will work with your ambassador to provide whatever evidence you require."

Another voice broke in on the speaker. "President Krasalov? This is Jeffrey Archer at the NSA again. Do you have access to satellite imagery at your location?"

Krasalov conversed for a few moments in Russian. "Yes,
Mr. Archer, I can receive photos here, why?"

"The next time one of your satellites passes over our east
coast, focus your cameras on the following location."

It was a set of coordinates Jeff Archer knew by heart.

SPECTATORS

Tony Broadman returned General Stoyer's pants, exchanging them for a gray HRT uniform and a black FBI ball cap. McMullin had insisted Broadman take a last look around the bunker before they left. He said it was critical for a former hostage's recovery that the last memory of their place of captivity be as a free person and not as a prisoner. He also hinted it would make Broadman's recollections clearer when it came time to be debriefed.

Broadman was glad McMullin didn't make him go back to the box cell where he had been confined. That area was now blocked off with screens. On the other side, forensic technicians gathered evidence before removing Pittman's body.

The hackers lined up on the lower level. The HRT troopers quickly frisked each of them before filing them out to a waiting bus. Broadman was surprised to see Yoshida among them, back in his orange jumpsuit. He winked at Broadman.

The sun was dipping beneath the tree tops when Tony Broadman and the FBI agents emerged from the garage. Broadman squinted at the light and sheltered his eyes. McMullin offered Broadman his sunglasses.

Broadman was stunned at the level of military force present for his rescue. Soldiers and federal agents with machine guns seemed to be everywhere. The noise of circling helicopters filled the air. The FBI agents escorted him past the shattered gates to a long line of law enforcement and military vehicles. Behind them, an army helicopter with medical markings lifted off from the compound.

"Tony!" a familiar voice shouted.

Ben Hawthorne emerged from one of the Suburbans, striding forward to embrace his friend. "Man, am I glad to see you!"

Broadman returned the embrace, the reality of his release still sinking in. "Same here," was all he could think of to say.

Hawthorne handed him a cell phone. "Here. Call Christina. Then we'll have the docs take a look at you."

The two HRT agents pulled away from the reunion, walking to the last FBI vehicle.

Patrick greeted them. "Good work. Where's Ken?"

McMullin jerked his head toward the bunker. "He insisted on staying with the hackers until they were released. He said something about a plan."

Patrick laughed. "That kid is a piece of work! Thank God we've got him back. Stoyer?"

"Trussed up like a Christmas turkey. Know any judges who might want to talk to him?"

"One name springs to mind," Patrick replied. "How many bodies do we have in there?"

"Eleven bad guys and one hostage."

"Have the SEALs bag them and put them outside, in plain sight," Patrick ordered.

The lines on McMullin's face deepened. "Begging your pardon, sir, but why?"

Patrick checked his watch, then scanned the sky. "Because in fifteen minutes we're going to have some very high-level spectators, and I want them to see the price we paid to clean this place out."

TOASTS

Marenko pulled the message from the printer. He regarded Joan Turner seriously, the paper hiding his smile.

"What?" Turner demanded. "What's happening?" The hour she had spent standing on the nuclear brink had seemed like days to her.

"I apologize that you will be going home without seeing the launch of one of our missiles," Marenko said, "but at least you will have a home to go back to. And you will have an interesting story to tell."

Turner shivered. "A little *too* interesting, if you ask me!"

Marenko smiled. "In your country they give awards for telling such interesting stories, do they not?"

Turner's eyes became distant. "Yes. Yes, they do." In her concern over her own survival, she had temporarily forgotten her ambition. But it returned to her soon enough.

Marenko helped her down from the command van. "Good!" he boomed. "Then we will drink to your story *and* to your awards!"

Colonel Sakavin was outside, waiting for his orders.

Marenko waved to his deputy. "Sergei! Tell the crews to put their missiles away! The men have been sober long enough!"

EPILOGUE

REUNION

"Tyranny is a lovely eminence, but there is no way down from it." - Shakespeare, *Pericles*

General Stoyer shuffled toward his cell, his hands and feet shackled. His orange coveralls and slippers were identical to those the hackers had worn, minus the monitoring tag. The FBI agent who had accompanied him from the bunker insisted on taking several photographs of him being stripped of his military uniform. The agent made sure the words "FEDERAL PRISONER" emblazoned on the coveralls would figure prominently in each of the photos. Bastard.

This prison was far different from the Hanoi Hilton. A new federal Supermax penitentiary, it was clean, well lit, and even reasonably ventilated. Reserved for the government's most high-profile cases, its prisoners were kept in solitary confinement most of the day. The few hours a week they had in the company of other inmates were tightly supervised, so the routine inmate fears of beatings and rape were not a factor here, he had been told.

That was no comfort to Stoyer. It took the full force of his will to prevent a POW flashback from overtaking him. In his mind, the gentle prods of the guard's baton became a bayonet, jabbing him in the spine. The catcalls of the other prisoners morphed into Vietnamese curses, assaulting his ears. He hunched over, flinching from the punches and kicks that would come next.

The prodding of the baton became more insistent. "C'mon, General, keep moving!" the guard growled.

A graying Hispanic man with immense shoulders stepped into their path. "Whatdya got there, Steve?"

"New arrival, Sarge," his guard declared. "The FBI wants a real short leash put on them. I was gonna stick him in C23, if it's okay with you."

"Did you just call him *General?*"

His guard passed over a clipboard. "No shit! He's the real deal! I don't think he cares much for his new uniform, though."

The sergeant's stare alternated between the clipboard and Stoyer, as if he didn't believe what his eyes were telling him. "It doesn't say here what you're in here for, General? Care to share that with us?"

Stoyer said nothing.

The sergeant grabbed the front of Stoyer's coveralls. "Answer me, dammit!"

"Whoa, sergeant!" the other guard cautioned. "Chill, man!"

Stoyer's eyes glazed over. "Stoyer, Jonathan! Captain, United States Air Force! Serial number..." was all he said before emptying his stomach onto the painted concrete floor. Only the first guard's grasp on the broad leather belt prevented Stoyer from sagging into his vomit.

"Son of a bitch!" the guard swore.

The sergeant seized Stoyer by the arm, almost lifting him from the floor. "Here, I got him!"

The guard had never seen his superior like this unless sorely provoked. In those cases he was truly dangerous. "Are you sure, Sarge? I can handle him!"

"I said I got him! Get a mop and clean that up!"

The sergeant grasped Stoyer by the collar and belt, pulling him bodily into the cellblock, toes dragging. Upon reaching cell C23, the sergeant deposited Stoyer roughly onto the bed. He jerked his prisoner upright until the General's eyes met his with an unfocused stare.

"What's the matter, General? Don't you remember me?"

Stoyer blinked dumbly.

"C'mon, General! Airman Ruiz, from the Hanoi Hilton! You remember me, don't you?"

Stoyer searched the man's face, but recognition wouldn't come.

"You remember Pablo Ruiz! I worked the ELINT panel on that old EC-121 you flew in 'Nam!"

Finally Stoyer bridged the memory of the wiry young man he had known with the hulking figure before him. "Pablo," he whispered.

"That's right." Ruiz extended his arm. Scars gnarled the dark flesh like the bark of an ancient tree. "You know, it's been so long, I can't even remember which of these are from that lousy crash landing you pulled or from the beatings the gooks gave me afterward."

Stoyer's lips trembled, mouthing the word "sorry."

Ruiz grasped Stoyer's arm, partially to keep him upright. "Hey man! Don't be sorry! Look what it did for you! You went from captain all the way to three-star general! Operation SNOWBLOWER was a real good deal for you, even if you count that year in the Hilton!"

Stoyer jerked in recognition of the codeword.

Ruiz smiled. His grip on Stoyer's arm tightened. "Yeah man, I know all about SNOWBLOWER. You never *were* going to tell me about that, were you? I went through *hell* to help you get those stars and all I got was that lousy fruit basket you sent me every Christmas! Well, one year a spook brother of yours delivered the basket personally and told me all about it."

Stoyer sucked in a ragged breath.

The grip remained firm. "Hey man, don't sweat it! He didn't tell me till two years after the Ruskies stopped using that code. He was one of your buddies who followed you up the ladder with SNOWBLOWER. Said he felt guilty about how the rest of us got used up and thrown away."

Stoyer swallowed hard.

Ruiz tightened his iron grip. "You know, I always thought it was weird the way you sprung me out of the stockade to fly on that mission. Then I figured it out. You were just making sure none of your lily-white academy buddies went down in flames with you. Nothing on that flight but blacks, spics, slants, and you. You even got that suck-up airman you liked off your crew. What was his name...Richter? Yeah, that was it. Kiss-ass Carl, that's what we called him."

Stoyer's lips moved, but no sound came out.

Ruiz ignored him. "But hey, look at you! You may be a three-star general, but you're in *my* world now! You won't *move* unless I say, you won't *eat* unless I say, you won't *sleep* unless I say. That's why you should always try to stay on my good side. You don't *ever* want to piss me off."

A demented wail came from an adjacent cell. It was Larry the Lunatic. Something about snakes and spiders in his cell. Whatever.

"You know, there are some really dangerous people in here," Ruiz hinted, "and I'm the *only thing* standing between them and you. If you think solitary is bad, just piss me off and

I'll let you have some *company*. Some of these guys are pretty lonely, if you know what I mean."

"Yo, Pablo!" came a shout from a cell across the hall. "Who's your new girlfriend? Is she sweeeet?"

Stoyer blinked hard, as if trying to wake himself.

Ruiz laughed. "Sorry, General! This ain't no bad dream!" He leaned close. "Actually, I hate to be the one to break this to you, but really you died, *and you didn't end up in the good place!*"

Stoyer started sliding backward down a long, dark slope. The lights of the world receded, swallowed by the darkness that had almost claimed him as a younger man.

Ruiz sneered. "You know, my old lady thought this whole prison guard deal was a bad idea. Before she left me, she even had me go to a shrink! That prick doctor said I had unresolved issues from being a POW, and he said picking this job was overcompensation. Can you believe that shit?"

Stoyer heard none of this. He stared into space, shaking silently.

Ruiz shook his head. "Well, I *may be* crazy, but just seeing you here today has made *every day* in this hell hole worth it. Don't you worry, I *promise* to keep you company! Every time you open your eyes, I'm going to be right here, ready to talk about old times. Just you and me!"

Terror contorted Stoyer's face. He began to speak, softly. Ruiz couldn't make out the words at first, but Stoyer said them again and again, louder with every repetition.

Ruiz finally recognized it as a Vietnamese phrase, begging for mercy. The Vietcong guards had taught them to say it when they had had enough torture and were ready to talk. An English-speaking VC Intelligence officer would be brought to the broken man and then the real fun would begin.

"Yeah, you and me are gonna have some *good* times, General!" Ruiz left Stoyer's cell. He turned the key that closed the thick motorized door. It muffled but did not silence Stoyer's cries for mercy, which echoed down the concrete corridor.

Sergeant Ruiz continued his rounds of the cellblock, whistling a happy tune as he went.

SECOND CHANCES

"The only justification for rebellion is success."
- Thomas B. Reed

It had originally been a camp for troubled youth, which was certainly appropriate. The Resistance had been able to acquire the property at a reasonable price. The previous owners had not run out of troubled youth, but of donors willing to help pay for their rehabilitation.

Patrick and Hawthorne pulled up to the gate. The battered wood sign overhead read "CAMP REDEMPTION." The property wasn't far from New York City but was isolated in every practical sense. In keeping with its rehabilitative history, Camp Redemption was miles away from the nearest source of alcohol, tobacco, or other form of debauchery to which its residents might desire to return. This also served to reduce any curiosity about Camp Redemption's current residents or their activities.

A lone figure appeared by the padlocked entrance. He unchained and opened the gate, then secured it again after the two FBI agents pulled inside. He climbed into the sedan's back seat.

Patrick reached over the seat. "Ken! Good to see you again!" He shook the younger man's hand. "So how did things turn out?"

A satisfied nod. "Not too bad! I convinced ten of them to join us. We're still arguing over goals and methods, but that's normal with any new cell group."

"That's part of why we're here," Hawthorne said. "We figured we could play bad cop--two shadowy guys with guns who show up and lay down the law. Then you can say you're just following the marching orders we gave you. If they don't like it, they can walk."

Yoshida chuckled. "Not damn likely. Several of these guys have very good reasons to stay disappeared. They were downright relieved *not* to be going home!"

"How's the operations center coming together?" Patrick asked.

"We're putting it in the chapel. Lots of space, dimly lit, narrow little windows. A perfect environment for computer work."

Patrick drew back in mock surprise. "Won't that interfere with your worship services?"

Yoshida laughed. "Yeah, right! Not exactly a pious bunch. I thought we'd start with a legitimate computer business, something to keep the guys busy and generate some cash flow. Then we can branch out into selective intrusions to teach them about Resistance work."

Patrick held up a cautioning hand. "Absolutely nothing illegal in the short term. Remember, you guys are President Adams's only alibi in this mess with the Japanese. And *you* are the best witness we have to convince the Russians that PANDORA was purely Stoyer's idea. So no Resistance business *at all* until Congress gets through with their hearings."

"Better tell them that in your lecture. These guys have gotten pretty good at mayhem and destruction, and they've got a king-sized beef against the government. I've had a hard time reining them in."

"Don't worry about that," Patrick assured him. "Reining them in is my job."

Hawthorne pulled the sedan up to the main lodge.

"Bad cop mode, Mr. Hawthorne," Patrick said to his driver.

Hawthorne curled his lip in feigned contempt. "Drop dead. Sir."

"That's the ticket! Let's do it."

Patrick and Hawthorne stalked in to meet the assembled hackers, scowling all the way. Yoshida trailed submissively along.

* * *

The trio emerged from the lodge twenty minutes later.

"How did I do?" Patrick asked.

"You put the fear of God into me, and I already know what a teddy bear you really are," Yoshida offered.

Patrick glowered at Hawthorne. "I save this guy's life and he *still* gives me no respect!"

"It's a shame, sir," Hawthorne agreed.

"So what happened to Dave Jackson?" Yoshida asked.

"My guys are keeping an eye on him until he heals up," Patrick said. "I may need to put him in witness protection after that, though. Think your guys would accept him, considering his former occupation?"

"The bullets he put in Richter should buy him a lot of forgiveness. I don't think it'll be a problem."

"Good. By the way, I heard that Stoyer's little prank compromised some kind of surveillance system we've been using to keep tabs on the Russians for years. Krasalov made the President pull the plug on it for good."

"So we try to save the world and it gets more dangerous instead, huh?"

"Sounds like it. Better keep those skills sharp. You may need them sooner than you think."

They pulled to a stop at Camp Redemption's gate.

"One more favor, sir?" Yoshida asked.

"I'm listening."

"The guys took a vote. They'd like to rename this place Camp Pittman. If anybody knew how to tweak the government, it was Bob. And he *did* give his life for the cause, in the end."

Patrick shrugged. "Fine with me. But you'll have to make your own sign. I cleaned out every account I own chipping in to buy this place. By the way, I may have to retire here. I've got no place else to go."

"My kids are going to college here, too," Hawthorne groused, only half-jesting.

Yoshida patted both men on the shoulder. "We'll try to make some of that money back for you. And if worse comes to worse, when we were in the Snake Pit we found some government accounts just begging to be pilfered."

"Easy, Ken. Remember, low profile."

Yoshida became serious again. "Always. And by the way, thanks again for the rescue. I never gave up hope."

Patrick's jaw flexed. "We never leave our own behind."

"We wanted to make an exception in your case," Hawthorne offered, "but we thought it would set a bad precedent."

Patrick motioned with his head. "Now unchain that gate before we get weepy on you!"

* * *

They drove for several miles before Patrick spoke. "With Ken heading up our computer operations, that makes you our new cell leader for New York City, Ben."

"I figured as much, sir. Thank you."

"You've earned it. The way you handled Tony Broadman's recruitment showed real initiative."

Hawthorne winced. "It tore my guts out to expose him like that."

Patrick's gaze shifted to the passing scenery. "I know. I didn't sleep for the whole time they had him. But without Tony we would have never gotten Ken back. And in the end we didn't leave either one of them behind, did we?"

Hawthorne pressed his lips together. "No, sir."

"Consider this," Patrick suggested. "If Ken had completed the recruitment process and talked Tony into chasing that MINTNET story, the NSA might have come after him anyway, right?"

"Probably, sir. I hadn't thought about that."

"So how's Tony doing?"

"He was pretty shaken up, but being a media darling is very therapeutic. You wouldn't *believe* the number of people trying to get an interview with him. Even had some producer from Hollywood calling about buying the film rights to his little adventure."

Patrick cringed. "I hope we haven't created a monster."

"His wife will keep him grounded. What's *really* important is that Tony's management forgot all about the Resistance story. We stay off the radar screen for now."

Patrick had *hoped* it would work out that way, but he knew how hard it was to keep secrets indefinitely. "There may come a time to advertise our presence, but I think we work best in the shadows for the time being."

Patrick's personal cell phone beeped, not the one he used for Resistance business. "Patrick."

Hawthorne could hear a woman's voice over the cell phone. Although Patrick tried to make the call sound like official business, it was apparent he was making an appointment of a more personal nature. Hawthorne tried not to eavesdrop, but the last phrase of the woman's call sounded suspiciously like "I love you."

Patrick cleared his throat nervously. "Um, yeah, you too." He flipped his phone closed with a pained "you didn't hear that, did you?" look.

Hawthorne smiled. "Sir, there's no need to be embarrassed. Even Resistance leaders and Assistant Directors are allowed to have personal lives."

"Yeah, I'm so used to sneaking around, I guess I don't know when to stop."

"Your secret's safe with me. It's too bad, though. Given our security, I'll probably never meet her."

A shrug. "Stranger things have happened. You'd like her, though." Patrick smiled, his gaze unfocused.

"You're history. You know that, don't you, sir?"

Patrick's head snapped left. "Am I?"

"Most definitely."

Patrick sighed. "Damn. And I was such a cool bachelor."

"Happens to the best of us, sir."

"This country, with its institutions, belong to the people who inhabit it. When they grow weary of the existing government they can exercise their constitutional right of amending it, or their revolutionary right to dismember or overthrow it."

- Abraham Lincoln

"The American people have to trust us, and in order to trust us they have to know about us."

- Lieutenant General Michael V. Hayden, USAF
Director, National Security Agency, 1999-2004

Printed in the United States
105874LV00001B/59/A